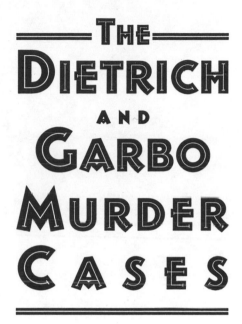

THE
DIETRICH
AND
GARBO
MURDER
CASES

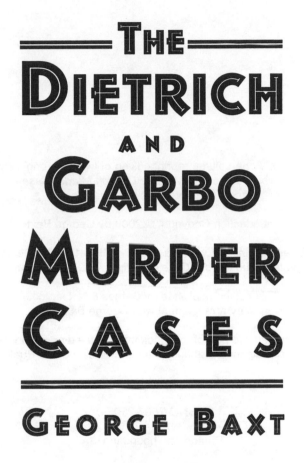

THE DIETRICH AND GARBO MURDER CASES

GEORGE BAXT

BARNES
&NOBLE
BOOKS
NEW YORK

CONTENTS

INTRODUCTION

Face it, dear reader, it's very exciting to have two of my own favorite books re-released. They star (to use a much-abused movie term) two of my screen favorites, Greta Garbo and Marlene Dietrich, whom were actually acquaintances back in the golden era....They played many sets of tennis together. Fate was kind enough to bring them into my orbit years after they left Hollywood, and I still tingle at the memories.

One New Year's Day, as I was en route to a cocktail party, I saw Garbo, looking in need of help, at East Fifty-second Street and First Avenue, where the snow was piled high and tough to maneuver across. I struggled across the street to her, held out my hand, and she wordlessly grabbed it. After I helped her across the street, she favored me with a faint smile (think of the effort it must have taken her!) and slowly ambled away. I remember sighing rather wistfully, but feeling anxious to get to the party to tell everyone I had rescued Garbo (well, it was a rescue, wasn't it?).

I had met Dietrich several years earlier when she was living at the posh Plaza Hotel, where I worked for a press agent. In a driving rainstorm (you gather I have my best luck in inclement weather), she was barreling down West Fifty-eighth Street, with a very chic floppy hat but no umbrella. To my disappointment, I could see she was knock-kneed. A little later, when we were alone together in the elevator, she made small talk about the "tewwible" weather, and my talk was even smaller.

Little did I think these ladies and I would meet again under happier circumstances!

I gave birth to the Celebrity Murders series in 1983, narrowly avoiding its being aborted. It was like this: I was in the fourth year of a deadly writer's block. One day, in a blessed flash, I conceived the idea to write a mystery using Dorothy Parker and some of the Algonquin Roundtable as characters who aid the police in solving a crime. I broached the idea to my agent (no longer), a southern gentleman "suh," and he looked at his door, awaiting some men in white coats to come and spirit me away. Far from discouraged, I went to a book signing for a friend at the Mysterious Bookshop and was hailed by Hope Dellon of St. Martin's Press, who in 1978 had tracked me down in Hollywood to buy the reprint rights to my first highly successful novel, *A Queer Kind of Death*. I grabbed the opportunity to tell her about my

Dorothy Parker idea, which, to my delight, the press also decided to publish (bless them). Hallelujah! I was back on track again.

Parker was a success, especially (don't ask me why) in Germany and German-speaking countries. Hope wanted more. In rapid succession, I gave her *Alfred Hitchcock*, *Tallulah Bankhead*, *Garbo*, and *Dietrich*. *Garbo* received fantastic raves in Germany, and shortly afterward, when the divine Dietrich went to her reward, I was free to use her as a character as well, pairing her with Anna May Wong, the lovely Chinese actress. They had played prostitutes in the 1932 movie *Shanghai Express*. For the Hollywood setting, I created detective Herb Villon (maybe descended from Francois Villon, who knows?); his sexy assistant Jim Mallory, who has a passion for movie stars (female); and Herb's girlfriend, Hazel, an alcoholic gossipmonger.

So the Celebrity Murders grew like Topsy, and there are now thirteen, with the fourteenth, *The Cary Grant and Jean Arthur Murder Case*, flashing around in my brain. I treat the celebrities with respect, reverence, and, hopefully, great humor. I select all my subjects with great care and, above all, for their sense of humor. (Yes, Garbo had a sense of humor, albeit a childish one.) I had great fun with all of them, but especially with Hitchcock, Tallulah Bankhead, and Mae West.

Doing a bind-up of *Garbo* and *Dietrich* is a truly inspired idea. I always felt that these two women should have done a movie together as wacky spies. After all, they both did films based on the life of Mata Hari (that sexy nincompoop, but what the hell, the pictures were success-ful....Garbo in *Mata Hari* and Dietrich in *Dishonored*, in which she kept the firing squad waiting while she careful-ly repaired her makeup).

So you can see why I find it truly exciting to have these books re-released together. Thank you for sharing the excitement with me!

—George Baxt
June 2000

THE MARLENE DIETRICH MURDER CASE

BY GEORGE BAXT

for
Robert Fletcher
and
Jack Kauflin

we remember the same things

◖◗ ONE ◖◗

MARLENE DIETRICH'S KITCHEN in her rented Beverly Hills mansion was a masterpiece of modern design. It was the kitchen that cemented her decision to rent the house. She had left Germany for the United States a month earlier and arrived in New York on April 9, 1930. After a whirlwind week of newspaper interviews, newsreel interviews, radio interviews, and being wined and dined by Adolph Zukor, who ruled Paramount Pictures (Marlene's new employers), with an iron fist, she had settled with a sigh of exhaustion and a sigh of relief into her first-class compartment on the Twentieth Century Limited.

A Hollywood star. The fantasy a reality. The dream come true. The script of her first American film, *Morocco*, on the seat next to her. Costarring with Gary Cooper and Adolphe Menjou. Gary Cooper. How she longed to sleep with Gary Cooper. Rudy wouldn't mind. Her husband, Rudolf Sieber wouldn't mind at all. He was content living with his mistress, Tamara Matul. Marlene was glad he was content. She was glad he had Tamara to love and amuse him. Marlene and Rudy had married six years earlier, and a year later she gave birth to her adored daughter, Heidede, more frequently called Maria.

This magnificent kitchen. For five days after arriving in Hollywood, accompanied by a Paramount representative, she had hunted for an appropriate house. Josef von Sternberg cautioned her, "Don't rent too expensive a place. Don't sign a long lease. If *Morocco* fails and you fail with it, they'll send you back to Germany."

Fat chance, she said to herself. She was a European smash in von Sternberg's *The Blue Angel*. She could act, she could sing in a voice husky with the seductiveness of the sirens of the Rhine. She projected a subtle eroticism and an exotic sexiness that appealed to both men and women. Fail? Me? Marlene? Lucie Mannheim and Brigitte Helm were two of Germany's biggest stars, but they lost Lola-Lola in *The Blue Angel* to me. Von Sternberg favored me over them, even though I was too heavy and needed to lose twenty pounds. But the way I looked at him at our first meeting, the look that promised everything but didn't deliver anything until I had a signed contract. Fail? Me? *Morocco* was a smash hit, a sensation. Dressed in a tuxedo in a nightclub in North Africa, I dared wrap my hands around a woman's face and kiss her full on the lips. I could hear the rest of the company on the soundstage gasp. Those sharp intakes of breath. The dark look on von Sternberg's face as he lit a cigarette. And my audacious query, "Didn't you like it? Shall I do it again? I can make it more suggestive." He kept the scene in the film. He knew it would give Marlene her much sought after celebrity, and it did.

And then *The Blue Angel* was rushed into American release and Frederick Hollander's "Falling in Love Again," which she sang with a contemptuous cynicism that would become her trademark, became her signature. And now she had her magnificent kitchen. What the world did not yet know was that this glamorous mother preferred to cook and bake and concoct exquisite soups, stirring the pot with the enthusiasm of

2

one of the three witches in *Macbeth*. Marlene reigned in the kitchen, and today, so did chaos.

"I smell something burning," said Anna May Wong, who was noshing on a plate of pickled herring.

Marlene hurried to one of her four stoves while brandishing a pot holder. She moved a pan of codfish balls from the flame and stirred the contents with a large spoon.

"They're fine, they'll be okay," she said with a small smile. There were five other cooks in the kitchen and all exchanged knowing glances. Had one of them come close to burning something, he or she would have been banished into culinary exile. Tonight was Marlene's big night. Over one hundred people invited to join her in welcoming the New Year, 1932. Nineteen thirty-one had been a glorious year. *Morocco, The Blue Angel,* and *Dishonored,* in which she again scored as a German spy based on the exploits of the notorious, albeit somewhat dumpy, Mata Hari. And now, with von Sternberg directing her for the fourth time in succession, she had completed her most erotic and suggestive film to date, *Shanghai Express,* in which she and Anna May Wong were a pair of extraordinarily unusual prostitutes who murder a Chinese warlord.

Anna May said, "Why don't you let these professionals do the cooking," gesturing to the five cooks, who awaited an explosion from Dietrich.

Marlene abandoned the codfish balls and pushed an errant strand of hair back into place. "Who said they're not cooking? There's plenty for them to do." She faced them with hands on hips. "Don't you have plenty to do?" The five busied themselves while Marlene continued, striving hard to overcome her tendency to supplant *r*'s with *w*'s. "Now really! All I'm cooking are my specialties. I am famous for my specialties." Anna May nodded in silent agreement. "Everybody in Hollywood looks forward to my specialties." And again Anna May nodded in tacit agreement. Specialties were indeed Dietrich's specialty. "Those codfish balls are a Scandinavian delicacy. A recipe handed down from the Vikings."

Anna May stuffed a cigarette into a holder decorated with jade chips. "I didn't know the Vikings were famous for their cuisine. I thought all they did was pillage and rape women."

"In between they ate," said Marlene with her usual logic. She pulled a chair to Anna May's side and sat. "Why don't you finish the herring?" Marlene chewed on a radish. Anna May blew a smoke ring. "What's bothering you?"

"Not working is what's bothering me. How many parts are there for Chinese women? And when there is one, it's played by Myrna Loy, who is from Helena, Montana, which is hardly a Chinese province.

"Nineteen thirty-two will be better. Mercury is leaving retrograde and the New Moon will bring a series of offers for you to work. Jupiter will be entering your house."

"He doesn't have a key. I'm thinking of going back to Europe. I was doing great in films and the theater until Paramount sent for me for *Daughter of the Dragon*." She added morosely, "That and *Shanghai Express* is all I've done in almost two years, besides redecorating my apartment house."

"Don't you own that apartment house?"

"Yes, but it's not a very big one."

"It's not the size that counts."

"All the apartments are occupied by friends and relatives, so I can't charge too much rent."

"Why not? Don't be victimized by parasites! Anyway, Carroll Richter predicts a wonderful 1932." Carroll Richter was making a fortune as astrologer to the stars and much of that fortune came from Dietrich. "You mark his words. Next year your ship will come in."

"I'm beginning to think my ship did come in but forgot to unload its cargo."

"What you really need is a love affair."

"That's all you seem to think about."

"It's such pleasant thinking. Now I shall prepare my Bavarian meatballs à la Schumann-Heink. I got the recipe from the great soprano. I've improved on it. I use chopped sirloin, not cheap chuck." A thought struck her. "Anna May, last April, when I came back from Germany with Rudolf and little Maria, we met this French actor on the train."

"I think you told me about him."

"Maybe I did. His name is Raymond Souvir."

"That doesn't sound familiar."

"Very handsome. Very charming. He must be very rich, I think. He lives very lavishly. He's coming to the party."

"And you plan to introduce us."

"Of course I do, but I have no ulterior motive, I assure you." She was quartering a sirloin steak and then subdividing the quartered sections. "He travels with a very select group, all European for the most part except for Dorothy di Frasso."

"I should have guessed the Countess di Frasso would have gotten her claws into him."

"Oh, Dorothy's not so bad. She's just pushy. Just a clever American girl who managed to marry into Italian nobility and walk off with a lot of her husband's wealth after she divorced him."

"She still doing it with Gary Cooper?"

Marlene shrugged. "It's too exhausting trying to guess who Gary's doing it to these days. Di Frasso or Lupe Velez, or this society girl he's been squiring, Sandra something." She was dropping chunks of sirloin into a grinder and pulverizing them. She resembled a cameraman the way she diligently ground away, and Anna May marveled at the contented expression on Marlene's face. Here was a true *Hausfrau*, if only she weren't so eaten up by ambition. "Anyway, Raymond is bringing a Chinese musician, a violinist. Now let me see, his name is Ding Dong something."

"Dong See," corrected Anna May.

"You know him?"

"Marlene," Anna May underlined her name with exaggerated patience, "Dong See is internationally famous."

"Well *I* never heard of him."

"I can't understand how come! He's appeared to great acclaim in all the capitals of the world."

"If he played in Berlin, then it had to be after I left. Anyway, he'll be here tonight; maybe you'll like each other."

"You mean because we're both Chinese?"

"Oh, for crying out loud, Anna May, from the time we met and became friends, I haven't been able to fathom your taste in anybody. You think Clive Brook is a bore."

"He is. Don't you agree? Those few love scenes you did with him in *Shanghai Express*, I expected icicles to form on your lips."

"You're right. He's a cold fish. But very charming. And what about Herbert Marshall? I saw him flirt with you at Ronald Colman's party. Does the fact that he only has one leg put you off?"

"Not at all. I think he'd be nice to have around if I needed to touch wood."

"What are you looking for in a man?" asked Dietrich with exasperation.

"I'm not looking for a man!"

"Then what *are* you looking for?"

"A job!"

Police Inspector Herbert Villon sat at his desk flipping through the pages of *Picture Play* magazine. Seated in a chair opposite him, Hazel Dickson, who enjoyed the dubious profession of selling gossip to newspapers, magazines, and their columnists, attacked a fingernail with an emery board. She heard Villon saying, "Oooh, what I'd like to do to Helen Twelvetrees."

"That's one of the things I like about you, Herb. You know, like the way you suck your teeth and clean your nails with toothpicks. I'm the lady who's generous with her favors, in return for which I get the occasional dinner, a couple of drinks, an invitation to the Policeman's Ball, and 'Ooooh, what I'd like to do to Helen Twelvetrees or Barbara Stanwyck or Ginger Rogers or Ruth Chatterton. . . ."

"Not Ruth Chatterton," said Villon, now ogling a photograph of Sally Eilers, "too old."

"I wish Chatterton could hear you say that so I could hear her sigh of relief. Will you put that damn magazine down and answer the question?"

"What question?"

"The one I asked you before you zeroed in on Twelvetrees. Are you wearing a tuxedo tonight?"

"Why?"

"What do you mean 'Why'? I'm taking you to Dietrich's big bash tonight. It's the most sought after invitation in town! Two dozen parties were canceled when Marlene announced she was giving hers."

Villon lowered the magazine. "You're chummy enough to call her Marlene?"

Hazel moved on to another nail, another enemy she assailed with vigor. "The last time I interviewed her she cooked me a Wiener schnitzel."

"Do tell."

"Don't be so snotty."

"I'm not being snotty. I'm being impressed. I'm even jealous. I'd like Marlene to cook something special for me too."

"Wear your tuxedo and make a good impression tonight and maybe she will."

"Do you think Helen Twelvetrees will be there?"

"How do I know?"

"Did Dietrich really invite you or are we crashing as usual?"

"Personal invitation by phone." She shifted in her chair. "She likes me. I don't peddle gossip about her."

"And how come you don't?"

"Because I genuinely like her. She's a great gal. With her, all that glamour stuff is a put-on. She thinks it's a big nothing. The only thing she likes about it is the money. She pulls down a hundred and fifty thousand a picture; where does that hit you?"

"If she wasn't already married I'd propose. And what about him living in Switzerland with a mistress?"

"It don't bother Dietrich, it don't bother me. Let me put it to you this way. I know plenty of dirt about her. Plenty of *real* dirt. But I ain't selling it to nobody. Let the others trade in on her. I value her liking me. She got me in good with Claudette Colbert where before Claudette would never talk to me, only to Florabel Muir of the Daily News Syndicate."

"So now it's Claudette."

"Well, you don't expect me to call her Shirley, do you?" She placed the emery board into her handbag, placed the handbag on his desk, folded her arms, which meant she meant business, fixed him with a firm look, and asked, "What about the tuxedo?"

"I'm a cop, honey. Cops don't wear tuxedos."

"What do they wear besides a sneer on their lips or a coffin?"

Villon lowered the magazine. He favored her with a sweet smile. "Hazel, why'd I ever get mixed up with you?"

"I'm not sure, Herb. I thought it was my mother you were after."

"She's got great gams for an old broad."

"The tuxedo, Herb. I blew a month's salary on a Coco Chanel."

"Maybe after the party you can hock it."

"Go to hell."

"I can't. We're going to Dietrich's party. And stop looking daggers at me. I'm wearing the tuxedo, okay?" She favored him with a look of contentment. "What real dirt you got on Marlene?"

"That's for me to know and you to never find out."

"What about her astrologer, Carroll Richter?"

"What about him?"

"He must have plenty on her."

"What makes you think that?"

"His crystal balls!"

8

In Marlene's kitchen, where she was now preparing several baking pans of apple strudel, Anna May was sipping a cup of tea and marveling at Dietrich's industry. It was a warm day outside and the kitchen was overheated. One of the butlers had opened all the windows and another had set up floor fans, which gave some relief to everyone working in the rooms. But the ovens were ablaze and would stay ablaze to keep the food warm through the party. Marlene was telling Anna May how an astrologer in Berlin, an Egyptian, had predicted she would have to cross a vast expanse of water before achieving true fame and fortune. And here she was.

"It's amazing."

"His prediction?"

"The way you believe in astrology."

"Don't you? The Chinese and the Egyptians were the first great practitioners of astrology."

"My grandfather was an astrologer, as a matter of fact. And he was pretty damn good at it. When Doug Fairbanks was looking for a girl to play the treacherous Chinese maid in his *Thief of Bagdad*, I was dying for a chance to audition but I thought he'd think I was too young. I was only fourteen. But my grandfather had my chart done for me and he said, 'You will play that part.' And I did."

"There, you see?" She shouted to no one in particular, "I need more white raisins!" and very quickly they materialized on the table where she was working. Anna May was deep in thought. Marlene caught her look and offered her a penny for her thoughts.

Anna May said, "My very good friend Mai Mai Chu. She's the astrologer who did my chart. Shall I ask her to the party? She's very very good. All the bankers and investment brokers swear by her. She predicted the '29 market crash."

"Oh yes?"

"My mother and her mother were great friends. Mai Mai lived in Paris for a decade or more. She knew the literary set. Hemingway, Fitzgerald, Sylvia Beach, all that gang. My mother suspected she might have been a spy for the Allies during the war."

"I wish I'd known that. She could have given me some tips for my part in *Dishonored*."

"She's been asked to work with Garbo."

"On what? Greta's doing a spy movie?"

"Don't you read the trades? She's doing *Mata Hari*."

Dietrich smiled and winked. "I got there first."

Anna May was crossing the kitchen to a wall phone. "I'm going to call Mai Mai now. If she's free, I'm sure she'll agree to come."

Mai Mai Chu was a petite woman of an unguessable age and delicately pretty features who lived in an elegantly furnished loft apartment on the perimeter of Chinatown. She was lighting incense in a little glass tumbler before a statue of Buddha. As smoke started curling out from the incense, Mai Mai said to Buddha, "Anna May Wong is phoning me." The phone rang. Mai Mai smiled. She said into the mouthpiece, "Hello, Anna May. So nice to hear from you."

"You're putting me on!"

"You know better than that. I sensed you and that's that. I've also been sensing Eleanor Roosevelt. I sent her a note assuring her her husband would win the Democratic nomination for president. And he's going to win. Actually, if they ran Rex the Wonder Horse opposite Herbert Hoover he'd also win. Nice people, the Roosevelts, but his mother's a harridan. I visited them at her Hyde Park estate this past September. Tastelessly furnished. What time is the party?"

"I don't believe this!" Anna May said to Dietrich, "She answered the phone with 'Hello, Anna May; so nice to hear from you' and now she asks, 'What time is the party'!"

Marlene was fascinated. "I'll have my car pick you both up."

"Wonderful. I hate driving on New Year's Eve." Anna May and Mai Mai agreed that the car would first pick up Anna May and then come for Mai Mai at her building on the outskirts of Chinatown. After a moment's silence, Mai Mai said, "There could be danger."

Anna May paled. "What kind of danger?" This drew Dietrich to Anna May's side, holding a glass of champagne and puffing anxiously on a cigarette. Anna May's hold on the telephone had tightened.

Mai Mai said, "The instruments of danger are a group of Miss Dietrich's guests."

Anna May repeated this to Marlene, who gave no reaction.

"Just a minute," said Mai Mai. She placed the receiver down on the table and pressed her delicate fingertips against her temples.

Marlene was disquieted. "What's wrong? Why aren't you talking? Has she hung up?"

"No no. She's done this before. She's probably placed the receiver on the table while she presses her fingertips against her temples. She does this when she needs to release tension."

Mai Mai returned. "It is nothing. Anna May, shall I expect you around nine?"

"Yes, I'll be there promptly at nine."

After she replaced the receiver, with delicate mincing steps, Mai Mai Chu wafted to her crystal ball, which rested on a purple velvet–covered cushion on a small table handcarved from ivory. She looked into the crystal ball and asked, "What shall I wear tonight?"

"Danger," whispered Marlene. And then her face was aglow, "How exciting!"

"Danger from some of your guests." Anna May's eyes were dark with foreboding.

"That is quite possible," said Marlene as she refilled her glass with champagne and filled another for Anna May, "I've invited the Marx Brothers."

ᦉ TWO ᦉ

IVAR TENSHA'S CUSTOM-BUILT orange Rolls-Royce smoothly made its way toward Marlene Dietrich's New Year's Eve party. To Tensha, it was like floating on a magic carpet to the palace of an Oriental potentate. He knew a lot of Oriental potentates, but he couldn't think of one as exotic and as glamorous as the glorious Marlene. He sat in the back of the magnificent machine with Countess Dorothy di Frasso and Monte Trevor, a self-styled film producer from Great Britain. The portable bar was well stocked with champagne, a brand bottled in France exclusively for Ivar Tensha. His signature was on the label. Nothing was too good or too expensive for Ivar Tensha, the Romanian munitions czar.

"Ivar, you have a very silly expression on your face," said di Frasso. Trevor was refilling their glasses. He didn't spill a drop, so smooth was the drive.

"I was thinking of Marlene," he said with a heavily accented voice.

"Marlene deserves better than a silly expression. Don't you agree, Monte?"

"I wish I could get her for a movie," said Trevor, "I dream of casting her as *Salome*."

"*Salome*," whispered Tensha, "the dance of the seven veils." Di Frasso expected drool to seep from his mouth, but none was forthcoming.

"And as Herod," continued Trevor, "I see this young actor Paramount has brought over from London, Charles Laughton."

Di Frasso agreed. "That would be very interesting. You'll need someone sexy for John the Baptist. How about Gable?"

"Dietrich and Gable. Now wouldn't that be a fascinating combination." Tensha licked his lips. If he wasn't so damned rich, thought di Frasso, he'd be repulsive. She wondered if there was a Mrs. Tensha, and if so, how to get rid of her.

Said Monte Trevor, "Louis B. Mayer doesn't lend his stars without driving a hard bargain."

"Whatever the money," said di Frasso, "it would be worth it for Gable. He's hot box office."

Tensha spoke softly. "I can get anything I want from Louis B. Mayer." Di Frasso thought she detected menace in that simple statement. Monte Trevor thought, here I am in the backseat of a Rolls-Royce owned by one of the world's wealthiest men, a man who seems to be actually buying my bullshit of producing a film about Salome. Maybe he's interested in putting up the money. I could budget it for two million and walk away with half a million for myself. That's how Alexander Korda operates in England, that shrewd Hungarian.

Trevor heard di Frasso saying, "Monte, your lips are moving but no sounds emerge. Are you all right?"

"Oh quite, quite my dear. I was just formulating a budget for *Salome* off the top of my head."

"Is that where you keep your money?"

Trevor laughed, but not heartily. This woman is dangerous, he thought, I wouldn't want her for an enemy. "I think *Salome* needs to be done on a lavish scale. The way Cecil B. DeMille would do it."

"How lavish?" asked Tensha.

"Roughly I'd say two million."

"Dollars?"

"He doesn't mean dinars," said di Frasso flatly.

"Even if it was dinars, it would be too much," said Tensha, who proceeded to light a cigar that to di Frasso resembled a miniature torpedo. Tensha's cigars were made especially for him in Cuba from tobacco grown on his own subsidized farm fifty miles outside Havana. The cigar bands of course carried Tensha's signature.

Trevor felt himself deflating, but he persisted as any good con artist would. "Don't you find the prospect of being involved with motion pictures exciting?"

"War pictures. I like war pictures!" Tensha's eyes were ablaze with fervor. "Bombs. Bullets. All calibers. Blood. Lots of blood. Maimed and mangled bodies. Explosions. Soldiers trembling and quivering on barbed wire. Women sobbing and screaming as their children are swept with machine-gun fire."

Di Frasso commented dryly, "I'm sure Monte plans on some spears and a few flaming arrows and perhaps a catapult or two hurling rocks onto parapets."

Tensha made a vulgar noise. "Too tame. By me, *Salome* is salami."

Trevor said in a tiny voice he didn't recognize as his own, "But what about the dance of the seven veils?"

Di Frasso interrupted. "Perhaps she could do it during the Battle of the Marne?"

"That," said Tensha, "could be very interesting."

"Yes!" said Trevor enthusiastically, "for each veil she sheds, she shoots an officer."

"From the hip?" asked di Frasso.

Trevor glared at her. She was busy renewing her face. They were almost at their destination. The cigar smoke was causing her eyes to tear. She asked Trevor to lower a window. While carefully rouging her lips, she eyed the chauffeur, who was staring at her in the rearview mirror. Not that young, thought the chauffeur, but what the hell. If she could be a ticket to a screen test. Gable got to where he is by using older women,

Pauline Frederick, Alice Brady, Jane Cowl. His first wife who taught him all he'd ever know about acting, Josephine Dillon, was twenty years older. And his current wife, Rhea, she's at least fifteen years older and rich to boot. His eyes sent di Frasso an unsubtle signal. She rewarded him with a raised eyebrow, which she hoped he recognized meant she was lowering her guard.

"My dear," she heard Tensha saying, "never with the hired help. It is so bourgeois."

She replied with a smile, "And where did you get the impression I'm descended from landed gentry?"

"My guests will be arriving any minute now!" shouted Marlene in her magnificent ballroom. "You must hurry!" She was yelling at a workman atop a ladder fixing clusters of balloons to the ceiling. His was the last to be set in place. At a signal, all the clusters of balloons affixed to the ceiling would fall at midnight. She had borrowed technicians from the studio to set up the electrical system that would release the balloons at the touch of a button. Her maid Gloria was urging her to return to her suite and finish dressing. Marlene waved her away impatiently as she spoke to the orchestra leader. "Not too many waltzes! Waltzes are for Marie Dressler's parties. And when I make my entrance down the stairs . . ."

"I have a magnificent arrangement of 'Falling in Love Again,' " said Gus Arnheim, the orchestra leader whose usually hefty fee she had beaten down to scale for him and his musicians. After all, wasn't it a privilege to play at Dietrich's party?

"No!" she boomed. "For my entrance you will play 'There'll Be a Hot Time in the Old Town Tonight'!"

Arnheim blanched. "We don't have the sheet music."

Dietrich bristled. "You're musicians, aren't you? You're professionals, aren't you? You can improvise! Improvise! Start rehearsing!" She hurried away to check the trays of hot and cold hors d'oeuvres stacked in the pantry.

Arnheim commanded, "Okay, boys, let's give the lady

what she wants." The drummer made a nasty noise, to which Arnheim said, "You'll never give her that."

Somewhere on a bumpy road in Benedict Canyon, a tired Hispano-Suiza dreaming of an imminent retirement after too many years of service coughed and chugged its way to Dietrich's party. The chauffeur prayed the old veteran would make it back to the Russian Embassy before breaking down. In the backseat, Gregory Ivanov, one of Russia's most skillful diplomats, held his wife's calloused hand. Natalia Ivanov had worked on a collective farm outside Minsk, where she guided tractors and maneuvered ploughshares and hoed and raked and seeded until her arm muscles were the envy of every male comrade she had bedded with unrestrained alacrity. The Russian word for 'nymphomaniac' is much too complicated, but Natalia was too simpleminded to be bothered by complications. On an official visit to her collective while Gregory Ivanov was still a small cog in the vast Bolshevik wheel, Ivanov took one look at her tensors and her threatening breasts and it was love at first sight. With the not-so-little woman behind him and pushing, he soon made his way into the diplomatic corps and rose rapidly to the top, like cream in a bottle of unpasteurized milk. There was no end to his ambitions, and wangling his post in Los Angeles by betraying three of his closest friends and his mother, who wrote odes to wheat and scythes, was just the beginning of the progression of his own five-year plan.

Natalia grunted.

"What bothers you?" asked Gregory Ivanov.

"I will look like a gnarled oak tree in a room full of movie stars."

"If so, Natalia Ivanova, then you will be an original. Movie stars! Poo! With their perfect bodies and their lacquered nails and their coiffured hair, can they compare to you?"

"No," she said darkly, "because I'm a mess."

"I love you the way you are, my beloved. Warts and all."

"I'm homesick."

"I know. But we can't leave until I have finished . . . you know."

She nodded. Although they spoke in Russian and the chauffeur was a college student who was hired because he claimed he didn't understand Russian, they trusted no one. But soon, if all went according to plan, he whispered to her, "We will rule the world."

She snuggled against his chest and smiled, revealing a row of brown stumps that passed for teeth. The chauffeur wondered as he stared at her in the rearview mirror if she enjoying gnawing tree bark.

Dietrich stood in front of a floor-length mirror, admiring the silver lamé dress designed for her for this occasion by Paramount's Travis Banton. Its line was simple and majestic. The neckline was trimmed with mink. Gloria, the maid, adjusted the mirror and Marlene admired the back of the dress. It was cut to the base of her spine, daringly sexy. She didn't need a brassiere. Her breasts were arrogantly firm. It would be years before they'd need an adjustment. She would wear no jewelry. She had no need to. She was a sun that had no need of satellites.

"Madam, you are exquisite," said Gloria.

"I know." Gloria was in her midtwenties and said she aspired to nothing but a husband, children, and a small house at the beach, any beach. She had been an extra in the nightclub scene in *Morocco* and caught Dietrich's attention when the star saw Gloria move another extra out of the way of an arc light that made Dietrich look five years younger. Dietrich was impressed, struck up a conversation with the girl, and offered her the job as her maid. Gloria was thrilled and accepted at once. Although she tended to shout a lot and raise her voice and demand perfection in everything, underneath it all Marlene was Mother Earth. She was kind to the people who served her and her daughter, and her generosity was legend. It was predicted by her advisers she would die a pauper, a prediction she responded to with a shrug. She believed

17

in herself. She would always overcome adversity. After all, wasn't she the only movie star in the world who could play a musical saw? Darling Igo Sym, he said she was his best pupil. She toyed with the idea of regaling her guests with a few selections tonight, but then tabled the idea as they might find it unsophisticated.

"Gloria . . ."

"Yes, Miss Dietrich?"

"Pour two glasses of champagne." She indicated the cooler that contained a chilled bottle of Dom Perignon of a vintage year. "I want us to greet the New Year now, alone. Go on. Pour them."

"Oh, Miss Dietrich!"

"Don't be silly, Gloria. I am a mere mortal, but don't you ever tell Garbo."

"You're driving too fast!" yelled Dong See. "Slow down, for crying out loud, you'll kill us!"

Raymond Souvir maneuvered the white Cadillac through the tricky and threatening curves of Malibu Canyon Road with the skill and dexterity of a professional competing in the *Grand Prix*. "I've never had an accident in my life, so relax."

"There's a first time for everything."

"Don't be frightened, be excited. Tonight you're going to meet the crème de la crème of motion pictures. I had tea with Marlene on Sunday and she let me see the guest list. There'll be everybody but Rin Tin Tin. Marlene doesn't approve of animals at large gatherings. Anyway, the dog's a has-been."

Dong See's fists were clenched, knuckle-white. There were tiny beads of perspiration on his forehead; he seemed paralyzed. He prayed in Chinese, English, and French, this an affectation. The speedometer continued to read eighty. He knew the car could do over one hundred. He prayed it wouldn't. "Please Raymond . . ."

"Oh shut up and think about sex. Marlene's arranging a test for me. She's going to do it with me, and von Sternberg's directing. What a terrific woman. She's nothing like what you see on the screen. Do you know when I was first brought to her house by Claudette Colbert, she was in the kitchen . . .''

"I know she's devoted to cooking . . ."

"She was on her knees scrubbing the floor! Can you imagine? Dietrich scrubbing her kitchen floor! Unbelievable!"

"Look out for that truck!"

"Why? Is it doing something unusual?"

The limousine transporting Anna May Wong and Mai Mai Chu to the party was upholstered with zebra skin. A closed window separated the passengers from the chauffeur, and Anna May was glad the man couldn't hear their conversation. Mai Mai was all doom and gloom. "There is no hope for our China," she said sadly.

"I'm a native American, Mai Mai. I was born here."

"Nevertheless, China is a lost cause. First overrun by the Japanese, who will torture the people and pillage the cities, and then the Communists will take command. A very grim scenario, very grim. I suppose Carroll Richter will be at the party?"

"And you will be very nice to him."

Mai Mai smiled her charming, delicate smile. "I am always nice to everyone. I was even nice to Gertrude Stein and Alice B. Toklas, and it is not very easy to be nice to them, although Gertrude is nicer than Alice, who is very possessive and very sharp-tongued and should either wax her mustache or shave it. Did you meet them when you were in Paris?"

"They were out of town looking for truffles."

"Of course, Carroll Richter is a fraud. He despises me."

"How do you know that?"

"I have done his chart. A mutual friend gave me his date and hour of birth. Actually, he doesn't make the most of himself. He should be writing a syndicated newspaper column."

"Perhaps one day he will. What's wrong?"

Mai Mai's eyes were closed, her tiny hands covering her tiny mouth. Then her eyes flew open and her hands dropped

19

slowly to her lap. "It's here again. The warning. Danger, Anna May, danger."

"Do you see Marlene threatened?"

Mai Mai's voice was sepulchral. "I see all of us threatened. All of us." She reached over and took Anna May's hand. "I have had this premonition before. In Paris, at a ball given by Ivar Kreuger, the match king. Of course you've heard of him."

"Of course. He had a scheme to rule the world. . . ."

"It seemed silly to a lot of people, but Ivar was a genius. And a group of very powerful people believed in his scheme and joined him in implementing it. But Ivar was a madman. He went out of control and had to be destroyed. Very little has been heard of the scheme since. But those people still exist. And my charts tell me they have reactivated. They are on the move again. Our very being is threatened, Anna May, the sword of Damocles hangs over our heads, waiting to fall and destroy."

Then she fell silent. Anna May said nothing. She looked out the window at peaceful Beverly Hills, at houses still illuminated with Christmas decorations, some of them sweetly simple, such as a creche with the Virgin Mother cradling the infant Jesus. Some of them vulgarly garish such as an expensive electrical depiction of the first Christmas supper with waiters dispensing separate checks.

Anna May's heartbeat was unusually rapid. By nature she was a calm and unflappable woman. Now there was heat in her cheeks and moisture on her upper lip and she dabbed at it with a lace-trimmed handkerchief. What Mai Mai had told her disturbed her. Mai Mai was a genius; her father had told her this and she had great respect for his judgment. If there was an opportunity later, she would share what she had heard with Marlene. Marlene was a practical woman, a very intelligent and a very clever one. Look at how she manipulated her husband and von Sternberg and Adolph Zukor and Ben Schulberg, who was the West Coast head of Paramount Pictures, but, according to rumor, not for much longer. People seemed to like to be manipulated by her, she did it with such grace and subtlety. The way she loved her daughter, but didn't dote on her or indulge her. The way she defied the studio when they insisted she keep Maria sequestered from the public eye, as the presence of a daughter might damage Dietrich's glamorous image. So Dietrich was the bellwether, and other actresses revealed they were mothers. Gloria Swanson, Miriam Hopkins, Constance Bennett, even when the legitimacy of their children was in question. Lots of actresses went to the desert for their health and returned many months later with "adopted" babies. Some could even name the father.

Yes, she would share this knowledge with Marlene, and the sooner the better, although she'd be hard put to explain what she thought Marlene could do about it.

Marlene was in her daughter's bedroom, where Maria's nurse sat in an easy chair reading Tiffany Thayer's racy version of *The Three Musketeers*. Maria was a beautiful child, and now, fast asleep, her mother thought she resembled an angel in repose.

"Did she enjoy her dinner?"

"Oh, yes. She's like her mother. She loves her food."

"She mustn't like her food too much. I have a fat problem and I don't want her to have one too. Now listen, if the party gets too noisy and awakens Maria, come and tell me and I'll send them all home."

"Nothing awakens Maria. She sleeps like a log."

"I wish I could say the same for me. Well dear, Happy New Year."

"And to you, Miss Dietrich." God, but she's gorgeous in that slinky, shimmery gown. And me, me in this damned uniform, alone on New Year's Eve reading Tiffany Thayer. Oh, what the hell, D'Artagnan's banging Milady deWinter. Some girls have all the luck.

Marlene went swiftly down the hall to a room at the rear of the house. She knocked lightly on the door and entered. An actor dressed as Father Time and a midget dressed as the New Year's baby sat playing cards and drinking gin.

"Everything all right, boys?"

"Everything's fine, Miss Dietrich. Dinner was great." Father Time was a once popular silent screen actor down on his luck. Von Sternberg had asked her to hire him.

"How's the diaper, Ambrose?"

The midget chuckled and said, "A perfect fit. The gin's great too."

"Go easy on it. I don't want the old year reeling out and the New Year staggering in."

"Don't you worry about us," said Father Time. "We're pros."

"Happy New Year." Marlene shut the door behind her. Father Time. Once he'd been the king of the mountain, and now he was at the bottom of the heap. What a cruel profession, what a cruel town. Well, they'll never do it to me. She moved to a balcony hidden by drapes that overlooked the ballroom. The guests were arriving. Soon she'd make her entrance. She would time it very carefully even if she had to wait for the very last star to arrive, and that would undoubtedly be Constance Bennett. Well, thought Dietrich, Connie darling, no bitch upstages Dietrich, especially in her own home. The orchestra was playing "Sonny Boy." Al Jolson must have entered with his wife, Ruby Keeler. Marlene returned to her suite for another glass of champagne. She found Anna May Wong waiting for her.

"Darling! Why didn't you send Gloria to fetch me?" Gloria was pouring champagne for them.

"I only just got here. I'm glad I got to you before you joined your guests."

"You're frightened. What's wrong?" Gloria distributed the glasses and then discreetly disappeared.

"You'll probably think I'm foolish. But you've got to hear what Mai Mai Chu told me in the car."

"Where is she?"

"She's downstairs studying the guests."

"What do you mean 'studying' them?"

Anna May took Marlene's hand and led her to a settee. "You've got to hear this. And when I'm finished you can tell me I'm either a damn fool or that you're as disturbed as I am. But Marlene, Mai Mai is no damn fool and she's very disturbed. And Mai Mai doesn't disturb easily. You remember what she said on the phone this afternoon, there will be danger in this house tonight. Well, it came to her again on the drive here, but Marlene, this time Mai Mai was truly frightened. . . ."

"Tell me," said Marlene, "tell me everything. And I mean *everything.*" She took a heavy swig of champagne.

◖◖ THREE ◗◗

HAZEL DICKSON'S ROADSTER was old but proud. For the past five years it had served her well, transporting her over many thousands of miles on the trail of a lead or nosing out the tidbits she would sell to the newspaper columnists who hoped to titillate their hungry and faithful readers. Although Hazel was carefully steering up the long driveway where stately rows of cedars of Lebanon formed an arboreal honor guard, the roadster seemed to know its own way to the stately front door. One of a dozen parking attendants replaced Hazel at the wheel, eyeing Hazel and Herb Villon with suspicion. Surely they were meant to use the servant's entrance. Herb was not at home in a tuxedo and Hazel was wearing her Coco Chanel, the latest in evening pajamas. It was a daring new style that Dietrich had introduced to America when she returned from Paris the previous April.

They could hear the orchestra treating Cole Porter's "You Do Something to Me" with reverence and respect as they passed through the entrance. The butler on guard at the doors recognized Hazel and wished her a Happy New Year. She would have preferred hearing him tell her how ravishing she looked, but a girl can't have everything. Herb was impressed by the huge foyer with its grand staircase leading up to the ballroom. Maids and butlers were flying up and down bearing trays of food and party favors. "There are four bars upstairs," Hazel advised Herb, who had muttered something about being thirsty.

"If Helen Twelvetrees is here, introduce me to her."

"And then what?"

"And then I shall ravish her on the dance floor in full view of everyone."

"And what will her husband be doing?"

"Keeping score, if he's a good sport."

Entering the ballroom, Herb had the good manners not to yell "Wow!" Instead he said to Hazel, "If they drop a bomb on this place, the only thing left of Hollywood will be walk-ons and extras." He recognized Maurice Chevalier. He assumed the woman with the French heartthrob was his wife, Yvonne. There was Fredric March with his wife, Florence Eldredge, looking as though he wished he were with somebody else's wife. March's lechery was a Hollywood legend. John Gilbert, holding what was probably a tumbler of whisky, had arrived with his young bride, actress Virginia Bruce, but Hazel spotted her dancing with a French actor recently arrived in Hollywood, Charles Boyer. John Gilbert was trying to act gay and insouciant, as though his star was not descending, the talkies being unkind to him and his once huge horde of fans dwindling as rapidly as sand falling through a sieve. Gloria Swanson, albeit only five feet tall, looked majestic in a black gown studded with multicolored paillettes, and artfully wielded a black ostrich fan that managed to sidesweep anyone in her immediate vicinity. Hazel heard a woman commenting on Swanson, "She has a classic profile. Very old."

Jules Furthman, the highly respected writer who had scripted *Shanghai Express,* was talking to columnist Sidney Skolsky, a diminutive man whose forte was telling his readers what the stars wore in bed, if they wore anything. Furthman was expounding on another writer, who was accused of stealing his latest plot from de Maupassant: "He'd plagiarize an obituary." Skolsky reminded Furthman that he'd lifted *Shanghai Express* from de Maupassant's *Boule de Suif*, to which Furthman responded swiftly, "Not all of it!"

An ardent young man reciting a Browning love poem to lovely actress Dorothy Jordan was overheard by the impeccable but drunk John Barrymore, who cackled to his stunning wife, Dolores Costello, "My dear, methinks I am hearing verses."

Herb, holding his second gin and tonic, was having a wonderful time eavesdropping on the stars and delighting in their uninhibited bitchery. Hazel had left him and was off in search of salable items. Herb heard director George Cukor, a recent arrival from New York with the sharp tongue of an avenging serpent, say of an actress long on ambition and short on talent, "She's ferociously fought and clawed her way to the bottom."

Dong See had downed several brandies, neat, to calm his shattered nerves. Raymond Souvir was anxiously looking for Dietrich, and a maid told him she had not yet made an appearance. The former silent screen star Pola Negri, who after a three-year absence was back in Hollywood to make her first talking film for Radio Pictures, *A Woman Commands*, had much of the room buzzing with surprise as she engaged in what seemed to be a very warm and friendly chat with her once arch rival at Paramount, Gloria Swanson. A lip-reader might have been delighted at what Negri was telling Swanson. "I roll the batter very very thin until you can almost see through it. Then I mash cooked prunes into the cottage cheese and spread a good layer on each individual square of batter. After I roll them and place them in a pan of lightly melted butter, I put them in the oven and *bake* them."

"Bake? Not fry?" Swanson looked so astonished, one might have thought she'd heard an option drop.

"Bake, my darling, bake. Believe me, are those yummy blintzes!"

Bela Lugosi of *Dracula* fame was apparently bemoaning his

fate to Hazel Dickson. "So what is fame, what is success, what is money without someone to love?"

Hazel was pragmatic. "Have you considered taking up a hobby?"

"What kind of a hobby?" asked Lugosi in world-weary tones.

"Of course, something that would interest you. Something you could sink your teeth into."

Countess Dorothy di Frasso swept into the room with Ivar Tensha and Monte Trevor in her wake. She accepted champagne from a waiter and an hors d'oeuvre from another and to her horror realized she was chewing on a disguised anchovy, and she despised anchovies.

"Is there anything else I can get you?" asked a waiter.

"A stomach pump." She grabbed a napkin from the waiter's tray and rid herself of the anchovy. A gulp of the bubbly had a needed cleansing effect, and then with an infectious joie de vivre she took to the task of introducing the munitions king and the British producer to all her friends and acquaintances, and they were legion. Within minutes Tensha and Trevor were swimming frantically in a sea of celebrity names and celebrity faces. From Edward G. Robinson to Evelyn Brent to Louise Brooks to Paul and Bella Muni. Soon they were hanging on for dear life to such familiar names and faces as Lilyan Tashman and Edmund Lowe and Victor McLaglen and then onward to Jackie Cooper and his mother and Mitzi Green and *her* mother and then to a sad young thing whose husband had run off to Mexico with her wealthy mother, di Frasso commenting sotto voce to her escorts, "The brute married her for her mummy."

Then di Frasso took egotistical delight in pointing out the many men who'd been to bed with her. Tensha asked with a rare twinkle in his eye, "Tell me, my dear, were you ever a virgin?"

Di Frasso laughed. "Ivor, I was a virgin way back when virginity was an asset." They were joined by Raymond Souvir and Dong See. Souvir commented on the presence of Gregory and Natalia Ivanov. Di Frasso explained, "Marlene specializes in eclectic guest lists. Actually, I suspect the Ivanovs are here because Marlene and Joseph von Sternberg have been haunting the Russian Embassy for research on the life of Catherine the Great. They want to do a film of her life with, of course, Marlene portraying the empress."

"I thought the Communists despised royalty," commented Dong See.

"Not when it could turn a profit," said di Frasso. "They certainly treasure the treasures they confiscated from the deposed peerage. They've been selling them throughout the world to finance their five-year plan." She addressed Tensha. "I'm told you've acquired some priceless religious articles."

"Oh, yes. I have a taste for icons studded with precious jewels."

Di Frasso said wearily, "While I have a taste for precious studs."

A buzz went up in the room. Constance Bennett was making her entrance, a dazzling creature in one of Gilbert Adrian's more unique designs, the dress daringly slit from ankle to thigh, and wearing jewels that were assuredly worth a movie star's ransom. Gloria Swanson, who loathed Constance Bennett, asked the star's sister Joan, "What will she do with all the wealth she flaunts? She certainly can't take it with her."

"If she can't take it with her," replied Joan Bennett, "she won't go."

Hazel Dickson said to Herb Villon, "Oh, thank God."

"For what?"

"Now that the Bennett bitch is here, Marlene will make *her* entrance."

In her suite, Marlene was pacing and digesting what Anna May Wong had told her. Mai Mai's premonitions were certainly disturbing. The delicate Chinese woman was not your ordinary, run-of-the-mill astrologer predicting that you will meet a tall dark stranger who will rape you; she was a psychic, a genuine psychic, a woman possessed of powers Marlene found both awesome and frightening. Marlene thought these were terrible burdens for a woman she knew to be small and seemingly defenseless. When a young actress in Berlin appearing with Max Reinhardt's celebrated and respected Theater Ensemble, she now remembered she had heard of the amazing Mai Mai Chu almost a decade before Anna May mentioned knowing her. Now she was here, under Dietrich's roof, suffering a premonition or premonitions she couldn't clearly decipher.

Danger.

"I see danger!"

Gloria, the maid, hurried into the room. "Miss Dietrich, Constance Bennett has arrived and Gloria Swanson is saying terrible things about her!"

"As well she should. Connie is a terrible woman. Come, Anna May, let's go downstairs."

Anna May was wise in the ways of Dietrich. "I'll go first. Give me a few minutes and then make your entrance."

She was out of the room before Marlene could politely demur and hurried down the stairs into the overpopulated ballroom. Dorothy di Frasso spotted her, "There's Anna May Wong coming down the stairs. She'll probably know the identity of the strange little Oriental woman wandering the room and staring at everyone. God knows what she's looking for."

"Perhaps an honest man," suggested Monte Trevor, not knowing any himself.

"There, look at her," cautioned di Frasso, "now she's staring at our group. Do any of you know her?"

No one replied.

The orchestra was spiritedly rendering "There'll Be a Hot Time in the Old Town Tonight" and the ballroom erupted into thunderous applause. Slowly, sensually, sinuously, a wicked and very worldly-wise smile on her face, Marlene Dietrich triumphantly descended the staircase into the ballroom.

Joseph von Sternberg sipped his drink. *You are my creation.*

I made you. I discovered you and taught you to be Marlene Die-
trich, the magnificent star, not the fat little frump I auditioned in
Berlin. I recognized that under those twenty pounds of fat there was
screaming for release the stunning creature descending the stair-
case. I too am that creature. Marlene, you are my doppelgänger.
The *doppelgänger*, the occult creature Germans believed was a
person's other self. Von Sternberg signaled a waiter for a
fresh drink.

Hazel Dickson said to Herb Villon, "She makes every
woman in this room look like Baron Frankenstein's creation."

"Oh, I wouldn't go that far," replied Herb, adding with
disappointment, "I guess there's going to be no Helen Twelvetrees."

"There's a Helen Twelvetrees," Hazel assured him, "but
not here tonight."

Hands on hips, Jean Harlow said to Joan Crawford, who
clung to the arm of a new boy in town, Franchot Tone: "Can
you beat that broad?"

To which Crawford responded, "The point is, Baby"—
everyone at MGM called Harlow 'Baby'—"you *can't* beat
that broad. My hat's off to her."

Natalia Ivanov was crying softly into a handkerchief. There
was no consoling her, and her husband refrained from trying.
Unlike Dietrich, Natalia could never ask the mirror on her
wall, "Who's the fairest one of all?" They would have been
surprised to learn that Dietrich never questioned her mirror.
She didn't have to. She knew the answer.

Kay Francis embraced Dietrich. "It's a tewwific pahty, dahling. And yaw so democwatic. Evewy stah from evewy studio
is hewe. But how did you dawe ask Connie Bennett and Lilyan
Tashman to the same pahty?"

"Why not? They're both friends of mine." She almost said
'fwiends' but she had greater control over her impediment.
Kay Francis didn't give a damn, not when they were paying
her seven thousand dollars a week.

"Didn't you know?"

"Know what?"

"Lilyan caught Connie in bed with her husband, Eddie Lowe. She beat the stuffing out of Connie!"

"That's all right. Connie has stuffing to spare. Forgive me, darling, I have so many guests to greet."

"Go wight ahead, sweetie. I want to meet Anna May's astwologuh fwiend. I think she's so fascinating." She wafted away on a cloud of Russian Leather.

Hazel waved at Marlene. Marlene wondered if the formidable-looking gentleman stifling a yawn was Hazel's policeman boyfriend. If there was truly danger tonight, she would find the presence of an officer of the law very comforting. Marlene and Hazel embraced. Hazel introduced Herb Villon, and Marlene recognized his name and said warmly and sincerely, "I'm so glad Hazel brought you." Villon felt good all over and was deeply in love with Dietrich. Hazel would be relieved to learn Helen Twelvetrees had been overthrown. Marlene swiftly and lucidly told them about Mai Mai Chu's dire prediction, and Villon, who had in the past resorted to psychics when at an impasse in a particularly puzzling murder case, was openly sympathetic to Dietrich.

"Perhaps it would be wise for you to send for reinforcements, Mr. Villon."

"Call me Herb. Why do I need reinforcements?"

"The danger!" exclaimed Dietrich.

"What danger?"

"The danger I just told you about! Mai Mai Chu's premonition." Hazel shifted from one foot to another while Villon explained to Marlene, "I can't call for reinforcements because of a psychic's premonition."

"Why not?"

"My chief would think I'm nuts."

"You can't be nuts. I can see for myself you're a highly intelligent person."

"Marlene, this is New Year's Eve. The entire police force is out keeping law and order. People go wild on New Year's Eve. They might send for me to go out there and help."

Marlene stared into his big brown eyes and at his craggy good looks and respected the intensity with which he spoke to her. "But supposing something terrible happens?"

"*Then* I request a backup and we pray there's a backup available."

Anna May Wong joined them. She knew Hazel well and was happy to meet Villon. She told Marlene, "Mai Mai is creating quite a stir. She either amuses people or makes them uncomfortable. She's foreseeing things and I think she's in a mood to perform. Would you like her to?"

Dietrich gave the offer some thought and then smiled. "Will she be outrageous?"

"She will be whatever she will want to be. I've seen Mai Mai in situations like this before, and I can assure you, she's never boring."

"I'm a bit of a psychic myself," said Dietrich, "and I have a feeling this will be a night to remember. Come. Let's get her started."

The ballroom was hushed. Mai Mai Chu sat on a plush chair on the orchestra platform. She looked like a porcelain statuette come to life. She spoke softly but clearly, and everyone in the room could hear her. Anna May Wong stood next to her. She addressed the guests.

"With Marlene's kind permission, I have asked my dear friend Madam Mai Mai Chu to perform for us tonight. Actually, Madam Chu volunteered. She has much on her mind that she wishes to share with all of us. Madam Chu is a world-renowned and respected astrologer . . ."—Carroll Richter stood stiffly at a bar clenching a highball and choking on the scream welling up in his throat—". . . and equally of importance, she is a psychic possessed of the most amazing, and perhaps to some of us, very frightening powers."

There was a buzz humming in the ballroom. It was a buzz familiar to veteran Hollywood party-goers. It consisted of amusement mingled with expectation peppered with cynicism and a dollop of incredulity. Hazel heard a dimwitted starlet ask her escort, "I thought a psychic was something you took when you have an upset stomach."

Anna May continued. "This afternoon, when I phoned from this house to invite Mai Mai to join the celebration tonight, she told me she sensed danger here."

Again the buzz, but this time one of increasing interest and curiosity. Dorothy di Frasso exchanged looks with Ivar Tensha and Monte Trevor. The Ivanovs had joined them and Gregory squeezed Natalia's hand. Dong See stole a look at Raymond Souvir, who was hypnotized by the look of anxiety on Marlene Dietrich's face. Out of curiosity, Herb Villon's eyes were two spotlights sweeping the room studying the reactions of various guests. Hazel knew she was on to a potentially great story and was glad Louella Parsons, the queen of Hollywood gossip for the Hearst newspaper syndicate, was ill with the flu and couldn't attend. More likely she and her physician husband had polished off one too many bottles of bootleg rye and were too sick to make it. Lolly Parsons paid handsomely for hot items.

"This evening, on our way here together," Anna May continued while wondering if a lecture tour with Mai Mai might prove handsomely profitable, "Madam Chu again was struck by the premonition of danger cloaking this house tonight. Since our arrival, she has been moving among you, studying your faces, and from some of you she has been getting what she refers to as interesting vibrations. She will also share with you some of what she has learned the past few days from her charts. And speaking from experience, when I despaired of being hired by Doug Fairbanks for *The Thief of Bagdad* when I was just an inexperienced youngster, she told me I'd get the part, and bless her heart, I did. Madam Chu has spent many years abroad in Paris, in Berlin, in Moscow, you name it, she's been there; in other words, she knows international acclaim and respect. My dear friend, Madam Mai Mai Chu."

Anna May accepted Dong See's arm as he assisted her from the platform. They had been introduced earlier and took an instant liking to each other. Madam Chu smiled at her audience and spoke reassuringly. "Do not be frightened by what I say. What I say to you is a guide, a warning, the opportunity to avert what is inevitable. There are those who scoff at astrology, yet there are those who live by it and thrive by it and learn from it. My psychic powers are true powers. I can no sooner deny them as I cannot deny the inevitability of death. And none of us can deny the inevitability of death."

She knew she had them; some were fascinated, some restrained an urge to scoff vocally, some believed, and some wanted to believe, anything to ease the misery of living.

Mai Mai said, "My charts tell me there are several disasters impending. Perhaps this New Year, perhaps the following year, an ocean liner will catch fire and sink off the Atlantic Coast. Many lives will be lost. A pleasure cruise that will turn into a horrifying nightmare. And also in the same vicinity, which is in the area of the state of New Jersey and the Atlantic Ocean, an airship will explode and burn and again many lives will be lost. This airship will be of foreign origin and the suspicion will be that the cause of the explosion will be the sabotage of a terrorist organization."

What she was saying was incredible to many, amusing to others, and to some, absolute hogwash. Groucho Marx had arrived with his wife when Mai Mai began speaking and asked Marlene, "Where's the other three jugglers?" Marlene gently put a finger on his lips and he just as gently kissed it as his wife pulled him away.

Now Mai Mai really disturbed the guests. "My charts tell me there will be a terrible second world war. There is a dangerous cancer growing in Europe in the form of a little man with horrifying ambitions to rule the world." Marlene clasped her hands tightly together. She knew this man. She had heard him speak at a street rally. He had seen her perform on stage opposite Hans Albers in the musical *Two Bow-Ties*. He had sent her flowers and invited her to dine with him but she rejected him; he frightened her. And his vast army of followers was increasing at an alarming rate. She had heard and seen this for herself on her trip abroad the previous April.

Mai Mai was saying, "I tell you this because it is possible to avert these disasters, this European holocaust. I am giving you knowledge, and knowledge is power when used correctly." She coughed a very tiny and modest cough and cleared her throat. "A national tragedy is imminent. My charts are very powerful where this is concerned. The child of an American hero is under the threat of kidnapping. The child will be murdered."

Director William Wellman shouted, "Do you mean Lindbergh?"

"The charts do not give names."

"Well, hell," said Wellman to actor Richard Barthelmess, "I know Lindy. Maybe I ought to tip him off."

"I wouldn't worry," said Barthelmess. "She's just a pretty good lounge act."

Anna May could see Mai Mai was thirsty and chose to send her a glass of champagne. Mai Mai was standing. "What I tell you now I did not read in my charts. It is what I sensed and felt as I walked among you this evening." Her eyes pierced ahead. "There is here tonight an actress who is marked for murder. Her killer will escape detection."

"That could be any one of us," Thelma Todd whispered to Nancy Carroll, who merely shrugged.

Mai Mai said, "There are several suicides in this room, and I say to these people, do not despair, there is always hope and friends to sustain you and—" She stopped dramatically. *"Danger!"* she howled, *"Danger!* It is right here with us, terrible *danger!"*

Marlene shivered, and Herb Villon put a protective arm around Hazel Dickson's shoulders. Mai Mai's eyes moved from one person to another but Marlene could not tell whom she was particularly looking at. When she returned her glance to Mai Mai, the petite woman was drinking from a glass of champagne.

Then from the rear of the ballroom, someone shouted "Happy New Year!" Mai Mai stared ahead into space as the glass slipped from her fingers. She heard the orchestra blasting "Auld Lang Syne" and in a misty haze saw multicolored balloons wafting down from the ceiling and then she heard Marlene shrieking "Catch her! Catch her!"

Mai Mai fell from the platform into Herb Villon's strong arms. He gently lowered her to the floor as Marlene and Anna May ran to Mai Mai. Mai Mai stared up at them, but she saw nothing. Marlene said, "God in heaven, she is dead." She did not realize she was speaking her native German.

Herb Villon said to Hazel, "Get the pieces of her champagne glass. Wrap them in a handkerchief. Don't let anybody step on them. And if somebody does, tell me who it is." But Hazel was quick. She had the pieces of glass carefully placed in her handkerchief and then safely placed the folded handkerchief into her evening bag.

Herb said to Dietrich, "Now Marlene. Now I call for an ambulance, the coroner, and backup."

The tableau that Herb and Marlene and Hazel and Anna May and the unfortunate Mai Mai formed went unnoticed by most of the revelers. The New Year had begun! Nineteen thirty-two was here! Everyone blew horns and wore funny hats and drank more bootleg booze and champagne, and the morning would provide one gigantic hangover.

Only the group surrounding the corpse stayed sober. Villon was led to a phone and he called headquarters. Anna May Wong and Marlene Dietrich stood with their arms around each other. They heard the Countess Dorothy di Frasso saying to her friends, "Why the poor dear! I guess the excitement was much too much for her! She's fainted!"

ᒪᓂ FOUR ᓂᒪ

THE NEW YEAR had aged thirty minutes before Herb Villon's backup arrived. His assistant, Jim Mallory, arrived in an unmarked car followed by two squad cars of detectives, sirens blaring, scaring the hell out of rabbits and coyotes and several of Dietrich's guests who had reason to fear the police. The coroner had preceded them, and Mai Mai's body was placed on a couch in the library across from the ballroom. Two butlers carried the corpse, Anna May accompanying them.

"What happened?" asked Miriam Hopkins. "Is she sick?"

"She's dead," said Anna May.

"How awful!" said Miriam Hopkins. "It must have been her heart. The excitement. Oh, the poor little thing."

Villon and Mallory were conferring after Herb had dispatched the other detectives to keep an eye on the exits and make sure no one left. "It's going to be hopeless questioning all these people." Dietrich had joined them. "The best we can do is get their phone numbers."

"My secretary can provide those," volunteered Dietrich. "I think it is pointless to detain anyone who wants to leave." She looked around the room. "Though it doesn't look as though anyone has any intention of leaving. Quite a successful party." They didn't miss the irony in her voice. "I never saw anyone give Madam Chu the glass of champagne."

"I thought it was Anna May," said Hazel Dickson.

"No," said Villon. "I saw her talk to a butler. She was probably telling him to get some champagne for Madam Chu. She was standing near Countess di Frasso and her entourage. They must have heard Miss Wong ask for the champagne."

"Strange," said Marlene, "it was like an optical illusion." Jim Mallory couldn't believe he was standing next to this great celebrity. He was mesmerized by her beauty, overpowered by her perfume, and hypnotized by her commanding tone of voice. Villon was puzzled by Marlene's statement, and Marlene was quick to explain. "I was fascinated, of course, by Madam Chu's predictions. But at the same time, I noticed she was always directing her eyes back to one group of my guests. I couldn't be sure which and I tried to follow her gaze. When I turned my eyes away from Madam Chu she was empty-handed; a few seconds later, she was holding the glass of champagne."

"Which group of guests do you think particularly interested Madam Chu?"

"Frankly, Herb, I think it was the Countess di Frasso and her entourage. Ivar Tensha, the British film producer. . . ."

"Monte Trevor," contributed Hazel.

"Yes. Him. Raymond Souvir, the young French actor. That's him talking to Nancy Carroll." Anna May had returned from the library. "The Ivanovs were standing near them and, oh yes, the violinist, Dong See. Anna May, are you all right?"

"I could be better. I phoned my father and told him what happened. He's contacting her family. They're in San Francisco. The coroner is examining the bod . . ."—she hesitated for a second—"is examining Mai Mai. I heard him say he suspected *nux vomica*. Herb, do you know what it is?"

Jim Mallory spoke up. "*Nux vomica* is the seed from which strychnine is extracted."

"Strychnine." Marlene's voice was ghostly. "How terrible."

Villon asked Hazel for the handkerchief with the champagne glass shards. He instructed Jim to get it to the police lab and have it tested immediately. Jim collared another detective and transferred the errand to him. He didn't want to miss a moment of Marlene Dietrich. He would treasure the memory and dine out on the story for the rest of his life.

"Di Frasso's friends, Herb. I have a feeling Mai Mai Chu might have met some of them before. Probably abroad when she lived there." Marlene had his undivided attention. "Perhaps they are the danger that terrified her. And she was truly terrified those last moments before she collapsed. I saw her face. I'll never forget the look. I've seen nothing like it before in my life. It was so awful."

"I saw it too," said Anna May. "And I think what it signified was the terror of her realization that the danger was to herself and to no one else. I think she recognized then that it was she, Mai Mai, who was marked for murder. And by then it was too late to protect herself; she had sipped some champagne."

Jim Mallory said, "All it takes is a sip of strychnine and whammo."

"Jim, spare us." Mallory blushed. Villon said to Marlene, "Is there somewhere I can question these people?"

"Yes, there's a study next to the library. Would it bother you if Anna May and I sat in on your inquiries?"

"Not at all. Listening to them might jog a memory. There was a hell of a lot going on in this ballroom tonight and I'll be damned if I can remember a fraction of what I saw or heard."

"I can," said Hazel, who had already phoned Louella Parsons's assistant, Dorothy Manners, to give her the scoop on Mai Mai Chu's murder. Hazel was promised a fat fee, to which Hazel said to herself, "A very happy New Year, Hazel darling."

Herb shot Hazel a look and then addressed Anna May. "Miss Wong, this is my assistant, Jim Mallory. Would you accompany him and point out the Countess, the Ivanovs, Tensha, Mr. Trevor, Raymond Souvir, and Dong See?"

"Of course," said Anna May.

"And Jim," Villon's voice was cautionary, "just say they're wanted for some routine questions; don't frighten the hell out of them or they'll clam up."

Marlene smiled at Anna May and then at Villon. "Don't worry, Mr. Detective, we'll help loosen their tongues. Between us, Anna May and I speak a lot of languages. We especially talk turkey." She led the way to the study. The orchestra was torturing "The Sheik of Araby" while a nasal tenor bleated the lyrics into a megaphone, a bad imitation of the popular crooner Rudy Vallee. Blissfully, no one paid any attention to him. Several guests watched with curiosity and suspicion as Marlene led the way to the study. The butlers who had carried the body into the library had spread the word that it was suspected Mai Mai Chu had been poisoned.

"Champagne!"

"But how?"

"Was there poison in the bottle?"

"My God! Supposing there's a madman loose at the party!"

"I don't think so. Chaplin's at home with Paulette Goddard."

William Wellman, the director, said to Gary Cooper, "I phoned Lindbergh ostensibly to wish him and his wife a happy New Year. I sort of matter-of-factly let drop Madam Chu's premonition about the possible kidnapping of a national hero's baby, and you know what that modest bastard said?"

"Nope."

"There are a lot of other national heroes around. Can you believe that?"

"Yup." Monosyllables were about as articulate as Gary Cooper ever got.

Seated on chairs arranged in the hallway outside the study, Monte Trevor asked Ivar Tensha, "Why do you suppose our group was singled out for questioning?"

"Possibly the police have recognized us as the privileged

class. Why does it worry you? Have you never been questioned by the police before?"

Trevor's face reddened. "Not seriously."

Natalia Ivanov clutched the crucifix she always carried in her purse, mouthing pleas for help to Saint Olga while under his breath her husband reminded her they were supposed to be antireligious.

"Not positively," said Natalia.

Dong See puffed on a scented cigarette while Raymond Souvir wondered if the body had yet been removed from the premises. Souvir had an abnormal fear of dying, having survived a train crash in Switzerland. His face paled as he saw the library door opening, and a few moments later two police attendants wheeled the body out and into the house elevator, where they were a tight squeeze.

"Oh, God," said Souvir while Dong See chuckled and thought, How anyone who drives a car as wildly as he does could be afraid of death is beyond me. Orientals were taught not to fear death but to welcome it as an adventure in a new dimension. On the other hand, he himself was in no hurry to cross the Great Divide and planned on a long and profitable life.

Inside the study, the Countess Dorothy di Frasso was a charming study of poise and cooperation. She sat in a comfortable chair facing Herb Villon, who sat behind a small desk that seemed much too delicate in construction for his large frame, while at his left sat Jim Mallory recording the interrogation. He was never without a looseleaf pad, and only he could translate his own peculiar scrawl of shorthand. Marlene and Anna May were on a love seat to the right of the desk, and Hazel Dickson perched on a window seat, which also afforded her an excellent view of the comings and goings in the driveway below.

Villon had asked the Countess if she had met Mai Mai Chu before tonight.

The Countess said, "I didn't even meet her tonight! No one introduced us. Every so often I did find her staring at us and

I was wondering at first if she disapproved of our not mingling with some of the other guests. But I'm sure you understand, Mr. Villain. . . ."

"Villon."

"Oh, do forgive me. Villon. Anyway, you know Hollywood and understand the pecking order. It's all so cliquey. I mean the Constance Bennett bunch doesn't mingle with the Norma Shearer bunch, and even at parties they tend to keep themselves apart from each other. It's really terribly tiresome. By the way, darling, where were Norma and Irving tonight? Surely you invited them."

"They had a previous engagement and Irving Thalberg tires so easily. They're with Helen Hayes and Charlie MacArthur."

"Oh, really?" The Countess looked chagrined. "And they didn't invite me?"

Marlene decided the question didn't deserve an answer. She couldn't understand why she had invited the woman to her own party. She wasn't particularly fond of her; in fact she felt sorry for her. Other than Gary Cooper, Dietrich thought her taste in men was execrable, especially her fondness for Italian gangsters.

Villon was talking to di Frasso. "Were you bothered by Madam Chu's rudeness in staring at you?"

"No, because I didn't believe she'd singled me out. She was giving equal time to other members of my group."

"You said your escorts tonight were Mr. Tensha and Mr. Trevor. Have you known them long?"

"I met Mr. Tensha in Rome a few years ago. It was at a state dinner given by Mussolini. Dear Benny, he's such a sweetie. And he's made the trains run on time, can you imagine that?"

"I suppose so. I'm not big with trains. You were living in Italy at the time?"

Her voice darkened. "I was married to the Count. We weren't in Italy all that much. I'm the restless type. I like to move around a lot."

"But you didn't move around a lot tonight."

"Tonight I was in a ballroom. Outside there's the whole world for me to play in."

"Did any of your group acknowledge having seen Madam Chu before?"

"Well, frankly, and I hope I'm not casting undue suspicion, but I had the feeling she knew or recognized several of my bunch. On the other hand, they've all had their pictures in newspapers and magazines. I mean, for instance, there have been the stories that Raymond Souvir is to be screen-tested with Marlene. And Ivar Tensha! My dear, he certainly is celebrated as the munitions czar. Dong See is a celebrated musician. I mean, the only frumps in the group are the Ivanovs, but I seem to remember even they had their pictures in the papers when they joined their embassy here. And as for myself, well," she flicked imaginary lint from her dress, "I'm always news."

"Did you by any chance see who gave Madam Chu her glass of champagne?"

"I don't remember that at all. I assumed it was Anna May because I heard her say to someone she thought Madam Chu was getting hoarse and could use a drink, something like that. Frankly, it seems rather ridiculous to me that anyone would choose to murder the woman. Her predictions were harmless. I mean, a madman who wants to rule the world! That's grade-B movie stuff. And as for World War Two . . . oh dear. I don't buy that at all. And then, to suggest someone in the room will be murdered and someone else will commit suicide, my dear Mr. Vill . . . *on*, anyone in this room could make those generalizations and sound mysterious and ominous. Everybody knows the two Johns, Gilbert and Barrymore, are drinking themselves to death. And I could think of several ladies out there I'd be only too happy to accommodate with assassination. "She smiled in the direction of Dietrich and Anna May. "Present company excepted, of course."

"Why?" asked Marlene.

"Oh, darling, you know we've never competed for anyone."

Dietrich wore an enigmatic smile. Everybody in the ballroom knew she and Gary Cooper had a red hot affair during the making of *Morocco*, which crazed von Sternberg and di Frasso, who had succeeded in stealing Cooper from the volatile Lupe Velez.

"What about Monte Trevor?"

"What about him?"

"Where'd you meet him?"

"Oh. Let me think. Oh, of course. In London. If I recall correctly, it was a party Gertie Lawrence was giving for the Prince of Wales and I recall Monte had the audacity to try to convince the Prince to star in a film of *Ivanhoe*. Well, he is terribly photogenic, don't you think, Marlene?"

"I've never met him."

"Oh, haven't you? He's a bit of a bore. Come to think of it, all the royals are bores. It's all that incest and intermarriage. I like Monte Trevor. He's an honest fraud. And he does manage to get a film made every now and then. Why Marlene, tonight he was trying to convince Ivar on the drive here to back a production of *Salome* to star you!"

"How flattering," responded Marlene, "and how apropos; like John the Baptist, many a man has lost his head over me."

Jim Mallory was salivating. If only to be given a chance to lose his head over Marlene Dietrich.

"Monte dangled the bait, but Ivar didn't bite. Anything else?"

"Did you know Raymond Souvir in Paris?"

"He insists we met at a dinner party at Feodor Chaliapin's, but I don't remember the occasion at all. And as for Dong See, we were introduced at a reception for him in Shanghai after one of his recitals, and I remembered because he was so charming and attentive. He's changed some since then, but then I suppose we all change over the years." There was a pause and she asked, "Am I sitting in what they call the hot seat?"

"Actually Dorothy," said Marlene, "you're sitting in an Adam original. I bought it at an auction for a very fancy price."

Hazel Dickson was starving. She wondered if she dared ask Marlene to send to the ballroom for some food. She knew Herb Villon was not thrilled about her sitting in on the interrogations and she was sure that by now the mansion was being besieged by reporters and photographers. She looked out the window and decided she too was psychic. There they were in the driveway, milling about anxiously, being held back by some of Herb's minions. Well, she'd beaten them all to it and knew that Herb would suffer some flak because of it. He was often being accused of favoring Hazel on a murder case.

"How else can I assist you?" asked di Frasso with exaggerated graciousness.

"You've been very helpful. Thank you. Would you ask Mr. Tensha to come in?"

"I'd be delighted."

Hazel wondered if she could ask the Countess to get her a plate of turkey and ham, but by the time she got up her courage, di Frasso was out and Tensha was in.

"Cigar?" asked Tensha of Villon, indicating a row of his brown torpedos in his inside jacket pocket.

"No, thank you," declined Villon. "I don't smoke them."

"And if you don't mind, Mr. Tensha," interjected Marlene, "I'd be grateful if you didn't either. The room is small and it's already quite close in here."

"Hazel," ordered Villon of his girlfriend on the window seat, "open the window." She did as requested.

Despite being deprived of a cigar as a prop, Tensha was quite composed. He said to Marlene, "This is a terrible thing to have happen in your home. And Miss Wong, we have not been introduced, but I know the deceased was your good friend and I offer my condolences."

"Thank you," responded Anna May softly. Such ye olde worlde courtliness, thought Anna May, such an anachronism coming from a man who profits from death and destruction.

Hazel could tell Herb didn't like Tensha. Offering the cigar was a mistake. Now if he could only produce a ham and cheese on rye she might fall madly in love with him. She heard Herb ask Tensha, somewhat facetiously, she thought, "You deal in munitions?"

"Indeed."

"Are you in this city for business or for pleasure?"

"Both."

"Have you ever met Madam Chu before tonight?"

"In passing and very briefly, I recall social occasions in Berlin and Paris and perhaps also in Rome when we were both under the same roof."

"You were not ever friends?"

"Oh, no. Madam Chu I understood to favor bohemian circles where I am very uncomfortable."

"You don't consider tonight a bohemian occasion?"

"No, tonight was quite delightful until Madam Chu's unfortunate murder. In fact, she fascinated me. The thought of a second world war! You can imagine how a prospect like that appeals to me."

Herb Villon positively hated him. Herb had served in the recent war in the infantry and had suffered a chest wound. He had seen his buddies dropping around him like ninepins in a bowling alley. There was many a night he awakened to the imagined screams of a comrade begging God to give him another chance at life. And this son of a bitch sitting on an antique chair with a pocket load of hundred-dollar cigars slavers at the possibility of a frightening premonition becoming a reality. Don't these people ever get struck by lightning?

"I can tell you that Madam Chu had won the respect and admiration of many dignitaries the world over. Albert Einstein adored her. I was told she warned the Romanovs to get out of Russia as the revolution was imminent, but I don't think that was a premonition. I think she got it firsthand from Leon Trotsky, with whom it was rumored she had an affair."

Both Marlene and Anna May arched an eyebrow upon

hearing this delightful gossip. Anna May whispered to Marlene, "I'm so glad for Mai Mai. I always had the feeling she wasn't getting much."

"But Trotsky!" Marlene suppressed a shudder.

Villon continued, "The others? Mr. Trevor, Dong See, Raymond Souvir, the Ivanovs?"

"The Ivanovs I met here at a reception at the Russian Embassy. He's a simpleton. She is very deceptive."

"How so?"

"I think she is a very clever woman. She professes to peasant origins and has the calloused hands to prove it, but she was smart enough to manipulate her husband into his present position in the embassy. I don't like the man. I think he's a pacifist and they are no use to me." He longed for a puff of a cigar. "As for Trevor, I met him in London. He's always out to separate me from some of my fortune. He's not smart enough. Otherwise, I find him quite harmless. Souvir I do not know. As far as I'm concerned, he's just another pretty face. Dong See is a gifted musician, but I do not travel in musical circles."

You don't travel in circles at all, thought Marlene; you are a smooth, calculating monster. Which is why you are a billionaire and I am not and never will be.

Villon said to Tensha, "I read in the papers you are negotiating to buy an estate here."

"I've bought it. I do a lot of business in the Near East and the Far East and I decided it would be less tiring to break the long journey with a place of my own in Hollywood. I have purchased the estate of a silent film star who apparently has been silenced forever by the talkies. Perhaps you have heard of Clara Kimball Young?" They had. "She was heavily in debt and I came to her rescue. The place needs a lot of work."

"Your group was standing near Madam Chu before her death. Did you see the person who gave her the glass of champagne?"

"I really don't remember. Wasn't it you, Miss Wong?"

"No, it wasn't."

Tensha said to Villon, "Perhaps it was a butler. I remember one passing among us with a single glass on the tray."

Marlene filed that statement away. *I remember one passing among us with a single glass on the tray.* And with all eyes focused on Mai Mai Chu, how easy it would have been for someone to drop a poisoned tablet into the glass. Her eyes met Villon's briefly. She sensed he too harbored a similar suspicion. She liked him. Hazel's a lucky girl. He's a good detective and he's a good man, and baby, let me tell you, a good man nowadays is hard to find. She surfaced from her reverie and realized Tensha had been dismissed.

"You didn't ask him to send in one of the others?" said Marlene, somewhat surprised.

"After him, I need a breather," said Herb.

"I need food and I'm going to get some. If I miss anything, you can tell me later." Hazel hurried out of the room and Marlene began pacing.

"Very interesting, Mr. Tensha," said Marlene.

"I loathe him," Villon stated flatly. "I expected dollar signs to flash in his eyes at the prospect of another world war."

"Don't be foolish," said Marlene, "we'll never see another one in our time. The world is too poor. This Depression won't disappear in the near future. But Herb, a few interesting things he said. A butler passed among them with a single glass." Herb smiled. The lady was smart. "The old trick of concealing a pill in the palm of the hand and passing it over the glass."

"That's probably the way it happened," Villon concurred. "But from whose palm did the pill drop?"

"You can discount Dorothy di Frasso," said Dietrich.

"Why?" asked Villon, as Jim Mallory feasted on Dietrich with feverish eyes.

"The only poison she dispenses is with her tongue. And besides, what would her motive have been?"

"Dorothy didn't murder Mai Mai," Anna May agreed. "But I feel certain it was one of the others."

"Mr. Tensha is so smooth. As for Dong See, he says he does not travel in musical circles. And I'm sure Dong See does not travel exclusively in musical circles. He's certainly not traveling in one tonight, unless you consider Gus Arnheim's cacaphony musical. Oh God, what a night!" She was at the door and opened it a crack. The noise from the ballroom was obscenely deafening. "Can you beat that! They have to know by now Mai Mai was murdered, but they go on celebrating as though murder among them is a common occurrence." She shut the door and faced Villon.

Villon said, "You look like a tiger about to pounce."

"Do I? All I want to know, Herb, is who's next?"

"You mean who's next to be murdered?"

"No, who's next to be questioned. There won't be another murder tonight. You know as well as I do Mai Mai was murdered because she knew too much about the backgrounds of some of the suspects. And it goes back to Europe where they first met. I think Mai Mai knew something terrible. I think Mai Mai, had she not been poisoned, would have revealed something very, very sinister. And how convenient of the murderer to have some *nux vomica* in his possession."

Herb asked winsomely, "Why, my dear Marlene, doesn't everyone carry some poison on them for an emergency? Well, let me tell you from a lot of past experience, professional killers are always well prepared. And one of this bunch I'm questioning tonight is a professional killer. And damned clever too. Jim, I want to see Monte Trevor next." As Jim went to get Trevor, Herb said to Marlene, "Marlene, you've got the makings of a good detective."

"I agree with you. It's a necessary talent when you deal with the kind of men I come up against. And let me tell you, Herb, you're pretty darned good yourself."

Monte Trevor preceded Jim Mallory into the room. He hesitated for a few moments, and Villon said, "Come in, Mr. Trevor and sit right there. There's no need to be afraid."

Or is there, wondered Marlene.

ᘛᕮ FIVE ᕬᘚ

MARLENE THOUGHT MONTE Trevor looked more like a greengrocer than a film producer. On the other hand, what was a film producer supposed to look like? Sam Goldwyn had been a glove salesman. Jesse Lasky had played a saxaphone in vaudeville. D. W. Griffith was both a failed actor and a failed playwright. Looks are deceiving, she reminded herself, and not only Trevor's looks are deceiving. There is someone here who is dangerously deceptive, who should look like a murderer, but again, what should a murderer look like? Tensha profits from death and should be the most obvious choice to be a murderer. But with his power and money, wouldn't he arrange for someone else to do his dirty work? He didn't look like a munitions maker, he looked like a puppeteer behind a Punch-and-Judy show in a Paris park. Could Raymond Souvir be a murderer? Why not? And why not Dong See? A hand that delicately wields a violin bow could just as delicately pop a death pill into a glass of champagne. And there's the Ivanovs. The Communists thrive on purges. They murder in job lots, hundreds at a time if the stories coming out of Russia can be believed. Natalia Ivanov is an ambitious woman, but what could there have been in this peasant's past that would have triggered Mai Mai's suspicion? Likewise her husband, an oaf in sheep's clothing. This is too exhausting, and she wasn't paying attention to Villon's questioning of Monte Trevor. She caught a glimpse of Jim Mallory's face and from his strange look wondered if he was suffering from an upset stomach.

"Madam Chu is not unfamiliar to me," Trevor was telling Herb. "I read an interview with her in the London *Times* . . . ooh, let me think . . . um . . . yes . . . some ten or more years ago . . . and I thought at the time she had possibilities as the subject of a feature film. But who to play her other than Miss Wong here, and she was not yet on the threshhold of her present celebrity. It would have meant casting an Occidental actress and expecting the makeup department to work a miracle."

"Did you make contact with Madam Chu?" Herb was toying with a pencil while staring at Anna May. He couldn't read a thing in her face. Truly inscrutable.

"As a matter of fact, we had tea at the Savoy. I think it was the Savoy. Maybe the Mayfair Club? The Dorchester?"

"The setting is of no importance, Mr. Trevor, only the cast of characters."

"Yes, of course, ha ha. You Americans do insist on cutting away the fat and the gristle. Well, as I said, we met and I broached the subject of filming her story. It seems I wasn't alone with the idea. A French director approached her in Paris, I think it was René Clair, and another had met with her in Berlin. But she said something quite sensible. I can't quote her accurately, it was so many years ago, but she said something like this. 'There is no story, Mr. Trevor, there are only my gifts, and how do you dramatize gifts?' Quite an intelligent woman, I'm happy to say. Anyway, truth to tell, a few years later I did a movie about a clairvoyant and it was a terrible flop."

"Has making films been your only interest, Mr. Trevor?"

"What do you mean?"

"Have you been involved in other schemes, something that might pique Madam Chu's interest in you?"

"I don't understand. Filmmaking is my life."

"Possibly not always all that profitable. I'm a Hollywood baby. Born and brought up here. I have met lots of film producers, and except for a chosen few, most of them are usually hard up for some green paper."

"Too true, oh yes, too too true."

Marlene whispered to Anna May, "The more nervous he gets, the thicker his accent."

Villon spoke. "So it stands to reason to get your hands on some eating money you from time to time dabbled in some extracurricular activities."

His face was red and the veins stood out on his neck. "I don't deny there have been some very ugly rumors about me in Europe. I have enemies. Doesn't everyone?"

"Can you repeat some of those ugly rumors?"

"They're too ugly to repeat!"

"You're among friends, Mr. Trevor."

"Friends don't cross-examine people without any provocation."

"You're not being cross-examined, Mr. Trevor. You're being questioned. No one forced you into this room. You could have refused to cooperate."

"Oh, ho ho ho!" There was no mistaking the sneer in his voice. "Haven't I heard *that* before."

"Then you've been questioned by the police before."

He leaned forward, angry. "Thanks to those bleeding ugly rumors spread by a jealous rival who thought I was having it off with his wife!"

Marlene laughed and couldn't resist asking, "And were you having it off with his wife?"

"I never denied it! But those rumors were inexcusable! And I'm so angry I'll tell you what those rumors were and possibly still exist." He crossed one leg over the other and clasped his knee with his hands. Marlene felt sorry for him now. Only too well did she understand what it was like to be victimized by ugly rumors. "Word was spread that I was financing a prostitution ring. Then there was a story circulating that I was profiting from an organization specializing in illegal adoptions. It was said I traveled the Continent and Asia setting up a ring to steal infants and then offer them up for adoption at very fancy prices."

"Dreadful," said Marlene.

"Dreadful indeed! Who has the time and the money for that kind of an operation? And then the rumors that I was an extortionist, that's how I supposedly largely financed the production of my films. Would you like to hear more, Mr. Villon? Can you digest some additional sordid details?"

Villon said with a small, not unfriendly smile. "You should write your autobiography."

"I am," he said. "I call it *So Help Me God!*"

"Madam Chu was particularly interested in your group. I'm sure you were aware of this."

"I most certainly was. I thought it was me who was the reason for her attention, so I introduced myself and reminded her of the time we took tea at the Sav . . . maybe it was the Grosvenor House?" He could see Villon was growing impatient. "Anyway, she remembered me and then absolutely floored me when she said, 'But do not plan on the realization of a film about Salome'! How about that. I'd been discussing that very idea with Mr. Tensha and the Countess di Frasso on the drive here, and Madam Chu sensed it just by looking at me. That's what she told me. She sensed it just by looking at me. I say, do you suppose she knew she would die tonight?"

No one responded.

"Oh, dear. It is a terrible thought, isn't it?"

"After that tea with her, you had no further dealings with Madam Chu?"

"None." He said it so softly, Villon and Marlene were sure he was lying.

"Tensha says he knew you in Europe. Likewise the Countess. What about the others?"

"I never met any of them until tonight." He had uncrossed

his legs, and the palms of his hands rested on his lap. Then he whipped a handkerchief out of his pocket and dabbed at his face. "That's all I can tell you."

Villon dismissed him and Trevor almost leaped out of the room, missing crashing into Hazel Dickson by inches. "If ever anyone looked like a fox being chased by the hounds. Did I miss much?"

"You missed the fox," said Marlene. And what a fox. She knew he spilled the ugly rumors about himself to show he had nothing to fear from them or from Villon's questions. She said to the others, "I think he was fun. Didn't you, Herb?"

"I wouldn't want him to marry my sister."

"Don't be mean, Herb," said Hazel. "You know she's desperate for anyone to pop the question. While I'm on my feet, can I page any of the remaining suspects for you?"

He asked for Dong See, who attacked upon entering with a volley of indignation about being kept waiting and how dare he be subjected to such treatment and how dare anyone think him capable of murder. He might louse up Paganini or Kreisler, but poisoning Mai Mai Chu was so unthinkable, so awful. He paused for breath and Herb jumped in.

"Am I correct in assuming, since both you and the deceased were celebrities on the international circuits, that your paths have crossed before?"

"Mai Mai was a fan of mine and I a great fan of hers."

"But you didn't have much conversation with her tonight, did you?"

"You are quite correct. When I first saw her I waved at her, but she looked right through me, or so I thought. Then I realized she was very preoccupied and probably having one of her visions. I decided I would wait until after her . . . contribution to the evening, when conversation would be easier. A tragic decision on my part. I never dreamt tonight was the last we would see of each other." He turned in his seat to Anna May. "At least we're the better for having known her." Anna May nodded in agreement, and Marlene put her hand over Anna May's.

54

Responding to other questions, Dong See said that on various occasions he had met Tensha, Trevor, and di Frasso abroad, but had never become intimate with them. To him, the Ivanovs were ciphers, and he totally disapproved of Communists; they didn't pay well. Raymond Souvir was something else. "We were good chums in Paris, good pals. He's a dangerous driver" was added as an afterthought.

"Is there anything else dangerous about him?" Villon asked.

"I think a woman is better qualified to answer that question." Jim Mallory thought his smirk most unbecoming.

"I hope you have no immediate plans to leave the city."

"I shall be around for several months. I'm composing a concerto and have rented a secluded house in the hills." Mallory recorded his address and phone number.

Dong See composing a concerto, Hazel was thinking. Not the greatest item in the world, but still, it might be worth something to *Etude,* the foremost musical magazine.

Raymond Souvir was a much more affable subject of interrogation. He bubbled with enthusiasm at the prospect of his screen test with Marlene, he adored Hollywood and wasn't the climate magnificent, not like the damp and wetness of Paris except in the spring when Paris was glorious and so conducive to romance. And so many beautiful women, how clever of you Marlene and also how brave to invite so many gorgeous creatures into your home to greet the New Year, oblivious of the fact that Marlene liked women and many women were her friends and she didn't give a damn if they were more beautiful and more glamorous than she, because they weren't and that's that. In little over a year she'd become an icon of the silver screen, rivaled only by the enigmatic Garbo, whom many predicted she would soon topple from her pedestal, a prospect that held little interest for Dietrich.

Right now she was wishing he'd shut up and let Villon get on with the questioning. She'd ignored her guests much too long, and by this time she was sure many wanted to go home. Happily, a detective entered with a note for Villon from the coroner and Villon instructed him to lift the embargo on the mansion and let the guests come and go as they pleased. He was pretty damn sure his killer was one of the favored seven suspects.

"How's my party going?" Dietrich asked him.

"Great! Nobody's leaving. And the food's terrific. Boy, those potato latkes!"

"The secret is to keep them thin, very finely grate the onions, and fry them only in Crisco."

With a bewildered look on his face, the detective departed while wondering if she was intimating that she herself had made the potato pancakes.

"Excuse me," Villon said to the actor, who realized he'd been talking too much and now sat placidly awaiting Villon's attention. Villon read the coroner's note, showed it to Mallory, and asked him to pass it on to Marlene. All outward symptoms of the victim pointed to strychnine and he was sure the autopsy would confirm it. Marlene shared the note with Anna May.

Villon studied Raymond Souvir's face briefly before starting his questioning. Dark, suave good looks, typical of a professional model, but he suspected a trace of fear in the eyes. Perhaps it was just nerves; probably Souvir had never been questioned by authority in his past, but who could be sure. Baby-faced killers were epidemic in America. He started the questions. Yes, Souvir had met Mai Mai in Paris several years ago when he was just starting out in show business and occasionaly sang at *Le Boeuf Sur Le Toit* and other popular clubs. Singing was his first profession after a brief career as a photographer's model, and it was Mai Mai who advised him he had latent acting gifts. So he studied with a succession of teachers and then won a lead in the Paris production of Elmer Rice's *Street Scene*, playing the naive son of a Jewish radical. This brought him a few screen offers, and he made three, which brought him to the attention of a Paramount talent scout who suggested that von Sternberg test him for the part of Dietrich's suave and wealthy protector in her next movie, *Blonde Venus*.

"Over the years," asked Villon, "have you kept in touch with Madam Chu?"

"No, not really. But Dong See might have told you, he and I became very good friends in Paris. He would tell me what Madam Chu was up to, and how frequently some of her premonitions displeased people. You know, like tonight, who wants to know there'll be another world war?"

"Tensha." It was Marlene who literally spat the name.

"Of course," agreed Souvir, "munitions." In response to Villon's question as to whether he had ever met any of the others previous to tonight, Souvir said, "I was once interviewed by Mr. Trevor for a film he was planning to do in Paris, but I don't think he remembers me. I met the Countess di Frasso at some parties, but I don't think she likes me." He looked embarrassed. "I once turned down an amorous advance she'd made." He laughed and it was a very nervous laugh. No, he did not see who gave Mai Mai Chu the glass of champagne, because at the time he was trying to signal a waiter to get a glass for himself. As to the Ivanovs, he shrugged and said, "They do not interest me. They are, well, they are peasants."

And where did you spring from, Marlene wondered, from what countryside and from what poor little village where papa probably had a small farm from which he scraped a meager living, where mama was an exhausted wife who had birthed half a dozen brats, most of them unwanted, and milked the cow and sowed the seeds and baked the bread and darned and mended the threadbare rags they wore the year round. Don't be so mean, Marlene admonished herself. He might also be the son of a wealthy manufacturer whose doting father had financed his career.

"Have you any idea which of you might benefit from Madam Chu's death?"

"*Monsieur?*" Souvir looked like a startled faun. Had he

only just realized that he was being questioned because he was a suspected murderer? "Are you thinking that I put the pill in Madam Chu's champagne?"

Villon leaned forward. "How did you know anyone put a poisoned pill in her champagne?"

"Why, why, it was discussed while we were waiting to be questioned. I, I . . . I think it was the Countess di Frasso who said if the champagne was poisoned it could only be with a pill because it would be impossible to pour a liquid into the glass even if the waiter was walking very slowly. As it is, I cannot imagine how one places a pill in a glass when there's danger of being seen by so many people. Oh . . ." There was a strange expression on his face. Villon waited. He knew he was about to hear something important. "Mr. Villon," he pronounced it *Vee-yon* and Hazel thought Herb's name was certainly sexier when spoken with a French accent, "you remember I told you I didn't see who gave Mai Mai Chu the glass of champagne because I was trying to signal a waiter for a glass of my own. But now I remember how it really was. I stopped the waiter who was carrying the champagne to Madam Chu and asked him to please bring me one too. He only stopped for a few seconds."

"More than enough time for someone to seal Madam Chu's doom." Maybe even you, Mr. Frenchman.

"Yes. I'm sorry. I didn't realize. How terrible. In a room so crowded, so noisy, so many of us pushed against each other, it is difficult to remember what one has seen or heard or said."

Villon said to Mallory, "See if di Frasso is still here. If she is, I want to talk to her again."

Souvir turned in his chair to Marlene and Anna May Wong. "I am *distressed!* That I might have been the instrument . . . it is too terrible for me to contemplate!"

Hazel was curious about Mallory's hasty departure. She caught Villon's eye and he signaled her to be patient.

"We all inadvertently make mistakes, Raymond." He wasn't reassured. Anna May was thinking, he stopped the waiter, he could have dropped the pill himself. That was exactly what Marlene, Villon, and Hazel Dickson were thinking. But soon the three would wonder what motive he could possibly have. Unless, as he himself said, he was the instrument. The person instructed to poison the champagne.

"Too ridiculous," said Marlene aloud.

"What's too ridiculous?" asked Villon.

"I'll tell you later."

"Tell me now."

"Later." Her tone of voice said, Don't mess with a Teuton.

"I'm so sorry," Raymond Souvir said in a sad, tired voice.

Nice delivery, thought Marlene. Even the way he's slumped in the chair, he has possibilities. Even if he is almost as pretty as I am. If he gets the part, the women might spend more time looking at him rather than looking at me, which is where they're supposed to be looking. But then, this is moviemaking. Von Sternberg will edit the picture to make sure they mostly look at me. Hell, they won't take their eyes off me after that number where the gorilla enters, makes threatening and subtly obscene gestures at the chorus girls, and then unscrews its head revealing its *me*, *Marlene*, wearing the gorilla suit. God it'll be hot under those lights.

Villon thanked Souvir. Marlene said to the actor, "Stick around for a while, darling, and we'll have a drink. I'll be finished here soon."

"Yes. I'd like that." He hurried out.

The Ivanovs as a replacement for the handsome, gentle young Frenchman were a culture shock. They entered with Jim Mallory, who told Villon he had found the Countess and she was damned annoyed at being recalled but was sitting outside smoking a cigarette and tapping a foot, but he didn't specify which. He brought a second chair to accommodate Gregory Ivanov, Marlene having winced with apprehension when Natalia settled onto the Adam, like a dirigible docking into port.

Hazel thought the Ivanovs were a great double act. If they could master a soft-shoe routine and a couple of choruses of "Dark Eyes" they might be a cinch playing specialty houses.

No, they didn't know Madam Chu personally but had seen her once at a reception in Moscow. They had heard she had once been a mistress of Trotsky's, but Trotsky was now in disfavor and living in exile in Mexico. Gregory asked if they knew that years ago he had been an extra in Hollywood films, and only Jim Mallory was amused by the non sequitur. Neither one of them saw Madam Chu accept the glass of champagne from the waiter, not that this information was necessary any longer, but it did elicit from Natalia that she remembered the waiter pausing briefly next to Raymond Souvir, as she also wanted another glass of champagne. No, they didn't know if Madam Chu had any enemies in Russia, but Gregory had sat behind her at a screening of *Thunder Over China* and she voiced disapproval of the treatment of Orientals in that film. Anna May told Dietrich that they should have heard what she thought of Warner Oland's portrayal of the evil Dr. Fu Man Chu and that Mai Mai was even sorrier that they shared the same surname.

When Villon told them they could go, they quickly thanked Marlene for her hospitality and for a most unusual evening and promised they'd soon be inviting her around for a bowl of borscht with a boiled potato and a dollop of sour cream.

"Yogurt is healthier," said Marlene, having the final word, as usual. Mallory fetched the Countess di Frasso, who was thoroughly annoyed at being brought back for further questioning and said so in no uncertain or polite terms.

"And really Marlene, a lot of your guests are wondering why you're ignoring them!"

Marlene replied, "I will apologize when I return to the ballroom."

"And I certainly don't understand why you and Anna May are privy to these questionings."

"Because I asked them to," said Villon. "I admire their minds and they're being very helpful."

And very decorative, thought Jim Mallory.

"How did you know a strychnine pill was dropped into Madam Chu's champagne?"

"I didn't know; I deduced. The whole party is buzzing that she was poisoned, and I heard one of your detectives mention *nux vomica* and I happen to know the seed of that plant is poisonous, so I had to figure out, and I gather quite correctly, that the pill was an abstract of strychnine. So I shared my knowledge with the others. I must say it didn't seem all that surprising a bit of information to any of them except the two Russian peasants, and I think they're still astonished by indoor plumbing. Is that all?"

"It'll have to be."

"What do you mean by that?"

"It means I got the information I wanted."

She stormed out of the room. Hazel asked, "Aren't any of you hungry? Marlene, the food is absolutely sensational. Your guests attacked everything as though they'd been victims of a famine. Well, Herb, what did you learn tonight that I might use?"

He said matter-of-factly, "One of them is a murderer."

Marlene was lighting a cigarette and Jim Mallory cursed himself for not having leapt in with his lighter. "I'm sure I'm not the only one who had a bit of trouble with some of Raymond Souvir's testimony. If he stopped the waiter, he had the best opportunity to doctor the champagne."

"You're not the only one," said Villon, "but there's no reason why he wanted to murder the woman, unless he, like all the others, is pulling off a pretty good masquerade. I've a theory, but if you're in a hurry to get back to your guests, Marlene, it can wait until tomorrow."

"I'm a firm believer in the present, Herb, such as there's no time like, etc."

"What kind of a threat Madam Chu posed, I do not know. But somehow, somewhere, she stumbled on information that put her life in danger."

Danger! There is danger!

"I think in the past she had small inklings of a plot that in some way links our suspects, and when she saw them together, she had a pretty good idea what was afoot. And someone knew she knew something, and she posed a threat. I think what she knew had been brewing in her mind for several years. She knew these people before at some point or another, and she served them premonitions, her kind of information. Probably seemingly harmless at first, but then as the scenario began taking shape and lengthening, she realized she was onto something more or less of a powder keg."

Hazel asked facetiously, "Sort of like an international plot of some kind? Something linked to that madman she predicted would one day try to take over the world?"

"He's very real, Hazel. He exists. His name is Adolph Hitler. And he is extremely dangerous." Marlene had Hazel convinced.

"Well, my dears," continued Hazel, "I didn't detect any Germans among tonight's septet of suspects."

"There's me," said Marlene. "I'm a kraut, and I can be pretty damned dangerous. And on the other hand, I've also been threatened. When Emil Jannings began to realize I was walking away with *The Blue Angel*, he tried to kill me. I can still feel those brutal hands around my neck. Fortunately, von Sternberg swatted him with a riding crop."

"Anna May, Mai Mai didn't manufacture some of these premonitions, did she?"

"Never. She sometimes misread the charts, but she never tried to marry her astrology to her psychic powers. Very often when she did a chart a premonition flowered, but that was the extent of it. Mai Mai didn't have a dishonest bone in her body."

"But Herb, nobody knew Mai Mai was to be here tonight. Only Anna May and I knew."

"Isn't it possible she spoke to someone on the phone who said they were coming here tonight, and she said, 'Oh, I'll be there too,' " asked Herb.

"Very possible," agreed Marlene, "and whoever it was

came prepared to kill her. Now, who among them did she know so intimately that she'd phone and say, 'What are you doing tonight'?"

"No one," said Anna May. "If I hadn't ask her to join me tonight, she would have spent the evening with herself and her charts. No Marlene. No Herb. Someone phoned her. It had to be someone who was desperate to see her and quiet her."

"How I adore puzzles!" exclaimed Marlene. "Let's keep thinking, and now I must return to my party. Young man!" Jim Mallory realized he meant her. His knees were turning to jelly. "Would you be a darling and escort me back to the ballroom? She put her arm in his and thought she heard him say *Ideedoonerd*. What he had said was, "I'd be honored."

Of course, the first step he took, he tripped.

ᴖᴗ SIX ᵍᵍ

BEDLAM REIGNED IN the ballroom. The reporters and photographers had invaded the premises once Villon ordered the security laxed, and most of Marlene's guests were cooperating with the gentlemen of the press. Marlene was immediately surrounded like a wagon train besieged by Commanches and as usual handled the reporters with tact, savoir faire, and good humor. Villon admired the way she fielded their questions while making sure the photographers were favoring her best angles. Hazel Dickson turned the other cheek to the sniping of her envious colleagues, the least nasty comment being called "Teacher's pet." Anna May bore the brunt of the inquiries into the personal and private life of Mai Mai Chu while Herb Villon told the press he had some good leads and hoped to have a more concrete story for them within the next few days.

Anna May and Marlene posed for the photographers in a variety of groupings, none of them particularly original. Marlene posed with Raymond Souvir and Joseph von Sternberg, and then Marlene was grouped with Anna May and Dong See. Ben Schulberg, the West Coast head of Paramount Pictures, managed to corner Marlene privately for a few seconds.

"What's going on? Are you in the clear? There must be no scandal!" Scandal, thought Marlene, what about you and Sylvia Sidney. What she said was, "Murder is always a scandal, Ben, and it's unfortunate it happened in my house, but since it did, there's nothing we can do about it. Make the most of it! *Shanghai Express* will soon be going into release and here are Anna May and I, both in the picture and both the center of a murder mystery. That should prove profitable publicity."

His eyes lit up. "You've got something there. I'll remind the press you're both in *Shanghai Express*. You're not under suspicion, are you?"

Said Dietrich wearily, "No, Ben, The detective in charge is a friend of a friend and I'm being cooperative. Actually, I'm enjoying the experience tremendously. I'm learning a lot about police work. Maybe we could do a movie with me as a detective."

"There's nothing glamorous about you as a detective."

"Why not? I could wear a low-cut holster." She saw Villon having a private conversation with Anna May and wondered what was going on.

Anna May was telling Villon about Mai Mai's loft downtown on the outskirts of Chinatown. "The keys must be in her handbag." Villon told her the handbag accompanied the body to the morgue. He signaled Jim Mallory to his side and told him to call the morgue and have them deliver the handbag to his office. He was looking forward to several hours in Mai Mai's loft.

Marlene's eyes caught Raymond Souvir deep in a discussion with Dong See. Souvir seemed agitated. Marlene longed to have a talk with the actor. She found Hazel Dickson and asked her to separate the two men. "I want a little time alone with Raymond," she explained.

"Who wouldn't?" asked Hazel as she set off to accomplish her mission. A moment later, Marlene had her arm through one of Souvir's and walked him to an isolated spot near the bandstand. A downbeat orchestration of "With a Song in My Heart" served as a background.

Souvir said, "I saw Mr. Schulberg talking to you. Does he know I'm a suspect?"

"Don't let it bother you, Raymond. Ben Schulberg has more serious problems at the studio. He may soon be out of a job."

"Oh my God, supposing his replacement doesn't like me? Ben Schulberg likes me. He told someone he did."

"Stop fretting, Raymond. The studio spent a great deal of money importing you for this test, and they will make the test. Von Sternberg wants the test and I want the test, and whatever Marlene wants, Marlene gets. Now tell me, before we're interrupted, have you ever had an astrological chart done for you?"

He said quickly, "No."

"Now, Raymond," she bore down heavily on his name, "Mai Mai Chu didn't forecast your stars in Paris?"

"I . . . I . . ."

"Raymond, this is Marlene. Never lie to Marlene. Marlene is a great believer in and respecter of the truth. The truth will out. Am I right in saying that in Paris, thanks to Dong See's friendship with Mai Mai Chu, she did your chart?"

He was deflated. "Yes. It was a birthday present from Dong. But that was two or three years ago. I haven't seen Mai Mai since, that is until tonight."

"Why did you try to hedge?"

"Because I'm afraid. I want nothing to do with this case. I didn't kill her. I swear on my mother's life."

"What was going on just now between you and Dong."

"Nothing was going on."

"I saw you, and my eyes are very good. You were upset about something. Did it have something to do with Dong's friendship with Mai Mai?"

"No! I told him how upset I was at being questioned by the detective. It could be bad publicity, and Marlene, I need to succeed in Hollywood."

"And if you don't?" His shoulders slumped. Marlene was sympathetic. "You'll always have a career on the Continent. And you're still young. If you fail this time, there's the chance of another try for the brass ring. Now tell me the truth, did you know there was a plot to kill Mai Mai?"

"No! I knew nothing about Mai Mai. I just happened to be here, that's all."

Dietrich decided on another tack. "When Mai Mai read your chart, did she reveal anything startling or unusual that the future held for you?"

"I don't believe in the stars, Marlene, I believe in myself."

"You don't believe in the stars and yet you want to be one."

"Please don't put me on."

"Raymond, I have had myself charted many times. I'm a Capricorn. What's your sign?"

"Taurus."

"Of course. The bull. Very stubborn. You must have had some prognostication from Mai Mai that you've never forgotten."

"Yes. She predicted that my success in France would continue. But that . . ."—he hesitated. She waited. ". . . that it would be interrupted. There would be a scandal."

"Wouldn't it be ironic that it might be Mai Mai's murder?"

"Yes, that's what I was telling Dong."

"Really? But you seemed so upset. If you don't believe in the stars, why be upset? Shrug it off and get on with your life."

"I had forgotten it until Dong reminded me. He thought he was being funny."

"I have learned from experience that humor wears many faces. Some cheerful, some nasty. You mustn't let it upset you. You mustn't let the fear of failure hang around your neck like a dead albatross. You live extravagantly, I assume you have a great deal of money."

"That won't last."

Marlene arched an eyebrow. "Oh?"

"What I mean is, I have to continue earning to live on the scale that I do."

"Don't we all, darling? They pay me one hundred and fifty thousand dollars per picture and I haven't a nickel saved. But my charts tell me my star will shine for many many years to come, so I don't worry." She smiled and said, "Dong See has found us. Don't look so upset. Laugh. Go ahead. Laugh." He laughed, a laugh that had the strength of an infant's burp. Dong See joined them. "Well Dong, I was hoping to ask you to play for us tonight, but I suppose now it's too late unless you chose to do 'Danse Macabre.' "

"Anything at this point would be an anticlimax," said Dong. "I'm tired, Raymond. Much though I'm not looking forward to it, please drive me home."

Marlene took each man by an arm and said forcefully, "Not until we've had a drink to the New Year. I think it's going to be a fascinating and exciting year. In fact, I don't have to think, the charts assure me that's how it will be." She was steering them to the nearest bar. "By the way, Raymond, by any chance was your father a farmer?"

"My father? My father owned a draper's shop in Rouen. That's where I was born." And he refrained from adding, And I wish I was there now.

No farmer, thought Marlene. Wrong again. At the bar, a young actor was wiping liquid from his shirt front with a bar towel.

"What happened?" asked Marlene.

"I tried to drink champagne from Carole Lombard's slipper. It was open-toed."

Jim Mallory watched the bartender pouring three glasses of champagne for Marlene, Souvir, and Dong See. How fickle she is, he thought sadly. She asks me to escort her into the ballroom, I trip and fall flat on my face, everybody laughs, and I look and feel like a damned fool. He felt an arm around his shoulders and looked into Herb Villon's sympathetic face. Villon said, "Don't ask for a star, Jim. You have the moon." And indeed, looking out a window, Mallory could see a full moon in the sky.

"That explains it," said Jim.

"Explains what?"

"Tonight. The edginess. The uneasiness. The murder. Full moon. Nothing goes right when there's a full moon. Madam Chu's handbag is on its way to your office."

"Good boy. How's for some champagne?" He led Mallory to the bar, where Marlene greeted them, raising her glass high and offering a toast. "To Mai Mai's murderer! May you catch him before he strikes again!"

Dong See asked, "You think there'll be another murder?"

"There has to be. One is never enough, isn't that so . . ." —she imitated Souvir—". . . m'sieu Vee-yon?"

"Not necessarily."

"If you catch the killer within the next ten minutes, then you're right. But you won't because he or she isn't about to confess or give themselves away, and you don't have enough evidence to pin it on anyone, so by the law of averages, the killer will strike again."

Villon laughed. "You've seen too many movies."

"I rarely go to the movies, Herbert Villon. The killer will strike again because he has to." She held center stage and showed she intended to make the most of the spotlight. "He's afraid that either he's been seen spiking Mai Mai's drink or there's someone who's a party to his crime and can't be trusted and must therefore be silenced. Right, Herb Villon?"

"I hope you're wrong." The bartender had poured drinks for him and Mallory, and Herb lifted his. "I can't stand a case cluttered with too many corpses."

"Can't you handle the traffic?" She was enjoying baiting him. She'd bet her bottom dollar that she and Villon were on the same wavelength. She hadn't told anyone yet, and she soon intended to tell Villon, but she was convinced that Mai Mai's murder was a conspiracy and she was convinced Villon had come to the same conclusion. "It stands to reason there has to be another victim, what with so many suspects involved. Oh Raymond, you're perspiring. You mustn't take me so seriously. It's the New Year and I haven't eaten and I'm feeling a bit light-headed, and look at Dong See, a masterpiece of composure. Where are the others? Let me see, the Ivanovs I'm sure have gone home. Too bad there's no snow; she could have whipped the horses mercilessly as their sleigh headed back to the embassy, fearful of being pursued by a pack of wolves with red-rimmed eyes. But no fear, Natalia Ivanov would wring their necks and skin them and stitch together their hides into a very handsome lap robe.

"Ah! Monte Trevor! He has trapped the luscious Miriam Hopkins and is probably offering *her* Salome. Look how eager she looks. Miriam is a true daughter of the south, all corn pone and hominy grits and thick slices of ham drowning in a sea of pineapple juice laced with brown sugar. Our Miriam sure does know how to play the coquette. *Gott im Himmel!* She slapped his face and there she goes flouncing off in a rage. He didn't offer her Salome, he offered her his very own extraordinarily revolting self for a romp in her boudoir. Good for you, Miriam, I see you in a refreshing new light, no longer the loud-mouthed, demanding, and insulting boor that we all know you to be.

"Who's missing? Let me think. Of course. Ivar Tensha and Dorothy di Frasso. And here's Hazel to claim her detective. Hazel? Have you seen the munitions maker and the gossip maker? Wait! There's the Countess worrying Gary Cooper! Oh, poor Gary, his vocabulary is as limited as his self-restraint. Unless my instincts betray me, he'll be her late snack and her breakfast. But wait, wait, who is the patrician beauty coming to claim him?" She sipped her drink. She was enjoying herself enormously. "I remember, the Sandra something to whom we are told he has offered matrimony. Don't hesitate, young woman, grab him. He is very very eloquent when horizontal. Aha! The Countess retreats! She's studying the stag line. The one at the end, darling, the handsome creature with the cleft in his chin. Cary Grant. Tallulah's already made a bid, but I don't think he's listening to offers. The Countess sees him. She is sashaying towards him. But wait. There's Groucho! He's loping towards her with his gorgeous leer."

Groucho pounced on Dorothy di Frasso, took her in his arms, and asked, "May I have this dance? You can lead, but let me guess where. Please dance with me. I'm a terminal case. I'm not sure which terminal. Union Station or Grand Central." The Countess tore away from him and with a shrug Groucho went in search of a fresh victim.

Marlene laughed and continued. "But where is Tensha? Could he have left without saying goodnight to his hostess, who admits that for a while she was a bit derelict in her duties. But it isn't every hostess who has the good luck to have a murder committed under her very roof and under her very nose. Surely Tensha would have sought me out to thank me for a perfectly wonderful evening despite a fatal flaw. Ah! As they say in very bad operettas, Here he comes now."

Ivar Tensha had the Countess on his arm, an obscene cigar in his mouth, and an anxious look on his face. The Countess di Frasso looked none too happy. Monte Trevor was coming up behind them with the kind of look that made Dietrich wonder if he was planning to make off with the silver. Tensha took Marlene's hand and kissed it. She planned to scrub the hand with a strong disinfectant. "Thank you for such a wonderful evening. Despite the unpleasantness, I had a very lovely time. Good night to all of you."

"I'm sure we'll be meeting again," said Villon.

Marlene cried out in despair, beautifully timed and beautifully acted, "But you can't leave so soon? It's the shank of the evening." It was one in the morning, but to Marlene any hour of the night was the shank. "There is still so much for us to talk about. I insist you have one more drink with me. I insist! Do not demur! Bartender?"

"Yes, Miss Dietrich?"

"Fresh drinks all around. In fact, there's something missing from the champagne!" She diplomatically refrained from suggesting that what was missing was strychnine. "A few drops of green mint in each drink. It does wonders for your sinuses. Will any of us ever forget this night? Will you, Dorothy? Or

71

you, Mr. Trevor?" She smiled at Villon, who could tell she was up to no good, and whatever it was he hoped it would take effect.

"May I join the party?" Anna May Wong looked wan and unhappy.

"Of course, darling. How terrible this has been for you. Anna May knew Mai Mai Chu since she was a child. Anna May, do you think Mai Mai read in her chart that tonight foretold tragedy for her?"

"She might have," said Anna May. They'd discuss the possibility earlier. What is Marlene up to, she wondered.

Marlene's eyes were like the beacon atop a lighthouse as they swept from face to face. "Have any of you who knew Mai Mai before tonight had their charts done by her? I know Monsieur Souvir had his read several years ago, a birthday gift from Dong See. Raymond is a Taurus. Taurus the bull. Very stubborn. He does not tell much. Dong, did Mai Mai read you?"

"I think so. I don't recall."

Anna May stared at him. Obviously she has read you and you remember what was important to remember.

"You, Mr. Trevor. You tried to get Mai Mai to star in a film about herself. I'll bet you dollars to doughnuts before rejecting your offer she did a chart and was guided by it."

"By Jove, come to think of it, she did do a chart and the bloody thing did work against me."

Anna May said, "Then she also did your personal chart."

"Actually, she did. But I couldn't remember the time of my birth, I was so young then. She chose the neutral hour of twelve noon."

"That's a common practice among astrologers when the subject doesn't know the actual time of birth. It doesn't make for too accurate a chart, but the approximation is serviceable." Anna May wondered if Raymond Souvir was feeling ill.

Marlene wasn't satisfied with Trevor's response and beamed her eyes at Tensha. "Mr. Tensha, why do I have a hunch Mai Mai once did your chart? I think tonight was not the first time you heard her predict another world war."

He took the cigar out of his mouth and stared at the ash. He knew better than to flick it on the floor. He couldn't stand the thought of Marlene ordering him on his knees and commanding him to wipe up the mess with a handkerchief. Though had he had a better view of the rest of the ballroom, he would have seen a vast expanse of untidiness that did not speak well for the community of Hollywood luminaries. "Marlene, you make me think of Cassandra. She was also a bit of a witch. Madam Chu did indeed read my chart several years ago and headed me off from what she predicted would have been a disastrous marriage. I was smitten with a German actress named Lya dePutti."

"It was *you!*" gasped Marlene.

"I gather you knew Lya," said the munitions czar.

"I adored her. She committed suicide. Was it because of *you?*"

"I choose to think not. I gave her a handsome settlement to release me from our marriage contract."

Hazel Dickson was telling Herb and Mallory that Lya dePutti had been Emil Jannings's leading woman in a brilliant German film, *Variety*, six years earlier.

The bartender had freshened Marlene's glass. "Tell me, Mr. Tensha, did she put you off anything else?"

"No. She did predict I would have a long and unhappy life. Does that answer you satisfactorily?"

"Not really. But it will serve for now. Dorothy? What about you? It seems to me there would have been at least one occasion when you might have looked for Madam Chu's services."

"I find your smugness most unbecoming, Marlene. I don't see at all what horoscopes have to do with Mai Mai's murder."

"Horoscopes, my dear Countess di Frasso, have everything to do with Mai Mai's murder. May I tell her why, detective Villon?"

Hazel stared at Villon with a quizzical expression. The son of a bitch has been holding out on me. He's told Marlene something but he hasn't told me. He'll sleep alone tonight.

Herb Villon's expression was neutral. He was like a car idling at a traffic light, waiting to shift gears. He didn't know whether to consider hugging Marlene or strangling her. At the same time, he knew there was no stopping her. She'd had a lot to drink, although he didn't know this didn't matter, as she could drink almost a case of champagne a day, and frequently did, without any telling effect. He said, "By all means tell her whatever you plan to tell her, but I don't remember telling you anything."

"That's quite right, Herbert, so stop staring daggers at him Hazel, he's perfectly innocent of whatever you think he's guilty of. So what I'm telling you, my dear Dorothy, is a deduction of my own, and I think it's a damned good one." She paused for dramatic effect, took a deep swig of the bubbly, let her eyes slowly travel from face to anxious face, wishing en route she could pat Raymond Souvir on the head to assuage his apparent anxieties, winning Anna May's admiration for the way she had the circle of people hanging on her every movement, her every word, and finally came back to Dorothy di Frasso. "In all these charts, I think Mai Mai predicted something involving the seven people she saw tonight before she was murdered. What she predicted was too terrible for her to try to handle. And I don't think she realized the enormity of the prognostication until she saw all of you together. She suddenly realized that on separate occasions she had made this same terrible prediction about all of you. But someone knew this could happen, especially when told that Mai Mai was being brought to my party by Anna May, and so it was necessary to plot to kill Mai Mai. And it didn't matter if she proved to be an immediate threat or not. She simply had to be eliminated as a precaution."

"Absolutely, utterly ridiculous!" said Dorothy di Frasso.

"That's what some nasty critic wrote about me in my first

film, *The Little Napoleon.* I don't know what's become of the critic, but I'm sure doing fine."

You sure are, thought Herb Villon, and whether you know it or not, you've just set yourself up as a target. He decided to try to take the curse off it. "Marlene, where do you get such outrageous theories?"

Marlene feigned sadness. "Ah, Herbert. Is it so outrageous? Is it any more outrageous then the Teapot Dome? The Boston Red Sox scandal? Your Jim Fiske's plot to destroy the American economy in 1879 or whatever the hell the date was?"

Ivar Tensha offered Dorothy di Frasso his arm, which she took willingly. There was obviously no Mrs. Tensha, and she was in need of a healthy bankroll. The crash of '29 had hurt her more than she thought. Marlene kissed Souvir goodnight and then made a swipe at Dong See's cheek but didn't quite connect. She shook Monte Trevor's hand and decided there was more strength in a filleted codfish. She caught the odd look with which Tensha favored her as he looked over his shoulder on his way toward the staircase. Dorothy di Frasso waved goodnight to several people as she passed them on the way out, and then she too took a last look at Marlene. Marlene raised her glass of champagne to her and then downed the contents.

Herb Villon said to her, "If you're looking for trouble, I think you've found it."

She looked coy. "Are you mad at me?"

Marlene Dietrich or no Marlene Dietrich, I'll slap her silly if she's after Herb, thought Hazel.

"You went a little too far, I think."

"I don't think so. I also don't think I know what I'm talking about, but the theory just came to me in a champagne flash and I just couldn't stop myself. Anyway, it made a lot of people uncomfortable. Maybe not all of them, but a lot of them. Now, whose got the keys to Mai Mai's place. It's somewhere near Chinatown, right Anna May?"

"She's amazing," Herb said to Jim Mallory.

Mallory said, "I'd go through fire for her without wearing asbestos."

"Herbert," commanded Marlene, "we must go to her apartment and search her files. I'm sure she keeps files. We must search her files for horoscopes, copies of horoscopes, and then we'll find out for sure if I'm crazy or not. Mr. Mallory, you don't have a drink! Quick bartender, champagne for the adorable Mr. Mallory and his adorable dimples. Quick, Herb, catch him. I think he's fainting!"

⦿ SEVEN ⦿

THE ORCHESTRA WAS playing "Good Night, Ladies" without much energy and even less enthusiasm. The few remaining guests who were still ambulatory took the hint and made their departures without so much as a 'good night' or a 'thank you' to their generous hostess. Marlene had indeed set a magnificent table, and never again would her guests witness the Niagara of bootleg booze and champagne she had provided.

What a waste of time, Gus Arnheim, the orchestra leader, was thinking. She could have thrown this bash at the Cocoanut Grove, one of the industry's most popular night spots, which was his steady venue, and there wouldn't be this mess to clean up. Not so much a waste of time as a waste of money. The party must have cost many thousands; what profligate spending in these financially depressed times. Then he reminded himself, Miss Dietrich is a queen, and queens are only happiest reigning in their own palaces.

Marlene urged Anna May Wong to spend the night in a guest room, and the emotionally exhausted actress was more than grateful for the offer. A butler escorted Anna May to the room.

Herb Villon stood in the hallway that separated the ballroom from the den and the library, obviously loath to leave. He'd sent Hazel home with Jim Mallory, Hazel trying her best not to be suspicious of why Villon was remaining behind.

From inside the ballroom, where she was pacing about in a wide circle, very deep in serious thought, Marlene saw Villon from a corner of her eye. She went to a bar, grabbed a bottle of champagne by the neck, dexterously maneuvered a grip on two glasses, and slunk her way toward the waiting detective with an exaggerated gyration of her hips. "I had an idea you'd hang around after the others left." She led the way to the library. "It's more comfortable in the library," she said, "unless Mai Mai's ghost is in there trying to make contact with you to name her killer."

"I don't think she knew who her killer was. In fact, I don't think she had much time to do much thinking. Strychnine works faster then a whore on the make."

Marlene handed him the bottle. "Here, darling, put your thumbs to work."

"You sure you want more of this stuff?"

"Darling," she said wearily, "let me hear the cork pop." She took a cigarette from a Tiffany box on a table, lit it, and then sank into an overstuffed easy chair. She heard the pop and was at peace. She watched him pour through smoke-fogged eyes. She accepted her glass and he sat opposite her in a Morris chair. They toasted the New Year for the umpteenth time, and Marlene kicked off her shoes. "Imagine being a wallflower at my own party. I didn't dance one dance tonight." She laughed. "Wait till I tell Maria in the morning. Anyway, Herbert Villon detective first class par excellence, you stayed because you don't think my conspiracy theory is all that farfetched."

"No more farfetched than the one I'm kicking around. My big problem is picturing these seven suspects as conspirators. I can't see them working in concert. Some of them don't seem to know each other that well."

"M'sieu Vee-yone," and she thought of Raymond Souvir's

moments of stress, "when I walk on the set of a movie the first day of shooting, I might have met some of the other actors at some time or other, but mostly, I haven't. In no time, in a few days or so, it's as though we've known each other for years. Shooting a movie is a form of conspiracy. We actors are working in concert under a director we hopefully respect and with technicians who we know will do their damndest to make us look good, and if the Gods are smiling on us, our conspiracy will result in nine to twelve reels of a very entertaining movie. When we're finished, we move on to the next conspiracy, probably never to see each other again, though in this town that's hardly avoidable. I hope I'm making sense."

"You're doing great."

"Let me continue. As to seeing these seven as conspirators, let's begin with the two who have come to us already professing great affection for each other as bosom buddies, though neither one of them has much of a bosom to speak off. Raymond Souvir and Dong See."

"Souvir's a frightened rabbit."

"And rabbits are great survivors. That's why they have so much time to multiply. Souvir is frightened, perhaps, yet according to Dong See he drives like a devil pursued. Reckless drivers have a very macho image of themselves, and I believe Raymond Souvir is mucho macho. He's also very ambitious. And I suspect he's also very ruthless. The French are usually very ruthless, which is why I adore them and plan to spend my fading years in one of the better *arrondissements* of Paris. Souvir is driven by ambition. His only real worry tonight was whether the powers-that-be at the studio would cancel his test if he were implicated in Mai Mai's murder." She took a deep drag on the cigarette. "I don't think you are reading Raymond's fear correctly. There are lots of kinds of fear. I think Raymond, like all the others, has been very glibly lying. Let's begin with his life-style.

"He rents a very expensive, furnished house on Doheny. He's at one club or another every night of the week except Sunday, I've been told, squiring a variety of beauties who have expensive tastes. Where does the money come from? His career in Europe? Let's examine that. He's had some success as a singer and made three films. I know the kind of salaries they pay in Europe. Nothing to compare to what we're paid here. Raymond hasn't been on the scene long enough to amass any impressive bank account or assets. The road to success is paved with parasites with their hands outstretched. So I suspect Raymond is being financed."

Herb was sponging up her information. "You mean somewhere in the background there's a rich sponsor."

"It's certainly not his family. They're middle class and like all good French people live strictly within their means. The only French person I know who's heavily in debt is Mistinguett, and that lady is famous for her legs, not her business acumen. My theory is that Raymond is financed by a group, a company, a corporation."

"Why?"

"How the hell do I know? We're only talking theory, right? Why is that bottle so far away. Put it on the table between us." Chore finished, Herb settled back in his chair. "Raymond and Dong See profess a great bonding between them. This is not unusual between men without the specter of sex rearing its delicious head. How this came about I can only speculate. The usual deduction, if they're not lovers, is they were introduced at some point, liked each other, and nursed the friendship along. But from the dark side of my speculations I see them assigned to like each other."

"They're good friends, strangers in a strange city, and yet they're not living together."

"Exactly, darling. Musical professionals are a drearily demanding and temperamental species. Living with them can be hell. And in Dong See I detect a very selfish, very single-minded young man who is terrified in Souvir's passenger seat. Musicians are very disciplined; they have to be or they're second-rate. Dong See is very disciplined. I'm sure he does as he's told."

"Meaning he knows how to take orders and follow through."

"That's my theory, mind you. I don't want to be charged with slander should you one day turn on me."

"I don't turn that easily."

"That's what I thought. Now the Ivanovs. They are Bolsheviks, not the best example of Bolsheviks, but they'll do until something more dangerous comes along. They are underlings and will go through life as underlings. They were born to obey orders, although I suspect Natalia, behind all those phony tears, is a very determined woman. If this conspiracy is international, then of course the Ivanovs are the cubs of the Russian bear. Actually, I'm rather amazed the Russians are participating in a conspiracy with members of the outside world, because the Bolshies are so isolated and so insular. They are very suspicious people, and trust my words, their isolation and suspicion will be their undoing. Maybe not in our time, but in time. Let's set them aside and save them for future reference."

"I hope for their sakes they turn out to be priceless treasures. They're both so nondescript I almost feel sorry for them."

"They should do something about their teeth." She paused, sipped some champagne, took another drag on the cigarette, and then, stifling a yawn, said, "Monte Trevor. Is he or isn't he?"

"Is he or isn't he what?" We know he's produced movies."

"Is he or isn't he a conspirator. And if he is, why?"

"Do you suppose it takes special credentials to be a conspirator?"

"I don't know. I've never been one, except as a member of an acting company." She laughed. "Come on, Herb. We're both thinking conspiracies are secret meetings in sinister old mansions with hidden wall panels leading to secret passageways that end in a heavily draped room with a solitary lamp in the middle of a round table, and sitting around the table a mysterious assemblage of people with black hoods masking their faces."

"I saw that movie and I hated it."

"I didn't see any movie. I made it all up. I don't think Monte Trevor could conspire to form a poker game. But here he is, arriving at the party in the company of the very socially prominent Dorothy di Frasso and the very powerful and fearsome Ivar Tensha. I don't see Tensha as a man who suffers fools easily, so Monte Trevor must have some kind of a certain something to attract Tensha to him."

"I should think Tensha's the type who needs a lot of errand boys, a master at demanding servility. I'm sure he has his henchmen deployed all over the world."

"Henchmen, hmm. Monte Trevor could be an ideal henchman, couldn't he?"

"Especially if it could mean raising the financing for a movie."

Marlene gestured at the bottle and Villon refilled her glass. "Dorothy di Frasso is a very shrewd, very calculating woman. She's been welcomed in international circles for years. She has a charming façade and is very democratic. She entertains royalty and commoners alike. Of course, she adores Mussolini, which makes her suspect in my book. Could she be a conspirator? And if so, to what purpose?"

"She has useful contacts, you say." Marlene nodded. "That's very important to a conspiracy."

"So we mustn't dismiss Dorothy too easily. Although I also suspect she has designs on Tensha."

"Why not?"

"She hasn't a hope in hell. Men like Tensha never marry, and if they do, they sequester the little woman in a villa in some forest or another where she takes up with her chauffeur or else spends most of her time developing housemaid's knee from all that genuflecting in church."

Villon said, "Tensha would have to be playing a very important, very powerful role. I don't see him taking a backseat or playing a secondary role."

Marlene was staring into her drink. Herb exaggerated clearing his throat and Marlene looked up. "I was thinking of Raymond Souvir stopping the waiter who was bringing Mai Mai her drink."

"Butler," Villon corrected her.

"Butler, waiter, they're all the same damn thing. Wait a minute!" She was on her feet. "He wasn't one in my regular employ. He was hired for the party along with several others. I got them all from an agency. My butlers weren't circulating serving drinks. I placed them in doorways so they could guide people to the bathrooms or whatever, take coats, keep out the uninvited."

"You think this man might have doctored Mai Mai's drink?"

"Why not?"

"Why yes? Could he have known Mai Mai? Highly unlikely."

"But he could have been paid to drop the pill. Isn't that possible?"

"In a case of murder, anything's possible." Villon's back ached, and he was beginning to long to get home and postpone further speculation to a time later in the day, but Marlene was just warming up and not about to let him escape.

"You need food. Let's go to the kitchen and scramble some eggs." She put on her shoes. He dutifully made his way with her to the kitchen, where the hired help were still cleaning up. Marlene grabbed Herb's wrist. "That's him. The butler. The one drying the pans."

The man looked tired but smiled affably when Marlene put her hand on his shoulder. "You did a very good job tonight. You all did." Her voice encompassed all the help, who managed to look pleased by the compliment. "Of course," she said to the man, whose name was Morton Duncan, "it was terrible that Madam Chu was murdered."

"It must be awful for you," commiserated Duncan, "having her done in right here on the premises. Being such a good friend of yours."

"Yes, it was sad she was 'done in,' as you so quaintly put it, but she was not a good friend; tonight's the first I laid eyes on her."

"Oh. I was under the impression she was an old friend."

Herb took over. "You brought the drink to Madam Chu, didn't you?"

Duncan looked uncomfortable. "Sir, I didn't know it was poisoned."

"I'm not saying you did. Who asked you to bring the drink to her?"

"Miss Wong. She took it from the bartender and placed it on my tray and asked me to take it to Madam Chu, but to use discretion when interrupting her dissertation."

Marlene said, "Anna May most certainly did not poison the drink. You couldn't possibly suspect her."

"I could suspect anybody. It's a free country." He asked Duncan, "And Mr. Souvir stopped and asked you to bring him a glass too, didn't he?"

"If you mean the Frenchman, he did that."

"You didn't see someone's hand passing over the glass?" continued Villon.

"Well, sir, in the moment or so that the Frenchman distracted me, that could have happened, but I didn't see it. There was such a crush of people around me, I was having difficulty getting through to Madam Chu. Believe me if I had seen anything that seemed out of sorts I would say so, Miss Dietrich. It pains me to know that I was the bearer of death."

Bearer of death. Marlene stifled a laugh. The ancients killed the messenger who brought bad news. They should kill critics who write bad reviews. She said to Duncan, "I'm sure it's a very painful memory. But you were just an instrument, don't blame yourself."

They left the man and Dietrich was soon busy scrambling eggs. Marlene asked Villon, "What do you think? Do you believe him?"

"I have to believe him. I'll do a check on him. See if he has any record."

"I hope he doesn't. I think he might be a poet. 'Bearer of death.' Wasn't that sweet? Can you imagine those words spoken by Erich von Stroheim? He'd really make you tremble at the sound of them." With a cigarette dangling from her mouth, she continued scrambling the eggs, into which she poured some cream, then added a dash of cinnamon and just a drop of curry powder. Villon heated ham, which he cut from the bone, a remnant of the party's buffet.

"You know something, Herb? I just had a terrible thought. There were so many people at the party tonight, maybe we're barking up the wrong conspiracy. Maybe one of the other guests is the guilty party."

"They weren't clustered around a waiter carrying a tray that held a poisoned glass of champagne. Believe me, Marlene, the killer is one of my seven suspects. . . ."

"*Our* seven suspects, Mr. Villon. I'm in on this with you, and don't you dare try to cut me out! Don't slice so much ham; we'll have to eat it all or it dries out. And there's nothing so appalling as dried out ham. Take it from me, I've worked with enough of them. Now, before I forget, what time tomorrow are we going to Mai Mai's loft? Not too early, we both need some sleep. Of course, Anna May must be there with us, in case there are things written in Chinese, and she can translate for us. And, of course, that darling assistant of yours, Jim Mallory. Now wasn't that strange, fainting the way he did."

"He was overcome with love."

"Love? Nobody has fainted because of love since the middle of the last century, and even then, I suspect it was all feigned. Who's he in love with?"

"You."

"Really? How adorable. But in a very nice way, you must tell him he'll have to step to the rear of the line. Herb, if only you knew what I have to put up with. Get the plates. The eggs are ready."

In the guest room, Anna May Wong was pacing the floor. She couldn't sleep what with Mai Mai's face contorted in the agony of her death throes reflected everywhere she looked. She could still hear her father's cry when she told him Mai Mai was dead, murdered.

"How often I warned her, how often I pleaded with her to exercise greater discretion with her premonitions. Why didn't she listen? She was always so headstrong, so foolhardy. She was not a true Chinese woman."

Poor father. A true Chinese woman. And what is that? Subservient, obedient, with bound feet. Thank God I never had to undergo that agony of the primitive custom of the binding of women's feet.

Always so headstrong, always so foolhardy.

Stubborn. Like Taurus the bull. Stubborn, like Dong See, a Taurus. Why think of him now? Strange, his friendship with Raymond Souvir. Such an unlikely pairing. But still, why not?

She found a negligee in the closet and put it on. She recognized it as one Marlene had worn in *Dishonored*. She left the room quietly in search of the kitchen to warm up some milk. When she reached the kitchen, there were Marlene and Villon eating ham and eggs.

"Oh good!" cried Marlene.

"What's good about not being able to sleep? I'm going to warm up some milk."

"Warm up some red wine. *That'll* make you sleep."

"No, thank you, I've drunk enough tonight."

"Tomorrow, Anna May, we go to Mai Mai's apartment. We need you there in case there's any Chinese that needs translating."

"Marlene, it's all in Chinese. She always did her charts in Chinese." They now had the kitchen to themselves. Anna May stirred the milk with a spoon. "My father said on the phone tonight, Mai Mai was always so headstrong, so foolhardy. If she knew something of such great importance, why didn't she take it to the proper authorities?"

Marlene placed her fork on her plate. "Maybe she did. And whatever authority she went to was the wrong authority. Isn't that a possibility, Herb? And of course it's a probability the wrong authority was a guest at my party tonight." Herb chewed thoughtfully. "Anna May, the milk's boiling over."

"So are all of our conjectures," said Herb. "We've got an awful lot on the plate. Now to sift what we've got and sort it out and then put it back together again in a different shape, which will show us the face of the killer."

Marlene looked at her wristwatch. "It's 4 A.M. If we meet again at two this afternoon, that ought to give us plenty of time to sleep. I've got several New Year's Day invitations, but the hell with them. Finding Mai Mai's killer takes top priority." She rubbed her hands together at the prospect of unmasking a murderer. "I wonder which of our suspects are boiling some milk to help them get some sleep."

⦿ EIGHT ⦿

SLEEP ELUDED DOROTHY di Frasso. She was annoyed when Ivar Tensha refused her offer of a nightcap. They had dropped off Monte Trevor at his hotel, the Beverly Wilshire, the producer accepting his dismissal reluctantly. Thankfully the bar was still open and catering to some noisy revelers. Monte had a horn blown in his ear and confetti flung in his face and tried to look good-natured about it, but barely succeeded. He ordered a highball with a double shot of scotch and settled onto a stool to rerun in his mind the reel of film whose subject was Dietrich's party and Mai Mai Chu's murder. *Dangerous. Very dangerous.*

Dangerous. Very dangerous. Di Frasso wore her most diaphanous negligee as she reclined on the chaise longue in her bedroom. She puffed on a Sweet Caporal and watched the smoke rising to the ceiling, which was decorated with several seraphs in various suggestive poses. She wasn't thinking of a least likely suspect, although a voracious reader of murder mysteries; she was thinking of a least likely victim. Mai Mai Chu. Strychnine. Dear God. She, di Frasso, came close to being the victim. Her throat was parched and she considered swiping the champagne from the tray while there was the opportunity when Raymond had the butler's ear for a few moments. Thank God she hadn't. Whoever dropped that pill was good, very damned good. She considered herself a highly observant person—one had to be to survive in the circles in which she traveled—yet she had not seen the hand that presumably passed over the glass, dropping its lethal potion like a bomb over enemy territory. To do that required nerves of steel and a deadly variety of chutzpah.

Chutzpah was a popular word in Monte Trevor's vocabulary. The definition of *chutzpah* was a man who murders his parents and then throws himself at the mercy of the court as an orphan. Monte was feeling like an orphan. He was always wallowing in loneliness and self-pity on holidays. He was a bachelor, and what little family he had were scattered to the four winds and did not keep in touch with each other. He had hoped the night would continue with Tensha and di Frasso; there was much to discuss and disseminate about the party and the murder. He recognized that di Frasso's priority was getting a romantic stranglehold on Tensha, and he also recognized that Tensha was not interested in falling under whatever spell she was hoping to cast. A more important thought possessed him: Why kill Mai Mai Chu in full view of Marlene's guests? From his point of view it was a foolish move, but he had to admit it took the courage of an egomaniac to kill her there. The bartender placed a bowl of peanuts in front of Monte, and the producer gratefully helped himself. He'd eaten nothing at the party. Villon's questioning had erased his appetite. Why didn't di Frasso find him appealing?

The Countess had poured herself a glass of chardonnay and was chain-smoking. How did Monte Trevor weasel his way into Tensha's good graces? She was surprised to find him in the car when Tensha came to pick her up. She'd known him in London and once almost succumbed to his entreaty for her to do a screen test for a movie he was planning about Lucrezia

Borgia, *With This Ring I Thee Kill*. That was another of his projects that never came to fruition. Had I done the role, would I be in a different position today? Would my star be shining as lustrously as Marlene's? I would have made it in talkies, I'm sure; I have a lovely voice and my speech is without impediments like the 'r' problem Marlene and Kay Francis have in common. Marlene does a pretty good job of masking hers, while Kay doesn't give a damn and knows her fans find it adorable when she calls to her beloved Wichard or Wobert or Wonald. Oh, to hell with those clever females. What have I gotten myself into? Oh Christ, it'll be headlines today. My face will be plastered on every front page of every newspaper across the country and probably most of the rest of the world. Those reporters and photographers were positively ruthless in pursuit of their stories.

Dottie! That news hen called her Dottie! How dare she! I am the Countess Dorothy di Frasso! Not Dottie! "Hey Dottie! Poison is a woman's weapon! Did you have it in for Chu?"

Rude guttersnipe. What desperation, what fear, what awesome fear did it take to compel Mai Mai's elimination in full view of all those people? I must say Marlene handled the incident magnificently. That crude detective person letting her and Anna May sit in on the interrogations, how irregular! Hmmm. I wonder if there's something going on between Marlene and that Herbert Villon. I gathered they only just met tonight, or last night as it's now five in the morning; could Marlene have operated that quickly?

Now who the hell is phoning me at this hour? The hell with them. I won't answer. They'll go away. They'll assume I have the phone turned off. How dare they have the *chutzpah* to call me at this hour of the morning and on New Year's Day of all things! Oh, but supposing it's Tensha. He can't sleep either and he's wondering if he might drop by for a spot of breakfast. She hurried to the phone.

"Hello?" Disappointment. "Monte, you're drunk. Sleep it off. *What?* How dare you make such a suggestion! *I could kill you!*"

Gregory Ivanov sat on a kitchen chair holding a glass of hot tea into which Natalia had dropped his usual four lumps of sugar plus a soupçon of slivovitz. Natalia shuffled about the room, which was as shabby and worn as the bathrobe she was wearing. The two-story house that claimed to be the Russian Embassy was equally shabby and worn, but the rent was gratefully cheap. The owner had reclaimed it from a prostitute whose specialty was bondage, and the basement was a wreck what with the all the chains that had to be pried loose from the walls, all the bloodstains that had to be scrubbed clean with a powerful detergent, and the cloying scent of lilac toilet water, which the prostitute had favored. Natalia was sipping from a snifter of brandy and smoking a cheap Mexican-made cigarillo, listening to her husband shlurping his tea.

Her voice was dark with foreboding. "It was wrong to murder Mai Mai at the party."

Gregory said with irritation, "What difference does it make where she was killed as long as the deed is done."

"Not there. Not in full view of all those people. That detective is no fool, he's not your typical dumb officer of the law we have seen in so many American films played by Tom Kennedy. Ha ha. Very funny."

"What's very funny?"

"Tom Kennedy."

"He's an oaf. We will be hearing from this Villon again, you know."

"You fool. We have diplomatic immunity. We could have refused to be questioned."

Gregory snorted and almost spilled some tea. "Wouldn't that have been clever. Then one or the other of us would surely be suspected as the guilty party. Poisoned pill! *Borshamoy!*" He knew his addressing God was pointless, as He had turned a deaf ear long ago to the revolutionaries who had overthrown and assassinated the Romanoffs. He was in the basement where the czar and his family had been herded together on that last day of their lives. He was recruited to be one of the killers. The little czarevitch was so brave, so hope-lessly brave as he stared at the soldiers who were about to pull the triggers. It mattered not to the boy, he was doomed to die soon of the deadly hemophelia with which he had been cursed at birth. And Anastasia, the beautiful child with her sweet, little puppy eyes. Was it possible the rumor was true that she had survived that massacre? But how? Gregory was, like Nim-rod, a deadly shot. He was positive he'd gotten her between the eyes, and what came dripping down her face was not mascara as he knew the czarina forbade her daughters the use of cosmetics.

Natalia now sat at the kitchen table, which was covered with a piece of peeling oilcloth; she said firmly, "Gregory, we must rise above this. We must prevail. We are here for a purpose that could make us both very powerful, and power is a tool which we can use to turn some formidable profits."

"You are talking capitalism!" he thundered.

"Gregory," she spoke his name with a caress, "if Madam Dietrich's life-style is capitalism, then I am more than willing to be seduced. Which of those two do you think dropped the pill?"

"Why so modest? Two? There are seven of us."

She favored him with a knowing look. He sipped his tea. She sipped her brandy. Both wished aloud there would be no suspenseful delay of further instructions.

The drive back from Marlene's was even more harrowing than the drive getting there. Raymond Souvir was like a ma-niac possessed as he took the hairpin curves on two wheels. Dong See shrieked and cried and pummeled the actor's shoul-der, but Souvir was impervious to his entreaties or the pain he was inflicting. When at last Souvir pulled up in front of Dong See's secluded lair in the Hollywood hills, Dong See surprisingly didn't fling open the door and make his escape. Instead, he said in threatening and measured words, "You have a suicide wish."

"I have a wish to get home in a hurry and think."

"You have a psychological desire to die. If the automobile doesn't kill you, fear will."

"I wish I hadn't come to this damn place."

"You wanted to be a star in this country. An international celebrity."

"The newspapers today will make me an international celebrity. Sooner than I expected. Oh Christ, there's no turning back. There's no getting out of it. Unless it's canceled, I have to do the screen test with Marlene. Even if it's just a screen test, she'll wipe me off the screen. I'll never get that part. It's so hopeless. It's no use. Mai Mai's chart said I wouldn't get the part."

"Mai Mai was always so right. Her charts don't lie."

"There's another reason I'll never get the part."

"What's that?" asked Dong See through a stifled yawn.

"I can't act."

"I thought you were rather nice in your last film."

"It was wrong to kill Mai Mai at Marlene's."

Dong See erupted. "I'm so goddamn tired of hearing that name! Mai Mai this! Mai Mai that! She shouldn't have been killed at the party! What would have made more sense? The Brown Derby? The balcony of Grauman's Chinese? The opportunity to kill her obviously presented itself, and so it was done. Now go home and drink a glass of wine and get some sleep, if you don't kill yourself en route!"

Very greedy woman, thought Ivar Tensha as he soaked in his bathtub scented with salts. The perennial cigar was jammed in his mouth and one could well wonder what Sigmund Freud might make of Tensha's passion for oversized cigars. On a stool next to the tub, there rested a glass filled with chopped ice and the Italian liqueur, *Strega*. *Strega*. The Witch. The Countess di Frasso. Indeed a witch, a very bewitching witch. He'd been tempted to catch the bait she'd dangled in front of him earlier. "Darling, wouldn't you like to come in for a nightcap?" But the nightcap she offered wasn't quite the right size. He never dared spend the night with women. Screw them and send them home in his car with perhaps a monetary token of both his esteem and his generosity. But spend the night with one? Heaven forbid. Tensha talked in his sleep and that could prove dangerous. One unfortunate young lady back in Bucharest had to be quietly eliminated because he'd made the mistake of falling drunkenly asleep before he could send her on her way, and did she get an earful. Very tragic. So young. So beautiful. She ached to enter a beauty contest. She might have been a contender. Now she was just a memory.

Monte Trevor is getting wearisome. He sticks to me like a barnacle on the hull of a ship. He does come in handy to run my errands, but sooner or later I might have to succumb to his entreaties to finance a film for him. Who knows? If I finally yield, the damn thing might show a profit. I suppose I could be interested if it's a movie about Jesse James or the Dalton Boys or any one of those western outlaws. I dote on the stories of their lives, even if they are vastly overexaggerated. After all, I have so much in common with those outlaws. I'm probably the biggest thief in the world. I have billions. Why do I want more? What can I do with more power? Could I finance a search for a cure for cancer? Would I finance such medical research? I hate doctors; I hate doctors as much as I hate chess and lawyers. What do I like? Who do I like? Who did I ever like?

Mai Mai Chu.

There'll never be another like her. Never. Impossible. After they made her, they shattered the mold. How well she understood me, she and those dreadful charts. How much I once loved her. The infatuation was brief but memorable. April in Paris with Mai Mai. She was not impressed by my vast wealth or my position in the world of finance. She liked me for myself. She made no demands. She was never jealous. She was too proud of her own niche, which she had carved for herself with her unusual gifts. Presentiments. Predictions. The stars. Charts. He was a Gemini. Gemini the twins. Two people. Mai Mai told him she usually liked Geminis, mostly preferring them over those born under the other signs. But reading his chart doomed his presence in her life and she quickly brought to a close their brief liaison. They remained friendly, but try as he may to revive the spark, there was no hope of renewing their romance.

Mai Mai was dead. Mai Mai was poisoned. That is not the way she should have died. Mai Mai was a delicate creature and she should have had a delicate death. A heart attack in her sleep perhaps. Or if it had to be by poison, then a poison less powerful than strychnine. But the opportunity fortuitously presented itself and had to be taken. Like the opportunity to foment the rattling of sabers. War is hell. War is highly profitable. Highly profitable? Don't be so modest. Immensely profitable. War in the Far East. War in the Near East. War in South America and Central America and in Mexico, where there was always some peasant with the ambition to be another Pancho Villa. Bring on another Armageddon! How he loved the sound of it. Armageddon. He would be forever grateful to Mai Mai for her prediction of a second world war. Had she known the plot was under way to make a deadly reality of her very accurate prediction, would it have provided her a measure of happiness as death quickly overtook her? Another major conflagration. To paraphrase a quotation from the Bible, his treasury would runneth over.

The cigar was dead and there was no match or lighter at hand with which to revive it. He placed the remaining half cigar on the stool, to be smoked later. Waste not, want not. The first light of dawn appeared. Another day in lotus land. This detective. This Villon. He will continue to be a nuisance. The investigation might prove very troublesome. It might be advisable to lead a lamb to the slaughter. Perhaps award a murderer to the eager Villon and have done with it.

Lazily, he added more hot water to his tub. He added more salts and savored the odor. He scrubbed his back with a brush while wishing there was a beauty sharing his tub who would lower her head and pleasure him erotically. Not like that starlet he had entertained several nights earlier, who rebuffed his request because she was a vegetarian.

Marlene slept fitfully. Twice she looked in on Maria, and the second time her daughter was smiling. *Liebchen* is having a sweet dream, how nice. Marlene quietly looked in on Anna May. Happily, she was asleep. Unhappily, there were signs on her cheeks that she had been crying. Tears for Mai Mai. A damp memorial. Marlene returned to her room. She went out on the balcony and watched a lovely sunrise. There was a balmy breeze and there was a busy afternoon awaiting her. She also had to learn her lines for Souvir's screen test, which was scheduled for the next day. Did Souvir have the stuff for stardom? Did Souvir have the stuff to commit a murder? Did Monte Trevor or Dong See? The Ivanovs? Natalia could commit murder, especially if there was a hammer or a sickle handy, but what would compel her? What motive? The seven suspects danced in Marlene's head and she knew they'd be performing there until the murderer was found. She wanted a bath. It was too early to disturb her maid. She could run her own and be at peace with her own thoughts.

Peace? Would she ever know peace again? A murderer at large. Mai Mai in a refrigerator in the morgue awaiting an autopsy. She wished they had known each other; they might have been good friends. Peace, hah! Von Sternberg's wife on the warpath threatening to sue Marlene for alienation of affections. What affections? Joe told her he had ceased loving his wife, Riza Royce, at least a year before discovering Marlene. Riza had begged for the lead in *The Blue Angel*, but she was a mediocre actress. Now she contented herself appearing in foreign-language versions of American films while contemplating separating von Sternberg from a large chunk of cash. The bathroom was steaming up and Marlene poured her special brand of bath salts imported from Italy into the tub. The hot water would relax her, invigorate her. She bunched her hair together and tied it with a ribbon. She lowered herself into the water. She admired her reflection in the mirror. But why was she frowning?

* * *

Morton Duncan's visitor to his apartment was displeased. "More money? We agreed on one hundred dollars."

"I didn't know the pill was poisonous. I didn't know it would kill her. You said it was a practical joke. It would make her uncomfortable, gassy, something like that. But it killed her. And I had a close call with Dietrich and the detective in the kitchen. I talked my way out of that one all right, but pretty soon they'll cotton to the fact that I was the only one who could have poisoned the drink. For crying out loud, man. Now I'm a murderer. Indirectly sure, but I could cop a stretch for it! That Villon is no fool. And Dietrich's a hell of a lot smarter than I thought. I've got a brother in San Juan Capistrano. I'm going there until this thing cools down. I want five hundred dollars. Not a penny less."

"Or else?"

"I'm making no threats. But I agreed to help with a joke, not a murder. Damn you, five hundred dollars!"

"I don't have that much on me. I have about two hundred. I'll get the rest to you tomorrow."

"It's tomorrow already."

"You're a pain in the ass. Can I have a glass of water?"

"In the kitchen."

"Show me."

Duncan led the way into the kitchen. He was filling a glass of water as his visitor found a carving knife and plunged it with ferocity into Duncan's back. The glass fell and shattered in the sink. Duncan clawed at his back with what little strength was left in him. He felt his knees giving way as his visitor stepped back out of the way as Duncan fell forward and lay spread-eagle. His visitor heard Duncan's death rattle and was satisfied. With a dish towel, he wiped the hilt clean. He tossed the dish towel aside and went back into the combination living room and bedroom. Why, he wondered, was Los Angeles squalor so much more squalid then any other city's squalor? He had traveled the world and seen slums too awful to describe. He'd seen rats the size of dogs chasing and attacking children. Not that the room wasn't tidy. There was neatness in its shabbiness. Duncan's murderer left the building cautiously. It was quiet in the streets. Dawn was just breaking, but the only activity he could see was a milkman with his horse and wagon farther down the street making deliveries. Duncan's murderer hurried around the corner, where he had parked his sports car, got behind the wheel, and leisurely drove away.

Wearing a terry-cloth robe, Marlene hurried downstairs to the ballroom. She continued down the hall to the room at the end. She had forgotten them in the confusion of the murder. She opened the door to the room and there they were. Fast asleep in easy chairs, Father Time and the New Year's Baby. Deep in alcoholic stupors. Marlene smiled. They had probably wiped themselves out with gin long before midnight. She went in search of her butler, found him tidying up in the study, and told him to pay them double the promised ten dollars and send them home in a car.

"Don't wake them up. Let them sleep it off. Give them another couple of hours." She continued on to the kitchen, eager for breakfast. Anna May Wong had preceded her there and was enjoying a cup of steaming hot coffee and a cigarette.

"Well, good morning early bird. Less than an hour ago I looked in on you and you were fast asleep."

"A very troubled sleep, let me tell you. Nightmares. Awful."

"Villon is meeting us here at two," Marlene reminded her.

"That'll give me plenty of time to go home, bathe, and change. Is your driver available?"

"He'd better be." She crossed to the intercom on the wall and buzzed the chauffeur's quarters above the garage. The voice that finally replied was heavy with sleep. He heard his instructions, and Marlene asked the cook for some whole-wheat toast and jam. She said to Anna May, "He's getting himself together." The cook brought her a mug of coffee into which Marlene spooned some honey.

Anna May sat back and commented. "How do you do it?

You've had almost no rest and you're as fresh as the morning dew."

"It's my Italian bath salts. Very restorative. I'll give you some to take home with you."

"I have restoratives of my own. My mother has them sent from China."

"Oh, yes? Maybe I should try some of those. Us girls can't have too many restoratives. Try some of this honey. It's local. I buy from a man who claims his bees are oversexed, which is why his honey is richer."

Anna May shuddered. "What won't they think of next."

The butler entered. "Miss Dietrich. You have a visitor."

"I do? I'm not expecting anyone."

"She apologized for dropping in unexpectedly. She says you were old friends in Berlin."

Marlene shot a 'heaven help me' look at Anna May and then asked the butler, "I presume she gave a name."

"Yes. Brunhilde Messer."

ᘒ NINE ᘓ

"BRUNHILDE MESSER!"

"That's the name she gave me, Miss Dietrich."

"Oh, that is indeed her name. Tall, stunning figure, strong features, and the inevitable monocle in her left eye." Anna May envisioned a very striking-looking woman. Marlene asked the butler, "Where is she waiting?"

"In the drawing room."

"Good. Bring my coffee and a cup for my guest and more toast and whatever cook has handy to impress a girlfriend from the old country. By the way, have the newspapers been delivered?"

"They're on the table in the drawing room."

"They'll give Brunhilde an eyeful. Anna May, my darling, I'll see you at two. You'll probably be gone before I'm through with Brunhilde."

"Brunhilde! How Wagnerian!"

"You're right on the nose. Brunhilde is a trained soprano, as were her mother and grandmother before her. Very strict and disciplined Junkers. I wonder what brings Brunhilde to Hollywood, and I can't wait to find out. See you later!"

Brunhilde Messer was indeed a very striking-looking woman, probably a few years older than Dietrich. She sat on a sofa reading the front page of the *L.A. Times*, which featured photos of Dietrich, Anna May, and Mai Mai. There was a photo of the body being wheeled out of Dietrich's mansion and a larger photo of a cross section of Marlene's guests, which was bound to annoy a number of stars caught in various stages of inebriation.

"Brunhilde!" Marlene entered with arms outstretched. Brunhilde dropped the newspaper and with a Wagnerian yodel of "Yo Ho Te Ho!" hurried to Marlene, and they hugged each other with joy. Brunhilde stepped back, adjusted her monocle, and said, "The camera doesn't lie. You are more gorgeous than ever."

"What brings you to Hollywood?" They sat next to each other on a sofa as the butler wheeled in a cart on which was laid out a carafe of coffee, toast, breakfast cakes, china, and cutlery. In a tiny Tiffany vase, there was a fresh carnation.

"Such a long story," said Brunhilde, and Marlene remembered to her regret that long stories were the soprano's specialty. "Most importantly, I'm here to see you. But first you must tell me about the murder! Have you seen the newspapers?"

"Not yet, not on an empty stomach." The butler placed the newspapers on the cart and Marlene picked up the one Brunhilde had been perusing. "Always the same damn picture with me displaying my legs. Wait until they find out I'm knock-kneed. Oh God, I suppose this will be going on for weeks." She put the newspaper aside and poured the coffee.

"Who would want to murder Mai Mai Chu? She was such a dumpling!"

"You knew her?"

"Knew her? When she was in Berlin last year she did my chart. She was introduced to me by my friend Adolph Hitler."

Dietrich was spooning honey into her cup of coffee, but

now both hands were frozen in midair. "Hitler's your friend?"

"Thank God. A very powerful friend. His star is very much in the ascendency in Germany. He has the president right here." She indicated the palm of her hand. "The president is almost senile. He will have to be deposed in the very near future, and when he is, mark my words, Adolph will become chancellor of Germany."

The butler was busy fussing about the room. Marlene said, "Just a moment, Brunhilde." She raised her voice so the butler would know she was addressing him. "That will be all, thank you."

"Yes, Miss Dietrich." He left the room hurriedly.

Brunhilde asked, "He eavesdrops?"

"Every domestic in Hollywood eavesdrops. It's a popular pastime, and frequently profitable if there's some gossip to sell to the columnists. So it was Hitler who introduced you to Mai Mai. I wonder if she ever did his chart."

"Of course she did. He's a fanatic about astrology. He doesn't make a move without having the stars consulted. You certainly remember I share the same enthusiasm. It's the stars that brought me to Hollywood."

"So you're looking for a career here."

"Not at all! I'm doing superbly back home. Haven't you heard? I'm producing and directing films. Leni Riefenstahl and I are now arch rivals. Leni isn't acting anymore."

"How foolish of her. She's Germany's biggest star."

"Not foolish at all." She held up a pastry. "What is this?"

"A Danish pastry."

Brunhilde was impressed. "All the way from Denmark?"

"No, all the way from Levy's bakery."

Brunhilde bit into the pastry. "Mmmm. Very nice. Prunes."

"There's also cheese and raisins and whatever. Tell me more about Leni."

"She's been winding up all her acting commitments to

make more of those mountain pictures she loves to do. You know, skiing, climbing, and all that physical activity I abhor."

"What sort of films have you been making?"

"*Power*. Films about power. Political power, financial power, the power of men over women and the power of women over men. I just finished one with Willy Forst and Hans Albers."

Dietrich laughed. "I had affairs with both of them. I did a film with Willy in Vienna, *Café Electric*, That's when Igo Sym taught me how to play the electrical saw. Believe me, my dear, that was one period when I was all charged up. Willy got mad at me when I returned to Berlin to do a musical with Margo Lion, *It's in the Air*."

"I remember that one. You and Margo played lesbians."

"Yes. The lesbians lost."

"Adolph intends the German film industry to be the biggest in the world. He has a tremendous amount of financial backing."

"Amazing. I heard him talk once. He was so nondescript looking, but I must admit his effect on the audience was hypnotic. And now he is becoming powerful." She thought for a moment. "Power can be very dangerous in the wrong hands. Very very dangerous. I wonder if Mai Mai accurately predicted his rise."

"Oh, yes. Indeed she did."

"You saw his chart?"

"No, but he read some of it at a dinner several months ago. She predicted truly astonishing things for him. Your friend Ivar Tensha was there."

"Tensha is not my friend. I dislike him intensely."

"But I see in the paper he was at your party last night."

"The Countess di Frasso brought him. I met him last night for the first time."

"Monte Trevor was here too. Isn't he a friend?"

"He came with Dorothy di Frasso and Tensha. Same story. I met him last night for the first time. You know him?"

"Oh, yes. He spends a lot of time in Berlin. He's looking to get a foot in the door of the movie industry. I'm sure he's still badgering Tensha to invest in films."

"Yes, I'm told that's going on."

"And everyone was here last night witnessing Mai Mai's murder! Oh, why didn't I try to reach you yesterday. I could have been here and seen all the fun!"

"Fun! Since when is murder fun?"

"You know what I mean! I should have called Raymond too."

Marlene was fascinated. Tensha, Trevor, and Raymond Souvir? "You know Raymond Souvir?"

"Yes, the darling boy. I brought him to Berlin to test for a film I'm thinking of doing about the flying war ace, the Red Baron. I saw Raymond in a play in Paris and thought he had the right boyish good looks. The Red Baron was only twenty when he was brought down in flames." She shrugged. "Talk about a misspent youth." She was lighting a cigarette. Marlene lit one too, while deep in thought.

Marlene said, "The three are suspects in Mai Mai's murder." She told Brunhilde about the seven suspects, which was interspersed from Brunhilde with "No!" and "You don't say!" and lots of tongue clucking. Finally Marlene said, "Souvir and Dong See are quite close."

"I'm glad to hear Dong See has recovered."

"Was he ill?"

"Automobile accident about half a year ago. He was badly smashed up."

"There was nothing in the newspapers about it here. At least not that I recall."

"Because it was kept out of the papers. His manager canceled his tour and Dong See was hidden in a sanatorium in the Swiss Alps. The accident occurred in Italy, where they are perfectly dreadful drivers. They drive their cars as if they were riding bicycles. Italians are children. They're lucky to have Benito Mussolini to direct their destiny. Well, at least Dong's recovered. I hope the accident hasn't affected his playing."

104

"He's in no rush to return to concertizing. He's rented a house here in the hills above Sunset Boulevard. He says he's going to spend the next three months composing a violin concerto."

"How ambitious of him. I had no idea he composed too."

"Many musicians give it a try."

"I must get in touch with Dong. And with the others too." Marlene looked at her wristwatch. "Am I keeping you from anything?"

"There's still time. I have a date at two with Herb Villon, the detective investigating Mai Mai's murder. Anna May Wong is joining us."

"I see her picture's on the front page. You've just done one together for von Sternberg, I read somewhere."

"Always for von Sternberg. How I ache to do something with Ernst Lubitsch or Rouben Mamoulian. A cheeky piece of froth in which I can show my audiences how funny I can be. But no, they keep me chained to von Sternberg, and he continues to trap me into one piece of exotica after another. In my next I'm exiled to the tropics. The tropics, for crying out loud."

Brunhilde adjusted her monocle and said firmly, "Fate has brought me to you. Marlene, I want you to come back to Germany and become the Fatherland's greatest star. Don't argue. Hear me out! You will do comedy with Oskar Karl-weis, operettas with your Willy Forst. . . ."

"Hardly *my* Willy Forst."

". . . or another erotic drama with Emil Jannings, another *Blue Angel.*"

"Work with that monster again? That mountain of *dreck?* Never!" She was on her feet and pacing, nostrils flaring. "Jennings is garbage! *Garbage!*"

"*Achtung!*" cried Brunhilde, flabbergasted by this sudden outbreak of invective.

Marlene swept her hair back and with hands on hips, towered over the seated Brunhilde and said, "I'll thank you to keep a civil *Achtung* in your mouth."

"Beloved Marlene. Come back to us. Come back to your roots."

"I have new roots, Brunhilde. They are here. In this country."

"In this house? Where a woman was murdered while your child slept under the very same roof?"

"Brunhilde, your monocle is slipping. It might fall to the floor and break."

"No matter," said Brunhilde, screwing the monocle back into place, "I have dozens of others." Marlene sat, and Brunhilde took her hand and pressed it gently between hers. "Marlene." The voice was now grave, dramatic. Marlene recognized something momentous was about to issue from her friend's mouth. "I have a personal message for you from Adolph. I committed it to memory." Now she was Adolph Hitler. All that was missing to complete the picture was his Charlie Chaplin mustache. " 'Fräulein Dietrich. I speak from my heart, a heart that is yours for the asking.' "

Marlene hastily lit a cigarette to keep from emitting an embarrassing guffaw. " 'I implore you to return. When I come to power as the Emperor of Germany, possibly the Emperor of Europe, possibly the emperor of the world, I will build you a palace. The walls and the ceilings will be imbedded with precious jewels. The fixtures will be of pure gold and platinum. I will build a movie studio especially for you. It will be the most magnificent in the world, the ninth wonder of the world. The world's greatest scientists will discover the formula for eternal youth, and it shall be yours. While Garbo and Crawford and Shearer and Harlow grow old and wrinkled and turn to dust, you shall be forever young.' "

Dietrich couldn't contain herself any longer. She howled with laughter while clapping her hands together. Her cigarette fell to the floor, and with a look of undisguised annoyance Brunhilde retrieved the cigarette and consigned it to her coffee cup. Dietrich's laughter soon subsided into a cough, and exhausted, she leaned back gasping for breath. "Brunhilde, you tell your beloved Adolph that I am flattered to know he thinks so highly of me. . . ."

"He worships you." She almost sang the words in high C.

"He mustn't worship a false god. Look what happened to the Israelites when they put too much faith in Baal. They ended up with Baal in the wrong court. No, Brunhilde Messer, no, no a thousand times no."

"That is your final word? You won't reconsider?"

"You've known me a long time, Brunhilde, and you remember, when I say *No*, it's *No*."

Brunhilde was polishing the monocle with a handkerchief. "How Adolph suffers. Just a few months ago he was shattered by Geli Raubel's suicide."

"And who was Geli Raubel?"

"His niece. The great love of his life."

"Good heavens!" Marlene feigned shock. "He was *shtooping* his own niece? That's incest!" She thought for a moment. "Isn't it?"

"If Adolph indulges in incest, it is on a rarified plain."

"*Liebchen*, incest is incest even if it's kept in the family."

"Now he has Eva Braun."

"Another niece?"

"No relation. She is madly in love with him."

"Good. Tell him to build the palace for her."

"Marlene." The voice was grave again. "You are taking this much too lightly. Adolph Hitler is not to be mocked or scoffed at. Soon, very soon, his voice will resonate through the world and . . ."

"Enough of this nonsense, Brunhilde. You didn't come seven thousand miles to bring me his offer. You could have mailed me a postcard."

"Well," Brunhilde sighed, "then I must have a talk with Garbo."

"You'll grow hoarse shouting."

"She's deaf?"

"No, she's in Sweden. Had you known, you could have

saved on the carfare. Tell me, Brunhilde, the Ivanovs, the Russians, Natalia and Gregory, did they ever take an excursion to Berlin?"

"He served in their Berlin embassy briefly before being assigned to Los Angeles."

"I presume you met them."

"They are peasants."

"Don't make sport of peasants. Without them there would be no crops."

"Gregory is very boring. He used to do card tricks."

"Oh yes? He has nimble fingers?"

"Very nimble fingers. I slapped them away twice."

"Where are you staying, Brunhilde?"

"You want to be rid of me. I am annoying you."

"On the contrary, you have been amusing me, but then you always did have a delightful sense of humor. Remember a performance of *Götterdämmerung* when Beniamino Gigli bowed to the audience and you pushed him into the orchestra pit and he fell headfirst into a tuba?"

"It wasn't Gigli. It was Lauritz Melchior. Gigli couldn't sing Wagner. He excelled at Puccini and Verdi. I'm keeping you from your appointment."

"I still have time. Would you like to see Maria? She's growing up into a very beautiful child."

"I'd love to see her."

"Now, don't be annoyed with me, Brunhilde. You descend on me unannounced . . ."

"I'm sorry. I was so eager . . ."

"It doesn't matter. I'm delighted you're here. And if you'll take the time to think about your Adolph Hitler's very amusing offer . . . yes . . . amusing . . . nothing more and nothing less . . . you will realize in the long run it's ridiculous and inappropriate, and wait until I tell von Sternberg. Ha! He could use a good laugh right now. Come!"

"Morton? Morton?" The landlady banged on the door with her fist. "There are a couple of flatfoots out here! They want to talk to you!" Her name was Bertha Gull and she looked familiar to Herb Villon and Jim Mallory, and Villon told her so. "You probably seen me in pitchers," she said with what she was sure was a beguiling smile. "I do a lot of extra work. So does Morton."

"I took a guess at that," said Villon, "That's how I tracked down his address."

"Morton also works as a waiter. He worked for Miss Dietrich last night. Morton doesn't do as much extra work as I do. I'm what they call a 'dress extra.' That's because I own some exquisite ball gowns, which I lifted from . . . which I bought at Magnin's with my savings. I get paid more then Morton does. I run this rooming house in case the movie industry suddenly collapses and disappears."

"No chance of that, I'm sure."

"Oh, no? Do you read *Popular Mechanics?* Well, it's my favorite read next to *Liberty* magazine. Well, *Popular Mechanics* had this here article on television, which is a combination of radio and movies, and they predict in another twenty or thirty years television will wipe out *both* movies and radio. *Morton!*" She was banging hard on the door again. "This isn't like him. I know he didn't go out because I sit by the downstairs window all the time, especially on a holiday like today, just to check the comings and goings of my tenants, y'know, if they snuck somebody in for the night, which I do not permit. I run a clean house. You want hanky-panky, sit in the top rows of the Hollywood Bowl. Morton has the best apartment. The Presidential Suite. It has its own kitchen. *Morton!*"

Villon was growing impatient. "Use your passkey."

"Well, all right, if you insist. This isn't like him. Maybe he's taking a shower and can't hear me. I don't want to frighten him."

"Please open the door, Mrs. Dull."

"*Gull.*"

"Sorry. New Year's Day whammies." He'd had very little sleep, and Hazel had hogged most of the bed and the blanket. Too much wine had taken its toll and his performance was way below par, and Hazel didn't hesitate to tell him as she stumbled to the kitchen to make herself a salami and provolone sandwich. The door was open and the detectives trailed the landlady into the seedy room.

"Well! He didn't sleep here last night at all! The bed's still made. Morton? Are you in the bathroom?" She looked inside the bathroom, but Morton remained elusive.

Villon shouted from the kitchen. "He's in here. But if you have a weak stomach, stay where you are. Jim, call for the coroner and some of the boys."

Bertha Gull screamed. She was standing in the doorway, with her hands on her cheeks.

"I told you to stay where you were," Villon reminded her.

She said in a tear-stained voice, "He owes me two weeks rent."

"Well now, why don't you look on it as a farewell gift."

"This is no time for levity, officer. Poor Morton. I recognize the hilt. That's his best carving knife. Stainless steel. He bought it at the Broadway. I was with him. We'd just come from a day on Connie Bennett's *Common Clay* at Fox. We each had a line, as a matter of fact." Jim Mallory was delighted to leave Bertha Gull to Villon as he went out to the unmarked squad car to radio headquarters. "I said, 'It was a delightful evening,' and I think Morton said, 'Charmed, I'm sure.' No chance he might still be alive?"

"Only if you believe in miracles." He was hunkered down examining the space between the body and the sink. He got to his feet and saw the broken glass in the sink. "Must have been getting himself a glass of water when the knife hit."

Bertha Gull said quite logically. "He wouldn't be getting himself a glass of water if someone was breaking into the place, would he?"

"You're right. Nice thinking, Mrs. Hull."

"*Gull.* Just think of flapping wings and splashes when they dive into the water for a fish."

"Sorry. I didn't expect to find him dead. Maybe a little shaken, but not dead."

"I read the paper this morning. I read about this here Chinese lady being murdered at Miss Dietrich's. Morton worked there last night, like I told you. You think Morton had something to do with it?"

"Now I'm positive Morton had something to do with it. Enough to get himself killed to shut him up."

"The boys are on their way," said Mallory as he came back into the apartment.

Bertha Gull asked, "Why would somebody want to shut him up?"

"To keep him from talking."

"Talking about what?"

Was she truly this innocent, Villon wondered, or was she slightly retarded? Mallory was smiling, the Bertha Gulls of the world would never cease to be a source of constant amusement to him. Mallory was also an innocent and therein lay his charm. Marlene Dietrich had recognized this, and as a congenital protector of innocents, took to him immediately at the party. Villon saw no harm in giving Bertha Gull information, unless it might turn out in a surprising switch that she was Ivar Tensha's mistress. "We think Mr. Duncan might have had something to do with the murder last night."

"Oh, don't be silly. Go away!" She dismissed the information with a disdainful wave of a hand. "Morton and murder, they both begin with 'm' but that's about as close as they'll get. Morton was a gentle soul. He attended Mass religiously, and he never went to confession because he had nothing to confess. Believe me, gentlemen, Morton Duncan was just about the dullest and most tiresome man I ever met, and I suppose I'll never see that back rent he owes me." They had abandoned Morton Duncan and were in the bedroom–sitting room searching in drawers. "Believe my word, you won't find a thing."

The bottom drawer of the dresser was filled with pornographic material. Villon and Mallory feasted as they flipped through magazines, postcards, and obscene comic strips featuring such old favorites as Tillie the Toiler, The Katzenjammer Kids, and Moon Mullins in acts that were eloquently filthy. "What have you got there?" demanded Bertha Gull. She was at Villon's elbow and could clearly see what was causing him to smirk. Her cheeks reddened and she backed away, looked at the corpse on the kitchen floor, and then said in a very small, sad voice, "Still waters certainly do run deep. Well, it's no wonder he met such a violent death. It was God's punishment for never confessing his guilt and taking his dose of Hail Mary's."

"Could you possibly spare a shopping bag?" Villon asked her. "These will have to be confiscated and taken to the station house."

"Oh sure," she said with a cynical sneer and left to find a shopping bag.

Villon leaned against a wall while Mallory settled into a chair. Mallory said, "Well, your hunch was right."

"That was no hunch, that was detective work. It had to be him who dropped the pill in the champagne because his explanation of not seeing a hand pass over the glass was too damned elaborate, too well thought out. He was paid to drop the pill, but I don't think he knew it was lethal. He was conned into thinking it was a joke, something like that. Probably slipped him a ten or a twenty, but when he realized she was dead, the price went up and who's to blame him? A smart prosecutor could have nailed him good. So at the party he said more money or else. They met here and again the price went up, probably from, say, a hundred to maybe five or more. So his visitor, who is no dummy, knows Morton Duncan is now dangerous and therefore expendable. So he asks for a glass of water, follows Morton into the kitchen, and good-bye Morton and don't forget to write."

"Poor Morton. I was so positive we'd get the name of who supplied the pill out of him. He looked like the type who frightened easily."

"Not movie extras. They're a tough bunch."

They heard sirens. "They made good time. We have to pick up Marlene and Anna May in half an hour and it's going to take that long to get to Marlene's place. Hello there, Irving, top of the morning to you."

The coroner threw him a filthy look. "I suppose this one's been poisoned too." He had performed the autopsy on Mai Mai Chu a few hours earlier and confirmed the poison was strychnine.

"No, Irving, this was a straightforward plunge of a carving knife into a back, leaving the stiff very stiff."

"Anyone we know?"

"You might recognize him if you saw a movie called *Common Clay.*"

The coroner, a movie buff, moved Morton's head for a better look at his face. "Oh, of course! He's the extra who said, 'Charmed, I'm sure.' " Villon's jaw dropped.

❦ TEN ❧

"STABBED IN THE back!" Anna May Wong was genuinely shocked.

"That's nothing new in this town," commented Marlene cynically. "So it was he who poisoned the champagne. Damn, just when I was going to cast suspicion on Gregory Ivanov." She caught Villon's questioning look and explained what she had learned from Brunhilde Messer. "He does card tricks. Very clever with his hands, very nimble fingers. But alas, he's in the clear."

Villon said, "Brunhilde Messer." He screwed up his face, prodding his memory. "Opera. Tall broad. Built like a wrestler."

Marlene elaborated on Brunhilde's visit and Adolph Hitler's bizarre offer, saving the best of her information for last.

Anna May said seriously, "If you became the queen of the German film industry, you could make them write good parts for me."

"Oh Anna May, how desperate you sound. Would you want me to betray my principles and accept Hitler's ridiculous offer?" She was enchanted by the way Mallory's lips moved as he read one of the newspapers. She sighed. "My countrymen will follow him like sheep. He offers them hope and a future and they are desperate for both. The country is sinking under a cruel recession. Bread is ten dollars a loaf! Can you imagine that? Bread! Thank God my mother and sister have me to send them enough money to survive. How the others manage I do not know." Her hands were clasped together as she shook her head from side to side. Then she laughed, a laugh tinged with bitterness and irony. "How the hell did I manage when I lived there? But together, Rudy and I were able to earn enough to live better than most. How often you have told me I'm too cynical, Anna May. But Germany breeds cynicism. Germany lost the war and now Hitler promises to lead them to financial recovery. He promises those poor humiliated people that soon they will raise their heads again with pride and take their rightful place again as a powerful nation. Who knows? Who am I to condemn him? I'm here in the United States. I make money. I live better than I deserve. And for crying out loud, why am I bemoaning the lot of Germany when right here in my adopted country there's a frightening depression and armies of homeless roaming the country, living in Hoovervilles of shacks with newspapers for blankets when they sleep. Men selling apples on the street, banks failing, and what the hell am I carrying on about? Anybody want a drink? We're not leaving for Mai Mai's just yet. I have lots more to tell you. Brunhilde Messer was a geyser of information." She paused. "Geyser, or geezer?"

"Geyser," said Villon, thinking she ought to know, having been erupting for the past couple of minutes.

Nobody wanted a drink. Marlene lit a cigarette and sat on a straight-backed chair next to an end table and an ashtray stolen from the Brown Derby restaurant. "My friends, all of our suspects are liars."

Mallory folded his newspaper and placed it aside while hearing Villon saying, "Aw, Marlene, you don't really think that?"

"Oh, all right, all right, Herb, don't be such a smart aleck.

115

Brunhilde knew them all in Berlin, where they all knew each other. And their center of gravity was Hitler. Monte Trevor was there trying to weasel his way into the film industry. The Ivanovs were with the Russian Embassy before being transferred here. Raymond Souvir was brought to Berlin by Brunhilde to test for a movie she's planning to produce and direct. Tensha was there and is possibly one of Hitler's financiers. Stands to reason for a munitions maker. Hitler wants power and you need an army to wrest power for yourself."

"Mai Mai's prediction." Anna May's voice was ghostly. "The second world war."

Marlene felt a chill. "I wonder if Nostradamus had any Chinese blood in him?"

"Nostra Who?" asked Jim Mallory.

"Nostradamus lived hundreds of years ago. He was a seer and he made some pretty knockout predictions for the future." Villon's hands were in his pants pockets as he slowly paced the room. "What about Dong See? Wasn't he in Berlin too?"

"Apparently not then. It seems he'd been in a terrible automobile accident in Italy and was so severely injured that he had to be sequestered in a Swiss clinic for six months."

Anna May said, "You'd never guess from the way he looked last night. Anyway, they say Swiss doctors and surgeons can work miracles. I've heard there's a new clinic that has perfected a serum that prolongs life. How do the Swiss find the time when they're so preoccupied with chocolate and cheese?"

"Did Miss Messer mention di Frasso?" asked Villon.

"No, but Dorothy is a butterfly. She flits from capital to capital as the whim strikes her. Last March she was on a safari in Africa. Before that she was found at an archaeological dig in Egypt. She also collects important people like other women collect charms for a bracelet." She did a scathing impersonation of di Frasso. " 'I just *adoooorrrre* Benny Mussolini. He makes the trains run on time.' " She crushed her cigarette in an ashtray. "She's a charmer, I have to hand her that."

Villon was now sitting and contemplating the view from the picture window. Marlene's daughter and the chauffeur were on the lawn throwing a beach ball back and forth. "Mai Mai Chu was in Berlin too?"

"*Ach Gott.*" Marlene slapped her forehead. "How could I forget *this?* She was not only there, but she read Hitler's chart!"

"Some girls have all the luck," said Villon. "I hope she kept a copy of that one." He chuckled.

"What's so funny?" asked Dietrich.

"I was thinking about what Hazel's missing. She's so busy doing the New Year's Day party circuit. From Marie Dressler to the Wesley Ruggles and then on to Ramon Novarro, even though she's heard Metro may not be renewing his contract."

"Ramon is so sweet, poor darling. Bi-lingual, bi-sexual, and now by-passed." She winked at Mallory and hoped he wouldn't faint. He had a very silly expression on his face, which reminded her of the comedian Stan Laurel, whom she considered funnier than Chaplin. "Well, my friends, what are we waiting for? There's nothing we can do here, and I say we get going downtown to Mai Mai's place." She was on her feet, and Mallory admired her slacks and jacket. Women wearing pants, what's the world coming to? "Well Herb, this is turning into quite a case, isn't it. Mai Mai murdered last night, the waiter murdered in his kitchen early this morning, and we have ten hours ahead of us for further interesting developments. Shouldn't we go in one car?"

Villon agreed. The ladies would travel with him and Mallory. Dietrich spoke on the intercom, advising Maria's nurse that she and her guests were leaving. Since her chauffeur would be free, she suggested an excursion to the Venice Beach amusement park. It was Maria's favorite place. It was the nurse's too. She especially loved the Tunnel of Love and especially with the chauffeur's arms around her.

"Maria's nurse thinks she's kidding me," said Marlene as she led the way out of the house. "She thinks I don't know she sneaks out to the chauffeur's room above the garage when the household is supposed to be asleep."

"Why not?" asked Anna May, who long ago had drawn a protective veil around her own private life. "As the title used to say in silent pictures, 'Youth calls to youth.' "

"In this case," said Marlene, "youth howls to youth." She added mournfully, "Ah, to be in the first flush of youth again." She laughed, "Although I was never all that innocent. How about you, Jim Mallory? Are you still a virgin?" His knees began to wobble. He held tight to the rear car door he was holding open for the ladies. Marlene patted his cheek and then settled back on the seat.

Anna May said to her as she sat, "Must you torture him?"

"Don't be silly, he loves it." Mallory was at the wheel of the car. Villon was speaking into the car radio, telling the precinct they were leaving Dietrich's house and heading south to Mai Mai's loft. The dispatcher gave him a message from Hazel demanding he join her later at one of the parties. The coroner left word that the knife that had sent Morton Duncan to his unjust reward had gone clean through his heart, causing instant death. *Charmed, I'm sure,* thought Villon. What a world. What a life. What a death.

Marlene spoke suddenly. "It can't be Hitler."

"You've lost me," said Anna May. "It can't be Hitler what?"

"Just because all the suspects were in Berlin and know Hitler doesn't mean he's in any way the reason why Mai Mai was murdered. It has to be something deeper, something more malignant. An abscess that needs to be lanced." She had their attention while cautioning Mallory to keep his hands firmly on the wheel and his eyes on the road ahead of them. New Year's Day meant New Year's Day drunks, and at the wheel of a car drunks could be lethal. "Why should anyone fear Mai Mai because she had seen them in Berlin at the same time? They were there legitimately to all intents and purposes. One for a screen test, another looking for a wedge in the film industry, two of them were gainfully employed in their country's embassy; and Tensha makes no bones about how he earns his money, and Hitler has a professional eye for finding financial backing. So what if Mai Mai *did* recognize them en masse? But . . ."—and now her voice darkened—"if Mai Mai knew there was something else involving these people, possibly also involving Hitler, something more awful than the rise of a would-be dictator, something, for want of a better expression, earth-shattering."

"Sounds reasonable to me," said Villon.

"It has to be reasonable. Why else murder Mai Mai? It's in the horoscopes. It has to be. Their gathering at my party was a tragic coincidence. Mai Mai was a last-minute inspiration on Anna May's part, so the plot to kill Mai Mai didn't exist until one of the seven phoned her to . . . wait a minute, wait a minute! The plot to kill Mai Mai *very much existed.* She'd been marked for murder for months. But finding out she'd be at my party was for them a blessing in disguise, they could try eliminating her that night. And what better setting? A crowded ballroom, an orchestra, lots of noise, a cacophony of voices and a strychnine pill that had been kept in reserve if other means of killing her were not propitious. Oh, poor Anna May, I'm upsetting you."

"No. It's not what you're saying. That's logic. But murder is insanity. I've read about it, I've played killers, but it has never come this close to me. You read about a murder in the papers, and reading about murder has its own fascination. Then you shrug it off and turn to the funnies. But now I realize people are reading about Mai Mai then shrugging her off and turning to the funnies. Now I know how terrible murder really is. Mai Mai was a real person, warm, loving, always laughing. But so were all the other victims we've read about. But one has to be cold about it, doesn't one, Herb? You can't sentimentalize murder because there's the killer to apprehend, and if you go soft then the mind grows lazy and logic evanesces."

"Herb will catch the son of a bitch," Marlene assured Anna May, not also realizing she was assuring Villon, who frequently had his doubts about nailing a murderer. "And Jim Mallory will be invaluable to Herb, as he has already proven to be, and watch out for that bastard coming up on your left!" Jim swerved in time to avoid a collision. "Well! We came within a hair of making headlines tomorrow!"

"You'd get top billing," said Anna May sullenly.

"Oh, Anna May." Marlene did not fear death; she frequently contemplated her own mortality. It was Maria she worried about. What would become of her? She doesn't know about Rudy's mistress. If Marlene died, would Rudy marry the woman? Would she and Maria like each other? Would she be the right person to raise Maria? Marlene groaned and Anna May shot her a look but didn't question her. Am *I* the right person to raise Maria? She has a nurse and a maid, and there are butlers and a chauffeur and there are bodyguards, and I am at the studio sometimes as long as twelve hours a day when I'm filming, and I'm away on trips and I can't always take her with me. Oh, what the hell, how many children in the world wish they could trade places with Maria, so there.

Marlene's thoughts sidetracked to the actors she'd hired to be Father Time and the New Year's Baby. How pathetic their distress to realize they'd passed out and never got to do their act. Father Time wouldn't take the money the butler pressed on him, and the butler had to fetch Marlene, who held the actor by his arms, insisting he take the money. The poor bastard. Washed up. Washed out. No hope for him. Maybe she could find a way to wangle him onto Paramount's talent roster. All the studios maintained a company of stock players contracted at a minimal weekly salary to be on tap to do bits and walk-ons. Metro had several silent favorites who had fallen on hard times on stock contracts. Aileen Pringle, May McAvoy, Marie Prevost, to name three. How often at a screening had Marlene heard a buzz from the audience when a former favorite flashed by and was recognized. Maybe a few years from now that would be her. Like hell, not Marlene. Marlene is a survivor.

"That's the building on the northwest corner. The one with the grocery store on the ground floor." The streets were almost deserted. This was the commercial area that abutted Chinatown, where they would find hustle and bustle if they were in search of it. But in this neighborhood on a holiday afternoon, all was quiescent. Villon knew that behind some of the façades there were illegal factories paying coolie wages to illegal immigrants. There were illegal fan-tan parlors where the Chinese who were compulsive gamblers played mah-jongg and fan-tan and blackjack and rarely escaped the bondage and thrall in which the gamblers held them because of their constant indebtedness. Some traded their daughters and their sons for their freedom, some even offered wives and sisters. They defied the tongs, who frowned on the practice. The tongs were family societies who looked after each other, benevolent societies who financed business ventures for their relatives. They arranged marriages and made sure their dead were given funerals befitting a respected member. The movies libeled and slandered tongs, depicting them as gangs of cutthroats and thieves constantly warring with each other. They did on occasion feud, but differences were usually settled over a pot of tea and honey cakes.

Jim Mallory parked at the entrance to the hallway leading to a small elevator that rose to Mai Mai's loft. Marlene was astonished by the lack of security. "She could have been killed *here!*" cried Marlene. "The door is unbolted. Anyone can get in."

"Marlene, many eyes watched this doorway, as many eyes are watching us now. Here Mai Mai was safe. This was her fortress, secluded and impenetrable. I never told you this before, I had no reason to, but Mai Mai was a princess. Yes, she was of royal blood. Her ancestry goes back so many generations. Tragically, she is the last of her line. She had no brothers. Let me lead the way."

Two of the pairs of eyes watching Anna May leading the others into the building couldn't believe what they were seeing. One spoke softly, "Honorable Fong Shen Un, do my miserable eyes deceive. Is that not Marlene 'Legs' Dietrich I see?"

The second pair of eyes replied, "I do not deserve to look upon her. She is too far above for this humble and unworthy nobody. It would be an honor to grovel before her and have her humble me with her feet in my face. Oh Gut Tsu Donk, how often I have dreamed of screwing her."

The hallway was beautifully papered with decorative designs. Anna May explained they were the work of a young muralist whose work Mai Mai had seen and admired in Hong Kong. Mai Mai had arranged to bring him to the United States, and when last heard of, Anna May said, he was laboring in a vineyard in the Napa Valley.

"How sad," commented Marlene.

"Not sad at all," countered Anna May. "He owns the vineyard."

The four squeezed into the elevator, which made its way slowly and laboriously to the top floor. It came to rest with an agonizing grinding of the brake. When the door opened, the four stepped into a paradise, a shrine to the zodiac, a magnificently appointed room with high ceilings and many windows draped with multicolored materials imported from the Orient. The twelve signs of the zodiac covered the walls. The furniture was lovely in its simplicity. There were sofas and easy chairs, and oversized pillows dominated the floor. At the furthest end of the room, away from the elevator, was a hallway, the entrance to which was camouflaged by a curtain of stringed bamboo beads. Anna May explained that beyond the curtain was Mai Mai's bedroom and bath, and a kitchen.

"This room was the center of Mai Mai's life. Here she entertained and here she did her charts. She worked at this desk." It was built into a wall next to a huge chart of the zodiac signs. Past the chart was a row of steel cabinets and behind their doors Herb Villon was positive they would find the copies of the charts they were seeking. From her handbag Anna May extracted a ring of keys. "These will open the cabinets. The honorable Mr. Gai Ah Veck, the leader of Mai Mai's tong, entrusted them to me. I saw him before returning to your house, Marlene, and he was glad to learn there would

be no rest until Mai Mai's murderer is brought to justice."
She gave the keys to Villon.

He chose the cabinet closest to the desk. After several tries
a key fit and he opened the door. He was faced with a filing
cabinet. "Mai Mai certainly believed in security." He pulled
open a drawer and Anna May smiled at the perplexed look on
his face. "I told you everything would be in Chinese. Let me
have a look."

Marlene wandered about the room, studying the portraits
of relatives and ancestors with which the tables were heavily
populated. The family, thought Marlene, the all-important
family. The Chinese worshipped their ancestors. Respected
them and revered them. It was an honor to be elderly in the
Chinese world. The elderly had a vast store of knowledge and
shared it with the young. The elderly were not shunted off to
nursing homes or abandoned to a miserable lot. The family
took care of the elderly and honored them. Not like us,
thought Marlene, to whom the elderly are a nuisance. The
Eskimos used to set them out on an ice floe to freeze to death.
My mother is lucky. Her apartment is steam heated, and there
aren't many of *those* in Germany.

Jim Mallory dogged Marlene's trail. They exchanged comments on some of the paintings that hung on the walls. Mai
Mai had good taste, not too eclectic, and some of the pieces
Marlene judged to be very valuable. She recognized an Ingres
and a Picasso of a period unfamiliar to her. The bookcases
contained what would prove to be many valuable first edi-
tions. There were volumes on astrology that Marlene was
sure were priceless. She examined several, the pages yellowed
with age. She told Jim Mallory they were priceless. He wanted
to tell her so was she, but that took the kind of courage he had
yet to develop.

Anna May was dismayed. "This may take forever. These
files must contain thousands of charts!"

Marlene and Jim joined Villon and Anna May. Marlene
took a chart from Anna May. "How delicate a design."

"Those aren't designs. Those are Chinese words. Our alphabet is very complicated. No A to Z for us. Oh dear, oh dear, oh dear. I may have to spend weeks translating these."

"We haven't got weeks," said Villon. "It's not going to be easy holding on to the suspects. And I've no reason to place them in custody. Tensha's arm probably reaches into high places in Washington, and I can't touch the Ivanovs or they'll claim diplomatic immunity. Don't you know any people who can help you?"

Marlene had a thought and crossed the room to the bamboo curtain. The beads tinkled a strange tune as she passed through them, or perhaps it was Mai Mai singing a song of encouragement. The kitchen was on the left and her epicurean curiosity got the better of her, delaying briefly the continuation of her mission. It was well furnished with cutlery and beautiful glassware and plates and dishes and bowls of excellent manufacture. There were numerous woks and a shelf of cookbooks of international origins. An herb chest almost brought tears to Marlene's eyes. There were jars of every exotic herb one might bring to mind. The pantry was small but contained cans and boxes of provisions, most of which were imported.

Finally Marlene stood in front of the refrigerator. It was the latest model, with the engine jutting out from the top and encased in white aluminum. Marlene rubbed her fingers together like a burglar about to attack a safe. She pulled the door open and almost collapsed with laughter. There was a half-eaten ham sandwich on a small dish, a box of chocolate-covered marshmallow cookies, a bowl of what looked like cream of mushroom soup, a half-filled bottle of milk, some jars of jam and peanut butter, and finally, wrapped in wax paper, a potato knish. Sighed Marlene, ah the enigmatic Chinese.

She crossed the hall to what had to be the bedroom. She opened the door and felt as though she was about to enter a shrine. The room was also colorfully decorated, as Marlene had expected it would be, but it was completely feminine. The double bed was covered with a knitted throw, which featured a green dragon, undoubtedly a symbol of protection. Half a dozen pillows were artfully arranged against the headboard and Marlene could tell they were handsewn. Astonishingly enough, they were not emblazoned with the signs of the zodiac. The dressing table was much like one Marlene had in her dressing room. It was a theatrical model with dozens of small bulbs ringing the mirror. There were perfumes from France, from Italy, from Spain, from India, and, of course, from China. Her hairbrush and comb and hand mirror were antique, decorated in pearl. Her closet was a large walk-in with dozens of shoes, magnificent dresses for all occasions, and, surprisingly enough, hats. Oriental women rarely wore hats. Only the peasant women wore the straw hats that tied under the chin to protect them from the brutal sun when working in the rice fields. Next to the bed was a table, which held a night lamp and a telephone extension and a stack of books. The table's twin was on the other side of the bed. On it was a stack of folders and atop the folders rested what were apparently Mai Mai's reading glasses. Marlene placed the glasses aside. She opened the top folder. As she expected, it was written in Chinese. Marlene counted eight folders and felt her heartbeat accelerating.

Horoscopes. Eight horoscopes. The seven suspects? Could the eighth be Hitler's? She lifted the folders and held them as though they were sacred. Before leaving the room, she took one last look, drinking heavily of the atmosphere in which a very great lady had reigned as the royal she deserved to be. Then quietly, as though walking down a church aisle, she went to rejoin the others.

This isn't chutzpah, thought Monte Trevor, as he guided his rented coupe toward Marlene Dietrich's estate. This is my European upbringing rising to the surface. In Europe when you have been royally entertained the previous evening, you call on your host or hostess the next day to thank them in person. The hangover that had hammered in his head all morning had blissfully abated, though the memory lingered on. He didn't remember too much of what had happened to him once he entered the hotel bar, but he did remember phoning the Countess di Frasso and telling her he hungered to nibble on her nipples. This did not sit well with the lady, if he remembered correctly, and damned if that isn't her coming out of Marlene's front door. He drove up and managed a small smile as she recognized him. He got out of the car and before he could greet her she snapped, "There's nothing to nibble around here, Monte, Marlene's not receiving."

"Oh? Still recovering from last night?"

"She's not in. She went out several hours ago. With Anna May Wong and the two detectives who entertained us in the study last night. So you'll have to go peddle your papers elsewhere." She walked to her Hispano-Suiza, which to Trevor's surprise she was driving herself.

Trevor followed her to the car, looking as forlorn as an abandoned lapdog. "The detectives? Were Marlene and Anna May taken into custody?"

She got in behind the wheel. "Don't be an idiot, though it's too late for you. From what the butler surmised, and he seems pretty astute at surmising, they were off to investigate Mai Mai's loft. Searching for horoscope charts is my guess. And don't tail me, Monte! I loathe being pursued in general, especially by nibblers!"

Monte Trevor stood solemnly in the cloud of dust made by the expensive foreign car as the Countess sped off, undoubtedly to the adventure of somebody's cocktail party.

Charts! He hurried back to his car and sped off in the direction from which he had just come. A telephone was what he needed, but a telephone in the privacy of his hotel room. Oh Mai Mai, he was thinking, why didn't you take my advice and destroy those copies? But no, you were adamant, you told me to go do the physically impossible, and now you have suffered the consequences I predicted you would suffer. Now you are officially an ancestor.

* * *

Marlene came through the beaded curtain carrying the folders. "Could these possibly be what we're looking for? I found them in Mai Mai's room along with her glasses. It occurred to me that, like so many ladies of a certain age, Mai Mai preferred to work in the comfort of her bed at night." She placed the folders on a table. "Come on, Anna May. Have a look. Maybe I've struck pay dirt. Ah, Jim! What a sweet expression on your face! You must have been a beautiful baby."

◖◗ ELEVEN ◖◗

ANNA MAY EXAMINED the contents of one of the folders. "This is very complicated. It is not easy to decipher. I will need time with them, but they're positively the charts we want. This one is Monte Trevor's. I'll take them home and start working on them at once."

"Just for the hell of it," Marlene asked eagerly, "see if the eighth folder contains Hitler's chart."

Anna May examined the title page of each folder. "Bingo. This one's Hitler's."

"I thought one of them would be. Ha! Now I know how a prospector feels when he strikes gold!" Marlene's eyes sparkled and her cheeks glowed; her enthusiasm was infectious. "Have I the makings of a good detective, Herb?"

"That was a damned good deduction thinking the folders would be in Mai Mai's bedroom."

"Mai Mai and I were sisters under the skin. I also do my best work in the bedroom."

Monte Trevor made his phone calls but did not connect with Dong See or Raymond Souvir. Ivar Tensha was surprisingly undisturbed by Trevor's information. "It was inevitable the police would look for the charts and find them. They are quite innocent. Mine reveals very little that isn't already public information. It sounded a bit simpleminded when Mai Mai read it to me."

"Mai Mai was a very complex and a very brilliant woman. She could be very devious, surely you knew that. It's what she *didn't* read to you that's dangerous."

"She has been silenced. She can no longer chart, she can no longer read, and, most importantly, she can no longer speak. She had her opportunity and she rejected it. I thought the long period of inactivity before we all met here in Los Angeles might have led her to believe the plot was abandoned. But unfortunately, Fate played a trick. Mai Mai saw us at the party. So her suspicions were restored and deepened. There's nothing more to say. We'll speak later, Monte."

Monte Trevor wasn't satisfied, but there was nothing he could do. He would have to wait for the police to make the next move. He glanced at his wristwatch. Ramon Novarro's party must have started by now. No use sitting around a hotel room and stewing. I may as well go there, continue playing the role of an independent film producer on the make. Tomorrow, with the holidays out of the way, business would resume. He had appointments with several of the most powerful men in Hollywood. At least one of would have to be interested in what he had to offer. The studios were badly hit by the Depression. Paramount and Universal were on the brink of bankruptcy. MGM was demanding salary cuts from all employees, especially their stars. The country was in chaos. Jack Warner was banking on his friend Franklin Delano Roosevelt to win the Democratic nomination and the election. Roosevelt had confided in him his planned financial reforms to stabilize the economy and reward his future constituents with a New Deal that promised new prosperity was "Just Around the Corner."

Herb Villon was hoping the solution to the murders was 'Just Around the Corner.' Back at Marlene's place, Anna May retrieved her car and with the folders resting on the passenger seat dutifully eschewed all New Year's Day party-going to head for home and get to work translating the charts. Marlene planned to spend some time with her daughter before changing into something stunning for Ramon Novarro's party. Villon and Jim Mallory were headed back to the precinct. A police team had been left at Morton Duncan's apartment to dust for fingerprints and the usual routine search for clues. Villon doubted they would turn up anything valuable. He told Marlene he'd probably see her at the Novarro party, which he would attend to keep the peace with Hazel, the quilt hog. Marlene sang to herself as she made her way up the stairs to her boudoir. She rarely used the small elevator the owner of the house had installed at great expense. Climbing stairs was good for the hips, she'd been told by Madam Sylvia, filmdom's illustrious masseuse, and so Marlene took every opportunity to climb stairs. She went to her room first to select a dress and remembered she had given her maid the day off. No problem. Marlene knew how to look after herself; she'd done it for years before American stardom helped her afford servants. She looked in on the nursery, but Maria and the nurse had not yet returned from Venice Beach. Returning to her suite, she met the butler in the hallway and startled him.

"I didn't know you were back, Miss Dietrich. The Countess di Frasso stopped in while you were out. And when she left, I saw her encounter Mr. Trevor. She obviously told him you were out and so he promptly left."

"Did the Countess leave a message?"

"No, madam. She said she'd probably run into you at a party this afternoon."

"More than likely. I'm not sure if I'll be in for dinner tonight, but tell the cook not to worry. I enjoy raiding the refrigerator."

Within a few minutes, Dietrich wore a negligee and sat at her dressing table, brushing her hair. There they were reflected in the mirror, Mai Mai Chu and Morton Duncan.

How glibly he had lied to her and Villon last night. The fool. He might still be alive today had he told the truth. But no, it was not to be. Greed was his undoing. In these terrible times, could you blame the man for wanting to earn some extra cash? He wasn't even around to blame himself.

And you, delicate Mai Mai Chu. How could so tiny a woman emerge as so huge a threat? What was the link in those eight charts that triggered your suspicion these people were creating a dangerous situation? What an eclectic group. What in the world could bring them together? The Ivanovs aren't in the same league as the others. She gave that further thought. She replaced the brush with an emery board and went to work on her nails. The Ivanovs. Maybe they are not what we think they are. Maybe they are secret agents. She brushed that thought aside as insignificant. Russian spies were a glut on the market; the whole world knows that and jokes about it. But they're here and involved in this plot, whatever this plot turns out to be. They are therefore much more important than we think.

Raymond Souvir? From Rouen. His father's a shopkeeper. Aspires to American stardom. He *must* be something else, and if he is, he's giving one hell of a good performance. The fear the studio might cancel his test if Mai Mai's murder led to scandal was convincingly played by him. Tomorrow I test with him. There will be plenty of time to spend with him and perhaps learn a few things he will inadvertently let slip. That should be amusing if not fruitful.

Monte Trevor. Well, what do I know about him? He *has* produced films, several of them quite good I've been told, so those credentials are credible. He fawns on Tensha, but then, so does everyone else. Tensha is a brilliant financial tactician. She had learned long ago in Europe that people like Tensha used their business organizations as a front. One cannot easily dismiss his role as a foremost munitions dealer, but that is the tip of the iceberg. He's known to have a network of financial and political interests that spread around the world like one vast spider's web. What is he doing in this hornet's nest of seemingly minor characters? And Dorothy di Frasso? Is she involved? She hungers for a share of Tensha's financial life, and I wouldn't put it past her to permit herself to become his tool if the rewards were ample and dazzling.

Dong See. Automobile crash. Six months in a Swiss clinic. What was it that Dorothy di Frasso had said when seeing him for the first time in ages? Marlene worried her memory and then it came to her. *He's changed some since then.* How changed? wondered Marlene. What a jigsaw puzzle. Was Brunhilde Messer another piece that could fit in here somewhere? Hitler's errand girl. Hitler. Well, he needs all the help he can get, and he will get it, because he knows how to get it. World domination, a very understandable ambition. It didn't pan out for Napoléon Bonaparte, but that doesn't mean another contestant can't take a stab at it. There's an awful lot of world out there to dominate. Wasn't there possibly someone skulking in the wings with an ambition to only rule *half* the world? Don't they say 'The Sun Never Sets on the British Kingdom'? Why aren't we bellyaching about them? They're all over the place. Africa, India, the Bahamas, Canada, for Pete's sake. That's a lot of domination.

This is all too complex for me. I must give my brain a rest or it will explode. She went to her wardrobe, selected a dress, took a quick shower, and was sure a cocktail party was what she needed to revive her spirits. Why do they need reviving? You found the charts in Mai Mai's bedroom. You struck gold. You could tell Herb Villon and that adorable Jim Mallory were quite impressed with your deduction. Deduction my eye. Feminine intuition is more like it. Ah, the water feels wonderful and it's deliciously warm, but why am I feeling a chill?

Ramon Novarro's house in Beverly Hills was beautiful in its simplicity of design. A bachelor, Novarro looked after his mother and his many sisters and brothers. He was shrewd with money and owned property in Malibu Beach and downtown Los Angeles. If his star was descending, he would not lack for the wherewithal to continue living in the style to which he was accustomed. His New Year's Day parties were legendary. Here the biggest stars mingled with those no longer too much in demand. Ramon was loyal to his old friends. Loyal to director Rex Ingram, who gave him his first break and to Ingram's stunning actress wife, Alice Terry, who wisely turned a deaf ear to the rumor her husband and Novarro were lovers. She liked her marriage; it was comfortable and for years they luxuriated in living and making films in the south of France. Their suns had set in Hollywood, but they, like Novarro, were financially secure. And they, like Novarro, were busy gossiping about the murder at Marlene's party. In fact, everybody was gossiping about the murder, and Hazel Dickson flitted from group to group like a moth in a closet full of appetizing clothes.

Ramon Novarro was with a group that included Basil Rathbone and his wife, Ouida Bergere, and Lionel Barrymore, who was standing and bravely enduring the arthritic pain that would soon paralyze his body. "To think she was murdered right there before our eyes," said Ramon. "And how ironic, she had earlier predicted some of us at the party would be murder victims."

"Did she name names?" asked Lionel Barrymore.

"Oh no, she was much to discreet for that. Imagine if she had pointed a finger at me and said, 'Ramon Novarro, you are going to be murdered.' Ha ha ha. I'm sure if she'd had, I'd have sued her for causing me mental distress."

Ouida Bergere said to Hazel, "Isn't detective Villon your heartthrob of the moment, Hazel?"

"Not if he doesn't show up soon." Hazel was working up to her third gin and orange juice.

Ouida continued, "Raymond Souvir told us you and Marlene sat in on his interrogations. Isn't that a bit unorthodox?"

"Oh, phooey. Everybody in town knows Herb gives me preferential treatment. It's no different than Irving Thalberg making sure Norma gets the best scripts at Metro. And Marlene sat in because the murder took place in her house and Herb felt she had every right to sit in."

"Well, come on," prompted Rathbone, "let's hear what went on."

"You can read it tomorrow in Louella's column."

"Hazel," said Rathbone, "start talking or you'll never get another item out of me or Ouida." Hazel was one of the few news hens invited to the Rathbone's frequent parties. She told them almost as much as she could remember while minimizing the importance of Mai Mai's charts. Lionel Barrymore wandered away in search of something to sit on and was grateful when Ruth Chatterton indicated she would love his company beside her on a sofa.

"I see Hazel's probably been filling you in on the murder, and don't ask *what* murder; today it's our only murder."

"No, as a matter of fact, it isn't."

"Oh?"

"Seems a man was found dead this morning, stabbed in the back with a carving knife. It was on the radio. It turns out he was a waiter at last night's party."

"Isn't that fascinating! Do you suppose there's a connection between the two?"

"Well, Ruth, I don't have much of a deductive mind, so it didn't interest me if there's a connection or not. There's a good man on the case, Herb Villon, and if there's a connection then he knows about it. I'm sure the authorities aren't too eager to release too much information about the murders, but sooner or later we'll have all the facts and if they're sordid enough, all Hollywood will wallow in them. Where's your husband?"

"You mean Ralph?" She was married to actor Ralph Forbes.

"As I recall that's his name."

"He's staying at his mother's."

"Is she ill?"

"No. I told Ralphie I wanted a divorce and he was so angry with me he packed his bags and went home to mother. Which made a great deal of sense as I couldn't very well pack my bags and go home to mother as mother's been dead for years and you don't pack your bags and go to a cemetery."

"I'm sorry to hear this. Ralph's a nice man."

"Oh, terribly nice. They don't come any nicer. Or more tiresome. I think Ralph will always be remembered for having passed through life without giving offense. How's the composing going?"

"Still slogging away at it. I don't get much time the way Metro schedules me in one picture after another."

"Have you met Dong See?"

"The violinist? Is he here?"

"Yes, he's over there by the buffet. I'll see if I can catch his eye."

"Oh, don't bother. He's with that Monte Trevor, and he had me cornered for ten minutes convincing me I should play Herod in his *Salome* movie."

"It looks like a pretty heated conversation. I wish I could read lips."

Monte Trevor had told Dong See about the group going to Mai Mai Shu's loft and his fears that the charts would reveal something incriminating. Dong See was telling him, "There was nothing that I found worrisome when Mai Mai read my chart to me."

"Did she let you read any of it yourself?"

"Of course not. I couldn't anyway. I caught a glimpse of it and it was written in a script I don't understand. Probably Mandarin."

"But don't you see, I suspect Mai Mai told us only what she wanted us to know. I tell you, there's going to be trouble if we don't do something about those charts."

"What can we do? If the police have them, forget it. It's out of our hands."

135

"If the charts are in Chinese, doesn't it stand to reason they may have asked Anna May Wong to help translate them and they're in her possession?"

"I suppose you've told all this to Raymond? Look at him. Now he's got Dorothy di Frasso all worked up."

The Countess di Frasso was wearing a dress with floral patterns and a matching hat and handbag. Ouida Rathbone had commented that she looked like a float in a holiday parade. At the moment, di Frasso's language was as colorful as her outfit. "Don't be an ass, Raymond. The earth won't open up and swallow us. When Mai Mai read me she didn't tell me anything I didn't already know. I mean, to tell me I'd be involved in a long series of love affairs is like telling a pickpocket he'd have his hand in a lot of things."

"I should not have let myself be seduced into the promise of a glorious future," said Souvir.

"Hogwash. You've been on the make ever since I met you. You're a very ambitious little twit, and while you may never admit it, I know you'll let nothing stand in your way. Do you think I'm blind to the way you're sucking up to Marlene? Getting her to do the screen test with you and no less than von Sternberg to direct it."

"I didn't get her to do anything," he stormed. "She volunteered."

"Lower your voice. People are looking at us."

"Let them look, and let them listen."

"Oh, the hell with you!" Di Frasso went in search of more pleasurable—and wealthier—company.

Dong See replaced her at Raymond's side. "You're behaving very foolishly, Raymond."

"I'm worried, and you should be too."

"There's nothing to be done. It's out of our hands. We have to wait and see what develops. And look, there's detective Villon."

"Oh my God."

"Leave God alone. He has too much to occupy his attention these days. Have a look. Villon is with his lady, the Hazel Dickson person. And she seems to be giving him a hard time."

Villon warned Hazel, "You make a scene and I'll walk out."

"Don't you dare. Did you find the charts?"

"Not now, Hazel."

"Why not now? Herb!"

"Because this is no time or place to discuss them."

"Are you kidding? That's all they're talking about here! It's Mai Mai this and Mai Mai that. I'm thinking it might be profitable opening a restaurant and calling it Mai Mai's."

"Good idea. It might take your mind off trivialities."

"Oh, so now I deal in trivialities." He walked away from her. "Where are you going!"

"To get myself a drink." She hurried after him. When she was after information, she was relentless. Villon was hoping Marlene would arrive. He had sad news for her and he wanted to tell her before she was seen by the other guests. Luck was on his side. Through a window near the bar he saw her car drive up and the chauffeur getting out to open the back door. Herb hurried outside while Hazel, seeing it was Dietrich he was joining, was wise enough to keep her distance. Marlene saw him and smiled.

"Herb! You look so handsome. Did you know Morton Duncan's murder was on the news today?"

"Yes, I heard it at the precinct. Listen Marlene, before you go into the party, take a walk in the garden with me."

"You'll make Hazel jealous. She's standing on the veranda watching us." She had a wicked notion and waved at Hazel. "Hazel, darling, I'll be with you in a minute." Then Marlene took Herb's arm while serving him one of her most dazzling smiles.

Hazel went to the bar for another gin and orange juice, her face grim, her request made through clenched teeth.

Novarro's garden was one of the most beautiful ones in Beverly Hills. It was dotted with a series of fountains designed

137

and built for him in Italy. The centerpiece of one fountain was *Venus de Milo*, and the centerpiece of another was an Egyptian houri. Marlene saw Adonis in one fountain and Apollo in another. They were unusually well endowed, especially for statues.

"You look so serious, Herb. You certainly couldn't have heard from Anna May this soon."

"No, it's nothing to do with the case. At least I don't think it does. Last night you hired two actors to play Father Time and the New Year Baby."

"How do you know? They never made their appearance. They had passed out in a room where I had them waiting. They drank an awful lot of gin and it was good stuff too."

"The midget told one of my men. He and the actor who was Father Time were living in the same boarding house. Father Time was Lewis Tate. He'd been a big name in silents once."

"Yes, I know that. A mutual friend implored me to hire him and his friend. Tate's in very desperate straits. Oh dear. Has he done something terrible?"

"Very terrible. He hung himself."

Marlene said nothing. She walked away from Herb and stared into a bed of jack-in-the-pulpits. It took her a minute before she could compose herself. Then she came back to Villon. "When Mai Mai generalized that there would be murder victims and suicide victims, do you suppose she knew her predictions had traveled upstairs and embraced a tired old man who probably knew then that this would be the last New Year he'd welcome? Well, welcome is hardly the appropriate word." She took his arm and headed him back to the house.

"I want to pay for his funeral," said Marlene.

"That's very kind, but we've made arrangements with the county."

"You mean bury him in a pauper's grave?"

"We can't trace a family. He's been living on welfare for the past couple of years."

Marlene was firm. "He will not have a pauper's grave. He

is Lewis Tate. He is a star. And he shall have a proper place in Forest Lawn and I shall order a stone to mark his grave, and on it will be his name and a reminder that he starred in films. Yes, that's what I shall do. His final billing. Come, I need a drink."

◖◗ TWELVE ◖◗

FROM THE MOMENT she swept into the house, Marlene Dietrich took center stage and held it. The room rang with many varieties of "Hello Marlene" and "Darling" in various octaves and "Loved your party" and "Wasn't it awful about Mai Mai Chu" and "Is it true you're working with the police" and "Are you sure you're not in danger yourself," and Marlene batted answers to the infield and the outfield until confronted by Ouida Bergere.

"What's wrong, Marlene? Why weren't Basil and I invited to your party?"

"But you were, darling. I'm positive my secretary sent you an invitation."

"Are you sure?"

"Would you like me to repeat the sentence in the presence of a notary public?" Dietrich, like so many women in Hollywood, didn't like Ouida Bergere. She was pushy and pretentious and a climber who kept her husband constantly in debt with her expensive parties and gift-giving and other extravagances.

Ouida realized she was behaving foolishly. "Well, communications are always being snarled up in this town. I see Basil needs me. I'll phone you tomorrow."

"What's with the human icicle?" Marlene turned and was happy to see her good friend Adela Rogers St. John. Adela was just about the best chronicler of life in Hollywood, and magazines across the world paid handsomely for her services. Her father had been the notorious and sadly alcoholic criminal lawyer Earl Rogers. But when sober, he was a genius in the courtroom. A *Free Soul,* which starred Norma Shearer and Lionel Barrymore, was based on Adela and her father and made a star of Clark Gable as the sadistic gangster who slapped Miss Shearer around.

"Very upset she wasn't invited to my blowout last night."

"And what a blowout, from what I read in the papers and heard on the radio."

"Why didn't you show up? You could have had it all first-hand."

"There were so many parties to attend, I took in the one closest to me and then promptly at midnight fled home without leaving a glass slipper behind. I'd like to talk to you about the murder; I could use a good story."

"The good story is what Herb Villon is looking for. He's the detective on the case. He's over at the bar with Hazel Dickson, his sweetheart, and she's very jealous of me."

"I'm very jealous of Hazel. Isn't Mr. Villon something?"

"He has an adorable assistant who's smitten with me."

"Every male I know is smitten with you. Be a good gal and introduce me to Mr. Villon."

"No problem. But I'm warning you, there's not much to tell you that you haven't already read about or heard."

"I knew Mai Mai. She was a great gal. If she was murdered, I deduce it had something to do with astrology and those weird predictions of hers."

"That's what we think."

"We? Have you joined the police force?"

"Let's just say Mr. Villon thinks I'm just about the best amateur detective he's ever met." She told St. John about the incident of finding the folders in Mai Mai's bedroom."

"Good thinking indeed," said St. John with sincerity. "Who are these suspects and why?"

"I can't tell you why because that information has yet to be unearthed. I can tell you who because you'll be happy to know some of them are here." She pointed out Monte Trevor, Raymond Souvir, Dong See, and the Countess di Frasso."

"Di Frasso doesn't murder women. She's a man killer," said St. John wryly. "Who's among the missing?"

"Ivar Tensha and a couple with the Russian Embassy, Gregory and Natalia Ivanov."

"Well, they're a mixed bag and I've seen lots of mixed bags in my lifetime. What about this waiter who was stabbed to death?"

Marlene didn't dare reveal the truth about his administering the strychnine pill.

She said matter-of-factly, "Villon has him under investigation now. I don't think he's learned anything yet."

Adela Rogers St. John was nobody's fool. She chucked Dietrich under the chin playfully. "I think he's learned plenty and you're just playing possum."

Marlene smiled. "Come, I'll introduce you to Mr. Villon. I assume you and Hazel have already crossed paths."

"And swords."

Herb Villon had read many of St. John's articles and pleased her when he praised her fine writing. Hazel kept a stiff smile on her face while the bartender poured champagne for Marlene. While Adela carefully and cleverly questioned Herb about the murders, Marlene decided it would be politic to engage Hazel in conversation.

"Hazel, I know so little about you." Hazel suppressed a hiccup. "As a child, did your parents urge you to do anything specific?"

"Run away."

Dietrich wasn't fazed. "And so you did and here you are."

"It took longer than that to get here. There was once a husband. I can't tell you much about him because his face, like his brain, is a blank. But he was Dickson and I kept his name because it was easier to deal with than the one I was born with, which has too many syllables and ends with a *ski*. All I remember is we lived with his parents and they treated me like one of the family. Miserably. Barkeep! Another gin and orange."

Marlene's and Herb's eyes met and they told each other Hazel had had too much. Marlene hoped Herb hadn't told her too much, if anything, about the afternoon's excursion to Mai Mai's loft. Alcohol loosens tongues and Hazel's tongue was rarely tied. Gently, Herb put his arm around Hazel while signaling the bartender to go easy with the gin. Hazel shrugged the arm away and leaned against the bar, drink in hand, looking like a "B" girl in a sleazy bar waiting for some sleazy company. "I don't like this party," she slurred.

"Let's go. I'll take you home," said Villon.

"I don't want to go home."

Adela suggested to Villon, "There's a guest bedroom on this floor. It's through that door at the end. Down the hallway the last door on the left. It'll be quiet and you can reclaim her when you're ready to leave. You don't want to go now, do you? The party's just warming up."

"Okay, Hazel baby, we're going for a little walk." He had a firm grip on her arm. Adela relieved Hazel of her drink and placed it on the bar.

"I know where we're going. This is the Last Mile. And there's going to be no last-minute reprieve from the governor. I'm innocent, I tell you, I'm innocent!"

"Demand a retrial, dahling," growled Tallulah Bankhead, holding a glass of bourbon with a little ice. "Some women drink much too much, dahlings," she said over her shoulder to Marlene and Adela. "As for myself, I can never get enough of it. Do you mind if I leave my group in the lurch, which is where I found them in the first place, and join you two dahl-

143

ings? Murder becomes you, Marlene. You should be framed and hung in the Louvre."

"I can take the compliment two ways." She smiled at Adela. "Framed and hung."

Tallulah roared with laughter. "Of course! Of course! Ha ha ha ha! But I truly meant it as a compliment, dahling. By the way, now that I've got you, why won't von Sternberg direct my next picture?"

"I don't know, Tallulah, maybe because he's already set to direct mine."

"It's really a terrific script. The *Devil and the Deep*. Gary Cooper's opposite me and there's a dishy newcomer, Cary Grant, in the brief role of one of my lovers, which is too true to life. All of my lovers have been brief, and most of them not brief enough. And for my husband they're giving me something from England called Charles Laughton. Talk about England, do you believe Winston Churchill once made a pass at Ethel Barrymore? Ethel claims he did, but she also claims she's the first lady of the theater, and where does that leave Lynn Fontanne and Helen Hayes? Although there are those who insist Lynnie's husband, Mr. Alfred Lunt, is the first lady of the theater. Talk about first ladies, how do you think Eleanor Roosevelt will shape up? I adore her myself and I'm exhausted campaigning for him, but I think she has a tendency to fade into the background. Come clean, Marlene, who murdered Mai Mai Chu?"

There was at that moment a sudden lull in conversation so that her baritone broke the sonic boon and all eyes were on the three women. Adela suggested they link arms and do a time step, while Tallulah suggested to Marlene, "Here's an opportunity to make a brief speech on behalf of the United Jewish Appeal." Most of the guests upon seeing Tallulah resumed talking to each other or whatever they were doing, assuming Tallulah was once again in her cups, not the ones keeping her breasts firm. "You'll have to forgive me, dahlings, but it seems I'm always prone to commanding attention when I least desire it. Now *there's* something I could desire."

Herb Villon returned and Marlene introduced him to Tallulah. Tallulah persisted. "All right, dahling. Who murdered that poor unfortunate?"

"I don't know."

"I hope you're not as simple as your answers!"

"Herb Villon is much more complicated than you think," said Marlene, coming to his rescue. "He's a brilliant detective and you must take my word for it; I've been working shoulder to shoulder with him the past twenty-four hours and I have nothing but respect and admiration for this man."

Tallulah said to Adela, "I suppose that's what drove his girlfriend to drink."

Monte Trevor descended on them. "Tallulah Bankhead and Marlene Dietrich under the same roof!"

"Why not, dahling? We were invited." Dietrich introduced them.

"How I would love to see you both in the same film," enthused Trevor.

"Why not *Uncle Tom's Cabin?* I'll do Topsy and Marlene would be a divine Eva. Or better still, why not round up Greta Garbo and Jean Harlow and we could do *Little Women.*"

"You're pulling my leg," said Monte Trevor.

"Don't hold your breath. And who's this dear little chap?" Dong See had quietly entered the scene. "You seem to resemble that violinist I heard in Carnegie Hall a few years ago."

"Permit me to introduce myself. I am Dong See, the violinist."

"Well dahling, you were nothing short of miraculous."

Marlene stepped in swiftly. "Miracles seem to favor Dong See. He was almost killed in an automobile accident." There was no expression on Dong See's face, and no lack of expression in Marlene's voice. "Why wasn't it international news at the time, darling?" She continued to the others. "He was so badly crippled, they feared for his life."

"Who is 'they,' dahling?" asked Tallulah, who was running low on bourbon.

" 'They' in general," said Marlene airily. "They hid him away in a Swiss clinic for six months. How did you endure it, Dong?"

"Where did you learn all this?" asked Dong See, not looking particularly pleased.

"A mutual friend is here in Hollywood. She probably hasn't been able to get in touch with you. She arrived last night. Brunhilde Messer."

"Oh. Brunhilde is here in Hollywood?" He might have been giving a stock market quotation, his voice was so dull and lifeless.

Marlene couldn't resist. She repeated Hitler's invitation by way of Brunhilde. Bankhead was impressed.

"I never ever get any invitations like that," said Tallulah mournfully. "Nobody ever puts me on a pedestal unless it's to measure me for a dress."

Marlene said to Dong See, "You don't sound terribly enthusiastic."

"Perhaps she gave you the mistaken impression that she and I are close friends. We met a few times in Berlin, but it was never more than that."

"How strange." Marlene handed Villon her glass and he went in search of more champagne. "She seemed so surprised that you were at my party. Even more surprised that you had completely recovered. Was there a rumor that you had been killed?"

"There are always rumors about me. They seem to favor me much the same as these miracles you attribute to me."

Our suspects are liars.

"Well, Brunhilde seemed genuinely delighted to hear you had completely recovered."

Herb Villon returned with Raymond Souvir in tow. Marlene accepted the champagne gratefully while Bankhead wandered off for more bourbon. Adela Rogers St. John was like a sponge, absorbing information and innuendos, and when the opportunity presented itself she introduced herself to Dong See. She had met Monte Trevor on another occasion and Novarro had introduced her to Souvir earlier at the party. She knew Marlene was up to something, and whatever it was Marlene had it in complete control.

Marlene said to Souvir, "Raymond, did you know Brunhilde Messer is in town?"

"Brunhilde Messer?" Dong See shot him a look that did not escape Dietrich. "Oh, of course. Brunhilde. It's been so, long!"

"Not all that long," corrected Marlene. "She said she recently brought you to Berlin to test for the part of *The Red Baron*."

"Yes, she did, but so much has happened to me since then, I guess I forgot." He cleared his throat. "Did she mention if she has abandoned the project?"

"No. I wasn't that interested. I would doubt that she has. I've known Brunhilde since I was a kid starting in show business. Brunhilde never abandons anything. Adela, do you remember her?"

"And how. Years ago she sang in San Francisco. I was there. Terrific voice. Has she given it up?"

"She is now a film producer and director."

"Aha! Following in Leni Riefenstahl's footsteps."

"Nobody follows in Leni's footsteps. She never leaves tracks."

Adela smiled at the group in general. "With so many international notables in town, sounds to me like there might be some kind of conspiracy brewing."

Marlene said grandly. "Adela is so wise. She doesn't miss a thing. You're one smart woman, Adela."

"That's a compliment I like, especially coming from another smart woman."

Villon finally spoke. "What kind of conspiracy, Adela? You have anything particular in mind?"

"Nothing really special. There are so many varieties and assortments. They're the kind of stories I try to specialize in. It brings in a wonderful cross section of scoundrels, rogues, and vagabonds."

"And murderers," added Villon.

"Oh, thank heaven for murderers," said Adela. "My father, who, if you didn't know, was the great criminal lawyer Earl Rogers . . ."

"I must do a movie about him!" cried Trevor.

He was ignored as Adela continued, ". . . and as a girl, I sat in on most of his trials. Trials that made his fortune, which as everyone knows he largely drank and squandered away. Murderers always fascinate me. But our American murderers don't hold a candle to your European ones. They're so much more colorful, so much more bloodthirsty, so much more imaginative." She indicated Raymond. "You French have one of the greatest mass murderers, Bluebeard." She zeroed in on Trevor. "And the British have so many, I've lost count. And you, Marlene, who can hold a candle to the Dusseldorf killer?" Dong See stood with his arms folded. "China has had more than its share of brutal murders. I can't say too much on behalf of Italy and the Iberian countries. They may be hotblooded but apparently they're coolheaded. And what have we got to show for it here in the good old U.S. of A.? Ruth Snyder and Judd Grey, two colorless drabs who kill her husband for his insurance. Why don't you do a movie about that, Mr. Trevor?"

"Oh, no. As you say, much too colorless and much too drab."

"Have you heard, Adela," Marlene was saying, "Raymond is screen-testing tomorrow."

"Good luck to you, Raymond." Adela's good wishes were genuine.

"My luck is with Marlene. She's doing it with me, and von Sternberg is directing."

"No kidding! Which one are you sleeping with?"

"Adela, behave yourself," Marlene remonstrated. Raymond was extremely uncomfortable, and Villon was enjoying himself immensely and glad that Hazel was out of the picture while sleeping it off.

"How I envy Raymond," said Dong See.

Marlene had that familiar wicked look in her eye again. "You know, *you* should be screen-tested too." Dong See was startled. "You're young, you're handsome, a violin virtuoso. That's what films are really lacking today, good, serious music. I'm going to talk to Ben Schulberg at Paramount. He must whip together a script for you and Anna May Wong. I noticed last night how much you complement each other in looks."

"I'm not an actor, Marlene," Dong See demurred.

"Oh, I think you are."

Careful, Marlene, careful, thought Herb Villon.

There was no stopping Dietrich. "Everybody's an actor. We professionals are in a class apart because we study, we train, we work hard to find a foothold in our profession, and once we've arrived we fight hard to hold on to our positions. But to the layman, whom we refer to as civilians, every day requires acting. It's all a world of make-believe out there. Husbands and wives have to act as though they love each other long after the dew is off the rose. Shopkeepers have to act all day as though they care about every customer with whom they do business. Professional men are constantly acting! The doctor telling a patient there's little hope. The dentist assuring a patient there will be no pain. A lawyer or a prosecuting attorney trying to convince a jury of someone's guilt or innocence. Children are the greatest natural actors in the world. You see, Dong, acting is lying. Just as writing novels and short stories is lying. Am I right, Adela?"

She concurred. "Everybody lives a lie. Look at Tallulah. She's making believe she's having a terrific time. She's hanging in because she probably has nowhere else to go except home. Look at the Countess di Frasso," and they all looked because it was the first that they were aware she had arrived. And she was heading straight toward them. ". . . Dorothy di Frasso kids herself into thinking she's one of the most desirable women in the world."

"I heard that Adela, and I don't kid myself about anything. Have I interrupted anything important?"

"We were discussing acting and lying," said Marlene. "I claim both are the same."

Di Frasso took a glass of champagne from a passing waiter carrying a tray. "And what brought on so profound a discussion?"

"I suggested Dong See should do a screen test," said Marlene, "and he protests he is not an actor. And I say he is, everyone is."

"Even me?" asked the Countess in the process of raising the glass to her lips.

"Especially you," said Adela, who took every opportunity to needle the woman she considered an opportunistic parasite.

"You're so brave drinking from that glass," said Marlene. "You don't know where it's been."

Di Frasso's eyes narrowed. "What about *your* glass?"

"Mr. Villon fetched it for me. He wouldn't want to poison me."

"You're sure?" joked Villon.

"Quite sure," replied Marlene.

Di Frasso found a smile. "I don't think my number is quite up . . . yet." She sipped the champagne. "And anyway, there were several glasses on the waiter's tray. They couldn't all be poisoned."

"Just one," said Dietrich, "sort of Russian roulette. Oh, drink your drink, you silly girl. I doubt if anybody is marked for death tonight."

Di Frasso's eyes widened as she asked, "Where's Anna May? I don't see her. Wasn't she invited?"

Marlene said, "She decided not to come. As you know, having dropped in at my house and just missing us, we spent a very tiring afternoon."

Liar. That was Villon's thought. But beautifully done.

Marlene continued, "So she went home to rest and to contemplate. She deeply mourns Mai Mai Chu. They were very very close."

"Why do I suspect Anna May is at home studying some astrological charts she found in Mai Mai's apartment?"

Marlene laughed. "Dorothy, there were *thousands* in Mai Mai's filing cabinets. If we were looking for any specific ones, it would have taken ages to locate them."

"My money's on you, Marlene. You found what you were looking for."

"You're so sure."

"If you hadn't, you and detective Villon wouldn't be here. You'd still be downtown searching. You don't give up easily, Marlene; I know that."

"Quite right. But also quite wrong. Herb, shouldn't you look in on Hazel? I'm not leaving just yet. Raymond, you should be at home studying your lines."

"I've already memorized them. I was hoping we could meet earlier at the studio tomorrow and go over the script together, rehearse a bit. I would so appreciate it."

"No need to worry about that, my dear. Von Sternberg is a martinet where rehearsals are concerned. Of course, he's a martinet where everything else is concerned, but that's another story that bores me. Dong See, why don't you come to the studio tomorrow and give Raymond some immoral support," Adela bit her lip.

Monte Trevor said jovially, "Well, it looks like we'll all be on the lot tomorrow. I've got a meeting with Cecil B. DeMille."

Making his way through the crowded room, Villon was thinking, Marlene Dietrich, you are a very dangerous lady and you could just be asking for some trouble you don't want.

"Cecil B. DeMille. How impressive," said Marlene flatly. "Adela, could I talk to you privately for a few minutes?" They excused themselves and walked out to the veranda.

Making sure that no other guests were within earshot, Marlene took Adela's arm and guided her down the stairs onto the lawn. "Adela, did you know Lewis Tate?"

"Good grief, I haven't heard that name in ages."

"Today he hung himself."

"Oh dear, the poor bastard."

Marlene told Adela of the circumstances leading up to Tate's suicide. "I think passing out at my party was the last straw."

"No, the last straw made its appearance a long time ago. But he kept hanging on, hoping for a comeback, a chance to prove he could make it in talkies. He even failed at a chance in radio, and that wasn't worth a hill of has-beens. You taking up a collection for his burial? I've got a spare twenty on me."

"No, I'm taking care of everything. I've arranged for a service in the chapel at Forest Lawn. The day after tomorrow at ten in the morning. Could you try to round up some people?"

"I'll do my damndest. I'll try to round up some of his ex-wives. There's enough of them to form a small crowd. Lewis Tate. Hung himself. Made a pass at me a couple of times. I'm sorry I didn't take him up on it, well, at least once. He was quite a guy in his day." They headed back to the house. "Marlene, what were you up to back there?"

"Up to? Up to what?"

"You know better than to try and kid me. All that stuff about everybody's a liar. You made an impression, honey; I could tell by the looks on their faces. And somebody especially didn't like the inference that he's a liar."

"That's good. That's very very good."

"It more than likely could be bad, very very bad."

"I don't think so. Anyway, Adela, I have a very special God who looks over me and protects me. Haven't you suspected that by now?"

"Oh, I knew a long time ago you stepped into a lot of that certain something that's supposed to mean good luck. But murder is something else. You're dealing with a steel-hearted killer."

"A conspirator?"

"It seems to be pointing in that direction."

"You make me feel more confident. I'm glad you're my friend, Adela Rogers St. John."

"I wouldn't have it any other way, sweetie." They rejoined the party in time to see Tallulah Bankhead attempting a high kick and falling heavily on her backside.

"Okay, you sons of bitches," she growled from the floor, "which one of you bastards pushed me?"

◖◗ THIRTEEN ◖◗

HERB VILLON, HAVING returned from looking in on
Hazel Dickson, helped Tallulah to her feet. "Thank you,
dahling, it's comforting to know chivalry isn't dead." She
now realized it was Herb who had come to her rescue. "Oh,
it's you, dahling,"—her voice was now a seductive purr—
"have you any plans for Passover? But let me finish my
story," as though there was any stopping her, thought Adela.
Tallulah said, for the benefit of Marlene, Adela, and Herb,
while the three were being scrutinized by Dong See, Monte
Trevor, and Raymond Souvir: "I was telling them about my
sister getting rid of her girlfriend with a swift boot out the
door. Well, dahlings, she had gotten to be a bit too much. An
absolutely slovenly slattern. She always left the toilet seat up.
What have you two been up to?" This was directed at Marlene and Adela.

Villon was holding a match to the cigarette Marlene had in
her mouth. Adela told Tallulah, "We were talking about
Lewis Tate's funeral."

"Tate is *tod?*"

"Very dead," said Marlene, "he hung himself."

"Oh, dear God. His agent must be shattered."

"He hasn't had an agent in years," said Adela. "The funeral's the day after tomorrow in Forest Lawn Chapel, ten in the morning. He was alone, Tallulah, absolutely alone. Abandoned by everyone. Friends, family, everyone."

"How dreadful. I shall be there. He was very nice to me years ago in New York when I was just getting started. I shall certainly be at the services. Who's catering?"

Marlene addressed the group surrounding them. "It would be nice if some of you could attend. He gave a lot to the industry; it is so little to ask that the industry give this in return." A few people assured Marlene they'd be there. Ramon Novarro promised to round up a group. Adela said she'd get a notice to all the newspapers, where her persuasion was very powerful. Marlene was pleased with herself and feeling very beatific. She didn't dare admit to anyone in the immediate vicinity that she loathed funerals.

Monte Trevor said to Marlene, "Lewis Tate. Dead. How tragic."

Marlene blew a perfect smoke ring and said, "For some people death isn't the tragedy. It's life that's the tragedy."

Trevor asked, "Nietzsche?"

"Dietrich." She moved away in search of a telephone and found one in the adjoining study.

Anna May Wong, wearing a traditional Chinese kimono, sat at a desk sipping tea, studying the eight charts that were spread out before her. She and the kimono were two of the few Oriental items in the apartment. Outside of family portraits and mementos scattered about on tables and shelves and sideboards, the apartment itself was predominantly art deco. Much of the furnishings the actress had acquired when traveling and working abroad. She had filmed in England, Germany, and France, where she was a great favorite. There she was an interesting exotic, whereas in her own country, although the only Chinese actress ever to attain recognition, she was relegated to playing mysterious women in thrillers or cold-blooded killers. She had worked steadily until the past year, and through thrift and excellent financial advice was comfortably well off. She longed to get back before the camera, but at the moment she had no prospects. So she welcomed the opportunity to decipher Mai Mai's charts. She was working on Dorothy di Frasso's horoscope when the phone rang. It was Marlene.

"Why don't you take a break and come to Ramon's party?"

"I'm sure I'm not missing a thing."

"You're missing Tallulah Bankhead."

"I'm not missing a thing."

Marlene laughed. "Actually, she's outrageous, but less than usual. In fact, she's rather subdued, like the aftermath of a hurricane. How's it coming?"

"I've got Dorothy di Frasso's in front of me."

"Anything revealing?"

"Listen to this prediction Mai Mai made. 'You will never be in want. The Lord will provide. And if he doesn't, your ex-husband will." Mai Mai specialized in giving care and comfort to abandoned wives, ex-lovers, and stray cats. Actually, though, there's something I think a bit out of the ordinary. Here and there certain words are underlined, but for the life of me I can't see why Mai Mai thought them significant. I checked the other horoscopes and they too have underlined words, but they tell me nothing."

Marlene was thinking. "Tell me some of the words."

"Believe me, Marlene, they are nothing special."

"Name a few."

"There's 'forever' and here's 'worship' and 'states' and 'squad.' "

" 'Squad'? You're sure it isn't 'squid.' Mai Mai adored cooking."

"I know that. No. It's 'squad.' But I'll double-check. Chinese is so complicated it might turn out to be 'squash.' Where can I find you tomorrow if I need you?"

"I'm at Paramount most of the day. Raymond's test. With

Joe directing, it's bound to be an all-day session. In fact, I'm positive it will be and he'll work me until I'm ready to drop. He's furious I didn't dance attendance on him at my party."

"Wasn't he aware there was a murder?"

"Yes and he'll never forgive Mai Mai for stealing the spotlight. Don't stay up late."

"If I can't reach you tomorrow, what about Wednesday?"

Marlene told her about Lewis Tate's suicide and the funeral. Anna May had worked with him in an adventure story, *Bound East for Shanghai.* "I'm coming to the funeral. I want to pay my respects. Hanging. He deserved better then that."

"Amen to that. Good night, darling."

Anna May arose and turned on the radio. She fiddled with the dial until she found a program of symphonic music. She entered her bedroom. In one of its three closets she found a cardboard box that contained photographs and stills representative of her career. She rummaged about and found what she was looking for. Lewis Tate holding her in his arms unaware of an Oriental villain lurking behind them. Written in ink at the bottom, she read, 'Why doesn't he mind his own damn business. I hope I go on ravishing your lovely self into eternity. I adore you. Lewis.' He had indeed ravished her, but not into eternity. A lovely redheaded ingenue had diverted his attention and she became his seventh wife. Anna May tried to remember her name. Minnie? Miriam? Melissa? Not important anymore. It had been important once and she brought her broken heart to Mai Mai in search of one of her miraculous cures. And Mai Mai waved the redhead aside with the prediction she would die of a social disease in a Honolulu brothel. Lewis Tate. Dead by hanging. She carried the photo back to the desk and placed it in a bottom drawer, where from time to time she would look at it and remind herself she'd been very much loved, if only briefly.

Margaret Dumont, who had won instant recognition in films as the tall, dignified, and majestic foil to the Marx Brothers, was inconsolable about something and Tallulah was trying to offer her sympathy and bourbon.

"Anything I can do, Tallulah?" asked Marlene.

"I don't think so, dahling. Margaret's come to Hollywood and found religion. One of those sects that seem to proliferate in this deadly climate. But now her group's been set adrift with the sudden death of their spiritual teacher, and dahling, a religious sect without a leader is a non-prophet organization. There there, Maggie dahling, don't take it so hard, have a sip of bourbon."

"Nothing to drink, Tallulah, I'll be all right. If only Mai Mai Chu hadn't been killed. Whenever I was under stress, she was always such a comfort." She was suddenly and mercurially no longer feeling distressed. "Marlene, is the gossip true?"

"Which gossip?"

"That you and Anna May Wong know who killed Mai Mai but you're not naming the killer until you have concrete evidence?" Marlene wondered if there was anyone in the room who hadn't heard her. Hers was a voice that could penetrate lead. Herb Villon rode to Marlene's assistance on an invisible white steed with an invincible lance in his hand prepared to joust an adversary.

"Forgive me, Miss Dumont, but Marlene and Anna May are as much in the dark to the killer's identity as I am."

"Indeed?" She drew herself up to her full height and produced a lorgnette, through which she studied Herb Villon and quite obviously liked what she saw. "And who are you?"

"Herbert Villon, the detective in charge of the case."

"How thrilling," she gurgled, "you're my first detective and it's such a pleasant experience. Do you know my friend Hazel Dickson?"

Villon said affably, "We've been introduced."

"Then you must be her inside dope."

"Oh, God," groaned Tallulah to Marlene, who now held a much-needed glass of champagne.

Dumont charged onward like a locomotive out of control. "Hazel says she's positive you think Marlene and Anna May know the killer's identity and it's all in some of Mai Mai's horoscope charts. And didn't the waiter who was stabbed in the back have something to do with it?"

"I don't really know," said Villon. "He was dead when I found his body so there wasn't much he could contribute to the case other than some added mystery."

"But Hazel told me you and Marlene questioned him in her kitchen. You must have learned something then."

"Yes, we did," said Villon, treasuring the look of expectancy on the face of the actress who was about to be deeply disappointed. "We learned he didn't know anything about the killing, or so he professed. At the time, I believed him when he said he didn't know the glass of champagne he was bringing to Madam Chu contained the poison."

"You have to be very careful with waiters," warned Miss Dumont. "Waiters can be terribly two-faced, on one hand recommending the *shrimps rémoulade* and on the other pushing the *moules marinières*, which I loathe."

Marlene said to Villon, "Herb, here comes Hazel. She's escaped."

Villon excused himself and went to Hazel's aid.

"She looks a bit done in," commented Miss Dumont, "as though she herself's been poisoned."

"If she hasn't," said Marlene, "she may soon be."

"I feel terrible," moaned Hazel as Villon led her to the veranda for some fresh air.

"What can I get you?" asked Herb. "You've already got a big mouth."

"Don't be mean. I feel awful. Why is everybody looking at me?"

"Your old buddy Margaret Dumont just got through telling the whole room that you told her Marlene and Anna May know the killer's identity."

"I did no such thing. You don't believe me. I can see it in your face. A puritan father ready to smack Hester Prynne with the Scarlet A. Let go of my arm. I don't want to go outside. I want a drink."

"I don't think that's a very good idea."

"I don't give a damn what you think. And Dumont isn't my old buddy. I don't have any old buddies. I don't have any young buddies either, come to think of it. If Dietrich doesn't wipe that smile off her face I'm going to wipe it off for her."

Adela Rogers St. John said to Marlene, "Our Hazel now resembles a basilisk."

"A what?"

"A basilisk, a fabulous creature with death-dealing eyes and horrible breath."

"Why Adela, dahling," interjected Tallulah, "I didn't know you knew Jeanette MacDonald."

Monte Trevor's impending departure had put Ramon Novarro in mind of one of the late Sarah Bernhardt's interminable farewell tours. Trevor was insisting, "But Ramon, you must seriously consider doing films on your native soil. You could become the emperor of Mexican film production. And wouldn't Dolores Del Rio complement you regally as the empress? I will be traveling to Mexico soon to visit some friends in high places and I wish I had your permission to tell them you're interested in returning there."

Marlene and Adela, standing nearby with Raymond Souvir and Dong See, exchanged glances.

Ramon was telling Monte Trevor, "Despite the rumors circulating that I'm about to be professionally beheaded by MGM, I have an ironclad contract that has another three years to go, so unless they pay me off with hundreds of thousands of dollars, I will not be available in the near future. And Metro does not part with huge sums of cash, even in an emergency. It was so nice of you to come to my party. *Goodbye.*" Novarro left Trevor in the isolation of his extended farewell, and somewhat embarrassed, Trevor waved at Marlene and the others and beat a hasty retreat.

Tallulah was saying to Raymond Souvir, "If you like, dahling, I can coach you in your lines tonight. I've got no immediate plans and I'd just adore coaching you, dahling."

Souvir's eyes beseeched Dong See's help but the violinist's

mind was elsewhere. Dong See saw the Countess di Frasso materialize at the other end of the room, after what seemed like a prolonged absence. With her was Brunhilde Messer.

Marlene said, "I didn't see her come in."

"See who?" asked Adela.

"The tall woman with di Frasso." She explained Brunhilde Messer.

"She looks like a national monument," said Adela.

"She intends to be. I didn't know she knew Ramon."

"In this town you don't have to know the host to crash a party," said Adela. "When I was first beginning as a reporter, I'd go to some shindig at Harold Lloyd's and just say I was joining Charlie Chaplin. Since I was only sixteen at the time and you know Chaplin's reputation for leching after girls fresh in their teens, it looked obvious that Charlie was somewhere in the house panting for my presence. Dong See's beaten you to Brunhilde."

"I don't want to get to her."

"She has Herb Villon fascinated. He's over there at the bar with Hazel Dickson, who's staring daggers at us. What could be eating her?"

"Me. She's jealous. She thinks I'm of special interest to her boyfriend."

"Well, aren't you?"

"Not the way she thinks. Poor Raymond Souvir. He looks as though he wishes the floor would open and swallow him. Aha! Brunhilde is waving him over. I don't believe she hasn't seen me."

"She has," said Adela, "about the time you first saw her. She was looking at us then. Very slyly, mind you, but I caught it."

"Let's join Herb and Hazel," suggested Marlene.

"Is it safe?"

"Adela, there's a special God who looks after me. I will always be safe."

"Such self-confidence in the face of Margaret Dumont

practically declaring you and Anna May the most likely targets for murder by the killer. After all, declaring that you might know his identity!"

"Why not *her* identity?"

"Of course. Di Frasso and the Russian lady."

"Natalia Ivanov."

"That's it. Ivanov."

"And Brunhilde Messer."

"She told you she got in late yesterday, too late to know about your party."

"That's what she said, but it doesn't have to be so."

"Marlene, if she had been at your house last night, you would have seen her."

"Not necessarily. I didn't join my guests until almost eleven o'clock. . . ."

"Of course. Outfoxing Connie Bennett."

"By the time I came downstairs, there was such a crush of party guests, it was impossible to know who was there unless they sought me out. When Mai Mai Chu got on the bandstand, the crush was even worse because those who were in the other rooms and on the other floors or outside in the garden came hurrying in to see Mai Mai do her bit. After Mai Mai's murder, I must admit most everyone was well behaved, but there were many who just went right on partying whether or not they realized they'd witnessed a murder."

"That's my Hollywood," said Adela. "The natives are always restless and self-occupied."

"Then I was with Herb and Anna and that adorable Mallory boy in the study for quite some time, and although for most of that period my guests were forbidden to leave, Herb soon relaxed the security and I'm sure several left almost immediately. In fact, I saw very few of them."

"Didn't you get to sing?"

"No, I left that to the suspects."

They had reached Herb and Hazel. Adela asked solicitously, "Feeling better, Hazel?"

"I'm just dandy. Who's the big broad with di Frasso. She's staring at us right now."

Marlene kept her eyes on Herb and Hazel and explained Brunhilde Messer for Hazel's edification. Hazel rejoindered with, "That ought to be worth a couple of items. So Hitler wants you to be his Queen of the May. I'm going to use that."

"I wish you wouldn't," said Marlene. "I do not wish to be connected with Hitler even in a joke."

"It's too good a story for me to pass up."

Adela said quietly and pointedly. "I'm passing it up. And when I speak to Louella, I'm sure she'll pass it up. And don't try leaking it to Skolsky or Jimmy Fidler or the international press or it'll be the last item you peddle to any of them."

"I'm not afraid of you." Hazel's voice was weak, the timbre unusually thin.

"There's no need for you to be. I'm just trying to let you know that there's a time in every business to practice ethics and understanding. To deliberately try to hurt Marlene's career . . ."

"That's baloney! I think it's a big laugh!"

"Then go have a chuckle somewhere and keep it out of print. You know this town as well as I do. An item like that can be turned against Marlene, especially if Hitler becomes all powerful and a person to be feared."

Villon said softly but forcefully. "Hazel's going to forget she heard what Marlene told her in what Marlene and the rest of us assumed was the strictest confidence, or I'm going to paste her one in the face."

"Oh dahlings, who's the lucky recipient of that paste in the face." She looked closely at Hazel as the bartender replenished her bourbon. "You, darling? You look as though you've already been pasted. Oops! Forgive me! I thought you were someone else. I'm not wearing my glasses." She turned on Villon. "You brute, dahling. You wouldn't strike a defenseless woman, would you? Not with a surname like Villon. Surely you've heard of François Villon, the poet. Dennis King

163

played him in *The Vagabond King*. The way he swishbuckled around, it should have been *The Vagabond Queen*. Now I know who that is with di Frasso. Brunhilde Messer. I heard her sing in London at Covent Garden. She woke me from a deep sleep with her "Yo Ho Te Hos." The opera's a perfect place for an insomniac." She paused, took stock of her somber-looking companions, and then said knowledgeably, "I'm sure one of you is grateful for my rude interruption. Marlene, are you well? You seem very strange."

"I'm tired. I've had little rest since the party. I'll have one for the road and then be on my way."

On the other side of the room, Brunhilde Messer was telling her group, "There is much to be done, despite the police investigation. They'll find out nothing. I'm sure I can rely on you all to befuddle them."

Di Frasso asked, "Supposing it's true; supposing Marlene and Anna May are on the right track."

"I don't believe it," said Brunhilde.

"Anna May has the astrological charts, *our* astrological charts. Monte Trevor insists they will be incriminating."

"Perhaps, perhaps not." She chose that moment to wave at Marlene, who acknowledged her with a flutter of her right hand. "Something's troubling Marlene. I can tell. I've seen that look before, many times."

Dong See interrupted. "I'm tired. I'm going home."

"I'll give you a lift." Dorothy di Frasso had a lot on her mind, and Dong See was the person she wanted to discuss it with.

Souvir said to the violinist, "I thought I was driving you home."

Dong See said affably, "You stay and enjoy yourself. Lots of pretty little starlets are starting to arrive. It looks as though Mr. Novarro's party is going to progress well into the late hours."

Brunhilde trilled at Souvir. "Raymond, darling. Why don't we join Marlene's group. I do so wish to meet Mr. Villon."

164

Adela said to Marlene, "She's headed this way with your French actor. Try a smile for a change. You look like Sylvia Sidney in anything, and she's always on the verge of tears."

Tallulah Bankhead said to no one in particular, "That young man is really beautiful. I wonder if that's all there is to him."

Marlene suddenly brightened; catching her second wind had brought with it a dynamite shift in her mood. "Brunhilde, I thought you'd never join us." She introduced Messer to everyone. Tallulah roared, "You woke me up in London!"

Brunhilde took a few steps backward, startled, expecting to be attacked, but Tallulah's face was wreathed in one of her most enchanting smiles. "And I'll be eternally grateful to you because I awoke to one of the most exquisite voices in the history of opera."

Brunhilde also wore a phony smile. "You are too kind."

"Not too often."

"So, Mr. Villon," said Brunhilde, "I hear you are up to your waist in murder. I knew Mai Mai. We were good friends. She did not deserve to die, at least not this way. And the waiter, obviously murdered to silence him. But he probably wasn't aware the pill was poisoned."

"Oh, so that's it!" blurted Hazel.

"Be quiet." Villon might have hit her with a whip. "Where did you get your information, Madam Messer?"

"What information?" Her voice was husky. Marlene had a tight grip on her handbag and Adela's instinctive nose for news told her there might be a story brewing here.

"About the waiter."

Brunhilde was cool and self-contained. "My friends just explained to me what they told you when you questioned them last night. That, and what I read in the papers and heard on the radio gave me enough hints to come to my conclusion. So, obviously I am correct and it annoys you. Why are you so upset?"

"I'm not upset. I'm delighted with what you said. Very delighted. Hazel, you should be very delighted. Here's an item

for you, in fact, a bit of a delicacy like broiled pig's snout."
Hazel said nothing and just glared at him. "Adela? What does
what you heard from Madam Messer imply to you?"

"That somebody should have kept their mouth shut, but
blissfully didn't."

Marlene was thinking, somebody thought the information
was safe with Brunhilde. It was Brunhilde who should have
kept her mouth shut, but she was so busy being charming and
enchanting with Herb Villon that she inadvertently supplied
him with the break he so desperately needed. He was right.
One of the suspects was Morton Duncan's contact. He killed
Morton Duncan because Duncan might tell who supplied
him with the pill if his blackmail demands weren't satisfied.

Hazel said, "You'll have to excuse me."

Marlene said, "There's a phone in the alcove under the
staircase in the hall. You can't miss it. There's a lovely paint-
ing of the Madonna and Child hanging near it." Hazel shot
her an unpleasant look and left.

Souvir had been chatting affably with Tallulah until he
heard Brunhilde's gaffe and was now dabbing at his brow with
a handkerchief. Marlene and Villon recognized his discom-
fort. Tallulah asked Souvir, "Are you warm, dahling? It is a
bit close in here, isn't it."

"Delightfully so," said Adela, who was making a mental
note to consider the possibility of a very long article about
this case for the *Saturday Evening Post*.

Brunhilde deftly changed the subject. "So, Marlene, you
are helping Raymond with his screen test. You are always so
generous."

"Just like you, Brunhilde," said Marlene with a sly smile.
"We are birds of a feather. I see the Countess and Dong See
left together."

"She offered him a lift home and he accepted."

"Did she really? But Raymond, I thought *you* were his
favorite chauffeur."

Adela asked, "Doesn't Dong See drive?"

Raymond said, "Not since his near fatal car accident last year."

Adela looked amazed. "But you can't exist in this town without driving a car. The public transportation is a myth and there were more covered wagons crossing the country than there are taxis to be found here. He'd better hire himself a car and driver. There are lots of those available." She paused. "I think Tallulah's lost interest in us. She's wandered away."

Souvir said nervously. "She wants very much to coach me."

"Is that how they put it these days?" asked Adela.

Marlene said to Herb, "I'm sure you're thinking what I'm thinking. And isn't it delightful. I'm going to phone Anna May and tell her when I get home." She remembered something and drew Villon away from Adela and Souvir. Adela was a good sport about it and engaged Souvir in a conversation about acting techniques, of which his knowledge was sadly negligible.

Herb was repeating what Marlene had just told him. "Certain words are underlined?"

"In all the charts."

"When we put them all together, I'm sure they'll spell 'murder.' "

"Aha!" said Marlene very eagerly, "you think they are a clue."

"Marlene, everything I look at, everything I touch and smell, is a clue. And believe me, it's not an easy thing to deal with. Do you suppose the soprano's aware she blew it?"

"Oh yes, but she covered beautifully. Well, at least we know the murderer is definitely one of them and not somebody we hadn't thought of, such as my chauffeur or my very boring butler. Oh dear, Adela is struggling to converse with Raymond. Let's rescue her."

Villon said, "Brunhilde just stands there staring at Raymond. Do you suppose she sees something we don't see?"

Marlene said, "More than likely, she knows something we don't know."

Villon stayed Marlene with a touch of his hand on her wrist. "Do you suppose Messer knew exactly what she was doing when she dropped her clanger?"

"It's possible. But somehow I don't think so. You see, it completely unnerved Raymond. You can't feign perspiration. If you haven't observed it for yourself, then let me tell you in very plain English, Raymond Souvir is a very frightened young man, and from the way Brunhilde is staring at him, I think his fear is contagious. Ah, you three! Forgive us for being so exclusive for a few minutes, but Herb wanted some advice on a birthday gift for his delightful young assistant and I made a suggestion. Did I make sense, Herb?"

"Marlene, you most certainly did make sense."

Brunhilde Messer was lighting a cigarette. She took a deep drag and exhaled a frightening cloud of smoke. Adela was reminded of a volcano in eruption, not realizing the analogy was right on the nose.

◖❦ FOURTEEN ❦◗

DOROTHY DI FRASSO drove like royalty. She demanded the road to herself, an impossible exclusivity. Her impatience with other drivers was nerve jangling, bearing down on the horn as often as she bore down on the gas pedal. Dong See was as uncomfortable with her driving as he was with Raymond Souvir's, but he said nothing. Her mouth had also accelerated and she was now busily grinding Brunhilde Messer into pulp.

"The big cow. They should never have sent her here. Using that preposterous offer for Marlene from Adolph as an excuse. Why are the Germans so unimaginative?"

"They only seem so," said Dong See. "Don't discredit them so rashly. There are some very impressive imaginations at work there. You'll soon be witnessing a rebirth of that country that will astonish the world."

"That cow would have to give the game away."

"She gave nothing away."

"Don't be dense. She confirmed for Villon the fact that one of us convinced the waiter to drop the pill into the champagne. He could have been kept floundering in the dark for ages."

"You mustn't underestimate him while overestimating yourself. The man's smart and he's smart enough to let Dietrich and Wong contribute. They're very smart ladies. I'm amazed at the large population of clever women in this town. Properly used, they could be very helpful. Adela Rogers St. Johns has a mind like a steel trap."

"She's a bitch."

"I like her. She's forthright and convincing. I can see where she can be a very dangerous enemy. I'm sure you're aware she doesn't like you."

"Very few women like me. I've been aware of that ever since I set out in the world to make my fortune. My family was dirt poor and I made up my mind at the age of seven, when I seduced the son of a candy store proprietor, that I was going to be a somebody and be in a position of purchasing candy instead of bartering for it."

"You've been bartering ever since."

"It becomes a pleasant habit after a while." She shouted out the window to a jalopy she finally managed to pass. "Hire a horse, you nitwit!" This won her an obscene gesture. "Marlene intensely dislikes me. We've been rivals in love."

"Dietrich doesn't strike me as a woman who will suffer the indignity of being the third point in a triangle. She accepts her husband's affair with Tamara Matul. Her bisexuality is an open secret; I can't imagine you two having been rivals for a woman."

"Of *course* not."

"I can't believe this offer of Adolph's was a sincere one. Doesn't he know her maternal grandfather was a Jew? Conrad Felsing. He sold jewelry. Hitler loathes Jews. You should read his book; it tells you everything you could want to know about him."

"I tried. I found it unreadable." She was bearing down on the horn again, and a little old lady pulled over and let her pass. She recognized character actress Beryl Mercer. "Those charts are beginning to worry me. I'm beginning to think they contain something that can be very injurious. Anna May was

Mai Mai's pet. She could have told her things or hinted at things that could add up to trouble. Like you said, Anna May's a very clever woman."

Dong See said, "I have a yen for her."

"It'll take more then a yen to get her. I've learned she's unattainable."

"Doesn't she like men?"

"Oh, very much. What little one knows of her involvements, they are of brief duration. She's the kind of woman Virginia Woolf champions in her essay *A Room of One's Own*. Anna May's a rebel who at an early age was determined to have her own space. Now that she's got it, she's holding on to it. What's this about Monte Trevor planning to go to Mexico?"

"Someone's needed there. Monte's the logical one."

"Villon will never let any of us leave town. Not while he suspects one of us is the murderer."

"Dorothy, it won't be too hard to slip out of here when it becomes necessary."

"What about Raymond?"

"What about him?"

"His test. Supposing it's a success."

"Good for Raymond. He goes under contract to Paramount, a major studio. This leads to major contacts. He could become even more important in the scheme of things."

"He's a pussywillow bending in the wind."

"Raymond has greater strength than you give him credit for."

"I can only judge by what I see. We have an expression in this country, 'weak sister.' Raymond strikes me as a 'weak sister.' He perspires a lot."

"At the wheel of a car he has nerves of steel. Christ! Must you use that bloody horn so often?"

"I have no tolerance for anything that gets in my way."

"Take the next right. That's my road. It's a dead end. My house is at the top."

"Raymond has me worried."

"There's nothing to worry about. Watch out for that rabbit!"

"Let it watch out for itself. It should look both ways before crossing the road!"

Ivar Tensha wished he found Brunhilde Messer sexually attractive. It had been days since he'd been favored with a woman's favors and if he didn't have one soon, he was afraid he'd break out in a rash. They were sipping brandies, having finished the dinner he'd ordered from room service. Ivar stared at Brunhilde as she lit a cigarette. The thought of bedding down a woman her size repulsed him. He had to remind himself she wasn't here for a romantic rendezvous.

"Why do you look at me that way? Is it the unfortunate slip I made before Villon?"

"You must learn to think before you speak, Brunhilde. You treat every place like it is the extension of a stage in an opera house. Everything you do is large, as though you're trying to be heard at the top of the second balcony. I must admit you're in the right place. Everything in Hollywood is larger than life, like you are. This Villon is no fool. He's no hick cop in a hick town. I have done a check on his past record and it is formidable. He is a favorite son of the movie industry. His superiors are never less than supportive. He has not been known to make a false move. His only apparent lapse in taste is this Hazel Dickson."

"He's a magnet for women. Tallulah Bankhead salivated at the sight of him. And I suspect Marlene is keeping him in reserve once she's had enough of Chevalier and Herbert Marshall. I don't know how she does it. She juggles lovers like she's center stage in a music hall. Well, why not, she began in music halls."

Tensha was lighting one of his torpedo-style cigars, and Brunhilde was finding it hard to mask her distaste. "I don't understand Mai Mai's foolishness last night."

"How so?"

"A few of her predictions were too close to the bone. Too

172

close to what she had learned in Europe. She was told too much." He sighed. "But we were so desperate to have her. She would have been such a valuable asset. It was Trevor's idea to go after her and I seconded it. She could have disseminated so much false information, she would have been invaluable. But no. She was a woman drowning in ethics and morals and was shocked that we would think she would even consider betraying her great gifts." He shook his head from side to side. "When will people learn that loyalty is much too expensive. Did Dietrich believe you when you said you only just arrived last night?"

"I'm sure she did. One thing I know you admire in me is how convincing I can be when I have to be. I'm a much better actress than Marlene."

"Marlene doesn't have to act. She has a face."

"I had the devil's own time keeping out of her way at the party last night. I'm positive Mai Mai saw me. She was on the bandstand and could see over everyone's head. Still, she might not have recognized me immediately in my red wig."

"You looked like Harpo Marx."

"That's terribly unkind."

"I'm too rich to be kind."

She sipped her brandy. "Something may have to be done about Raymond."

"I like Raymond."

"I think he's frightened. He perspires more than usual."

"It's the little boy in him. Try mothering him. He'll respond."

"He doesn't interest me that way. I like big boys. Very big boys. Is there no way to kill this investigation?"

"There is, but I prefer to see it expire a slow death. Villon won't rest until he's caught the guilty party."

"That means you could be trapped here indefinitely!"

"If necessary, we'll give him a murderer."

"Who do you have in mind?"

"At the moment, no one in particular." His smile was crooked and ugly. "There is no dearth of candidates. On the other hand, if Villon solves the case quickly, we'll be spared any unpleasantness among us."

"If Villon succeeds, there could be another kind of unpleasantness. An explosive one."

"Silence can be induced. I wonder how Miss Wong is faring with those charts? Mine sounded amusingly simple when Mai Mai read it to me. Of course, I now suspect strongly she was guilty of the sins of omission." He was on his feet and pacing, cigar in mouth and hands clasped behind his back. "Damn her for her fidelity to herself. She even quoted Shakespeare at the time. Shakespeare! That hack!" He boomed the quote, " 'This above all, to thine own self be true.' Polonius in *Hamlet*."

Brunhilde made a face as she helped herself to more brandy. "I never liked the character of Hamlet. He had terrible taste in women. Ophelia and his mother."

"Unfortunately, my dear Brunhilde, Hamlet had to suffer the manipulations of his creator."

"What happens now?"

"My dear, we continue to follow the blueprint. I haven't too much time to spare. I must get back to Romania. There's a new gas we're developing that will soon be tested in northern Tibet. It's safe to test there. Nobody cares if entire villages are destroyed in outlands like northern Tibet. I considered an Eskimo community in the North Pole, but you can't be sure there's not some party of explorers in the vicinity who might survive and report the infamy. You know, Mai Mai predicted I would be involved with a tragedy in an outlying territory. I wonder if she meant Tibet or the Moon." He sat and folded his hands in his lap. "I have some interesting plans for the Moon. But they'll have to wait. Pour me some brandy, Brunhilde, this one should give me the glow I desire."

After leaving the party, Marlene and Herb made a detour to Anna May's apartment house. Hazel had been condemned to coventry by Herb for her miserable behavior at the party, much to Marlene's displeasure.

"You can't let her drive in the condition she's in," insisted Marlene. "Get one of Ramon's hired help to take her home."

"Marlene, Hazel's car knows the way back. Don't worry about Hazel. I'll follow you to Anna May's, and don't go too fast. In this darkness I might lose you."

"Herb, when I don't want to be lost, it's not easy to lose me."

When they arrived at her apartment, Anna May led them to the living room, where there was champagne cooling alongside a hot plate of egg rolls and spare ribs.

"I thought you'd like a little nosh," said Anna May. Marlene was no advocate of art deco but had to admit Anna May's apartment seemed more comfortable than bizarre. Anna May had the horoscope charts laid out on a dining table, and while sipping champagne and nibbling at egg rolls Marlene and Herb examined them. Anna May translated more of the underlined words for them but they could make no sense of them.

"This isn't going to be easy," despaired Villon. "If they form some kind of cryptogram, then I'm finished. They had me working in decoding when I first joined the army, but they soon shifted me elsewhere. What do you make of it, Anna May?"

"I haven't given it that much thought. I've been too busy interpreting the Chinese characters. For a woman with a very orderly mind, Mai Mai wrote very disorderly charts."

"Perhaps disorderly to you, but they obviously made a great deal of sense to Mai Mai. All of us have a shorthand all our own. Mine is terribly complicated to everyone in my household when I write them notes. The cook did guess that 'en em liv' meant no more chopped liver appetizer for a while, for crying out loud, but she's a wiz at things like crossword puzzles." Marlene was at the cooler helping herself to more champagne. "We haven't told Anna May about Brunhilde Messer."

Anna May looked surprised. "Was she at the party?"

Marlene said, "Was she ever." She had Anna May's complete attention.

Having absorbed Marlene's information, Anna May said, "She's no fool, and on the other hand she's never been known to be a mental giant. Still, here she is and I think you're right, Marlene. I have a feeling that silly offer from Hitler is a smokescreen."

"And where there's smoke," said Marlene, "to use a boring but appropriate cliché, there's fire."

Anna May refilled Villon's glass and then attended to her own. "I've been having a lot of thoughts about Mai Mai and the charts. The deeper I get into translating them, the more I'm growing suspicious there's more to them than the innocence of having their astrological charts mapped. I think Mai Mai was offered some kind of involvement with these people, and Mai Mai offered to read their charts not for their edification, but as protection for herself."

Villon said, "Christ, I hate that word."

Marlene was bemused. "Which word. You've spoken five."

"I'm speaking it now. Conspiracy. I hate that goddamned word. I think I prefer 'plot.' " He said to Anna May. "You think Mai Mai was offered the opportunity to become a member of whatever this bunch is up to?"

"It stands to reason," said Anna May. "She was very much a part of their circle in Europe. She was highly respected. I'm sure her psychic gifts were seriously considered of paramount importance to them. Coupled with her brilliance at charting the future, Mai Mai would have been invaluable. But she refused them, obviously." She leaned forward. "Before refusing, she learned a great deal. She learned too much. And now she had to be eliminated. It must have taken them some time to realize she must have consigned what she knew to the charts, not just as protection for herself, but as information to be deciphered after her death. I'm positive Mai Mai knew she was to be murdered."

Marlene was aghast. "And she didn't go to the police? She didn't seek protection?"

"She didn't need the police. She had the tong. You'll forgive me, Herb, but the police are no match for the tong."

"They were nowhere to be seen this afternoon."

"In which lies their genius."

"Why didn't they protect her at my party?" Marlene was more indignant than confused. "If she knew she was in danger, why did Mai Mai consent to attend the party? It was a last-minute invitation. She could have given you any number of excuses why not to attend. Aren't I logical, Herb?"

"Very logical, Marlene. I wasn't going to, but I'm going to tell you what I omitted from the coroner's report." Marlene had a feeling she knew what was coming. "Mai Mai was terminally ill." Tears formed in Anna May's eyes. Marlene had guessed right. She handed Anna May her handkerchief. "She would have been dead within a few months."

Anna May needed a few moments to compose herself, after which she said, "I'll tell you something ironic. Mai Mai swore if she ever became fatally ill, she would kill herself. She couldn't see herself consigned to a hospital at the mercy of the medical profession. She didn't wish to end her days as a burden, as she put it to me, with her family and friends wishing she would die and be out of not only her misery but their misery." She dabbed at her eyes. "Mai Mai had poison pills. They were given to her by the tong's apothecary with the tong's approval. They were strychnine."

Marlene slammed her fist on an arm of the chair. "Irony or no irony, murder is a heinous crime. The other one, Morton Duncan, he wasn't terminal, was he Herb?"

"I haven't read his report yet. The coroner delayed it. He had tickets to a football game. But I doubt if Duncan had a serious illness."

"He looked and sounded awfully healthy when you questioned him. *Ach Gott*, I'm so weary, I can't think clearly. What to make of the underlined words, what?" She returned to the dining room table and stared at the charts. She transferred her attention to the few pages Anna May had translated, with their underlined words.

" 'Forever.'

'Worship.'

'States.'

'Squad.' "

Those were the words Anna May told her on the phone. Now there were others.

" 'World.'

'Future.'

'Clouds.'

'Monsters.' "

She repeated them aloud.

"Anna May, do you have a piece of paper?" Herb Villon had his fountain pen ready. On the slip of paper Anna May gave him, he jotted down the words, which Marlene repeated for him. She read them slowly and with what Villon considered was a great deal of unnecessary feeling.

Anna May asked Marlene, "Do you want a copy for yourself?"

"Not necessary, darling. I've committed them to memory." Marlene was known to be a fast study. She took great pride in the fact that she could commit a script to memory in just one day of concentrated study. This was a gift generally attributed to child actors, who usually memorized not only their own lines but everybody else's so they could provide them with the dialogue they couldn't remember. Child actress Mitzi Green had made an art of it, and there was a collective sigh of relief at Paramount when they dropped her option. "And when I get home," said Marlene, "I must commit to memory the dialogue for the scenes I'm doing tomorrow with Monsieur Souvir. What's worse, I have to be up at the crack of dawn. But oh well, at least I will have breakfast with Maria." A thought struck her. "Anna May. The tong."

"What about it?"

"Does it protect you?"

"I could ask them to. Do you think because of Brunhilde, our lives are in danger?"

"Herb? You're the authority. Do you think we're marked women?"

He thought for a moment. "It's a possibility. But still, if they tried to score a hit on either one of you, they know I'd put them all behind bars and throw the keys away."

Marlene asked, "Isn't that unconstitutional?"

"Probably," said Herb, "but who among us can recite the Constitution?"

"Herb Villon, within you there breathes a rogue and a knave. Are you off to make peace with Miss Dickson?"

"I've had enough of Miss Dickson for one day. Anna May, just for the hell of it, bolt your door after we leave."

"Herb, I'll do that, but trust me, it's not necessary. All the other apartments are occupied by relatives and friends. One yell out of me and they'll be up here like a swarm of killer bees."

Marlene reminded them she employed bodyguards. "I also have a handgun and I'm a deadly shot." Villon believed her. "Come Herb, and thank you, Anna May. The food was delicious. Herb, do you really think I might be in danger?" He reassured her he didn't think so. He didn't tell her he had two detectives tailing her and two tailing Anna May. In the elevator, Marlene stifled a yawn and asked him, "Herb, is detective work always this exhausting?"

"It is when you're drinking champagne."

"But Tallulah, please! That's not in the script!" Raymond Souvir was backing away from the formidable Bankhead, who, having enticed him to her rented house for some coaching, had changed into a flimsy negligee and was now setting about enticing him into bed.

"Of course it isn't, dahling, it's an improvisation. The sort of thing that Russian person Stanislavsky is so fond of. Have you never seen the Russian Art Theater?"

"You mean the Moscow Art Theater?" He was perspiring profusely. Tallulah was dabbing at his face with a dish towel, which she was grateful to find protruding from under the couch, where she had kicked it several nights earlier while trying to cause an effect with a studio electrician she'd invited up to inspect her wiring.

"The Moscow Art Theater. Of course. They're always improvising. In fact, they're known to rehearse a play for a year before exhibiting it before the public. Now come over here, Raymond. You may have done some films and some theater, but what little I've heard from you tonight tells me you're still wet behind the ears and I'm determined to dry them. Now then, in the film you're Marlene's protector, she having sold herself to you to get the money she needs for her husband, who has one of those deadly diseases you'll never find in a medical dictionary but is attributable to the highly underworked mind of a Hollywood scriptwriter. So she gives herself to you and rightly so, as you're absolutely divine. And I haven't seen anyone so beautiful since I tried to coach Lew Ayres. Oh, do sit down, Raymond. The way you're flitting about the room you're making me think of Lillian Gish trapped in that damned closet in *Broken Blossoms,* and believe you me the last thing I want to think about at a time like this is Lillian Gish. You poor boy, you're still perspiring buckets, you're a nervous wreck; I know just what you need to calm you down." There was a dish of white powder on a table with a spoon at the side. She scooped up the powder and advanced on Raymond with a devastating smile. "Sniff this, dahling. It'll calm you down. It's the best cocaine this side of the Mexican border. Come on, dahling, *Sniff!*"

Herb Villon sat in his underwear in his favorite easy chair, positioned so that he could look out the window at the lights of Hollywood, a twinkling carpet spread below his apartment at the top of a building in the Hollywood Hills. He had much to think about. The two murder victims, the seven suspects, incredible women like Marlene and Anna May, the astrological charts with their underlined words, Lewis Tate's suicide—which he knew had no connection to the murders, but the tragedy gnawed at his gut. Brunhilde Messer. A kettle of fish he could do without, but there was the possibility proposed by Marlene that she could have been at the party New Year's Eve. He thought more about Brunhilde and Marlene's party. It wasn't a masquerade ball, so she couldn't have been there in disguise. Getting out of the party might have posed a problem until Herb decided to relax the security, but how did she get away with Marlene not recognizing her? He prodded his brain mercilessly until a thought came to him that caused him to snap his finger. He looked at his wristwatch. Not yet midnight. Marlene couldn't be asleep yet. She's probably at her dressing table meticulously removing her makeup with cold cream and then sponging her face with alcohol. He'd read somewhere that was her nightly ritual. He gave her number to the operator and hoped he wouldn't meet with a blockade known as the butler.

Marlene answered on the third ring. "Oh, Herb! This is extrasensory perception. I've been thinking of you and wishing I had your home number. Listen. I have a thought. How Brunhilde wasn't easily recognizable at my party. Herb, she could have been wearing some kind of a wig."

He smiled. How he loved her. "Marlene, that's why I called you. I got the same idea."

"Darling," said Marlene, her voice seductive and exciting as it caressed his ear, "what's that they say about two great minds?"

⦿ FIFTEEN ⦿

THE COFFEE IN Herb Villon's cardboard container looked as though it had been drawn from a Louisiana bayou. Jim Mallory's container of coffee had long been drained of its contents and Jim finally got around to dumping it into the wastepaper basket. Both detectives had arrived early at the precinct and immediately closeted themselves in Herb's office. Brunhilde Messer as a fresh entrant in the suspects sweepstakes displeased Herb. Last night's phone conversation with Marlene lasted almost an hour. Brunhilde's wig stoked their adrenalin and it led to a discussion of a great many facets of the case, which Herb had shared with Mallory over the better part of an hour. Brunhilde, Herb and Marlene had agreed, was probably a red herring. As Marlene succinctly put it, Brunhilde could bore you to death, but she'd never use a weapon. Yet they were not too quick to dismiss her. She most certainly had to know about the plot to kill Mai Mai and, as she had put it to Marlene the previous morning, she didn't want to miss the fun. A very strange woman, Marlene explained to Herb, a very ambitious woman, a very jealous woman, she couldn't bear not to be in on things. And that's probably what her presence in Hollywood was all about, she didn't want to be left out of the action. Marlene concluded that Brunhilde had messages to deliver of such importance that they needed to be conveyed in person by someone who could be trusted. Power, that's what Brunhilde's films were to be about, power. Murder is power.

"Murderers are like rapists," Herb said to Marlene. "They're cowards." And he repeated this to Jim Mallory, who was entertaining a vision of Marlene Dietrich spoon-feeding him apple pie.

Herb had been writing on a yellow-paged legal pad, and he sat back in his swivel chair to survey his work. "Okay, let's start at the top again and see what we've got. Come on, Jim, get that dumb look off your face and concentrate. Seven suspects and the Messer broad we keep in reserve to one side. First we have Ivar Tensha. He'd never have stabbed Morton Duncan in the back. That's dirty work and Tensha hires people to do his dirty work for him. The Countess di Frasso. I don't see her meeting up with Duncan in that dump of his, especially in that part of town. Also, I don't see her plunging the knife."

"Not even in a fit of anger?" Mallory remembered his mother flinging a pot of boiling coffee at his father, and then her thankfulness that she had missed.

"No knives for di Frasso," said Herb. "Her tongue would be more lethal. So, to continue. Dong See. Yeah, he could kill. Musicians are very temperamental. They're worse than hairdressers. He was out of action for six months. Badly smashed up in the car accident. I wonder if he was driving. He doesn't drive now. Or I assume he doesn't. Souvir's been chauffeuring him around, and last night the Countess took over the job, driving him home from Novarro's party. At least I assume she drove him home. That brings us to Souvir. Could he murder?"

"The manual says everybody's capable of committing murder." Jim lived by the detective's manual.

"Souvir's a devil behind the steering wheel, but does he have enough of an evil streak to commit murder?"

"He could have stabbed Duncan."

"Now we come to my personal favorite, Monte Trevor. He's not only a producer, but I suspect he's a damned good actor. The way he goes about trying to convince actors they're right for his movie. When you've got the cash with which to pay them, actors don't need too much convincing to accept a job. He's been trying to get money out of Tensha for his movie. Why should he have to? They've known each other a long time, I'm sure of that. Why not just say, 'Hey, Ivar baby, I need half a million for a new movie.' So maybe Ivar doesn't like movies, ah, who the hell knows. And back to Souvir, where's he getting the money to live the way he does? Marlene says he couldn't have earned all that much in Europe, and I believe Marlene."

"You're right. She's so believable."

Mallory was lucky Herb liked him tremendously. Herb was beginning to have his doubts about putting up with much more of Mallory's schoolboy-like infatuation with Dietrich.

"Natalia and Gregory Ivanov. They could use a knife. That Natalia could penetrate an elephant's hide with a salad fork. That's one powerful lady. Gregory would do as he's told. He was born to take orders and carry them out." He scratched his chin while staring at the revolving ceiling fan. The fan was of little use; all it did was rearrange the warm air so it wouldn't grow tired of remaining in the same position. "So what have we got? We've got a gang of people who we know are up to no good, but what that no good is we'll never dig out of them, so we have to wait and see what Anna May comes up with. Got any other ideas?"

"I was thinking why haven't we tried to find out where the suspects were when Morton Duncan was murdered."

Herb laughed. "You really want to bother? You want to listen to and file some more double-talk? Take it from me, they've composed perfect alibis. I've played this scene before. I'll wait for someone to slip up. Jim, we're going to have to enter through the back door of these crimes to find the killer.

Somebody's going to slip up the way Brunhilde did last night."

"I thought you and Marlene thought she blabbed deliberately."

"As of my phone conversation with Marlene last night, she's rewritten that theory. Brunhilde was never one, in Marlene's experience, to think before she spoke. Marlene said something funny about her. Brunhilde Messer needs to hear cues." He arose and looked out the window. Palm trees. Nothing but effing palm trees. Rats nest in them. Who needs sterile palm trees? They don't flower. They don't bear fruit. It costs the city a small fortune to keep the fronds trimmed. He hated palm trees. "I wonder how the screen test's going? And why do I give a damn?"

There wasn't an unoccupied soundstage on the Paramount lot. The studio had to grind out fifty-two films a year to keep its chain of theaters supplied. Contract stars were expected to film a minimum of four films a year. One actress remembered shooting three films at the same time. She worked for one director from eight in the morning until lunchtime. She had time to grab a sandwich and coffee while having her hair restyled to work for another director all afternoon. After a hasty dinner of soup and a hamburger, she was driven to another soundstage to do pickup shots for a film she'd completed a month earlier. She feared there'd be no continuity with her performance in this one because she'd forgotten her interpretation of her character.

Most features took from two to five weeks to complete. An occasional epic such as one directed by Cecil B. DeMille usually took ten to fifteen weeks to complete. The westerns were shot on the back lot or on a rented ranch in the valley. These were filmed in five days. Marlene's films were the most expensive, and that was because Josef von Sternberg was painstakingly meticulous and demanded sets that were elaborate and expensive. For *Shanghai Express*, an entire village and miles of railroad track leading into it took months to construct. The sets were never to be used again.

Expenses could also mount with screen tests, especially if they were personally directed by any of the studio's "A" directors (so called because their films carried the heaviest budgets and topped the bill when double featured). "A" directors included DeMille, von Sternberg, and Ernst Lubitsch.

Raymond Souvir's test was definitely going to cost more than the studio planned to spend. Von Sternberg was the martinet to Raymond Souvir's martyr. Marlene stood by helplessly as von Sternberg shouted and raged and struck furniture with his riding crop to emphasize his unreasonable dissatisfaction. Earlier that morning Marlene could no longer contain her equanimity and exploded.

"This is not my screen test! It is Raymond's! I'm already under contract! Stop bullying us!"

Von Sternberg shouted back at her, and while the two roared and snarled at each other like kings of the jungle battling over the carcass of a fallen wapiti, Raymond Souvir's already frayed nerves further unraveled until a makeup woman, on constant call for facial repairs, feared the young actor would fall victim to a nervous breakdown. The front office had already received a communiqué from a spy that things were not going well with the Souvir test and the suspicion was hinted that von Sternberg was deliberately sabotaging Souvir's chances as a means of satisfying his current vendetta against Dietrich. He had been told that morning that after his next film with Marlene, *Blonde Venus*, she would do *Song of Songs* with Rouben Mamoulian directing. ("Marlene is mine," he screamed at studio head B. P. Schulberg, "I am the only one who directs her! I discovered her! I created her! Without me she is nothing!")

The makeup woman busied herself wiping Souvir's perspiration away and hoping he'd stay dry enough for her to apply a fresh layer of makeup. There were an unusual number of visitors on the set, which aroused the interest of the technical staff. Perhaps Souvir was more important than they thought.

After all, von Sternberg is directing and Dietrich, a big star, is playing opposite Souvir. Marlene was also surprised. She was even more surprised that von Sternberg hadn't ordered all visitors off the set. He was probably too busy being troublesome to notice.

What in God's name are the Ivanovs doing here? And who are those three people with them, two men and a woman who looked as though they had just returned from fighting a campaign in Afghanistan. Marlene had to satisfy her curiosity. "What brings you to the studio?" The very fact that a great star chose to mingle with them made the Ivanovs bristle with self-importance for the benefit of their friends.

Gregory explained, "We are entertaining these very important visitors from our country. Please to meet them as I'm sure they'll be very thrilled."

"I'd be delighted," said Marlene while smiling at Monte Trevor, who was there killing time before his meeting with DeMille.

Gregory pointed to the woman. "This is Masha Smetana, chairman of the Tractor Committee of the province of Georgia. And here I am pleased to introduce Bronislaw Gerbernya, who manages the largest collective farm in the Ukraine. This trip is his reward for having produced over half a million dozen eggs, three quarters of a million bales of hay, a million bushels of corn, and cultivated thousands of acres of alfalfa and garlic. And last but surely not the least, Vladimir Gehoggurt of our secret police and the conductor of numerous successful purges."

"So," said Marlene to Gehoggurt, "you are the conductor of numerous successful purges. How do you sleep?"

Natalia explained, "He has no English."

"He also has no humanity," said Marlene.

Gregory said quickly, "Your studio was very kind to give us permission to visit today. We are so surprised to find so many acquaintances are also here."

Marlene wasn't surprised at all. Countess di Frasso had arrived a few minutes earlier on the arm of the studio's newest hopeful, Cary Grant. He was surprised Souvir was testing for the part of Marlene's protector in *Blonde Venus*. He'd been told the previous week the part was his. He'd have to have a word with B.P. about it. Dietrich wasn't in the least bit surprised to see Brunhilde Messer with Ivar Tensha. Marlene had an assistant director apprise Tensha that smoking was not permitted on this soundstage. His foul cigar offended her.

"Marlene, *liebchen*. Raymond asked me to give him moral support so here I am with Ivar, who was curious to see how the studio operates," simpered Brunhilde.

"It is not unlike a munitions factory. The films that are produced here are the ammunition needed for huge profits. Of course, because of the Depression the studio is hurting badly, the whole world is hurting badly, but the people need films to take their minds off the bad situation. Some films explode into fantastic successes. Appropriately enough, they are known as blockbusters."

"I find the analogy most interesting," said Tensha, having ground the life out of his cigar under the heel of a shoe. "When I think of filmmaking in those terms, I'm almost interested in thinking of investing in the cinema."

"Ah!" cried Marlene. "The person I've been waiting for! Dong See, where have you been? Poor Raymond is being put through hell by that beast with the riding crop. I want you to meet him."

"I don't think there's much I can do to help."

She took his hand and led him to von Sternberg, who—remembering they had met at Marlene's party—was suddenly a picture of charm and good manners.

"Here he is, one of the world's leading musicians. He belongs in *Blonde Venus*. Joe, you must test him. Look at his wonderful features. That bone structure. Where's that violin I asked for? Ah! Thank you, darling." The assistant director brought the violin to Marlene. Dong See's face was a mask. Marlene fingered the strings and brought forth a melody. "You don't know I'm a trained violinist," said Marlene offhandedly, "Mother made me study very hard. I've even mastered the musical saw. I don't play anymore. This looks like a very fine instrument. It's not an Amati, but I know the magic of your fingers will make it sound like one."

"No."

"No? Then perhaps you will enrapture us with what might sound like a Stradivarius."

Dong See backed away a few feet.

"Why, Dong See. You look absolutely terrified! The instrument won't bite you! The violin is your friend; it is your life's blood. Here . . ."—she held it out to him—"take it, make love to it." She signaled the cameraman and the sound engineer. "Boys! This is a take!" Von Sternberg stood with the cameraman, eyes blazing. Again she was usurping his position. Again she was sticking a finger in his eye. How she will suffer for this. What's wrong with this Chinese fiddler? Why does he shy away from the violin? I recognize that expression on Marlene's face. I've seen it often enough. It's that look she gets when she's proven something to herself. What is she up to now?

"Does this violin displease you? Now, don't disappoint me, darling. I promised myself I'd get some film of you and you mustn't let me down."

Raymond Souvir watched the scene taking place in front of the motionless camera amidst an embarrassing silence. Dong See was on the spot, and Souvir knew him well, knew and feared his temper.

"I cannot play," said Dong See.

"You mean you won't play here, for the camera." Marlene smiled. "You're not prepared. I should have realized that."

"I can't play because my fingers were shattered in the accident. They will never be the same again."

"How terrible." Marlene placed the violin on a table. "That's why your tour was canceled."

"That's right. I'm finished as a musician." He walked away from her.

Von Sternberg shouted, "Can we now get on with the business of making a screen test?" The set buzzed and hummed again.

Marlene brightened on seeing Herb Villon and Jim Mallory standing near the soundstage door. She hurried to them. "Did you see the scene I just played with Dong See?"

"I wish I had it on film," said Villon.

"So do I. Very heartbreaking. I'd burst into tears but I mustn't ruin my makeup."

"Why, Marlene Dietrich, you're a heartless beast."

"Not where this person who says he can't play the violin any longer is concerned. At my party, Dorothy di Frasso said something about this Dong See that I can't get out of my mind. She said something about not having seen him for quite some time, but that he'd changed some since then. Last night because I could not sleep, our talk, you darling man, was so exciting and stimulating"—Herb restrained from preening while Jim Mallory's eyes were green with jealousy—"I got to thinking about everyone involved in the case. My mind was a motion-picture projector and the film unreeled them, and when I thought it necessary I stopped this film and studied my subjects carefully; I dissected them. Dong See worried me the most. I kept coming back to him over and over again. There's so much goddamned noise, let's go over there behind the backdrops." They followed the leader.

"Won't they be looking for you?" asked Herb.

"They'll find me. Von Sternberg's on my back. He's poking around wasting time and money and I'm afraid poor Raymond isn't coming across at all. A robot has more animation."

"Let's get back to Dong See," Villon prompted.

"I studied his face hard. A thought kept coming to me. He was in an automobile crash so terrible that it caused him to be confined to a clinic for six months. Now think, what had the crash done to him?"

"Shattered his fingers for starters," said Jim Mallory.

"While he told us this, I had a good look at his hands. There are no scars."

"There was probably plastic surgery," said Villon.

"Those fingers had no plastic surgery. His face has had no plastic surgery. The process is not all that infallible. It leaves scars. Have you noticed Carole Lombard's left cheek? She too was in a terrible automobile accident and had extensive surgery for months before being given any hope she would be able to work in front of a camera again. She still has a scar on her left cheek. It's barely noticeable because our makeup men here are magicians."

"She's gorgeous," said Jim Mallory, then feeling like a traitor.

"Of course, darling, that's because her makeup is borrowed from mine. I shave my eyebrows and use a pencil; so does Carole. My makeup emphasizes hollows in my cheeks; so does Carole's. But so what, our personalities are totally dissimilar. Listen to me, boys. It is not easy to reconstruct shattered bodies and shattered faces. There are hospitals in Europe where tragedies are quartered. Men whose faces were so badly destroyed and deformed that they are kept hidden away from the public eye."

"Dong See was one of the lucky ones." Jim Mallory looked innocent enough to betray, thought Marlene, and hoped the future would be kind to him.

"This Dong See has had no plastic surgery, Herb. Trust me. Believe me."

"But six months in a Swiss clinic. What was that all about?"

"What's it all about? It's a trumped-up story, that's what it's all about. There was no six months in a clinic. This person is perfectly healthy. Don't you get it? Why do you think I planned this scene? And if I must say so myself, I pulled it off brilliantly. Boys, I had to see and hear him play the violin. I had to trump up getting him here and putting him on the spot. This man can't play the violin. He is not Dong See."

"Are you thinking of confronting him with that suspicion?"

"Of course not. He'll just continue playing his act as beautifully as he did just now, when he weaseled out of a tight spot. You mark my words, gentlemen. The real Dong See is probably dead. There probably was an accident and it killed him. Why wasn't it in the newspapers? Dong See was world famous. News of his terrible accident should have spread around the world. This man is not Dong See. He's an imposter. He's an agent. He's an instrument. Impersonating Dong See opens doors for him that would be shut to any ordinary Oriental. And these people are seeking to have doors opened.

"Herb, are you allowing Monte Trevor to leave the city?"

"Like hell I am."

"Ramon Novarro told me Trevor is planning a trip to Mexico. He tried to convince Ramon to consider returning there and helping resuscitate Mexico's film industry. I phoned Dolores del Rio and Lupe Velez and they confirmed that Monte Trevor made the same pitch to them. Herb, Monte Trevor acts the pushy pest, but it's an act. He's a very clever man, I'm positive. He must be. Why else does he have Tensha's ear? Check him out and you'll see he's not had a money-making film in years. He stays in an expensive suite. Who's paying for it? Raymond Souvir lives and spends like an emperor. Who's paying for it? How did the Ivanovs move to such important embassies as Berlin and Los Angeles if they are the bourgeois dolts they appear to be? And Dorothy di Frasso. She flaunts wealth as though she really has it. That mansion she lives in. That expensive car she drives."

"I thought she got a big settlement from her ex-husband."

"Yes, it was a handsome settlement that soon began to lose its looks, the way she spends. Gary Cooper told me she tried to borrow money from him and at a time when Gary wasn't making the kind of dollars he earns today. Who supports this Dong See effigy? Herb, these people are *subsidized.*"

"Tensha?" Herb knew as he spoke the name it was a waste of breath.

"No, darling, I doubt that very strongly. Oh I suspect Ten-

192

sha is heavily involved financially in whatever is going on. Herb, if you haven't been thinking about it, then I urge you to contact Interpol about these people."

Jim Mallory smiled as Villon told her, "What was that about two great minds?"

Marlene laughed, threw her arms around Villon, and kissed his cheek. After which she decided to give Jim Mallory equal time, not realizing he'd be days recovering from the shock. "Let's see what's going on out there. God, we'll never finish this bloody test."

Von Sternberg was supervising a fresh camera setup at the top of his lungs. Hazel Dickson, chatting with Monte Trevor, saw Marlene, Herb, and Mallory out of the corner of an eye and abruptly left Trevor. "Well, well, well, the unholy three," said Hazel.

Marlene oozed charm and concern. "I'm so glad to see you got home safely last night, Hazel."

"I didn't know I was in any danger. I suppose you've seen the papers."

"I haven't had the time, darling. Von Sternberg has kept us hopping, the sadistic bastard."

"Lewis Tate's made headlines. I mean, forgotten by the press and the public and the powers that be all these years, and so he goes and hangs himself and all of a sudden he's big news. The poor slob, if he were alive somebody would probably offer him a contract."

God bless you, Adela Rogers St. John, thought Marlene; God bless you. Lewis Tate may be dead, but today he lives, more alive than he has ever been.

Hazel was speaking directly to Marlene. "I hear I missed a hearts and flowers episode between you and Dong See. What was it all about?"

"Let Herb tell you."

"Herb can't tell me anything." Villon winced as each word struck him like a pellet shot from a BB gun. "I got a hot item out of Monte Trevor. He's been asked to come to Mexico to help pump some new life into their dying film industry. God, they make lousy pictures. Oh oh, di Frasso's got her tentacles around Cary Grant. He'd better be careful."

"I'm told he can take care of himself," Marlene reassured Hazel. "I don't see Raymond. I should go over some lines with him. Poor baby, I'm sure he's learning to his sorrow that working in Hollywood is a far cry from working in Europe. I'll see what I can do to pump some energy into this test. Ah! There's Dong See with Brunhilde and Tensha. I must apologize to him."

Von Sternberg was shouting. "I am ready! Marlene Dietrich!" She kept walking toward Dong See without missing a beat. "Where is Mr. Souvir? Are we making a test here or is this some kind of tea party?"

Herb Villon thought, If it's a tea party, it's more the Mad Hatter's than one given by his Aunt Hattie. He watched Marlene as she spoke to Dong See. Smooth as silk. What a woman.

"I do understand," said Dong See with charm. "I know you didn't mean to embarrass me."

"Still, no longer being able to play. What a loss. What a tragedy. I'll never forget your "Flight of the Bumble Bee." That bee was so real, I remember looking around for a fly-swatter."

Von Sternberg shouted her name again. Marlene shut her eyes, clenched her fists, and took a deep breath. Brunhilde whispered something to Tensha about expecting fireworks, while Marlene opened her eyes and past Brunhilde and Tensha she saw Raymond Souvir holding a paper cup, clutching his stomach and staggering forward. Marlene shouted for Villon, and he and Mallory hurried to her on a trot. She rushed to Souvir's side and Villon and Mallory were too late to catch him. He fell face down, crushing the paper cup beneath him. Villon and Mallory turned him on his back and Marlene knelt and shouted Souvir's name over and over again. He didn't respond. His eyes were half-open and from what she could see of them, Dietrich told Villon they reflected no life.

"He's dead. Look, those beads of perspiration. Poor soul. Poor Raymond. He's perspired his last."

ᗰ SIXTEEN ᗕ

"WHAT FOUL FIEND destroyed this beautiful youth! Who did this to Raymond! Oh my poor child, cut down in the prime of life!" Tallulah Bankhead beseeched God to strike the unknown killer with lightning and thunderbolts. Word of the murder had spread through the studio like brushfire, and Tallulah's anguished cry in the fitting room caused the walls to tremble. Her secretary drove her to the soundstage where the test was supposed to be shot and Tallulah swept into it like Medea satisfied at her success in polishing off her two brats. With fingers intertwined and a loosely tied dressing gown showing two incredibly well shaped legs, she stood staring down at the corpse, which had been covered with a blanket.

Marlene wisely stood aside with Herb Villon and Jim Mallory and let Tallulah take the spotlight. Outwardly Marlene looked unaffected by Souvir's murder; inwardly there gnawed at her stomach the fear that Souvir's murder would trigger others. She had shared this intuition with the detectives while Villon retrieved the crushed paper cup and entrusted it to Mallory for safekeeping until it could be gotten to the lab for tests.

"Oh, how I coached him last night and oh, how he adored my coaching, once he relaxed, dahlings. I saw his potential and I promise you it was large, very very large. Didn't you see it too, Marlene?"

"No darling, it hadn't shown itself." The coroner arrived with his assistants, followed by several plainclothes men. The coroner flung the blanket back. Very businesslike, he pulled an eyelid back. Then he pried open the mouth and studied the tongue. Next he went south to the fingernails. In between he made little grunting noises, difficult to discern whether they were of dismay or pleasure. Marlene recognized him as the same man who had attended Mai Mai's body. She commented to Villon, "He's terribly efficient." The coroner heard her and smiled gratefully. He instructed his assistants to wrap the corpse and take it to the morgue and file it in a refrigerator box.

"Poison," he told Villon and Mallory. Mallory handed him the crushed paper cup and the coroner sniffed it. "Something of the nightshade family, but that's just a guess. Let me take this; I'll turn it over to the lab boys. Well, Miss Dietrich, ha ha, it seems you have a fatal attraction to homicides." He indicated the visitors to the soundstage, who stood about in groups, nervous, worried, anxious, and shocked, "You holding them for questioning?" he asked Villon.

"That would be as useful as applying iodine to a knife wound. I'll have the boys take their names and addresses and then we'll get in touch with them individually."

Marlene was smoking a cigarette. "Of course, there are the old familiar faces who need no further introduction. Look at them. Tensha keeps glancing at his pocket watch; he's anxious to be out of here. Di Frasso is touching up her lips. Dong See looks a bit sad the way he watches the body being wrapped for shipment, perhaps he does mourn his old pal. Monte Trevor and Brunhilde look as though they're waiting for an orchestra to begin the next dance, and from the look of the Ivanovs and their guests I suspect they might be holding a conference on the decadence of Western civilization. Hazel is scribbling away on her pad while Tallulah has von Sternberg cornered, undoubtedly demanding he be her next director. Poor Raymond, he is written off, but perhaps his memory will linger on. After all, he had a great deal of coaching. I look at all of them and it reminds me of a quotation from *A Midsummer Night's Dream.* 'The lunatic, the lover, and the poet are of imagination all compact.' There are many lovers here and I presume one among us is a poet, but the lunatic is yet to be trapped. I must phone Anna May and tell her before she hears it on the radio. Ah! Von Sternberg has escaped. Tallulah is heading our way. I think it's you she's after, Herb."

"Mr. detective person," she bellowed, "I must have a word with you. You can stay, Marlene, this will interest you too." She paused for effect. "Give me a drag of your cigarette, Marlene." She inhaled and forced the smoke into her lungs and then slowly exhaled. At last she spoke, darkly dramatic. "Raymond Souvir had a presentiment last night. He knew he was going to die soon." She paused to give that line time to sink in. "Between coaching, he did a lot of talking. Occasionally I'm a very good listener, thank God last night was one of those rare occasions." She asked Villon, "Forgive me, dahling, but what's your name again?"

"Villon, and this is my assistant, Jim Mallory."

Her eyes widened as though she was just now seeing Jim Mallory. "Isn't he divine looking. Dear young man, do you want to be an actor? I'd be delighted to coach you."

Jim was tempted to tell her he'd prefer being coached by Marlene, but instead said, "I'm very flattered, Miss Bankhead."

"Tallulah," said Marlene, exerting great patience, "Raymond Souvir."

"Of course. His presentiment. He told me it's in his astrological chart. Mai Mai said there was a break in his lifelines."

"You find lifelines in the palm of the hand, Tallulah." Marlene was lighting another cigarette.

"Well, whatever its equivalent is in the zodiac, she predicted where his life was concerned, he was doomed to be

197

shortchanged. Raymond was involved in something that he intimated would mean his death if he tried to defect. Am I making any kind of sense at all? We both did a lot of heavy drinking last night, not to speak of the heavy breathing, dahlings, so you'll understand I'm telling you as much as I can remember of what he told me."

Marlene stepped in. "See if I've got it right."

"Go ahead, dahling, I'd appreciate some help."

"Mai Mai told him he'd die young. He's involved in . . . for want of a better word . . . some sort of conspiracy. Something big, something very very big."

"Enormous. It covers the world, like the Red Cross."

Marlene continued, "He wanted to get out of it. Am I right in saying this was no sudden decision? He'd been entertaining it for some time now?"

"Exactly!" Tallulah took Marlene's cigarette, which had one last drag left in it, and Bankhead made the most of it. "He was worried what would happen to him if his screen test failed."

Marlene was quizzical as Bankhead crushed the cigarette butt under her shoe. "Are you saying he intimated his life depended on the success of his test?"

"His usefulness." She folded her arms. "Now, what do you make of *that?*

"A great deal," said Marlene.

"Oh really, dahling? You're light-years ahead of me. I thought he was being just another insecure juvenile positive he'd never be offered another job." She smiled at Mallory. "Aren't you glad you didn't let me convince you to be an actor? Anyway dahlings, there was a bit of a show of bravado, not terribly convincing but I think he enjoyed the sound of it. It was something like this. He's not afraid. There's a lot he could tell. And something about Mai Mai had to be silenced even though they knew she was dying. Was she? Oh the poor dahling. Robbed of the chance to put her house in order."

"She left her house in order, Tallulah," reassured Dietrich.

"Oh I'm so glad, dahling. I can foretell mine will be a mess. Have I helped?"

"You've been a great help, Miss Bankhead." Villon thanked her. Tallulah bummed another cigarette from Marlene and then hurried back to the fitting room. She saw Villon's men getting names and addresses, and Bankhead spoke to one who she was sure would want her phone number and gave it to him.

Marlene was saying to Villon, "I'm not much of a writer myself, Herb, but I think together, we could contrive a scenario that would help us in getting the murderer to give himself away. What do you think?"

"I think I'd like to know what progress Anna May has made. But first, I'd like a word with Monte Trevor."

"I'll be in my dressing room. It's that blue caravan at the end of this street. You can't miss it; it's baby blue, like Jim Mallory's eyes."

Mallory didn't realize he was fluttering his eyelashes until Villon brought it to his attention.

When Villon called his name, Monte Trevor excused himself from a group that included Hazel and di Frasso and Ivar Tensha. Di Frasso said, "I think Mr. Villon has heard Monte was thinking of making a bolt to Mexico. Any bets?" She had no takers.

Trevor was huffing with indignation. "But you can't keep me here indefinitely! I have urgent business in Mexico City. It means my livelihood."

"Mr. Trevor, let me remind you that you are a suspect in a murder case. If necessary, and don't force my hand, I can take you into custody."

"Don't threaten me. I have powerful connections."

"So do I. They're called handcuffs. You're forcing me to put a tail on you, Trevor, and that costs money. I'm a penurious son of a bitch and I don't like to spend money unnecessarily."

"You make me very unhappy, Mr. Villon."

"Don't force me to make you unhappier."

He walked away from the producer, with Jim keeping pace. They went in search of Marlene.

Ten minutes later, Dietrich had changed into a smart linen suit and was telling them Anna May needed to see them right away. "She's made tremendous progress but didn't want to tell me on the phone. I promised her we'd be at her place within an hour. But first, Herb, what stupidity prompted the killer to murder Souvir here on the lot, on a soundstage, for crying out loud, in the middle of a screen test?"

"It wasn't stupidity, it was necessity. Look, Souvir's been perspiring buckets ever since I met him. Because of the screen test? Hell no. Because he was afraid for his life. He could have breezed through the test if he hadn't become such a nervous wreck. Where does all that perspiration fit in with the speed demon? On the surface he's tough as nails, even instilling fear in Dong See, whether this guy is or isn't in his passenger seat. What I think, Marlene, is that it was important to this gang to have powerful people in Hollywood allied with them. If they couldn't convert them to their side, then they'd create their own. Don't be so dense, Marlene. Brunhilde positively came here with an offer for you, but it was disguised as one being made by Hitler."

"Supposing I'd fallen for it?"

"You'd be a very powerful lady, but not for very long."

Marlene crossed her legs. "So failing me and Greta and whoever else they were out to conscript, they groomed Raymond in Europe with those three French films and his German screen test. *Gott im Himmel*, who knows how many others like Souvir they may have planted in our midst."

"Who knows?" Villon's hands were outstretched, palms up.

"Herb, do you suppose my confrontation with Dong See had something to do with hastening Raymond's departure?"

Jim Mallory suddenly said, "It might hasten Dong See's departure."

"It's a consideration," agreed Villon.

"I don't know about that," said Marlene. "I think Raymond knew his time was running out." She laughed. "Maybe he was spending too much money. Oh dear, that's a bad joke. The poor thing." She had a new thought. "Nobody cried."

"When?" asked Villon.

"When they saw Raymond was lying there, dead. Nobody cried. There was no sorrow from anyone. Dong See, or whoever he is, did look a bit sad, but the others, there was no sound of sorrow from any of them. I can't wait to hear what Interpol turns up on these people. We better get started to Anna May's. I worry she's alone in the apartment with the charts."

"She's well protected," Villon assured Marlene.

"There were a lot of people on the soundstage, but Raymond was poisoned. Nightshade. Could he have committed suicide? Why not? If what Tallulah told us was indicative of his frame of mind, then from what he was accomplishing in front of the camera, which was pretty disappointing, he may have decided to select his own time of departure and be done with the awful, the awful waiting of knowing you're marked for extermination."

"Marlene, he was murdered. Someone gave him a paper cup of water and there's no point in asking our suspects, because they're hardly about to incriminate themselves. Like I told Jim before, they've got themselves covered. I mean Marlene, if you found a one hundred dollar bill on the floor of a restaurant, you wouldn't ask if somebody lost a one hundred dollar bill."

"I wouldn't ask because I never find anything of value," responded Marlene.

"A common ordinary paper cup," said Mallory.

"Darling, you'd be hard put to find cut crystal around here. You should see how many forms my secretary has to fill out to get a roll of toilet paper. Come on boys, let's get to Anna May's."

* * *

"You poor man," Hazel Dickson was saying to Dong See as she gave him a lift to Chinatown, "I heard about that stunt Dietrich pulled on you."

"She didn't know I could no longer finger the strings."

"Still, it must have been terribly embarrassing. How awful to be robbed of your gift. Um, what plans do you have for the future?" Come on baby, give me an item. Any item. Baby needs a new pair of shoes.

"I'm trying my hand at composing a violin concerto."

"That clinic in Switzerland must have put a pretty big hole in your pocket."

"I'm not hurting," he said in a monotone that should have told her she should try minding her own business. But he didn't know that minding other people's businesses was her own business.

"I've heard of that great sanatorium outside Lucerne. Were you there, by any chance?"

"Miss Dickson, could we talk about something else?"

Hazel was never fazed. "Sure. Let's talk about the murders. Who do you suppose did them? What guts it took to kill Raymond Souvir while he was shooting a screen test. You were the best of friends, weren't you?" Dong See said nothing. "You must be terribly broken up, but you're not showing it because you're inscrutable, you know, what they say about you Chinese."

She didn't notice that his hands looked as though he was about to strangle her. He saw Chinatown ahead and his hands relaxed.

"Where do you want to be dropped."

"At the corner would be fine. This is very kind of you."

"I wonder who's next?"

"What?"

"I didn't mean to startle you. Who's next. First Mai Mai Chu, then Morton Duncan, and today poor Raymond Souvir, don't you think there'll be more murders?"

"I don't know. I haven't given it much thought."

202

"Has Souvir's family been notified?"

"I don't know."

"Well, they should be. He may have left some money. He lived as though he had plenty. I'm sure Herb Villon is looking into it. Hey! Good-bye!" Dong See slammed the door shut and disappeared into the crowded street. "What a rude little bastard!"

In the privacy of her home, Anna May Wong wore traditional Chinese dress for comfort. She was pointing to underlined words. "Why none of us noticed it last night, I'll never know. But it came to me this morning. See?" She indicated the words in several charts. "These are underlined in red. And they are most significantly underlined in Mai Mai's chart. So I worked on it all morning and I've typed out the most significant sentences."

"But I didn't find Mai Mai's chart," said Marlene.

"We weren't looking for it. I phoned the secretary of the tong and he found it and brought it to me. It occurred to me it might hold greater significance then any of these others, and it does. It's frightening. What I'm about to read to you duplicates in the other charts with the words underlined in red."

"She was taking no chances," said Marlene. "If somehow her chart were to be destroyed by unfriendly hands, there remained her clever duplication."

"Exactly," said Anna May. "Mai Mai's chart is dated six months ago, when she returned from abroad. I'll generalize some things, such as her awareness she would soon be dead. Here she has written: 'At last the doctors and the stars are in agreement. My time is running out. I am ready. I have the pills, though there is every likelihood the Devil's Syndicate, as I choose to call them, will do their utmost to cut my sentence even shorter. I have refused to join them and I know too much. Indeed these are devils. They worship the evil god Molech.'"

To Mallory's perplexed look Marlene explained, "This god demanded the sacrifice of children. He is also known as Moloch. He accepted the sacrifices of other people too. He was very democratic about it."

"Notice," said Anna May, "the word 'worship' is underlined elsewhere in red. Let me continue: 'I was clever, probably too clever in retrospect, but I led them to believe I was an excellent prospect. They wanted my mind, they wanted my gift of prescience, my astrological genius. They also want the world. They want to enslave the world. They plan to begin by spreading their poison in the United States. The stock market crash was the beginning. To cripple the country financially is to become a malignancy that will spread across the world. Their disciples are puppets. I know Raymond Souvir, Dorothy di Frasso, Monte Trevor, Adolph Hitler, Ivar Tensha, the Ivanovs, and this Dong See, who is not the musician but a cousin whose resemblance to the original is remarkable. What they have been trained to be are recruiters. Monte Trevor is to recruit the great powers of the world's film industries; Ivar Tensha has a network of his own that controls powerful industries in all corners of the world; Raymond Souvir is a celebrated prostitute and has been to bed with many members of world governments, who will one day rue their brief relationship with him; Dorothy di Frasso is an ambitious climber, and ambitious climbers can wheedle their way into the trusts of the mighty.' " Anna May paused. The look on their faces varied from disbelief to shock to total cynicism. Villon couldn't swallow it, Jim Mallory was horrified, and Marlene was convinced this conspiracy was marked for failure. "You will see 'world' and 'states' are underlined in the other charts in red. Actually, every word I'm reading to you shows up in the other seven charts. How dense we were not to realize it would all be wrapped up in Mai Mai's chart, which, Marlene, was also in her bedroom but in a drawer tucked away under her lingerie. Fortunately, she shared the secret with Tu Low Hung, the tong's secretary."

Anna May continued reading. " 'The Ivanovs represent the Bolsheviks, but I do not think they are fully trusted. Stalin loathes Mussolini, whose interests are represented by his good friend the Countess. These people are but a fraction of their recruits. There are conspirators at work in the Latin Americas and throughout Asia, in Great Britain and Ireland. I have contacted Washington, D.C., and warned them the future president's life is at stake, but their secret service has found no corroboration and they are inadequate fools. An assassination attempt will be made and it will fail. Roosevelt will live to witness the next world war. This will be Adolph Hitler's contribution.' "

Anna May put the paper aside. "The point is, much as I loved and respected Mai Mai, how much of this can we believe? Was her illness affecting her mind? The American secret service are far from fools. What's it really all about?"

"It's all about power," said Marlene, "and as cynical as I am about the chances for this so called conspiracy to succeed, we have seen for ourselves the machinations of these puppets, we have seen Mai Mai and Raymond Souvir murdered because they became threats with the danger of exposure. The point is, my friends, if we show this document to the proper authorities, will they believe us or take us for a group of fools? I think what's most important, Herb, is to trap the murderer. I'm sure we both suspect the same person. And Anna May, again we must turn to you. Darling, I'm offering you what might be the greatest role of your life."

Anna May had lit a cigarette and there was a trace of a smile on her face. "Mai Mai names the most likely candidate to be her murderer. But of course, from her it is pure conjecture. And whoever you and Herb suspect, Marlene, as they say in all the most mediocre cop movies, 'You ain't got the goods on him.' You need the proof to get him and convict him. And the only way is to get a confession out of him."

Marlene said, "You can do it. I could see it in his face he's attracted to you. Are you game?"

"Sure I am. I want to be a recruit. I want to be powerful. I want to be up there with the big boys taking control of the world's finances. I want to make sacrifices to Molech. Who's got Dong See's phone number?"

⟋ SEVENTEEN ⟍

VILLON READ MAI MAI'S words for himself. When he was finished, he flipped through some other pages and said to Anna May, "This isn't really her chart, is it? It reads more like a diary."

"I refer to it as her chart for want of a better word. I suppose diary is more to the point. She has pages of comments about everyone, including me. Astrologers don't really chart themselves, but in Mai Mai's case, there was her gift of clairvoyance. This made her special, and she made notes on everything she predicted. You see there's a date on every page, or next to a prediction. This way she could check back on her degrees of accuracy. She was thinking of writing a book about herself and her gift. Several publishers were interested."

Marlene said, "Why don't you finish the book? Well, why not? Don't look so skeptical. I'm sure her heirs would be all for it and it'll give you something to do until an offer finally rears its lovely head."

"It's a thought, isn't it. Meantime, I have a much more important job to do. As you said, Marlene, it might be the greatest acting job of my life."

Villon said, "You're sticking your neck out, Anna May. This could turn nasty and be life threatening."

"You'll rescue me. Believe me, I'm neither worried nor frightened. Well, my friends, we have a lot of preparations to see to, so let's get to work."

Jim Mallory was on the phone talking to the precinct, watching Marlene, Anna May, and Villon hatching the plot with which they planned to snare the killer. When he was finished with the phone, he interrupted them to tell Villon that dispatches from Interpol were awaiting him. Villon was anxious to get back to the precinct.

"I'd like to come with you, if I may," asked Marlene. "I'd like to see what goes on at police headquarters. I have plenty of time. After all, I thought I'd be spending all day with Raymond's test. I wonder who will claim his body."

"The Interpol dispatch on him is bound to name his family and their whereabouts. Otherwise, we'll contact the French Embassy."

"I hope there will be someone to mourn him," said Marlene.

"This is no time to be morbid, Marlene," cautioned Anna May. "This is time for action and I'm all keyed up. Dong See will be here tomorrow at seven. If you three really worry for my safety, then make sure we're fully prepared and pray there'll be no slipup." Marlene had a sly smile on her face. "What's going on behind that smile, Marlene?"

"I was wondering if I shouldn't be playing the scene with Dong See tomorrow. I'm an old hand at dangerous situations."

Villon said, "I'll take the folders with me for safekeeping." Anna May gathered them and gave them to Mallory.

Anna May said to Marlene, "Don't try to rob me of my first good scene in ages."

"And what if nothing comes of it?"

"Something will come of it. I won't let us down."

"Anna May, you'll be brilliant." They embraced.

When she was alone, Anna May phoned her cousin who

occupied the apartment directly below hers. "Lotus Blossom, can you come up for a few minutes? I have something terribly important to discuss with you. Yes dear, I have lots of gin."

Arriving at police headquarters, Marlene parked her car next to Mallory's unmarked squad car. There was a twinkle in her eye as she said, "Herb, I'd like Jim to escort me inside." She took Mallory's arm. He was trembling. "Relax," said Marlene, "I'm not all that special. I'm just a world-famous movie star that millions of men and a certain breed of women dream about. And I'm only flesh and blood."

But *what* flesh and blood, thought Mallory.

Marlene continued, "Stop behaving like a schoolboy and straighten up, shoulders back, head held high. That's it. That's right." Villon thought she could have been one hell of a drill sergeant. "Now forward march. I know this is a big moment for you and you'll never forget it for the rest of your life." She laughed. "And neither will I! Boy, do I have an ego! And if I didn't, I'd still be Louis and Wilhelmina Dietrich's chubby little daughter and probably married to a sausage maker. Okay my friends, let's make an entrance."

It was one of the rare moments in the precinct's history when time seemed to have ground to a halt. Her cheery and sexy "Hello boys!" caused Villon to believe that such a thing as mass hypnosis was entirely possible. The desk sergeant seemed frozen to his chair. Several patrolmen and plain-clothes officers looked with either disbelief or incredulity.

Villon broke the spell with, "Relax, men, it's Marlene herself. She invited herself down to see how we operate, so start operating." She signed autographs, she pinched the desk sergeant's cheek, she chatted amiably and asked intelligent questions about their jobs. Had she been running for office she would have garnered a lot of votes. Finally settled in Villon's office, she lit a cigarette as he sifted through the pages transmitted by Interpol. Occasionally he handed a page to Mallory, whose poker face, Marlene decided, would have made him a great card player.

After several minutes of silence, Marlene said impatiently, "Come on, boys, share it with me."

Villon said without taking his eyes from the paper he was reading, "There's nothing all that startling. Mai Mai left most of the same stuff in her log. This is interesting about Raymond Souvir." Marlene leaned forward. "He's not French, he's an Arab. Born in Cairo. And he does come from a lot of wealth. Daddy owns oil wells all over the place. Daddy's also a *gonif*. He has successfully maneuvered the downfall of rival emirates. It seems daddy very much would like to rule the world or be a party to a worthwhile partnership. It doesn't say where to contact him. Maybe we'll ship the body care of American Express."

Marlene grimaced. "That's awful."

Said Villon, "We'll track down daddy. Wait a minute. Maybe we won't have to bother. Di Frasso and Brunhilde should know where to get hold of him. He's had affairs with both of them." He began whistling nothing recognizable as he continued reading. Finally he said, "Nothing new on Tensha except he's a good buddy of Souvir's daddy and they're in business together on a couple of ventures."

"Such as?" asked Marlene.

"Brothels all over the world and Arab slave trading. Christ, does slave trading still exist? I guess it does with the Arabs."

"What about the Ivanovs?" asked Marlene.

"More or less what we got from Mai Mai. Gregory is very thick with Stalin. Natalia was once Stalin's lover. Apparently he rewarded Gregory with Natalia for services rendered. Some girls have all the luck." Suddenly his eyebrows shot up. "Now how about Monte Trevor!"

Marlene was lighting a new cigarette. "Something juicy, I hope."

"Juicy but unproven. It's suspected he engineered the murder of Ivar Krueger."

"The infamous match king?"

"The one and only and never to be forgotten. The suspicion remains unproven, but it seems the match king financed a couple of films for Trevor, who fiddled with the budgets, and most of the money apparently ended up in his pockets and not on the screen."

"A lot of that goes on in pictures," advised Marlene. "What about Dong See?"

"Interesting. Our Dong See, as Mai Mai wrote, is the true Dong See's cousin. Their fathers were brothers. The families lived together. The boys were inseparable until Dong See exhibited his musical talent and was whisked away to be a child prodigy. Our See is named Li Po See and became the protégé of a powerful warlord, another man who ruthlessly pillages and destroys anything in the way of his path to power." He screwed up his face. "What do you do with power? I mean how much power is enough power? You got a theory, Marlene?"

"A very simple one. Power is sought by megalomaniacs. Mussolini, Hitler, Stalin, Napoléon, Alexander, Rasputin, Louis B. Mayer. Sooner or later it destroys them."

Villon set the papers aside. Jim had placed the folders on Villon's desk. Villon stared at them and then looked up. "Now to get the machinery in operation for Anna May's date with Dong See."

"I still wish that was my scene," said Marlene. "I've more strength than Anna May. I could walk into a cage of lions without a whip or a gun."

"Marlene, I think you'll find that beneath Anna May's seemingly fragile exterior, there lies a core of solid steel."

"I hope you're right." She exhaled a smoke ring. "I assume Anna May's cousin will cooperate."

"She'll cooperate, Anna May told me, or she'll get a dispossess notice. You see what I mean by a core of solid steel?"

"Herb, was there a car crash? Was the real Dong See killed?"

"There was a car crash," said Villon. "The brakes were doctored. Dong See refused to be recruited by his cousin. He threatened exposure. The musician was wanted by the organization as an influence on his following and the many important people he knew that could have been of use to them. Dong See survived the crash. And he *was* in a Swiss clinic for six months. It left him shattered in both body and mind. He remembers very little except his music."

"What's become of him?"

Villon handed her a sheet of paper. Marlene read it. "Oh, how sweet. I hope he's happy." She said to Mallory. "He lives in a small village in Palestine near the Dead Sea. He gives violin lessons to yeshiva students."

At ten o'clock the next morning Marlene arrived at the chapel at Forest Lawn cemetery. She had engaged a nondenominational cleric to conduct the services, as there wasn't a clue to Lewis Tate's religion. Anna May decided not to attend but sent a floral wreath, which was prominently displayed near the closed coffin. Marlene was surprised and touched by the attendance, which almost filled the chapel. Marlene wouldn't learn until later that the majority of those present were curiosity seekers who made a profession of attending celebrity funerals. Several former silent greats had volunteered to speak on Tate's behalf. There was Herbert Rawlinson and Mae Marsh, and Bess Flowers spoke a touching eulogy. The background was prerecorded organ music. Marlene was soon lost in her own thoughts, thoughts of the police engineers wiring Anna May's living room and connecting the wires to those in her cousin's apartment. She knew the microphones would be well hidden and that the police technician in Lotus Blossom's apartment would carefully record the conversation between Anna May and the bogus Dong See.

Marlene had phoned Anna May the previous night and told her what the Interpol dispatches contained.

"So he's Li Po See. There was a very famous poet named Li Po, Marlene."

"Yes, I know. Don't trip yourself up and call him Li Po."

"It is Li Po who will trip himself up. Trust me."

"I do, my dear, I do. But I'll be a nervous wreck in your cousin's apartment."

"Don't let her drink too much gin. You'll know she's had enough when she suddenly gets down on one knee and sings 'Mammy.' "

Marlene was shaken from her reverie by the cleric's asking the gathering to join in prayer. Marlene prayed with sincerity. For Lewis Tate she wished a better world for him in the hereafter, and if there really was an afterlife, about which she had serious doubts, she hoped Lewis Tate would find a very good agent. For Anna May Wong she prayed for success and safety, and for herself, she prayed for a thorough rewrite of the script for *Blonde Venus*.

Raymond Souvir's autopsy was completed about the same time as Lewis Tate's coffin was lowered into his final resting place. The coroner was positive it was poison and so went through the motions by the numbers, stifling numerous yawns and anxious to get away to a lunch date in Brentwood.

Hearing that Souvir's body was claimed by Dong See, alias Li Po See, gave Herb Villon cause for speculation. The mortuary attendant who called for the body informed Jim Mallory it was to be cremated and the ashes sent to an emirate in the Near East. All day until it was time to take up his position with his men in Lotus Blossom's apartment, Villon entertained misgivings about the dangerous position Anna May would be in, and the misgivings were far from entertaining. The plan was to rendezvous in the cousin's apartment at six o'clock, one hour before Anna May expected Li Po. Marlene arrived promptly at six with several bottles of champagne. Lotus Blossom, who had been told Marlene would honor her humble abode, greeted her with subdued warmth and was more than glad to chill the champagne for the great star.

"Quite an impressive setup," complimented Marlene as she saw the recording apparatus ready to be manned by the engineer wearing a set of headphones.

"Let us now cross our fingers and pray," said Villon as he glanced at his wristwatch.

"Will we be able to hear what's going on upstairs?" asked Marlene.

"There's bound to be some bugs," explained the engineer. "There always is especially if they're moving around, but Anna May has created a seating arrangement in which the microphone is in a bowl of flowers on a coffee table set equidistant between them. We've tested it and it's working fine."

Marlene thought to herself, the best laid plans of mice and men often go astray. But this isn't mice and men. This is an actress and the police. It has to work. It has to.

"I hope it's dry enough," said Anna May, as Li Po See sipped the martini. She had poured herself a glass of white wine. Now they sat across from each other, the vase between them. Anna May wasn't surprised when he arrived and asked to be shown through her apartment. She knew he must be harboring suspicions and wanted to make sure he and Anna May were alone in the apartment. He told her he liked the decor and asked how long she'd been living there.

"I bought the house five years ago. It was in a terribly run-down condition so I got it very cheap. I've put a lot of money into it." She explained about her relatives and friends and Li Po sympathized. There was a plate of hors d'oeuvres on the table and she offered it to him but he refused. Downstairs, Marlene wondered how long the small talk would continue when suddenly she realized where Anna May was leading the man. Villon looked tense. Jim Mallory had a quizzical expression.

"I'm thinking of selling the house and moving to Europe. I'm not very happy in Hollywood anymore."

"I thought you were very successful."

"I was once, but not anymore. Most of the good parts I can play are given to Occidentals. Don't you realize the prejudice against minorities in this country? In this profession? Black actors are never given parts that have dignity. They're always maids or Pullman porters. Oriental actors are always villains, and the women are servants. I'm sorry, but you see, I'm in a desperate situation."

"Were you hoping I might offer a solution?"

"Perhaps. I've read the charts. I know what you're involved in. What Mai Mai calls 'The Devil's Syndicate.' " He said nothing. He waited. "Why she had to be eliminated. She foresaw her own murder."

He said softly, "She had a truly remarkable gift. Anna May, what are you after?"

"I want to be recruited. I want to join your movement. My name opens the doors of the high and the mighty and I'm fed up being treated like a coolie and scrabbling to make ends meet. I've sold most of the valuable pieces that decorated this room."

"Does Marlene Dietrich know how you feel?"

"Do you think I'm mad?"

"Where are the charts? Are they here?"

"They're back in Mai Mai's apartment." She smiled. "They proved to be useless."

"Useless? Are *you* mad?"

"No, I'm not mad, I'm desperate." There was a cunning smile on her face. "I gave Mr. Villon false translations. I made what Mai Mai wrote sound innocent. Oh, there were certain predictions that were innocent enough, but I did not tell him about the plot to destroy the world's economy. Those charts, in the wrong hands, could be very dangerous and very very incriminating."

"I want them. You must get them for me. I must have them. This man Villon is very clever."

Downstairs, Marlene silently applauded Villon. He didn't like what he was hearing. It wasn't what Anna May had outlined earlier. She was off on a different tack altogether. He suspected what was coming and he dreaded it. Although he didn't share his fears with Marlene, she could see in his face that he felt something was going wrong. *Anna May. Nothing must happen to Anna May.*

"You're very right. He is very clever. He knows who the murderer is."

"Really." His voice was hoarse.

"He lacks the proof but he says he will soon have it. There were fingerprints on the knife that killed Morton Duncan . . ."

"Bullshit!" shouted Li Po. "That hilt was wiped clean and . . ."

Downstairs, Villon said, "That's it!"

Marlene waved him quiet. Anna May was plunging ahead, treading where angels fear.

Anna May spoke softly. "So you killed Morton Duncan. And it was you who paid him to poison Mai Mai. Raymond Souvir could no longer be trusted, so you poisoned him."

Li Po's eyes reflected menace. "Sadly, Anna May, only you and I know this. I don't think I can trust you to keep quiet."

Quietly and unseen, Marlene slipped out of Lotus Blossom's apartment and hurried up the stairs to Anna May's.

"Of course, you can! You're going to help me. You need me."

"Anna May, you're a very good actress. There were no fingerprints on the hilt. Where are the police? On the roof?"

Marlene knocked on Anna May's door and shouted, "Anna May, it's Marlene. Let me in! I'm sorry I'm late."

Anna May picked up her cue. "You're always late." She was staring at the gun Li Po was holding. "What's that for?"

"Let her in."

Anna May persisted. "Why the gun? I don't like guns. Put it away."

Damn Dietrich, thought Villon. "We can't use the stairs. Miss Dietrich had to get into the act! The fire escape! Quick!"

As they hurried out of the room into the bedroom that led to the fire escape, they heard the familiar strains of the Al Jolson favorite. Lotus Blossom was on one knee serenading the recording engineer, "Maaaaaaammmmmmmyyyyyyyy!"

In Anna May's living room, Li Po grabbed Anna May's arm and forced her to the door. "Open it," he commanded as he stepped back.

"Anna May, why don't you open the door?" pleaded Marlene.

The door opened. "What kept you?" Marlene remained in the doorway. Anna May faced her, shielding her. Li Po stood directly behind Anna May. Marlene did not see he had a gun aimed at Anna May's back. "Dong See, how good to see you again! Anna May, you look absolutely terrified, what's the matter?"

Anna May said, "You shouldn't be here, Marlene." Villon and Mallory entered stealthily through the window with guns drawn. In the street, the unmarked squad cars instructed to take up positions after Li Po entered the building were in place and waiting. In the apartment underneath, the recording engineer carefully wrapped the incriminating disc and placed it into a container while Lotus Blossom continued her serenade, enthusiastically but sadly off-key.

"Why shouldn't I be here?" asked Marlene. "You invited me for a drink."

Li Po moved swiftly. He grabbed Anna May around the waist, using her as a shield. He said to Villon and Mallory. "I suspected you'd be coming up the fire escape. You're very brave Miss Dietrich to set yourself up as a decoy, but I'm leaving here with Anna May and I don't think you want to be the cause of her death."

"Murder comes so easily to you," said Dietrich.

"I was trained by a master. Get out of the doorway."

Villon commanded, "Come inside, Marlene."

She entered slowly. She and the detectives were of the same mind. The recording engineer was hearing everything that was going on. He was a detective. He had a gun. Li Po was unaware of his existence. He had no idea Villon and Mallory had materialized from the apartment below. He had to assume they climbed up from the street. Marlene was their decoy. A

216

very glamorous one. Marlene was at the table examining the hors d'ouevres.

"Anchovies. I adore anchovies." She popped an hors d'ouevre into her mouth. Villon and Mallory couldn't believe their eyes. The woman was amazing.

Li Po, with Anna May as his shield, backed out into the hallway. Marlene asked him as they went, "I don't know why you had to kill Raymond. He was a nice boy. Of course, we know you didn't like the way he drove."

Her hands flew to her face as she heard the pop of the engineer's service revolver. Li Po cried out and dropped the gun. Anna May moved away as he fell to his knees. Villon and Mallory moved swiftly. The engineer was a crack shot. He'd hit Li Po in the right shoulder.

Anna May said, "All right, Marlene. You can look now."

Marlene looked, was relieved at seeing Mallory handcuffing Li Po, and she and Anna May embraced. "Anna May, you fool!"

Villon said angrily, "Marlene, you fool."

Dietrich said, "Don't be ridiculous. I had to cause a diversion. I knew you'd come up the fire escape behind him. And besides . . ."—she opened her handbag and showed them a handgun—"I borrowed this from one of my bodyguards. And I'm one hell of a shot."

The backup detectives had arrived and two were leading Li Po away. He was cursing them all in a Chinese dialect. "What's he saying?" asked Marlene.

Anna May said wearily, "Marlene, better you shouldn't know."

An hour later, in a booth at the Brown Derby, Marlene asked Villon, "What will you do with the others?"

Anna May and Mallory waited for Villon to answer Marlene. "By me, you mean the police? We do nothing. My job was to catch a murderer, and thanks to you two babies I've made my pinch. As for the others, that's up to the Feds. I'll make some guesses. I'm no Mai Mai Chu, but here's what I predict. The Ivanovs will declare diplomatic immunity, Tensha will envelop himself in the protective cloak of his billions. . . ."

Marlene added, "Of course, Trevor will be permitted to flee to Mexico, where he will be punished with a severe attack of the *turista* and spend much of the time on a different kind of throne than the one he envisioned. Countess di Frasso will have an excellent lawyer who will get her cleared of the charges that she was an accessory to murder. Brunhilde will be deported and will try to sell the film rights to her story, and I'll probably be offered the chance to play Brunhilde, which I will decline with alacrity. And Li Po? I suppose he will be tried and convicted."

"He will die," said Anna May.

"I'll sing no sad songs for him," said Marlene.

"Li Po will never stand trial. *They* will have him killed. It's in his chart, and Mai Mai is rarely wrong."

Villon made a mental note to increase the security guarding Li Po.

"Mai Mai Chu." Marlene spoke the name reverently. "Now there's a part I'd love to play."

"You see," Anna May exploded. "She wants the part of Mai Mai Chu! *I* should play it, not you, Marlene, *I* should play it."

"Calm down, sweetheart. They'll never let me play character roles. They'll make me go on playing the one part I play the best." She raised her glass of champagne in a toast. "And that part is familiar to all of you. It's known as Marlene Dietrich."

She sipped and then winked an eye at Jim Mallory. He winked back and felt wonderful.

The Greta

G A R B O

Murder Case

George Baxt

for
Hope Dellon
and
Eleanor Sullivan
with love and gratitude

One

She wanted to scream for help, but didn't dare. If someone came to her rescue, how would she explain her situation? Could she dare admit she was spying? Eavesdropping on a conspiracy, or what she and her employer suspected was a conspiracy. Real blood-and-guts stuff, grist for the mills of the dime pulps. She paused in her flight to catch her breath and remove her sandals. It would be easier to run along the sand barefoot. She looked behind her and saw nothing, heard nothing. But still, they could be there, not too far behind, pursuing her, and if they caught her, they'd kill her. They were without mercy, these conspirators. In time of war, mercy is redundant. And the United States was at war, with Nazi Germany and with Japan. Was it only a month since the infamy of Pearl Harbor? God, how time flies when you're in danger.

She climbed a dune and then hunkered down for a moment to gain her bearings. Under the Pacific blackout it was almost impossible to see anything. Only the stars were twinkling, as only the stars over Santa Monica could twinkle. There was a curtain of haze over the moon, and the waves breaking against the shore sounded like the staccato of gunfire.

Garbo. What the hell does Garbo have to do with this? While eavesdropping in the tastelessly furnished mansion just a few hundred yards past Marion Davies's immense beach house, she'd heard Garbo's name mentioned several times.

"Garbo would be perfect." A man's deep baritone, German accent. Although with the war on, nowadays for German you could read Swiss or Austrian.

"Isn't she a bit old?" Woman's voice, continental, but which brand of continental? Hard to detect.

"Is thirty-seven so old?" Pleasant voice. European too, but what part European? France? Hungary? He repeated his question. *'Is thirty-seven so old?'*

"I don't give a good god damn how old she is, we *need* her." The deep baritone, very officious. Undoubtedly used to giving orders and demanding and receiving respect.

"Why not Dietrich?" The woman, continental voice.

A derisive snort was followed by the baritone's, "You think Garbo's too old? Dietrich's forty-three, God bless her."

"Oh, she can't be. She's so divine looking." A new country heard from. Possibly Italy, British educated. Male.

"I want Garbo." The baritone nailed his demand to their ears.

"Hush." The woman, continental voice. "I think someone's out there."

The woman held her breath. She had managed to raise the window slightly without their hearing her. What had she done to give herself away? Oh Christ, it was a poodle. A nasty black poodle with ribbons in its elegant, expensive coiffure. It wagged its tail and licked her face while she gave it a rough shove away from her. Roundly insulted, the dog gave voice, and, fearful of discovery, the woman took off. Luckily, the dog didn't pursue her. But she heard a door open and a voice shout, "There! Over there! Heading toward the dunes! I see something!"

"Here! See! The window is slightly open. Someone's been listening."

"Stop shouting! Quiet! You'll wake up William Randolph Hearst."

"It's about time someone did." Possibly Italy, British educated.

"Wh-wh-wh-what the hell's g-g-going on out there?" Marion Davies was a vision of middle-aged dissipation, standing in the enclosed garden of her Santa Monica beach house, one hand on her left hip and the other holding a fresh highball.

"I don't hear anything," said her melancholy guest, her voice smoky and husky and reeking with despair.

"I w-w-wonder who's living in that b-b-b-big dump."

"I only hear the crashing of the waves." Her chuckle was dry and brittle. "Better to hear the crashing of waves then the crashing of careers. No, Marion?"

"Y-y-y-yes Greta."

"Marion, why is it you never stuttered on screen?"

"S-s-s-self c-c-control. Have another sherry."

"I still have some."

"Have more. We're up to our hips in amontillado. The old bugger knew there'd be a war so he had gallons of it imported from Spain or wherever it comes from."

"You're not stuttering."

"It comes and it goes."

"You're a fraud."

Davies smiled. She admired her guest's unique beauty. William Daniels, the cameraman, had said of her, "Greta Garbo doesn't have an unphotographable angle. You can place the camera anywhere and she'll emerge on film more breathtaking than an old master."

"Why didn't you marry John Gilbert?" Davies asked Garbo.

"He wanted children."

"So?"

"Somewhere there's an unborn child who's terribly lucky I'm not its mother."

"What a terrible thing to say about yourself."

"Why haven't you had children?"

"Out of wedlock? Are you mad?"

Garbo's laugh was like an explosion of dynamite. "All these decades living in sin . . . ha ha ha . . . and you wouldn't consider mothering a bastard?"

"I *am* mothering a bastard. He's asleep upstairs. What are you staring at?"

"Worms."

"What kind of worms?"

"Insignificant ones, I'm sure. Without a care in the world. They don't face a meeting with Louis B. Mayer tomorrow morning."

"You still under contract to Metro?"

"On paper, yes. In my soul, no."

"You haven't done a picture in a year. I thought *Two-Faced Woman* was kind of cute."

Garbo got up from her chair and stretched her arms lavishly. "There were two great cataclysms in 1941, Pearl Harbor and *Two-Faced Woman*. She leaned over and resumed staring at the worms. "Marion?"

"Yes, dear."

"I wonder how worms make love." Davies suppressed a shudder and swigged her highball. "Don't you suppose they repulse each other? And yet, there are so many worms, billions and trillions of them. I should imagine, come to think of it, worms must be very sexy."

"Greta, if you ever decide to go into analysis, can I sit in on a few sessions?"

Garbo now concentrated on the haze-covered moon. "Look at the moon."

"I've already seen it."

"Look at the haze. They call that a Bomber's Moon."

"Is that a fact?"

"Yes it is. It is perfect for raiding airplanes. Not too bright to give them away, not too dull to obscure their targets."

"Where the hell do you pick up stuff like that?"

"The *Reader's Digest,*" came the world-weary reply. "I think I'll go home."

"Why, for crying out loud? It's early yet."

"I must be up early to run on the beach."

"What an exhausting idea. You Swedes beat hell. No wonder there's such a high rate of suicide in Sweden."

"Thank you for dinner, it was lovely."

"Oh?" asked Davies through an alcoholic haze, "Did we eat dinner?"

Fifteen minutes later, Garbo sat alone on her patio facing the ocean, deep in thought. As she did too frequently, she dwelt morbidly on the past. Her abusive, alcoholic father. Her passive and permissive mother. Then she thought of Marie Curie and wondered why Louis B. Mayer was no longer interested in filming Curie's life story.

"Nothing happens!" Mayer had insisted at their last meeting. "She discovers radium. Big deal!"

"But you made *two* pictures about Thomas Edison."

"They both lost money!" Mayer puffed ferociously on his cigar. "For a while there I considered your doing something really different, like playing Mother Goddam in *The Shanghai Gesture*. Y'know, Von Sternberg's bomb. But then I figured, what the hell, you've played enough whores. Even though a Chinese whore would've been a change of pace." He smiled benignly. "So I didn't bother you with the idea."

"Thank you for having the good taste to spare me your bad taste."

And tomorrow morning there was to be another confrontation with the despised head of Metro-Goldwyn-Mayer. I am thirty-seven years old, she thought, and I am still a beautiful woman. I am very wealthy, I need never want for the rest of my life. This tiresome war, how long could it possibly last? A year, maybe two, and then I could resume traveling. The Far East, how I yearn to travel to the Far East. Damn the Japanese. Damn the Germans. Damn Louis B. Mayer.

"Who's there?"

She heard a noise coming from beneath the patio. She looked over the railing, and saw what seemed to be the figure of a woman emerging from behind a rose bush and running across the sand toward Peter Lorre's house. She thought of alerting the police and just as quickly scrubbed the idea. The house swarming with police was not her idea of absolute privacy. Probably some young girl playing hide-and-seek with her lover.

Lover. How long has it been since I've had a lover? And if I had one now, how would I handle the situation? My career teetering on the edge of oblivion, a world at war and I'm not cut out to be a soldier. I could be a leader, but never a follower. What shall I do? What shall I do? She snapped her fingers. I'll make some Ovaltine.

Peter Lorre was urbane enough to smile charmingly at his unwelcome guest.

She had scrabbled at his back door and for a moment he thought it might be a neighbor's dog come to beg for scraps. On the other hand, it could be the police. He hastily secreted his stash of cocaine in its hiding place in the butler's larder when the scrabbling became more insistent. He crossed to the back door and opened it a crack. "Yes, what do you want? Don't you know there's a blackout?"

She pleaded, "Please let me in. I've lost my way. I need to call a cab."

It was a young voice and young voices usually emitted from young faces and young faces usually belonged to young bodies and Lorre was partial to young bodies. "Hurry." He pulled the door back and she hurried in. She was carrying a purse and a pair of sandals, and the windblown hair partially obscuring her face could not camouflage her beauty.

"Thank you, you're very kind." Then she recognized him. "You're Peter Lorre."

"Yes," he acknowledged eagerly, "and my wife's away."

"If you could show me the phone."

He wanted to show her something else, but Jack Warner had only recently cautioned him about his indiscretions with young women. "I'd be delighted to show you my phone. I think you'll find it quite attractive. It's lilac, the only lilac-colored telephone in all Hollywood." She followed him into the tastefully furnished sitting room with what was usually a spectacular view of the Pacific Ocean, but now was heavily draped to keep the light in and the view out. "You look all tuckered. Has someone been chasing you?"

"I'm not sure. I think so. I was walking on the beach. . . ."

"That's very dangerous in the blackout. . . ."

"I do it frequently. Nothing untoward has ever happened."

You've never met Lorre before, he was thinking, and then silently admonished himself. He said, "You were walking on the beach, and . . . ?"

"I suddenly heard these noises behind me, you know, that slop-slop noise shoes make when they're running on sand."

"Oh yes. I'm a slop-slop *maven.*"

"Maven?"

"Connoisseur, Yiddish version." His real name was Laszlo Lowenstein.

"Maven," she repeated solemnly. "I like it."

"Shall we go back to the slop-slop noise?"

"If you insist. Well anyway, I began to run. I just panicked. I ran past Marion Davies's place. . . ."

"Why didn't you ask for help there?"

"I couldn't find the back door."

"Marion is always misplacing things."

"And then I hid behind a rose bush under a patio. . . ."

"That sounds like Greta's place."

"Garbo?"

"Hardly Rabinowitz."

"I should have liked to have met Greta Garbo."

"Well, apparently you've shaken your pursuers." There was a firm knock at the back door. "Apparently you haven't." He indicated a door to her left. "The only person who looks in that closet is my wife. Closets are her secret vice and on indiscreet occasions my undoing." The knock was now firmer.

"Perhaps it's your wife."

"Goodness no. She has a key. She even knows how to use it." She slipped into the closet as he went to the back door. He opened it and recognized one of the private policemen the community had hired to patrol the area since war had been declared.

"Why, Thomas Toth, I do declare. What brings you to my back door at this hour?"

"Have you seen a young woman?"

"If I had, I wouldn't tell you."

"That's usually Groucho's line."

"What kind of a young woman did you have in mind?"

"One on the run. She was last seen by Miss Garbo's neighbor darting around under her patio."

"Anyone would be safe under Greta's patio."

"Obviously you haven't seen her."

"Obviously. Is this my cue to invite you in for a drink?"

"No, thanks. My partner's waiting for me near your dune."

"It's a very comfortable dune. I designed it myself."

"Mr. Lorre, you sure are a caution." He disappeared into the darkness and Lorre shut the door, hoping the light from the kitchen hadn't attracted any Japanese bombers cavorting overhead in wild abandon. He hurried back to the living room and opened the closet door. She wasn't there.

"Hello?" He shut the door and crossed to the adjoining library. She wasn't there either. He went from room to room, but there was no sign of his night visitor. He said aloud, "She doesn't exist. It was all my imagination. I better go easy on the cocaine."

At ten o'clock the following morning, Greta Garbo sat across from Louis B. Mayer. His good right arm and master spy, Ida Koverman, sat near Mayer. Garbo wondered if Koverman's perpetual smile had been plastered onto her face.

"Now Greta darling," Mayer said cozily, "we certainly wish to continue making pictures with you, but you have to understand, they can't carry big budgets anymore." Garbo said nothing. A sphinx never speaks. "Your major market is lost to us." He was uncomfortable. "Europe is gone. You're big in Europe, very big, but you've lost your American audience. But darling, we'd like to continue starring you and we'll stockpile these films and when the war is over, we'll bombard Europe with them."

She finally spoke, mournfully. "Poor Europe. Always bombarded."

"You agree, don't you, Ida?"

"Oh yes," piped Koverman, who had years ago mastered the Hollywood art of saying yes.

"So you see, Greta, we can't spend too much money on your next films. We have to bring them in on the budgets we have for the Andy Hardy and the Doctor Kildare series."

"I see."

"But we can do some very lovely subjects. We have an idea for one where you play twin sisters. . . ."

She moaned, "But I just played sisters and it was a disaster."

"But they weren't really sisters," interjected Koverman, "it was a woman making believe she was her own twin sister. . . ."

"Please Ida, don't remind me."

Mayer stepped in swiftly. "These twin sisters are very different. One is a schoolteacher in Brooklyn and the other is a Nazi spy. And the schoolteacher is mistaken for the Nazi and she's in trouble with Conrad Veidt. . . ."

"It is not for Greta Garbo, Louis."

Mayer rubbed his eyes. "We have a play by Noel Coward, *We Were Dancing*. Norma Shearer wants to do it, but I think I can talk her out of it."

"Please don't. I hear she's having a hard time with Mickey Rooney."

"That's a lie!" roared Mayer.

"Oh Louis, I don't care if she is or she isn't. Noël Coward is very droll. I am not droll. I am sad."

"Well, I'll tell you. Jack Warner has a movie coming up called *The Conspirators*. All-star cast. Of course you'll get top billing. He asked for Hedy but I know if I tell him you're interested, he'll be beside himself."

"You wish to loan me out to Jack Warner?"

Mayer spread out his hands. "Why not?"

Garbo said forlornly, "Louis, I don't want to be a loan."

$\mathcal{T}wo$

Later that day, sharing the patio with her closest friend and confidante, Salka Viertel, Garbo asked mournfully, "What's to become of me now that I'm forgotten and forsaken?"

Salka smiled as she applied a match to a cigarette. "You'll never be forgotten and you'll never be forsaken." A Polish refugee, the woman had struggled her way to Hollywood and in no time learned English and became one of the film industry's highest paid scriptwriters. She had worked on several of Garbo's films and was one of the few people to win the star's trust and admiration.

"Mayer wanted me to be Andy Hardy or Doctor Kildare."

"How dare he!" Salka's indignation smouldered, waiting to erupt. She loathed Louis B. Mayer.

Garbo smiled. "Not really. He just wanted me to make very inexpensive films." She folded her arms across her chest and contemplated the beautiful sky. "So after all these years, I am no longer an MGM star."

Salka's eyes widened. "He canceled your contract?"

"By mutual consent. Divorce is always the best when it is useless to continue a dying marriage."

"Ha! Every studio in town will be after you now!"

Garbo's housekeeper, Lottie Lynton, stepped onto the patio and asked, "Shall I do tea, Miss Garbo?"

"Oh yes," said Garbo enthusiastically, "let's have tea! You would love tea, wouldn't you, Salka?"

The writer said dryly, "Why, I'd kill for some."

Garbo said to the housekeeper, "With some biscuits, chocolate-covered ones. And maybe some of those funny little finger sandwiches you make with cucumbers and radishes. Would that be too much trouble on such a beautiful day?"

"No trouble at all, ma'am." She retreated, not happy at having overheard Garbo was no longer with Metro. She knew her employer was rich but she also knew she suffered from wanderlust. But still, with a war on, where was there for her to go except possibly Yosemite National Park and she couldn't quite imagine Garbo hiking trails and frightening the animals.

"I have never played a nun. Mayer wanted me to do *The White Sister* years ago but I said no, Lillian Gish had already done it beautifully as a silent. So Helen Hayes played the nun."

Salka recognized the preamble to what would be some startling revelation.

"Perhaps I should become a nun."

"In what order?"

Garbo ignored the mockery staining her friend's voice. "In no particular order."

"You could never be a nun." Salka blew a smoke ring and then left her wicker chair to join Garbo on the wicker couch. She took her friend's hand and held it gently. "Now look, darling, you're still much too young to continue sequestering yourself."

"I feel that God needs me."

"I don't know if you've noticed, but God has been very tiresome lately. Though even He must know that somebody needs you. Get out into the world."

"The world is at war. Ah! I could be a nurse! You remember how I nursed people in *The Painted Veil.*"

"*That* stinker."

"But Salka, it was one of your babies! You helped write it."

"It's one of my babies that should have been stillborn. Now stop being so fey and start being practical."

"I am practical, which is why I am so lonely."

"You brought that on yourself. Now's the time to come out of your shell and join the war effort."

"I could be a very good soldier. I'm a very good shot. Shall I enlist?"

"Greta, I wish you'd hang a FOR RENT sign on cloud nine and come down to earth."

Garbo was on her feet and pacing restlessly. "It's no good, Salka. I can't do bond tours the way Carole Lombard and Dorothy Lamour do because crowds terrify me. I can't visit hospitals and cheer up the wounded and the dying because the wounded and the dying make me ill. I wouldn't know what to say to them. I can't dance with the boys at the Hollywood Canteen because I'm not a good dancer."

"You're a marvelous dancer."

"Clark didn't think so."

"That cluck. What does he know?"

"Do you think it would be difficult to get to Switzerland?"

"What the hell do you want with Switzerland?"

"It's neutral. I'd be safe there."

"You're safe here, for crying out loud."

"No I'm not. Last night there was a prowler."

"Really?"

"It was a woman. She was under my patio, behind the rose bush."

"I see. You were over at Marion's, drinking again."

"It was only sherry. A presumptuous amontillado. Why do rich people buy cheap wines?"

"Why do rich people drink them?" Her sly thrust didn't escape the actress. "Did you report your prowler?"

"Of course not. The police would have invaded my privacy."

"If there *was* a prowler, you could have been robbed or even killed."

"There most certainly was a prowler." They recognized Peter Lorre's distinct voice immediately. Both smiled. They adored him. Just about everyone in the industry liked the pixieish actor with his wicked sense of humor. He came up from the beach and chose a perch on the wooden railing that protected the patio. "It was a woman. A very pretty woman." He told them about his encounter the previous night.

"And she disappeared into thin air?" Garbo's hand was at her throat, a moment borrowed from one of her silent films, *A Woman of Affairs.*

"Poof!" said Lorre. "Mr. Saloman reported her."

"Saloman? The old man next door?" Saloman's house was situated between Garbo's and the Marion Davies beach house. His was becomingly modest, as became a retired insurance man.

"He happened to be opening a window to let some air in when he saw her under your patio. It seems she'd been hiding behind your rose bush."

"You see, Salka!" Her eyes sparkled victoriously. "I was not hallucinating!"

"I didn't say you were hallucinating."

"You didn't have to say it, but you implied it. Thank you, Peter, thank you. I might have been incarcerated in a lunatic asylum."

"I hope that never happens," said Lorre, "you'd drive them crazy."

"What's in that envelope you're carrying?"

"A script."

"Have you read it?"

"Yes."

"Is it a good script?"

"It's a very good script."

Lottie Lynton arrived with the tea wagon and three cups and saucers, having heard Lorre's entrance. "Shall I pour, Miss Garbo?"

"No, thank you, Lottie. We'll look after ourselves." The housekeeper withdrew and Salka Viertel took command of the tea service. She wrinkled her nose at the plate of dainty sandwiches, preferring heartier repasts just as any good Pole would. "So, little Peter, what is the script about?"

"The Maid of Lorraine."

"Joan? Joan of Arc?"

"The kid herself."

Garbo said, "But who would care to see Joan of Arc portrayed on the screen today? I mean hers was such a teeny tiny war compared to today's Armageddon."

Salka interjected, "She's one of the great symbols of freedom. I happen to think she was a rustic nincompoop who pulled off one of the greatest con acts in history. Even so, more power to her. After all, they nominated her for sainthood and she won the poll by a landslide."

Garbo now stood tall and majestic, her hands crossed on her bosom. "I shall be a saint."

Lorre smiled as he lit a cigarette. "You'd be a most imposing saint."

"I really mean it, Peter. I too can be a martyr."

"I brought this script for you to read."

"Lemon, Peter?" asked Salka.

"It is not. The script is very good."

"I meant in your tea, dear. Lemon or milk?"

He chose milk, wondering why the rich never offer cream.

"Why do you want me to read the script? Ah, yes! There's a good part in it for you and you want my opinion. I am so flattered."

"Listen, Greta, cut the Peter Pan act and let me talk some sense into your head."

"Bravo, Peter, have one of these odious little sandwiches."

Peter dismissed Salka with an abrupt wave of his hand. "Greta, you would be magnificent as Joan of Arc."

"I'm too old."

"Crap. You can play anything you want."

"I can't play Ginger Rogers."

She was offered no argument. Lorre said, "Ginger couldn't play Joan of Arc."

Salka snorted and said, "Try telling *her* that."

"Still, I'm too old. Joan was a frisky young colt. A very foolish and self-willed creature who succeeded because she dealt with people who were dumber then she was. I mean, take the Dauphin of France. . . ."

"I have," said Lorre after sipping his tea and finding it tepid and distasteful. "I'm playing the part."

"Really? But you're much too old."

Lorre said to Salka, "She's a broken record, this afternoon. Too old, too old, too old. Sarah Bernhardt triumphed as Hamlet when she was sixty and wore a wooden leg!"

"Still, she was much too old." She selected a chocolate-covered biscuit. "I suppose with a good cameraman, say, William Daniels, I could . . ." The rest of the sentence drifted out to sea, caught in the surf, on its way west. Salka winked at Lorre. They knew Garbo was hooked.

Greta curled up on the wicker couch nibbling at the chocolate biscuit like a well-brought-up mouse. "Which studio is producing?"

"It's an independent."

"Oh please, Peter, I have read all about these independents proliferating out here. They always run out of money."

"This one could never run out of money. The producer and backer is Albert Guiss."

Salka whistled. Garbo's mouth formed a moue. Then she said, "What did *Life* magazine call him? The international figure of mystery."

"His money's no mystery," said Lorre. "The film's budget is five million dollars."

"Don't be ridiculous," scoffed Garbo. "You could make five lavish productions with that kind of money. Why *Gone With the Wind* cost about a third of that to produce!"

Said Salka, "Without even reading the script I can tell you one million would be more than enough to put Joan on film. Possibly more if they really want Greta. She doesn't work for lunch money."

"They're offering Greta one million dollars," said Lorre.

It was Garbo's turn to whistle. "That's obscene."

Lorre shrugged. "It's the kind of obscenity I wouldn't mind indulging in."

"Albert Guiss." Coming from Garbo, the name sounded Wagnerian. "Have you met him?"

"Oh, yes. He has a fabulous connection for getting me cocaine."

"Oh, Peter," Garbo groaned, "someday this addiction will kill you."

"Don't be ridiculous. It's just a pleasant habit. Everybody in the industry knows I use it."

"It will be your downfall."

He laughed. "Bela Lugosi uses more than I do, and he never stops working."

Salka advised him, "Bela's an even bigger fool then you are. Look at what he's sunk to doing. Poverty Row horror films for a fraction of the salary he could be earning."

"I've got big news for you. Just this week Universal Pictures put Bela back under contract at his original money. Thanks to the war, horror thrillers are back. *Dracula, Frankenstein, The Wolf Man.* They tried to get me but Jack Warner wouldn't sell them my contract, bless his dreadful hide."

"But he's letting you do this one for Guiss," said Salka.

"Nobody says no to Albert Guiss."

"Is there a director signed?" asked Garbo.

Lorre set his cup and saucer down and waved away Salka's offer of a refill. "An old friend of yours."

"Oh yes? Who?"

"Erich."

She thought for a moment, and then her eyes widened, like Pandora opening the box. "Von Stroheim?"

"You're joking." Salka was genuinely astounded.

"It's his chance for a big comeback."

Greta stroked her chin, deep in thought, and then said, "No wonder it has a five-million-dollar budget. Erich will spend every penny of it."

"He will make a brilliant film."

Garbo nodded. "Yes. That is possible. Erich can be very brilliant. Even his failures are larded with his special genius. He will act in it too?"

"No. He's strictly behind the camera, that was a firm stipulation by Guiss."

"Good for Guiss. Score one for him. What's the shooting schedule?"

"Three months."

"There are many battle scenes?"

"A great many."

"Three months, then, will not be long enough for von Stroheim. He'll need six months. And you know what a stickler he is for realism!" She was back to pacing the length and breadth of the patio. "He will demand real corpses! Ha ha ha!" Salka laughed too, but Garbo wasn't kidding. She knew the reputation of the arrogant and profligate von Stroheim. "There will be real blood spilled. No tomato soup for von Stroheim unless it's piping hot for his dinner. Ha ha ha!" Then she paused and her hand flew to her throat. "And my God! When Joan burns at the stake . . . !"

"Stop that, Greta," cried Salka, upset. "He wouldn't dare burn you at the stake. He'll need you for retakes."

"There's a wonderful bunch lined up for the Inquisitors." Lorre had regained their attention.

"Boris Karloff's playing the chief inquisitor."

"Oh good, good, that is very good." Salka nodded her approval as Garbo continued to speak. "The industry has never given him a chance to show what a truly fine actor he really is. Who else?"

"Jean Hersholt."

"Also good. We were together in *Susan Lenox*. He's good to work with. He isn't selfish. He gives."

"Victor Jory."

"Another one misused by the industry. It's all very impressive. Still . . ."

Lorre said gravely, "Greta, sit on your doubts."

She continued pacing in silence. Then she placed her hands on the wooden rail and gazed out at the Pacific Ocean. Her face illuminated nothing but its breathtaking beauty. She saw dolphins cavorting, but her eyes reflected nothing. It was a replica of her final moment in *Queen Christina* when she stood at the ship's railing after the death of her lover, feeling nothing, hearing nothing, saying nothing, her mind and her face a blank. Finally she spoke. "I will read the script."

"Read it several times," implored Lorre.

"I will read it and I will think about it. You don't realize, Peter, but in my seventeen years in films, I only worked for one studio, for Louis B. and Metro." Her eyes misted. "It was my home. They looked after me. They catered to my every whim. I was a daughter there such as I never was to my own father and mother. But now I have been banished, I'm an orphan. I must choose my next set of parents with great care and discrimination." She looked away from the sea to Peter Lorre. "I don't know if I want Albert Guiss for a father. I really don't need a mother". She smiled warmly at Viertel. "Salka is a good mother. My good mother." She crossed to the older woman and placed her hands on her shoulders. Then abruptly she withdrew her hands and resumed pacing. "They talk about refugees and displaced persons. They whisper about concentration camps. Look at me! I'm a refugee! I'm displaced!" She made a sweeping gesture with her hand. "And this is my concentration camp!"

Lorre commented wryly, "At least you've got hot and cold running water."

"Don't mock me."

"Don't mock yourself. Enough of these self-indulgent dramatics and read the script."

"I'll read it tonight after my lonely dinner."

"I'll join you for dinner if you like," the actor offered.

"I prefer to be lonely. Are you going, Salka?"

"I've got to get back to the script I'm working on." She crossed to Garbo and kissed her lightly on the cheek. "Phone me when you've finished reading the script. Come on, Peter."

When they were out of Garbo's earshot, Lorre asked Salka, "What do you think? Do you think she'll do it?"

"Joan's a challenge for her. And you know Greta."

"Does anyone know Greta?"

"A few of us do. She dotes on challenges. And don't believe that crap about being orphaned by Metro. She loathes the place. She's delighted to be free. She dreaded the thought of doing another film for them. Now then, what about this woman last night?"

"Well, it was the strangest thing." He warmed up to the subject. "She was quite beautiful, and I have a suspicion she was European. Her English was unaccented, but it had that lovely lilt foreigners have when they learned their English in England. You know, like me."

"By you that's a lovely lilt?"

"Don't be unkind."

"How old was this woman?"

"Her early twenties at the most. But she was genuinely frightened. Marion Davies thinks she has something to do with that ugly mansion adjoining Marion's estate."

"Who lives there?" asked Salka.

"That's it. Apparently nobody. At least no one's been seen entering or leaving it since the Wolheims moved out so hastily last November."

"Oh yes. The Wolheims. A strange family. If they were a family."

"You knew them?"

"Only by sight. Greta and I saw them a few times when we walked on the beach. Father, mother, three sons and a daughter. At least that's what we assumed they were, father, mother, sons and a daughter. Yet none of them resembled each other."

"Perhaps the children were adopted."

"Peter, you think of everything." They arrived at her car in Garbo's driveway. "Tell me, dear. How did you get to Albert Guiss?"

"Albert Guiss got to me."

"Really, how so?"

"He sent a man named Werner Lieb to see me; he and a woman named Risa Barron are to be the actual producers of the film. Guiss will act as executive producer. Lieb is quite a charmer. I think he's German originally but he said he was educated in Italy and England. His is another of those weird accents I can't place. Me, you know I'm from Germany. You, I know you're from Poland. But this fresh breed of refugees pouring into the country, they're such hybrids. I mean even Guiss is hard to place. But that deep baritone of his. When he speaks, the room trembles. I think even his whisper could shatter glass."

"Why Joan of Arc?" asked Salka. "Why something so dark and heavy? Greta's proven in *Ninotchka* she can play comedy, why not something light and graceful co-starring with Cary Grant or Fred MacMurray? That's what Greta really needs in a vehicle at this stage of her career. Peter, she's at a dangerous crossroads and she's well aware of it. Greta's no fool. She has no delusions about herself. She's a complete realist despite the misinterpretations about her."

"Werner Lieb put it to me this way and you'll have a few surprises when you read the script."

"Oh yes?"

"Oh yes. Lieb says what Guiss has in mind is an inspiring and very patriotic film. This Joan is very fresh and sassy. She even tells saucy jokes."

"Does she die laughing?"

"This is an inspirational Joan. No long-winded speeches about hearing voices. She's a very democratic young lady out to do battle against the oppressors of her time. I find the script delightful, and I haven't found many delightful scripts lately."

"I can't wait for Greta's reaction." Salka got behind the wheel of her car. "I suppose the Dauphin's part is a very meaty one."

"Oh it's delicious. I get to do many wicked things."

"Who wrote this masterpiece?"

"Something named Gustav Henkel. A very pleasant fellow."

"Henkel. Sounds German to me."

"I thought so too, but when I asked him, he said he was Hungarian."

"You can't trust Hungarians."

"Actually, the script does need work. I suggested they get Bertolt Brecht to do a polish on it."

"Henkel didn't object at the suggestion of another writer being brought in?"

"Quite the contrary. He seemed quite affable about it."

"He can't be a real Hungarian. They are mostly objectionable."

"Why are you so hard on Hungarians?"

"One of them stole my virginity." She started the motor, while Lorre refrained from commenting, Petty larceny.

Greta Garbo, from her living room window, had been watching Salka and Lorre deep in conversation. Lottie Lynton entered and asked, "Is there something I can get you? I've cleared away the tea things."

Garbo said huskily, "I wish I could read lips."

Three

Chief Inspector Herbert Villon of the Los Angeles Police Department was awaiting the visitor the desk sergeant had just announced. He was reading Louella Parsons' gossip column in the Hearst newspaper and frowning. Lolly, as Louella was known to the industry, was taking Greta Garbo severely to task for not contributing to the war effort. Lolly's rival and archenemy, Hedda Hopper, had beaten her into print that morning by announcing in the riveting prose usually attributed to illiterates that Queen Garbo had been dethroned by the powerful Louis B. Mayer and was now just another unemployed actress. Hedda was a personal toady of Mayer's, and he gleefully fed her the tidbit of Garbo's defection.

Mayer had said to her over the phone, "Make it read like no other studio is interested in her."

"That won't be easy, Louis," said Hedda while examining her reflection in a hand mirror and reappraising a millinery horror positioned atop her head. "Your son-in-law wants her for an adaptation of Robert Hichens's *The Paradine Case.*"

"That *momser* is doing it just to annoy me. With all the eligible men in Hollywood my daughter had to choose to marry David O. Selznick. *O* for *Oy vay*."

"Warner wants her for *The Conspirators*."

"Too late, I gave them Hedy and it's a firm deal."

"Herb Yates at Republic is prepared to offer her *Lady from Louisiana* opposite John Wayne."

"Fat chance she'll do that. He'll end up with Ona Munson or some other half-baked *shlepper*."

"Funny," said Hopper as she laid the hand mirror on her desk, "I can't imagine Metro without Garbo. It's like an opera without arias."

"I know, I know. But she wouldn't compromise. She wouldn't take a cut in salary. She wouldn't settle for smaller-budget films. That Swedish bitch called my bluff! But just you wait. She'll see what it's like working for those other bums. She'll come crawling back."

"My money's on Greta."

Mayer exploded. "I thought you were my friend!"

"I am, Louis, I am. But Greta's always commanded my respect. She was always kind to me when I was down and almost out."

"Didn't I keep you eating with small parts? Didn't I?"

"Yes, Louis, yes, as you constantly remind me."

"Be a good girl, now. Let her have it with both barrels."

"Yes, Louis."

What emerged from Hopper's typewriter was a tad more merciful then Mayer demanded, yet it was still painful to read. But Parsons let go with a full salvo, forgetting that Garbo was one of Marion Davies's personal favorites, and Davies was her boss's mistress. Later, when both Hearst and Davies admonished her severely, Parsons took the reprimands bravely, which didn't prevent her from taking occasional potshots at Garbo in the future.

Chief Inspector Villon threw the newspaper in the wastepaper basket as his visitor knocked lightly on his door.

"Come on in!" shouted Villon.

The man who entered was tall, blond and thirtyish, with a strong face. His smile was almost shy and boyish. He shut the door and crossed to Villon, who had stood up to greet him, with his hand extended. "Arnold Lake, sorry I'm late."

"Sit down, Arnold." They both sat. "When'd you get in?"

"After lunch. The train was six hours late. We kept being shunted onto sidelines to let troop trains go through. They warned me when I left D.C. the trip would be no picnic."

"Couldn't you hitchhike a ride on an army plane?"

"The brass don't like that. Everybody's overheated with spy fever. You're not a spy, are you?"

"No, I'm just a movie-struck cop. Did you read Louella Parsons today?"

"No, I use her paper to wrap up my garbage."

"She attacked Greta Garbo." It sounded more infamous than the attack on Pearl Harbor.

"Why don't you punch her in the mouth?" asked Arnold.

"I couldn't hit a woman." Then he recognized he was being kidded. He laughed. "You know, living here in L.A., born here, brought up on the movies, it's like everyone in the industry is an old buddy of mine, whether I've met them or not. And I go back to the silents. But Garbo. You don't attack Garbo. She's an icon. A goddess. A living legend." He paused. "I must sound like a movie-struck kid."

"You sound very refreshing. Anyway, shall we get down to it?" He spread a dossier on the desk. "My credentials." Villon gave them a cursory examination.

"Fine. So they sent you here to lock horns with Albert Guiss."

"I always get the fun assignments."

"Have they any proof he's working for the Germans?"

"None whatsoever, only a scintilla of a suspicion. I just had a quickie sandwich with one of my associates. You'll get to meet her eventually."

"Pretty?"

"Very?"

"Can't wait."

"I thought you were married."

"It ended due to artistic differences."

"Anyway, my associate has been tailing a woman named Risa Barron, who's very close to Guiss."

"How close is close?"

"Mistress close."

"That's close."

"Last night, she followed her to a house on the beach at Santa Monica. She managed to overhear a plot to do something that might involve your goddess."

"Garbo?" Villon almost hit high C. "Garbo involved with spies?"

"They're trying to get Garbo involved. And we don't know if they're spies or not. There was a lot of palaver about Joan of Arc and they must have Garbo. . . ."

Villon leaned back in his swivel chair. "That's movie talk, Arnold. That's not spy stuff."

"Don't be too quick to dismiss it. The personnel at that meeting were exclusively heavy with foreign accents."

"So's every other movie coming out of the studios these days."

"The meeting was conducted by Albert Guiss."

"In person?" Villon straightened up.

"It wasn't a reasonable facsimile. And why conduct a business meeting under cover of darkness in an uninhabited beach house?"

"Can you beat that? Cloak-and-dagger stuff right under my nose. But listen, Guiss is known to be a perfectly normal eccentric."

"That's an oxymoron."

"I don't care what kind of a moron it is. Guiss has been under suspicion as a Nazi sympathizer from almost the inception of the movement," Arnold explained, "But nobody's been able to get the goods on him. He operates through dozens of phony setups and organizations. We think he has a brilliant operation going through which he launders monies into fifth-column hands. We're positive he was Franco's angel in Spain but we can't get the goods on him."

"And America has welcomed him with open arms."

"Why not? He has billions invested here. Does the thought give you a chill that he's probably silent-partnered in any number of defense industries?"

"It'll take months for my spine to thaw." They were silent for a few seconds. Then Villon continued, "So now he's going into the movies."

"That's right. But we can't figure out why. This movie he's involved in is about Joan of Arc."

"Joan of Arc? Aw, come on now. Ingrid Bergman's more right for that than Garbo."

"I don't think so."

"Come on, Arnold. Ingrid's younger than Garbo, she's much more right for it."

"I thought you were a fan of Garbo's."

"Oh until death do us part, but much as I love her, one has to be realistic about casting her. She's just too damn old for the part."

"Anyway, why argue? Bergman's under contract to Selznick and she's hot as a pistol and he'll never lend her to an independent."

"Don't kid yourself. He's short of cash, I hear, and . . ."

Arnold Lake held up his hands. "What are we arguing about? Who gives a damn who plays Joan? They can give it to Hattie McDaniel for all I care. I'm here to nail Guiss if he needs nailing."

Villon wiped his forehead with a handkerchief. "I get so heated up about casting. It's more fun than homicide. Okay, Arnold, so I'm to provide you with a cover. That's no problem. You're here on a special assignment working with me. What about your girl?"

"They almost caught her snooping last night. She managed to pry open a window, the better to hear them, but someone wised up to it and gave chase. She eventually ended up in Peter Lorre's place seeking refuge."

Villon melted in front of Arnold Lake's eyes. "Peter Lorre. My hero. Did you see him in his first American movie, *Mad Love?*" Without waiting for an answer, he was on his feet mimicking Lorre. " 'I, a poor peasant who have conquered science,' " his simulation of Lorre's voice was uncanny, " 'Why can't I conquer love?' "

"Bravo," said Arnold softly, wondering if some men wearing white coats were waiting in the corridor.

"I do impersonations occasionally," said Villon with a slight tinge of red in his cheeks. "So Peter Lorre rescued her."

"Well, not quite. When Lorre was occupied elsewhere, she high-tailed it out of his place. You see, she suddenly realized that not only was Garbo's name being noised about at the secret meeting, there was much ado about Peter Lorre."

Villon's chin dropped. "Peter Lorre a spy?"

"Why not?" countered Arnold with a sly smile. "It's perfect casting."

Garbo walked alone along the beach, a large floppy hat pulled down over her head until the brim obscured her face, her body wrapped in a grey oilskin windbreaker. Seagulls flapped overhead, squawking at her intrusion, and in the distance, a foghorn sent out mournful, depressing signals. If anyone else was about, she was oblivious to his presence, so deeply absorbed was she in her private thoughts.

Joan of Arc.

Peter Lorre.

Albert Guiss.

Erich von Stroheim.

Louis B. Mayer.

Salka Viertel.

Quite an impressive assemblage. Of not much box-office value on a movie theater marquee, but with the addition of Greta Garbo, it at least bespoke quality.

I am thirty-seven years old. I own a huge area of this seafront. I own large parcels of land on Rodeo Drive in Beverly Hills. I own an estate in Sweden, an apartment in New York. Ha, apartment *houses* in New York. I own my house here on the beach. I have furs and jewels and stocks and bonds and equities and my health, why shouldn't I retire from films? Why should I do Joan of Arc? She was probably a lesbian, and there's enough innuendo in my life about lesbianism. But still, can I retire with that dreadful *Two-Faced Woman* as the final film by which I'm to be remembered? Have they forgotten my *Camille*, my *Ninotchka*, my *Anna Karenina?* Some say it is tragic I have never been given an Academy Award, but so what? Luise Rainer won two years in succession, and now no one will hire her—Louis B. Mayer saw to that when she left Metro. And now he seeks to poison me the same way with the help of the gossip columns. Poor Hedda. Louis cracks the whip and Hedda jumps. Poor Lolly, with her uncontrollable bladder and alcoholic husband, who is she to cast the first stone, or even the second stone, or any stone at all?

The sigh she sighed was heavy enough to topple a wall. She took the hat off and stood still, like a lighthouse offering guidance to lost ships, but there were no ships in sight. It was after six in the evening, almost two hours since she'd been with Salka and Peter Lorre, and the curtain of darkness had descended. There were the moon and the stars to guide her back to her house, but where were the moon and the stars to guide her into the future?

In Peter Lorre's house, the grandfather clock in the downstairs foyer chimed six o'clock. Behind the bar, the actor poured himself a large scotch and water. He guarded his whisky supply zealously now that liquor was in short supply. He crossed the room to his favorite chair, intending to reread the script of *Joan the Magnificent* (as it had recently been retitled), when the doorbell rang. He muttered an oath, placed his drink on an end table and went to the front door. The door was covered with a heavy black drape to conform with the blackout law. He moved the drape aside a bit and then opened the door a crack. He recognized an old friend wearing a black trilby hat and a black velvet cape, presumably designed by a vampire.

"Bela," said Lorre, "how nice of you to drop by." Pleasant, but insincere.

"Good evening, Peter," said Bela Lugosi in his well-oiled Hungarian accent. "I have come to throw myself on your mercy."

"Come in. Quickly."

Once inside, Lorre guided Lugosi to the living room where Lorre's drink awaited him. As he followed in Lorre's wake, Lugosi said with a sweet smile, "Is it possible I could borrow a cup of cocaine?"

Lorre froze in his tracks. "A cup? That's a half year's supply!"

"Cup is merely a metaphor for my distress. I've been away on location and in my absence, my supplier was found floating in the ocean off the pier in Venice, a section of clothesline around his neck. Apparently he displeased someone who lacked a sense of humor. My supplier was a very funny man." He was referring to the Venice community just north of Santa Monica, a hotbed of male body builders who occupied an area dubbed Muscle Beach.

"Have a seat, Bela. Would you like a drink?"

"Some red wine?"

"Of course." Lorre went to the bar for the drink. "I'm a bit low on my cocaine supply. The war, you know, it makes importing a bit difficult."

"Yes, I'm well aware. The federals have quadrupled their guard of the Mexican border. Of course, one could always arrange to take a trip down there and bring a good quantity back, but that's a risky business."

"Especially so when you're foreign born. If you're caught, you get a fine and a jail sentence. This is followed by deportation, and this is hardly the time to be parcel-posted back to Hungary."

"No time is the time to be sent back to my native land." He took the wine from Lorre and sipped. The lascivious look of pleasure on his face had Lorre expecting to hear in the distance the plaintive howling of wolves, Dracula's Children of the Night. "Delicious. But then, you have always been a connoisseur. But what is this?" He'd espied the *Joan the Magnificent* script.

Lorre told him about the upcoming production. "They want Garbo to play Joan."

"Garbo?" Lugosi drew out her name like he was pulling at some chewing gum. "I was with her in *Ninotchka*. A very charming recluse." He thought for a moment. "She's too old to play Joan. They need someone younger, like Jane Withers." He heard Lorre choking on his drink. "Are you all right?" Lorre sat down, gasping for breath. "Is there something in it for me?"

"As a matter of fact there might be. The part of the jailer. It isn't big, but it's showy."

"It would be nice to be part of a prestige production again. I'm back at Universal."

"I heard. Congratulations."

Lugosi shrugged. "It's a living. I'll never die a rich man, but still, I can keep up the mortgage payments. . . ."

". . . And the cocaine payments. . . ."

Lugosi shrugged again. "There are no wars or dropped options in my cocaine dreams. Will you be able to help me out, even a soupçon?"

"I'll help you, of course. Do you know Erich von Stroheim?"

"Not terribly well. Why?"

"He's going to direct the film. You'll need his approval."

"Why shouldn't he approve me?"

"Erich is a very strange man. He is pursued by a unique set of grotesque private ghosts. Hard luck favors him."

"How can you say that when he is signed to direct this million-dollar extravaganza?"

"The gods tease him. On one hand, they reward him lavishly, and with the other hand, they doom him to bankruptcy. I hope this works for him. We'll see. I'll get the cocaine." He left Lugosi alone. Lugosi picked up the script and began to read. He chuckled. Then he laughed. Then he roared. "My, my, I didn't know Joan of Lorraine could be such a scream. I suppose for more than one reason she was the toast of the town."

Greta Garbo was reading the script. As usual, first she frowned, then she uttered a *huh,* then she turned a page and smiled, then she said a quick *ha,* and, to no one in particular because she was alone in the room, she said, "They don't need me, they need Fanny Brice." Pause. "She's also too old."

Four

Erich, how good to see you again." Greta's hands were outstretched to him and he took them while bathing in the warmth of her affectionate greeting. "It has been too many years."

"Not since *As You Desire Me,*" he reminded her.

"Oh my yes. And Hedda was my sister-in-law in that one!" They shared a laugh, seeming to have forgotten that von Stroheim had arrived with Gustav Henkel, the author of the script. Lottie Lynton was hovering in the background waiting for instructions from Garbo. Garbo acknowledged Henkel. "And who is this?"

"Good heavens, Gustav, forgive me. On the few occasions that I see the great Garbo, she strikes me with awe and leaves me with amnesia."

"Erich, you're too kind." She took Henkel by the hand and led the undistinguished-looking young man into the living room. "You are Gustav Henkel and a very fine writer."

He said in an undistinguished voice, "You are too kind."

"Not at all. I'm grateful for having read a fairly decent script at last."

Von Stroheim stiffened. "Only 'fairly decent'?"

Lottie Lynton trembled. She sensed a hidden danger in the man.

Garbo smiled at von Stroheim. "It's not as though Mr. Henkel has written the Bible."

Von Stroheim scoffed. "What would you know about the Bible? I'm sure you've never read it."

"Not all of it. Just the racy parts. Ha ha ha. Lottie, see what our guests would like. Drinks? Tea? Something to eat?" Wine was requested and Lottie went to work. "So, Erich." They took the seats she indicated. "You think this script is perfect?"

"Of course not, Greta. Gustav acknowledges it needs work."

Gustav spoke. "Oh yes, it does need work. The problem is, I don't know exactly what kind of work it needs. You see, this is my first attempt at writing a screenplay."

"So? Well then it's quite good for a first attempt. If a bit giddy. I mean, I don't quite see Joan playing craps with her jailers. I don't even think craps existed in those days."

Henkel smiled, dazzling them with a display of what looked like Roquefort cheese. "I worked very hard for the irreverence. I think we take our saints too seriously. I mean, before being elected to their eminence, they were quite ordinary people. I think if most of them were alive today, they'd be bemused by all the fuss."

"If they were alive today," said Garbo somberly, "we wouldn't need them." She waited while Lottie served the drinks and returned to the kitchen. "Well Erich, this is quite an undertaking. Five million dollars. Almost enough to rebuild Dresden."

"Not quite, but still a generous, staggering sum. Albert Guiss wants this to be his monument, much as *Birth of a Nation* is Mr. Griffith's."

"You like this Mr. Guiss?"

"So far I haven't found anything to dislike."

"So much has been written about him, all so arcane, so enigmatic, so like . . . like . . . ah! Orson's *Citizen Kane!* Why are we always fascinated by men like Albert Guiss? Mr. Henkel, how well do you know Albert Guiss?"

Henkel stared into his Chardonnay, but there was nothing written there to prompt him. "He has been very kind to me."

"He paid you well for the script?" Then hastily, "I take that back. It's none of my business."

"I got a very decent sum, for a beginner."

Von Stroheim took center stage. "Tell me what bothers you about the script, Greta."

She sipped her Bordeaux, set the glass on the coffee table, crossed her legs, and fixed her gaze on the director. "The construction needs improvement. Joan is lost for at least ten pages midway into the script and that's much too much. Not because it is the star part, but because what takes place while she's offscreen is hardly very interesting. Who cares what her family thinks about her taking command of the army? It is enough to see Joan leading them into battle. Families don't care about successful children, only about the sums of money they can send home."

"I see. That's valid. Henkel?"

"What? Oh yes. Valid. Very valid. Families are boring."

There is something unreal about this little man, thought Garbo. Little men. Henkel, a small man. Von Stroheim, a small man. Lorre, a small man. She heard von Stroheim ask, "What else, Greta?"

"Much of the dialogue is terribly amusing. In fact, Mr. Henkel, a few times I laughed out loud, and for me that is very rare." She cleared her throat. "But too often the jokes are unnecessary. I mean, if you are looking to do a farce about Joan of Arc, then Joan must be played by someone like Martha Raye."

Henkel smiled. Garbo didn't notice it. How had she guessed he adored Martha Raye?

"On the nose," said von Stroheim. "There's an overabundance of levity."

Garbo leaned forward, fingering the string of pearls around her neck. "Erich, shouldn't we consider restoring her being burned at the stake?"

"If we did, wouldn't you be disturbed by my paranoia for realism?"

"Only the critics dare burn Garbo." She cocked her head to one side. "Think about it, Erich. If it's truly unnecessary, then we'll do without it. Falconetti was so magnificent in her version, but then, it was silent, wasn't it?"

"And excruciatingly slow and boring. My Joan shall move at a steady pace," von Stroheim said, underlining his statement with a machine-gun—fire snapping of his fingers, "zip, zip, zip, so the audience won't have a moment to let their minds wander. You must understand, Greta, that we cannot undertake any revisions until you are firmly committed to the project. By that I mean your name on a contract, signed and sealed."

"Of course, of course."

"Have you discussed this with your agent?"

"I have dismissed my agent. I suspect he was allied with Louis B. Mayer in the recent unpleasantness. I am my own agent." Von Stroheim flashed a "heaven help us" look at Henkel. Garbo was known as a shrewd trader who could drive a very hard bargain. "Peter Lorre says Guiss will offer me a million dollars."

"Yes, that is so."

"Mayer says my only value is in the European market. But there is no European market. So where will Mr. Guiss recoup his investment? Or doesn't he care, he's so wealthy."

"He cares. He's a businessman. But in this instance, he is more of a patriot. He feels Joan is a valid symbol of the struggle against oppressors, in this case, the Axis villains." Garbo saw Henkel's eyes blinking wildly, like semaphores running amok.

Garbo said, "I find it hard to envision Albert Guiss wrapped in a flag of patriotism. Surely the man is a country unto himself."

Henkel said hotly, "Mr. Guiss is a great patriot. A very great patriot. He is a very great man."

"Cool it, Henkel," cautioned von Stroheim. "What about us, Greta?"

Her eyes widened, puzzled. "What about us?"

"Will we get along?"

"How will I know until we start working together?"

Von Stroheim smiled. "And you call Guiss enigmatic. Are you joining us?"

"I'm inclined to. But I have to discuss this with someone."

"But Peter Lorre told me Salka Viertel urges you to do this project."

"Yes, she does. But there's someone else. An old and trusted friend who is also psychic."

He threw up his hands. *"Ach!* Psychic! I hate that word!"

Henkel said in his copyrighted nondescript way, "I'm sure you'll be interested in meeting Albert Guiss. I know he's a very great fan of yours."

"For an investment of five million dollars, he should be!" She said it with good humor, and Henkel did something with his face that she suspected might be a smile. She was glad he hadn't parted his lips. She dreaded the sight of those awful teeth. If she did the film, she would insist his teeth be capped or removed.

Peter Lorre entered from the patio. "Am I interrupting?"

Von Stroheim was glad to see him. "Peter! Help me convince Greta to be our Joan."

Lorre looked at Garbo as though she were a naughty little girl.

"But of course you must do the film!" He sat on the couch next to Garbo. "There are so many of our refugee friends down on their luck who'll be put to work." Garbo couldn't bring to mind any names; all the refugees she'd met in Hollywood seemed to be doing quite well, especially the untalented ones. Lorre said to von Stroheim, "Haven't you told her Hanns Eisler is to compose the score?" His eyes pounced on Henkel. "And we will ask Bertolt Brecht to improve the scenario. And for supporting roles in addition to those I mentioned to you yesterday, Greta, there will be Fritz Kortner, Alexander Granach," he ticked off the names on his fingers, "Hertha Thiele, Albert Basserman, his wife Elsa . . . oh so many more. We literally need a cast of hundreds, don't we, Erich?"

"It's a tremendous cast."

"I'm overwhelmed," said Garbo.

Von Stroheim said to Lorre, "Greta is afraid our Joan is a little too frivolous."

Garbo clapped her hands. "Listen. I have had a thought about Joan as to how I might play her, but I was afraid you might find it, well, a bit outrageous."

Von Stroheim said staunchly, "But I love outrageous. *I* am outrageous. Tell me, tell me quickly, how do you think you might play her?"

Garbo stood up, towering like Gulliver over three Lilliputians. "I think it is quite possible that Joan was really a man." Lorre bit his lip. Von Stroheim felt the blood leaving his face. "A transvestite!" Henkel was wearing his awful smile and Garbo turned her back on him with revulsion. "What if I was to play the part androgynously?"

Von Stroheim finally found his voice—it was a rare occasion when he lost it, even briefly. "Greta, we have to think of the Catholic Legion of Decency. Those watchdogs of American morals are very strict and very dangerous. If they refuse us a seal it will cost us hundreds of thousands of dollars in lost attendance."

"I see." She stroked her chin. She had a solution and shared it. "They couldn't stop me from thinking I'm androgynous, could they?"

"No they couldn't," said von Stroheim.

"Well then, that will be our secret. If I play it."

"If if if!" raged Lorre. "Of course you'll play it!"

"Peter, don't push me." They heard the danger in her voice, and Lorre mustered his familiar pixie grin.

He said, "It's just that we're all so anxious to get going."

"I know. I know. But don't burden me with your anxiety. I've just rid myself of one albatross around my neck. I have to think twice before trying another one for size."

Von Stroheim stepped in swiftly. "This is not an albatross, Greta. This will be a milestone in film history. Your Joan will be exalted!"

"Even by *The New York Times?*" Her eyes twinkled.

Von Stroheim put his hands on her shoulders. "In *As You Desire Me,* we acted together. Ever since, I have wanted to direct you in something. In my exile in France, I thought of trying to talk Gaumont into letting me direct you in *Madame Bovary.*"

"Ah! Why didn't you?"

"I was too late. They were already doing it. But now, Greta, now, with Joan of Arc, here is the opportunity for my dream to come true. Greta, make my dream come true. I will never have an opportunity like this again."

"Yes you will. If I do it and it's a success, they'll be knocking down barriers to get to you. Tomorrow, Erich. Tomorrow. You will have my answer tomorrow."

Von Stroheim persisted, "You will never have an offer as magnificent as this one."

She cocked her head, as she usually did when amused. "Oh no? Supposing I tell you I already have received a very magnificent offer, although it was several years ago."

Hands on hips with exasperation, Lorre asked, "And what was that?"

"Adolf Hitler asked me to marry him." They were stunned. "Didn't you know I'm one of his three favorite stars? He sent the offer through the German ambassador here in Los Angeles. Of course I refused. I had already lived in Germany back in 1925. It was awful. Do you know who his other two favorites are?" She paused for effect and then told them, "Marlene . . . and Minnie Mouse. Ha ha ha ha ha!"

"You took a foolish chance last night," said the young man whose name was Martin Gruber. He and his companion sat in the booth of a coffee shop in the Culver City section of Los Angeles, just a few streets away from the imposing MGM studios that bordered Washington Boulevard.

"I was doing my job," said Lisa Schmidt. "How did you find out about it?"

"Guiss was discussing it on the phone this morning."

"And you guessed that the woman was me?"

"I don't know anyone as rash and headstrong as you. I wouldn't try it again."

"Why did they use the house?"

"It's the only property of Guiss's the FBI hasn't bugged. They don't know he owns it."

"They do now."

Gruber chuckled. "He'll find someplace else. He's really marvelous."

"Does Guiss trust you?" asked Lisa.

"Of course not. He trusts nobody."

"Not even Risa Barron?"

"Hardly Risa Barron. She's ambitious. She wants power. I gather he enjoys her in bed. So he makes her the film's co-producer. It's only a title."

"And a fat fee," said Lisa flatly.

"Guiss is very big with fat fees. He can afford to be. He has billions."

"Who *is* Guiss?" Lisa asked.

"Who is he? He's his own invention. And he astonishes and frightens an awful lot of people."

"Doesn't he frighten you?"

"Sometimes. He doesn't seem to notice me very much. I'm an employee and as such I have my uses. I'm unobtrusive. I don't ask questions other than what pertains to my work. I like working for him." Lisa was looking at her wristwatch. "Are you in a rush?"

"In a while. I'll have a spot more of coffee."

"A pressing appointment?"

"As a matter of fact, yes. It's for a job."

"But you have a job," said Gruber.

"I have time for another." The waitress he had signaled refilled her cup. "If I can get it, my boss wants me to take this job."

"What doing?"

"It's work on a film going into production soon." Gruber suspected Lisa was playing with him, and she was.

"Doing what?"

"Assistant to the director."

"And the name of the film?"

"Joan the Magnificent." She sipped her coffee, her eyes meeting his over the rim of her cup.

"You're insane."

"No more insane than you as Guiss's personal secretary."

"Lisa, please. Don't do it. Get out of this. Last night you were lucky. The blackout was on your side. But this new madness . . ."

"Martin, my darling, I can look after myself. And just think, if I get the job, I will not only be working with the mad Erich von

Stroheim, I will get to meet the magnificent Garbo. Luck is on my side, Martin. I feel it. I know it. Cheer up, Martin. This is all a magnificent adventure, the opportunity of a lifetime."

He added gravely, "Of a very short lifetime."

She sipped her coffee and looked away from him. A very short lifetime. He was possibly right.

Five

Small people, thought Garbo, suddenly I am surrounded by small people. She sat across from the diminutive yet exotic Mercedes de Acosta, Cuban born, now a Hollywood scenarist, and once, briefly, her lover. Mercedes's tastefully furnished apartment was in a new highrise on Doheny off Sunset Boulevard, and it afforded a magnificent view of Hollywood. It was ten in the morning and they were drinking strong coffee weakened by strong cream.

"How's for an onion roll and cream cheese?"

Garbo shook her head No. "Why do I have such a presentiment about this picture? I am so uneasy. It's as though heavy heavy hangs over my head. And yet, the more I think about it, the more I am compelled to undertake Joan."

"You're too old for it, but then, you were too old for *Camille* and you were brilliant."

"Too old, too old. Ah me, soon I will be at an age where there will be very little available for me to play. In three years I'll be forty. What will I do then?"

"In three years there may not be a world existing, so take hold of the present and with both hands. What you need is a lover."

"Oh God no." Garbo's voice was so powerful a chandelier shook. "I have my hands full coping with myself."

"What about Guiss? Have you met him yet?"

"No, but I have made discreet inquiries. There are those who find him above suspicion. And there are others who consider him beneath contempt. Why should I care about Guiss? He's the financing, I'm the artist. I am so torn. It hurts me so to feel that Hollywood is turning its back on me."

Mercedes snorted. "Why do you give a damn? Hollywood is only a state of mind where insincerity is an art."

"I will have no friends."

"You can always buy new ones."

"That's cruel."

"That's Hollywood. Do the movie."

Garbo brightened. She needed to hear the woman's support. She respected de Acosta, who had a quick mind and remarkable taste and a unique talent for friendship. She wrote well too, but had yet to equal Salka Viertel's success. Salka and de Acosta had a guarded friendship, colored by their possessiveness toward Garbo. Garbo was the important thing they had in common. They worshipped her, they treasured her, their lives were all the better for knowing her.

Garbo was happy, and when she was happy she looked a decade younger. "You really want me to do it? You really do?"

"Absolutely. Think, Greta. You'll be working. You'll have a reason to eagerly greet the morning, to get up and go to the studio and reign like the queen you are. Believe me, my beloved Greta, you'll never be equaled. You will be the legend they will speak of in cathedral tones."

"Could I become a saint?" Garbo's hands were clasped as she watched an inquisitive pigeon make a three-point landing on the balcony.

"Why not?"

Garbo smiled. "There's a pigeon on your balcony. Do you suppose it has brought a message?"

"It's brought filth is what it's brought. Shoo, you filthy thing," Mercedes cried as she clickety-clacked onto the balcony in a pair of absurd shoes in which she could barely maintain her balance. The pigeon stared at her in defiance for a few seconds, then flew to the railing and, with a haughty toss of its head, soared off in search of hospitality elsewhere.

The doorbell rang, and Garbo was annoyed. "You didn't tell me you were expecting anyone else."

"I'm not. It might be the concierge with the mail. He usually brings it up himself. Now stop fretting and pour yourself some more coffee. It's pretty damned good this morning if I must say so myself." She opened the door. "Alysia!"

"You're surprised? Did you forget you invited me for coffee?"

"Oh my God. Forgive me! It completely went out of my head. Greta needed some advice on a script and . . ."

"I could come back later, if you like." The woman was in her forties and her clothes would have been stylish a few years earlier. She nervously clutched a threadbare handbag and her shoes were badly in need of repair. Her accent, Garbo decided, was definitely German, and her voice was brimming with sadness and disappointment. Garbo was on her feet and said generously:

"Mercedes! Bring your friend inside. There's plenty of coffee for all of us."

Mercedes smiled the smile that had enchanted so many lovers. "Come in, Alysia. Greta's in a sunny mood. Let's make the most of it. It's an historical moment." The woman followed Mercedes into the living room, where Garbo stood with a warm smile decorating her lips.

Oh good, thought Garbo, she's as tall as I am. This could be a sign, a reversal of my fortunes. "Hello," said Garbo, "I'm Greta," as though the woman needed to be reminded.

Mercedes took over. "Greta, Alysia Hoffman is an old friend of mine."

Garbo gasped. "Alysia Hoffman! But of course! How stupid of me not to recognize you! We were in *Gösta Berling's Saga* together in Sweden!"

Hoffman laughed. "You remember! Oh how wonderful!" She said

to Mercedes, "Mine was such a small role I'm flattered Greta remembers me. And Mauritz Stiller, who directed, was so good to us all."

At the mention of Stiller's name, Garbo's face darkened. Mercedes saw the change at once and asked, "What's wrong?"

Garbo swiftly smiled again. "Oh, nothing. I still get sad when I hear Stiller's name. Even though he's now dead over a decade, I still remember how badly he was treated here." She said to Alysia, "When Metro wanted him back in 1925, he wouldn't sign the contract unless they took me too." She sat, and Alysia sat across from her. Mercedes brought a cup and saucer for the new arrival, and the three became cozy around the coffee table. "He was so brave and so foolish, we were both so broke, we couldn't pay our hotel bill." She laughed. "But after many delays, *Gösta* finally opened, and at last Stiller got the acclaim he deserved. And Louis B. Mayer, wouldn't you know, was in Berlin at the time and made him an offer. But Stiller loved me. . . ."

"I thought he was a homosexual," interrupted Alysia.

"But not seriously. He only dabbled in it. You know, the way you occasionally dip into a collection of essays. Mauritz loved me and only me. He wanted to marry me. I was so innocent and so *fat.*" The three laughed. "I really was, how do you say, *zaftig.* When Mayer finally agreed to take me, I had to agree to lose fifteen pounds. I lost twenty. When I got to Hollywood and saw how Stiller was being mistreated, I lost my appetite. I became an insomniac. I tried to fall asleep by counting producers." She looked past the two women, out the window, past the balcony, into the blue beyond where memories were surfacing from a long dormant suppression. "Then I met Yonnie."

"John Gilbert," Mercedes interpreted for Alysia.

"Oh well, that's all water under the bridge. So tell me, Alysia, how long have you been here in America?" Garbo was genuinely interested.

Alysia placed her cup and saucer on the table. "I came in through Mexico. That was over half a year ago. It wasn't easy, but a friend had a friend who was very influential, and I finally got my visa."

A friend had a friend who was very influential, thought Garbo, and was disturbed that her mind had conjured up Albert Guiss. "And are you acting?" Just as quickly as she asked the question, she regretted it. She could see the poor woman was enduring sorry straits.

"I'm trying to act. I've had two bit parts, but two bit parts can hardly sustain a career. It's not easy, after having graduated to leading roles in Germany. I played opposite Connie Veidt, Jannings, Werner Krauss."

Garbo said quickly, "Don't mention Connie's name in the same breath as the other two. They're Nazis."

Alysia spread her hands and said softly, "To me, it is more important that they are artists. Anyway, now I do part-time work. I sit for babies, I help a seamstress—thank God my mother taught me how to sew. Do you have anything that needs repairing? I could give you a special price."

Garbo was embarrassed. Having known poverty in her youth, she didn't care to deal with the poverty of others. She said, surprisingly enough, "We must try and find you something in my new movie."

Mercedes smiled. That was it. She must phone Salka and Peter Lorre. Garbo positively will play Joan.

Alysia Hoffman's eyes were misting. "What is your new movie?"

Mercedes swung into action. When enthusiastic she was a dynamo. In less than three minutes, Alysia Hoffman heard about the movie, the director, and who would probably be in it, and Alysia was enthralled.

Alysia said to Garbo, "Perhaps I could be your stand-in. We're the same height, we have similar coloring. . . ."

"Wouldn't you rather be in front of the camera?" asked an astonished Garbo.

The woman replied pragmatically, "A stand-in works through the time it takes to shoot the film. A part," she said wistfully, "that could be a matter of perhaps a few weeks, or even a few days."

Garbo thundered, "This is von Stroheim directing. The film will take an eternity. We shall watch each other growing older under his despotic direction." She laughed. "Every day we'll examine each other's faces for fresh wrinkles. My frown marks shall deepen into ditches and I shall develop an ulcer."

"Charming," said Mercedes dryly. "That attitude won't get you very far."

"Don't worry about me, Mercedes," said Garbo, "you should understand my strange sense of humor by now. After all, even though I'm a Swede, don't they call me The Melancholy Dame? Not very funny, is it. Well, go to it, Mercedes."

"Go to what?"

"To the phone and dial Salka and Peter Lorre and probably von Stroheim, and you hadn't forgotten you had invited Alysia for coffee this morning, as she was needed to underline the sadness of the refugee actor. . . ."

"Don't be cruel, Greta," snapped Mercedes.

"I am not being cruel. I'm glad my mind is made up." She rose to go. "Alysia, you will soon be working in the studio. I promise you that, although I'm sure the promise was made by someone else in line ahead of me."

The woman stood up. "I'm sorry. I didn't mean to offend you."

"But I'm not offended at all. I think it's very funny—ha ha ha. Now I must go and immerse myself in Joan of Arc." She marched to the door. She opened the door and then faced Alysia with a smile that was almost beatific. "Really, I'm delighted my mind was made up for me. Now I have a purpose for the next six or seven months." And this was followed by a heavy sigh. "But oh God! What do I do after that?" She slammed the door shut behind her.

Alysia Hoffman said, "Isn't she amazing?"

Mercedes replied, "She likes to think so. Well Alysia, that was a lovely performance on your part. What would you have done if she had offered to bring you an armload of dresses for repairing?"

"Repaired them. I really *can* sew. You wouldn't have an onion roll in the kitchen, by any chance?"

A few hours later, Herbert Villon and Arnold Lake were lunching in a Chinese restaurant with Lisa Schmidt. Lake couldn't take his eyes off the woman, he found her beauty so breathtaking. He found the courage to ask, "Why didn't you try acting?"

"What . . . and starve to death?" She watched Villon shoveling moo goo gai pan into his mouth with a pair of chopsticks. "You know, Arnold, you asked me that very same question over a year ago when I first joined the department."

"I don't remember."

"Understandable. You were so drunk. It was in your apartment, about ten minutes before you tried to rape me."

"I didn't!"

She smiled at Villon. "He did. But I made it easy for him, he was so adorable."

"I still am," said Arnold.

Villon had stopped eating and now drank of Lisa's beauty. "A cutie like you shouldn't take such chances."

"Live dangerously, that was my father's motto. He was a high-wire walker with the circus."

"And now the daughter walks the high wires," said Villon, "figuratively speaking."

Arnold asked Lisa, "When do you start work for von Stroheim?"

"Tomorrow, you'll be happy to know."

"Whether they've got Garbo or not?"

"Von . . ." She smiled. "He asked me to call him that when he patted my knee. Von. Anyway, Von is positive she's going to do it. All the big guns are aimed at her and this morning she was getting an opinion from her friend Mercedes de Acosta, who has been primed to convince her to do the film. What's bothering you, Arnold?"

"I think Miss Garbo is about to be in very grave danger," said Arnold. Villon dropped the toothpick he'd been using to excavate between his teeth. "They're too anxious to get her, and only her."

"She's a very big name," said Lisa, "even if her last movie was a dud. The picture stands to make a fortune in Europe once the war ends. Albert Guiss can certainly afford to wait to recoup his investment."

Arnold asked, "Can you trust Guiss's secretary?"

"Trust Martin? As much as you can trust any paid informant. Martin has the morals of an alley cat. He's apparently very good at his job or Guiss wouldn't have him. It's the first time he's had a male secretary. Before Martin, they were always women."

"What made Guiss switch?" asked Villon.

"From what Martin could gather, a couple of them sold information to magazines and newspapers, and I know one had a fling with him and then died during the abortion. Anyway, Martin's been with him several years now and let's be grateful . . . ," she smiled coquettishly, ". . . that he also appreciates my beauty."

"Be careful he doesn't cross you," warned Arnold.

"Let him try. I'll separate him from his privates. Anyone for tea, gentlemen?"

Samuel Goldwyn's studios were in the heart of Hollywood on Santa Monica Boulevard, and Goldwyn was happy to rent space to independent producers. It was here that *Joan the Magnificent* would be shooting. Goldwyn had rented them space on a three-month lease with monthly renewals.

In his well-appointed office, Goldwyn said to his faithful assistant, Sophie Gang, "You better believe me, Sophie, this lease with Albert Guiss is going to be an annuity. He has to have a shoe loose in his head to let von Stroheim direct."

"Von better not get wind of how you feel about him. He can become very nasty."

"Oh yes? If I hear he said something off-color about me I'll sue him for defecation of character. You better believe me, I'll swear that on a stack of bubbles. Now let's get back to business. What's next on the magenta?"

Sophie's eyes crossed and then just as quickly uncrossed. "Gary Cooper isn't crazy about playing Lou Gehrig."

"Goddammit!" roared Goldwyn. "That Gary is becoming a milestone around my neck!" He pushed his chair back from the desk and crossed to the window. He drank of his kingdom and once again felt content. "Thank God I own this studio lox stocks and barren. It's my Garden of Eden, Sophie. My paradox."

The *Joan the Magnificent* company occupied a large suite of offices on the Goldwyn lot. In Erich von Stroheim's freshly painted, redecorated and refurnished office, the director was pacing the room attacking the air with a riding crop. He wore magnificently tailored jodhpurs and a brown turtleneck sweater that made him look even shorter than he was. Greta Garbo sat in an easy chair, wearing beautifully tailored navy blue slacks, a pink blouse and a beret arranged devilishly on her head. Lisa Schmidt, soberly dressed in a skirt and blouse, with her hair pulled back and kept in place with a blue barrette, sat in a chair next to von Stroheim's oversized desk and took notes.

"Noted and agreed," dictated von Stroheim, "Miss Garbo is to have Adrian design her one outfit required for the role of Joan."

Garbo formed a bridge with her fingers. "Why aren't the producers here?"

"They aren't necessary. They're just figureheads. *I, von Stroheim,*" he said, beating the air mercilessly with the riding crop, "am the real producer of this epic. Now what else?"

"There's an actress named Alysia Hoffman. I want her for my stand-in."

Von Stroheim stopped in his tracks. "I usually choose the stand-ins."

Garbo said firmly, her chin rigid, "I want her."

Von Stroheim asked sternly, "Is she the right height? Is her coloring favorable?"

"Yes and yes." Garbo snapped each word. She could see Lisa Schmidt was relishing this test of wills. Two Olympians locked in combat; she was delighted.

"Have her come in and see me. Miss Schmidt," he barked her name, "set an interview with this Alysia Hoffman."

"You may set the interview, because you certainly should meet her, but I won't appear on the set if she is not my stand-in."

"Miss Garbo! You have signed a contract!"

Miss Garbo, thought Lisa, not Greta? We *are* annoyed.

"Miss Garbo wants Miss Hoffman. And if Miss Garbo doesn't have Miss Hoffman," she said, shifting in her chair for emphasis, "Miss Garbo shall be taken severely ill and confined to her home."

She raised her voice. "It doesn't matter a damn who's my stand-in."

"It most certainly matters to me! Everything in my productions must be perfection!"

"I have no use for perfectionists. They never accomplish anything, they're so preoccupied with being perfect. Oh let's get on to other matters. I've been invited to dine with Guiss tonight and I'm not looking forward to being on exhibition."

"You are his star. You owe him the courtesy of dining with him."

"Wealthy people make me uncomfortable. I'm sure he's a megalomaniac, a monomaniac and a Seventh-Day Adventist." She propped her chin on the palm of a hand. "This project is beginning to fill me with a disturbing melancholy. I can't work if I'm not happy."

Lisa watched von Stroheim's face. It was chiseled in stone. Then, quite suddenly, it was wreathed in a smile that was as genuine as a four-dollar bill. "All right, Greta. You shall have your Alysia Hoffman." He turned his back on her and crossed to a window. Garbo looked at Lisa and winked. "Alysia Hoffman. Wasn't she pretty big in Germany years ago?"

"Yes, she was pretty big."

"She's now willing to be a stand-in?"

"She's poverty-stricken. She has put her pride in mothballs. Maybe you could also give her a part. It would be a blessing."

"Yes. I'll see what I can do. I'm sorry I made such an unnecessary fuss."

"That's all right, I enjoyed the exercise. Shall we continue?"

Garbo's return to films made headlines across the nation. Hedda Hopper and Louella Parsons were almost hospitalized with the gastronomic disturbances brought on by having to eat their words. Louis B. Mayer, in a rage at the news, decided to cancel several contracts, and so Joan Crawford, the formidable Norma Shearer and Myrna Loy were soon to join the exodus from the lot. Newspaper editors were almost buried under a mountain of letters decrying the profligacy of a five-million-dollar budget for a film in these dire times. Garbo was criticized in several quarters for accepting the one-million-dollar fee, though she had every intention of donating a large percentage to several war agencies—except the Red Cross because she didn't like the color. The Internal Revenue Service was drooling at the prospect of the taxes it would collect from all participants in *Joan the Magnificent*.

In Herb Villon's office, he and Arnold Lake carefully studied the personnel lists clandestinely slipped to them by Lisa Schmidt with every name submitted to Washington for security clearances, regardless of their standing in the industry. Arnold lit a cigarette and asked Villon, "Why do you suppose Garbo was so adamant about getting Alysia Hoffman as her stand-in?"

"You heard what Lisa said. A clash of wills. Score one for the great Garbo."

"They aren't great buddies. Garbo knew her briefly in Sweden back in '25. Until the de Acosta broad brought them together again, they hadn't been in touch."

"Garbo isn't big on being in touch."

Arnold blew a smoke ring. "Nineteen twenty-five. Garbo's in Germany making a movie, *The Joyless Street*. Nineteen twenty-five. Hitler's Nazi party is emerging on the political scene."

"Now come on, Arnold, you're not trying to tell me you suspect some kind of a link then? She was young, naive, an innocent kid of twenty. She knew from nothing. She's even apolitical today. She doesn't vote."

"She can't. She's not a citizen."

"Oh."

"Oh. I'm not accusing the lady of anything. I'm just thinking out loud. Anything's a possibility in the espionage racket. So she's finally getting to meet Guiss tonight."

"Yeah. Dinner at his Bel Air mansion. Very secluded, highly guarded."

"Just the two of them?"

Villon referred to a memo on his desk, information from Lisa Schmidt by way of Martin Gruber. "There's to be Guiss's girlfriend, Risa Barron. Then there's the guy who's supposed to be co-producing, Werner Lieb. Figureheads, of course. Von Stroheim has already made it quite clear that he's in charge."

"They sat still for that? No ego problems?"

"Not according to Lisa, and that girl of yours is good, she's very good," said Villon.

"Strange. Still, these are only the preliminaries. Let's see how they behave when the actual shooting is underway. Who else?"

"Gustav Henkel, who wrote the first script." Villon rubbed his chin.

"There's a second script?"

"It's in the works now. Bertolt Brecht's writing it."

"What's a Bertolt Brecht?" asked Arnold.

"Brilliant German writer. *The Threepenny Opera* and a couple of others."

"What's *The Threepenny Opera?*"

"I don't know. I never saw it. And then there's William Haines."

"The movie comic? He hasn't been heard from in years. Where'd he crop up from?"

"After he was washed up in pictures eight years ago . . . too many boys. . . ."

"One of *them?*" Arnold might have been alluding to an alien from outer space.

"Right. He took to interior decorating, and thanks to Joan Craw-ford, who gave him his first crack at it, he's found a whole new career for himself. He's one of the few guys Garbo ever spends any time with."

Arnold asked, "What about the secretary, Martin Gruber? Do you think he'll be in attendance?"

"Very much so."

"That's good. I don't trust him."

"That's good and you don't trust him. So what's good about it?"

"It's good because he passes on the word to Lisa."

"For a nice price."

"And it's bad," elucidated Arnold, "because informers are rats to begin with and I don't trust any of them. Somewhere along the line he'll foul up."

"Maybe he won't."

"All informers foul up sooner or later. They get too cocksure and they then slip up. Guiss has run through an impressive list of secretaries, not one of whom came to a good end except one broad named Ilse Koch who's running a concentration camp in Germany." He rubbed out the cigarette in an ashtray. "It'll happen to Gruber. Sooner or later he'll make a dumb move. They always do." He shook his head sadly. "They always do. Aren't any of the picture's big hitters invited?"

"You mean von Stroheim or any of the cast? Not as of this memo from Lisa. I think Guiss wants Garbo all to himself. He's a big fan of hers. He drools at the very mention of her name. Come to think of it, what wouldn't I give to be there myself?"

Six

It was later that afternoon when von Stroheim had his meeting with Alysia Hoffman. Lisa Schmidt had efficiently tracked down the actress after getting her phone number from Mercedes de Acosta, and the shrewd de Acosta had advised Alysia to stay home near her phone, foreseeing an imminent summons to meet the Emperor von Stroheim.

Still pretty, thought Lisa as the receptionist ushered Alysia into the office. The crow's feet are beginning to appear around the lips, the eyes have a strange hardness, probably brought on by the hell she must have gone through getting out of Europe, but her height and her coloring are right.

Von Stroheim was surprisingly gentle with her and the actress was admirably composed. "You are an old friend of Greta's?" He was slapping the riding crop gently against the palm of a hand. Alysia told him they first met in Sweden nineteen years ago when she had traveled from Germany, where work was scarce, to see if there were opportunities in the burgeoning Swedish film industry.

"You speak Swedish?"

"In silents it didn't matter," she said with a smile. "Once my career shifted into high gear, I made films all over Europe. France, Italy, Austria. We all did."

"Of course," said von Stroheim. "I myself had many offers, but I was too busy here then. So you want to be Greta's stand-in."

"I need the job."

"Your height and your coloring are right. You agree, Schmidt?"

Lisa considered saluting him but swiftly thought better of it. "I think Miss Hoffman would be perfect."

"Women." He spat the word contemptuously. "You always stick together."

"I wouldn't take that as gospel," said Lisa slyly. She could see the actress was now uneasy.

"Don't be impertinent." His eyes shifted back to Alysia. "Miss Garbo suggests it might be generous on my part to also find a supporting role for you in the film."

"She's so kind."

Von Stroheim refrained from making an ugly comment about the star, still bristling over her firm demand that Alysia be hired as her stand-in. "There's a small but interesting part that you might be right for. A heretic, a follower of Joan. She gets stoned to death by a mob." He said it with such relish, Lisa expected him to cackle with glee.

"I know I can handle it."

"Of course you can." He was on his feet and pacing. "But remember this, I'm a fanatic where realism is concerned. I plan to use *real* stones." He bent over, his face against hers. "*Real* stones. You don't flinch? You don't protest? You don't say thank you very much but I'll remain behind the cameras? I don't frighten you?"

"Mr. von Stroheim," she said calmly, evenly, in a voice that won Lisa's admiration, "after what I've been through these past two years, nothing can frighten me."

He was back behind his desk. "I am satisfied. You are hired. Miss Schmidt will make the necessary arrangements. You will have the shooting schedule a week before we will begin."

"And when is that?" She couldn't disguise her anxiety. Lisa wondered if she ought to offer to lend her a fiver.

"That will be decided within the next few days. We only moved into the studio at the beginning of the week. We are still casting. And I'm awaiting the decision as to whether or not we shoot in Technicolor." He said with gusto, "Can you imagine what Technicolor will do to enhance the battlefields? Rivers of real red blood flowing past the dead and dying, the agonizing cries of the horses as they are brought down and crippled, the geysers erupting from decapitated bodies, oh by Christ this will win me the Academy Award those bastard cretins have denied me for years!"

Lisa Schmidt excused herself and hurried to the bathroom to throw up.

"Lottie." Garbo spoke her housekeeper's name gravely. Garbo was in her Spartan bedroom sipping a cup of bouillon, preparing to bathe and dress for Guiss's dinner party. Her housekeeper was laying out the ensemble Garbo had chosen to wear. "The coming months may be very difficult for you."

Lottie looked up from the slipper she was polishing. She said quickly, "Nothing is easy, I always say."

"Ah Lottie, so you are a philosopher!"

"Miss Garbo, from the time I decided to go into service, I knew there'd be a rough go ahead of me. Do you mind if I tell you how I feel about myself and others in my position?"

"But no, of course not. It would be such a privilege!" She might have just heard she'd won the Irish Sweepstakes.

"Well, ma'am. I think we're unique. It takes a special kind of person with a special kind of personality to decide to wait on others. You know what I mean? Maids, butlers, housekeepers, we're special. And good ones are damned hard to find, as you well knew when I finally landed on your doorstep."

"Oh how well I knew. You have been so good to me, Lottie."

"And you've been good to me, ma'am, and very generous. I'm the only domestic in Santa Monica who owns a frayed chinchilla opera wrap." She smiled, which she did infrequently. "I love parading around in it in my bedroom."

"Oh I'm so glad you like it. I wore it in *The Temptress,* oh, so many years ago. . . . It was a silent movie."

"I know. I saw it. You were great." She cleared her throat. "You see, we go through hell when we're interviewed for jobs. When I came here two years ago . . ."

"Is it that long we're together?"

"Yes ma'am, two years. I remember telling my parole officer, 'Garbo'll never hire me. When she hears I did time in San Q. she'll get turned off.' "

"But I didn't, did I? I was so fascinated! To have someone working for me who had the courage to poison her husband." Garbo's hands were clasped and the look on her face was sheer ecstasy.

"Poison. The son of a bitch took forever to die."

"Oh you have found that out too? How difficult it is to rid ourselves of people who no longer amuse us. Oh, if only I had your courage. How you must have agonized before finally lacing his soup and cocoa. . . ."

"Hot chocolate."

"How you must have agonized before deciding to kill him."

"I didn't agonize at all. The only thing that drove me nuts was how long it took him to die. Of course I'd read up on poisons and then it was hell getting enough of it to prove fatal. He would just slurp and slurp and ask for seconds and I tell you, that was so damned frustrating! I really began to get this feeling of inadequacy. I mean some friends were with me when he suddenly looked up from my special lentil and split pea number . . . the bacon and the thinly sliced leeks are what do the trick," she winked conspiratorially, "and he gasped, 'Holy shit!' and fell face down into the soup. Well I was so relieved I said, 'Well it's about time' and my big mouth did me in. Anyway, I had a real shrewd lawyer—Isadore Marino, half wop, half Jew—and he saved my neck. Anyway, you were saying? The road ahead's going to be a tough one to travel?"

"Yes. A very tough one. Joan is a very difficult character to interpret, and von Stroheim is a very difficult man to work with. And I must cope with this strange smorgasbord of co-producers and writers and musicians and refugee actors, all of them undoubtedly with a method all their own. *Ach* God how we shall clash!"

"My money's on you, Miss Garbo." Lottie was attacking the slipper with fresh gusto.

"Is it really?"

"Miss G., when you're on the screen, everybody else gets wiped off."

Garbo was sad. "Not always. Constance Bennett stole my last film from me. And she's such a terrible person."

"It was such a terrible picture. Oops. Sorry."

Garbo laughed. "Don't be sorry. Your honesty is refreshing." She looked at her wristwatch. "I must start dressing. The car will be here soon."

"You've got plenty of time. It's picking up Mr. Haines first. He's miles from here."

"And now they tell me the film will be in Technicolor. I have never filmed in Technicolor. I will insist on tests. Technicolor is for musicals. I must make sure I do not look like Betty Grable." She crossed to her floor-length mirror and stood with her back to it. Then she looked over her shoulder at her mirror image, a familiar Grable pinup pose. After a few moments she was satisfied she would never look like Betty Grable.

Guido's was an unprepossessing and inexpensive Italian restaurant near the Goldwyn Studios. In a quiet booth toward the rear of the establishment, Lisa Schmidt sat having dinner with Alysia Hoffman, both having settled on veal piccata and spaghetti.

"This is so good," yummy-yummed Alysia. "How really kind of you to invite me to dinner."

Lisa twirled pasta on her fork. "To be perfectly honest, I didn't have anything else to do and I was in no mood to sit around my apartment reading Fannie Hurst. Anyway, I like the way you handled von Bastard."

"Is he really all that terrible?"

"I'm sure it's mostly affectation. He's still living back in the old days when he made his masterpieces, even though the studios butchered them."

"Still, how many directors have been capable of those masterpieces. *Greed* is soul-stirring."

"Are you Jewish?"

"What?" Alysia almost dropped her fork. Lisa's steady gaze never left her companion's face. "Jewish? Me, not at all."

"Then why did you have to leave Germany? You're still a big star there. Why give up your career to go through an exile's hell?"

Alysia sipped some Chianti. "How do I make you understand?"

"It's not important, really. I mean I'm a nosy bitch and I know I ask too many questions. . . ."

"No no no no. It's a perfectly valid . . . valid, is that right? Valid?"

"Perfectly valid." The veal was stringy.

"Good. It's a perfectly valid question. You see, Lisa, Jews are not the only refugees fleeing Hitler. I was . . . how do you put it? Yes a rebel, a firebrand. I rebelled against the Nazis and what they stand for. And I was very outspoken. Foolishly, I suppose."

"I think you have guts you haven't used yet, Alysia."

"Guts?"

"A colloquialism for strength, bravery."

"Ah yes. How nice. Thank you. So I was outspoken and I started to get into trouble. Goebbels, who has control of the movie industry, warned me time and again about my overactive mouth. Well, I thought I was big enough a star to pooh-pooh his threats. But *ach* no. Soon I was being followed, my mail was being opened, and they investigated lovers who might have been yids and some of course were. . . ."

Lisa placed her fork quietly on her plate and studied the woman who was talking and eating ravenously.

"And then they were questioning my friends."

"What about your family?" asked Lisa.

"I have no family. I was married back in '26 but that didn't last very long. I haven't the vaguest idea where he is now. His name was Heinrich, he was a prize fighter."

"Like Max Schmeling?"

"Oh not so good, though Schmeling has capitulated to the Nazis, I heard, when I was in Mexico."

"It must have been hell getting to Mexico."

"Of course first I tried to get a visa into the States, but I was rejected. I made a deal to do a movie in Spain for Franco, a terrible script but it was a good excuse to get me out of Germany. While in Spain, I had an offer to do a film at the Cherubusco Studios in Mexico City with Luis Buñuel. You've heard of him?"

"Yes. He's brilliant."

"Well, this film never got made. But it wasn't cancelled until after I arrived in Mexico City, so I was safe. The authorities let me stay. But there were no more offers of work. My money was running out and soon I was scratching about to survive. It wasn't easy."

"But it helped improve your Spanish."

Alysia laughed. "I was already fluent in Spanish. I was always very good with languages. Soon my English will be better, no?"

"I'm sure it will be. Dessert?"

"Oh I don't think I have room!"

"You've got to try Guido's zabaglione. It's one of the few things on the menu he doesn't have to be ashamed of. Go ahead and order, I have to call an actor I've been trying to get in for an interview tomorrow. Order me a pot of espresso, honey."

Alysia lit a cigarette as she watched Lisa cross to the wall telephone on the opposite side of the room. So beautiful, she was thinking, so very beautiful. Somehow she seems miscast in the role of von Stroheim's assistant. Still, it was good to be friendly with her. She had learned soon after her arrival, you can never have enough friends in Hollywood.

William Haines, former MGM star and now a successful interior decorator, couldn't contain his enthusiasm for the young man chauffeuring this splendid limousine. And it was splendid indeed. There was an impressively stocked bar and a small refrigerator with hors d'oeuvres, peanuts and pretzels, several decks of cards, a checkers set and a chess set and a Parcheesi game. And there was the young man propelling the car smoothly on the road to Garbo's home in Santa Monica. That profile, those broad shoulders, a splendid youth, even if his accent was by way of the Katzenjammer Kids.

Haines crossed a leg and began his campaign. "What's your name?"

"Ludwig."

"Like in Beethoven?"

"Oh yes, sure."

"How long you been in this country?"

"Not long."

This is hard work, thought Haines. But quite a challenge to an old campaigner. "How long have you been driving for Mr. Guiss?"

"Long time."

"Oh. So you worked for him in Europe."

"Long time I leave Europe."

Haines thought, Get your story straight kid, I'm not. He was beginning to enjoy himself. "Since you're not long in this country and you've been driving a long time for Guiss, what have you been doing in between?"

"Driving."

Smart cookie, thought Haines. "Is that all you do? Drive?"

"I only drive."

"Don't you ever putt?"

"Pardon."

"Forget it. Inside joke." He slumped down in the seat. He was looking forward to seeing Garbo but not looking forward to the cast of characters he suspected would be their dinner companions. Like anyone else with a healthy inquisitive nature, he was glad for the opportunity of a firsthand look at Albert Guiss. He was glad Garbo was going to do Joan, because there was something he wanted her to try and do for him.

He hated asking another favor. After his fall from grace eight years earlier when Mayer set out to destroy his career and his credibility in Hollywood (I wonder if the old bastard ever found out I serviced Gable a few times?), Garbo had been one of the few people who had come forward on his behalf. At the time he had thought she was barely aware of his existence. They'd been working on the same lot for almost ten years, but never once did she say a word to him when they passed each other. True, she was aloof to just about everybody else in the studio ("She's very shy, Bill. Don't be upset.") but after all, didn't she appreciate he was Metro's court jester? Always clowning around, always saying campy, outrageous things about everyone and anyone, until he himself was the butt of cruel laughter and derision.

Joan Crawford had always been a pal and remained steadfast. Of all people, Norma Shearer, wife of the powerful Irving Thalberg, went out of her way to ask him to their parties despite her husband's admonitions. But the morning Garbo called and invited him to lunch, *that* was overwhelming. Thinking about it now it brought tears of sentiment to his eyes. She'd invited Marion Davies, Salka Viertel and Mercedes de Acosta and they all got high on gin and orange juice. And thanks to Davies, there were kind words in Louella Parsons's column a few days later that he was now busy considering offers from independent producers. Independent indeed. Poverty Row. And he did a few quickies because he needed the money. Greta had come through, another of her occasional contradictions. She wasn't an iceberg. She did have a heart. He once saw her pat a gatekeeper's little boy on the head. That must have taken quite a bit of courage on her part.

"What? What did you say?" The chauffeur had penetrated his reverie.

"We're here. Miss Garbo's."

"Oh. Well that was fast. I'll go get her." As he opened the limousine door he said over his shoulder, "Now don't you be funny and drive away or I'll cry."

The chauffeur watched Haines cross to Garbo's front door and press the doorbell. Under his breath he voiced a vicious epithet and then sat back, dreaming of returning to Germany and the war, dreaming of the glory that would be his when he would decimate the enemy with bullets and bayonets and hand grenades and his bad breath.

"Oh Billy, darling, Billy, why are we going to this suffocating dinner party?" She was sipping vodka on the rocks and Lottie was ready for him with his usual scotch highball.

"Because you have to and I'll be your immoral support." He raised his glass high. "Here's to absent friends."

"That is so sad," said Garbo. "It makes me think of obituaries. The first thing, Billy, the first thing I read in the newspaper is the obituaries." Her face was wreathed in a pained expression. "Do you read the obituaries too?"

"I'd be dead without them."

"Have you noticed lately how many obscure nobodies are dying? It shouldn't be permitted. Shall we be fashionably late to the dinner?"

"Yes. Come sit by me." She joined him on the couch. "Sweetie, you've been a wonderful friend."

"Oh please."

"You have. And I'm remembering you in my will."

She laughed. "Please don't. I have so much of my own. Leave it all to your boyfriends!"

"Those ungrateful sons of bitches? Let them all starve to death. Now let's get serious."

"And Roebucks?" He glared at her. "Don't you like my little joke?"

He patted her hand. "It's adorable. Let's be selfish and keep it to ourselves."

"I should never tell jokes. Salka always says I don't know how to tell a joke. You're getting impatient with me. Don't. I'm very nervous about this dinner. I'm very nervous about the whole project. I've made a terrible mistake and I can't back out. If only I was capable of a nervous breakdown."

"Greta, please listen. I'm doing so well with the decorating that now I'd like a chance to branch out."

"Branch out? But where?"

"Set dressing. Let Cedric Gibbons and the rest design the sets, but let me choose the furniture and the decorations. Don't you think I'd be great at it?"

"Oh Billy. You could be great at anything you choose to be. You could be president of the United States if you weren't so odd."

He took her hand. "Speak to them about me. Maybe they'll give me a chance."

"You mean von Stroheim? God." She was up and pacing. "I've already defeated him on the hiring of Alysia Hoffman." She told him about the Hoffman problem that had been decided in her favor. "Now you ask me to defy the dragon in his cave again." The look on his face was now so little-boy-lost, she put her drink down and threw her arms around him. "I enjoy defying the dragon. It stimulates my adrenalin. I will do it for you, Billy." She withdrew her arms, looked at her wristwatch, and stood up with her arms outstretched. "How do I look?"

"Sensational."

"You think the cut of the back is not too daring?" There was no back and it was indeed daring.

"There are them in which it could bring on a heart attack."

"I will fascinate Albert Guiss?"

"From what I can gather, he's already fascinated. Interested in landing yourself a mysterious billionaire?"

"I don't know." Lottie held the front door open for them. "I have to see what he's like in person. I must study him very carefully. I must converse with him. And he already has a mistress."

"I'm sure there's room for one more."

"Ha ha ha ha. Don't wait up for me, Lottie. I'm not sure when we'll be back. If God is good, it will be early. So darling, just set out a glass of milk and some Hydrox for me."

ᏚᎬᏉᎬᏁ

Ihe atmosphere was charged with electricity. Garbo felt it the minute the massive front doors swung inward to admit her and Haines. She had felt it when the limousine drove up the road leading to the castle, and it was surely a castle, in the exclusive Bel Air compound. When they reached the wrought-iron gates that protected Guiss's castle from unwanted invasions, an electric eye found them and triggered the gates to open. Haines was surprised there were no armed guards. On the other hand, the ramparts and turrets of the magnificently imposing structure could easily camouflage any number of dangerous gunmen.

Garbo commented with equanimity, "Very impressive." She had had her share of castles. She had portrayed Sweden's Queen Christina. The limousine parked at the bottom of a wide flight of stone stairs.

Haines counted thirteen as they ascended. Sweet. Somebody isn't superstitious. And then the massive doors swung inward. There was no burst of organ music and Haines was disappointed. But there was a butler and six footmen and four maids and Haines wondered if they had been choreographed.

Surely the butler was from Central Casting, a replica of the celebrated character actor Gustav von Seyffertitz. His accent was pure Herman Bing, Bing being an actor who played mostly comedy waiters. The manner in which he directed the footmen and maids had to be a God-given gift. His name was Kriegman and when Garbo was curious about his origins he told her his family originated in East Prussia.

Kriegman led them up a long flight of richly carpeted stairs, surrounded on both sides by tapestries whose values she was sure had to be estimated in six figures or more. She whispered to Haines, "A bit ostentatious, don't you think?"

Haines nodded and wisecracked out of the side of his mouth, "The big showoff. What do you bet the main dish is frankfurters and sauerkraut."

"Oh I do hope so!" she said with sincere enthusiasm, "I do hope so."

Haines asked her, "Where'd he get the extras holding the spears?"

The spear holders loomed ahead of them standing on each side of a set of double doors to which Kriegman was leading them. They wore black uniforms trimmed in gold braid, and Haines wondered when a soprano and a tenor would appear. As the three approached the doors, the guardsmen became animated and swung the doors open. Garbo suppressed a gasp. The huge room was a dazzling display of somebody's magnificent taste.

"I'm jealous," said Haines.

Garbo knew at once that the tall, elegant, impeccably dressed man approaching her with arms outstretched was Albert Guiss. "We meet at last," he said in a voice meant to be seductive. "I'm Albert Guiss." He kissed both her hands. "I see you are overwhelmed by the decor, but you dwarf it all with your own special brilliance."

What a line, thought Haines, I'll bet it has caught a lot of fish. He could see Garbo was somewhat hypnotized.

"Mr. Guiss . . ."

"Oh please. You must call me Albert."

"And you must call me Greta." Her teeth sparkled like her smile. "I want you to meet my friend, William Haines."

"You must call me Billy," said Haines with his celebrated smirk which some innocents accepted as a smile.

Guiss stepped between them and took Greta by her right arm and Haines by his left, and guided them to the other guests. "Here Greta, seated on the love seat, are your two producers, my watchdogs, heh heh. Risa Barron and Werner Lieb."

Lieb stood up and bowed stiffly from the waist. Risa Barron extended her hand, which Garbo touched slightly in friendship. Haines wondered how Risa could raise her arm, it was so weighted down with jewelry.

"Miss Garbo, at last," said Risa Barron.

"Greta. Everyone must call me Greta. After all, we'll be working together for many many months, we must be on first name terms and become good friends."

"You wonderful woman," said Risa, sounding like steam escaping from an overheated radiator. Billy Haines wondered how so many ugly features could be set together to create a fascinating face. She had a long nose, wide mouth, a pointed jaw, and eyes with an oriental cast to them. Her lips were ruby-red luscious and there was just enough eye shadow to give her a suitably mysterious aura. This babe knew how to sell herself, thought Haines with admiration, and he could understand her conquest of Guiss. The head happened to be on top of a very stunning body.

Werner Lieb was something else. Haines thought he should be an assistant checker in a sausage factory. He was pale, slim, wore his evening clothes with panache and managed the monocle in his left eye like a veteran of monocle managing. He too kissed Garbo's hands, gushing, "This is a dream come true, Greta. To meet you at last, but also to work with you."

"Thank you. I'm sure the film will be more than memorable for all of us. But look, Billy! An old friend of mine!" Gustav Henkel stood near the massive fireplace holding a glass of champagne. She prayed he wouldn't smile. He did. "This is Gustav Henkel, who wrote the script which Brecht is rewriting and it does not seem to bother Gustav. See! He's always smiling!"

"Kriegman!" barked Guiss, "Drinks for Miss Garbo and Mr. Haines." She asked for champagne and Haines asked for his scotch highball.

Greta took Guiss by the arm and walked him around the room, pausing here in front of a Tintoretto, here in front of a Picasso, here in front of a Renoir, then a Degas, and surprisingly, a few moderns like Max Ernst and Salvadore Dali. "What a fabulous collection, where did you acquire your unique taste?"

Haines wished he could find out where he acquired his unique fortune, but instead busied himself in small talk with Risa Barron. "I'm stunned by your emeralds."

"Thank you. What about the rubies?"

"Blood red and knockouts." He wondered if they were gifts or trophies.

"Billy? Weren't you the movie star William Haines?"

"Ah yes, back in the Middle Ages."

"But why did you stop acting? You were sometimes funny."

"That about sums up my career, sometimes funny." He accepted his highball from Kriegman, who he thought could use a pair of roller skates to get across the enormous length of the room to Garbo before her champagne went flat. Haines asked, "Excited about producing the film?"

"Who wouldn't be? It was so wonderful of Albert to ask Werner and myself to co-produce." She bent her head and whispered, "Of course there is von Stroheim to contend with." She laughed. "I have contended with worse. Hitler and Mussolini, for instance."

Haines was impressed. "You knew them?"

"But of course," was the matter-of-fact reply. "Hitler wanted me for his mistress. This was before Eva Braun. But I could not live with a man who sucks his teeth. Now there is a price on my head. I am on Adolf's hit list. Oh well, let us hope that is not my epitaph."

Garbo was saying to Guiss, "Yes, I am delighted we'll be shooting in Technicolor, but von Stroheim must make tests of me. I must have Westmore devise suitable makeup for the color cameras. After all, Joan can't be rosy-cheeked with orange lips and green eyes. True, the script is witty here and there, but Joan must never be an object of fun, or else how can we expect the audience to sympathize with her?"

"That is absolutely true. I'll convey all this to Von. By the by, now that we're doing it in color, he's thinking seriously of your suggestion to show her burning at the stake."

She laughed. "Of course he would. Joan roasting in glorious Technicolor. A riot of cerise and orange and brown and yellow. Von Stroheim will revel in it. Someone who knows Technicolor must be brought in to advise and moderate him. He will go too far."

"I know that." Guiss lit a cigarette and then jammed it into a pearl-studded holder.

They were standing next to a Botticelli. "Albert," said Garbo, "how come you settled on von Stroheim? Don't get me wrong, we worked together once as actors and it was fine. But no one else in the industry will buy him as a director, and along comes generous you giving him five million dollars to play with."

"He better not play with them." The eyes were narrow and the voice rasped and Garbo took this as a sign the man was not playing the dilettante. The sudden flash of cruelty sent a small tingle jogging down her spine. In a more genial tone he advised her, "Believe me, von Stroheim was not my first choice. First I approached the most obvious man for the job. Cecil B. deMille."

"Of course, he's so deliciously banal."

"He did consider it for awhile. It seems he'd already done Joan as a silent with Geraldine Farrar."

"Oh yes? I must try and find a print. I'd like to see it."

"I've seen it. Terribly primitive. I tried many others, even Alfred Hitchcock, but he waved me away with a very cryptic, 'There's no suspense.' "

"True. Like *Hamlet*, there's no changing the ending," Garbo said.

"My next choice was Josef von Sternberg."

"And he wanted Marlene to play Joan."

"Oh not at all. They barely speak these days. He wanted Ingrid Bergman."

"Oh? But you couldn't get her?"

"I didn't even try. I wanted you and only you." His voice was smooth and seductive. He took her hand and caressed it while his eyes devoured her face. "And now I have you."

"You have Greta the actress."

"And if I want Greta the woman?"

She saw another guest arrive and cut him off abruptly. "Who is that man?"

"Martin? Martin Gruber is my personal secretary. He is late because I sent him on an errand. Martin! Come meet Greta Garbo." Gruber hurried across the vast expanse to join them.

"Poor man," said Garbo. "He'll be out of breath before he reaches us. What a vast expanse. Was it once a ballroom?"

"No, the ballroom is in the north wing. I plan to throw a party there when the film completes shooting."

"That could be years from now," she said mournfully.

"Miss Garbo! Miss Garbo! You leave me speechless." Gruber never shut up. "I am one of your greatest admirers. I have seen all of your films at least a dozen times."

"Really? No wonder you wear such thick glasses."

"I have an awful myopia." He said to Guiss, "I have taken care of the matter."

"Good. I see Kriegman has opened the doors to the dining room. We are ready to serve dinner."

"*Wunderbar*. Frankfurters and sauerkraut!"

"Frankfurters and sauerkraut? What ever gave you such an idea? Such food is for walk-ons and extras," he said proudly. "Tonight I am serving pheasant under glass and chateaubriand and trout Marie Antoinette."

Garbo said, "I have never heard of trout Marie Antoinette."

Guiss smiled suavely and said, "That's trout with the head removed."

They found their place cards and were seated. Garbo could tell, from the number of empty glasses and the amount of silverware at each place setting, that it was going to be a very long evening. Already before her was a plate of paté de foie gras with truffles and gherkins ("alive alive oh," whispered Haines to Risa, who was quite befuddled) and she dug in with her celebrated enthusiasm.

"Greta does love her food," said Haines to Risa. "If she'd been born in Africa, she'd have been a cannibal."

Martin Gruber feasted in equal parts on the paté and Garbo's face. He was enchanted by her throaty laugh, the way she seemed so riveted to every word Guiss said and how she gently touched his sleeve every so often. If she was insincere, he was witnessing a truly magnificent performance.

Werner Lieb cursed Guiss silently for having placed him next to Gustav Henkel. The scenarist preferred his fingers to a fork and showed little respect for the royal truffles. He ate with his mouth open, accompanied by ugly sucking noises that recalled to Werner the ugly noise of the automatic dredges on his grandfather's farm in Alsace. Werner attempted conversation. "Have you seen any of Brecht's rewrite?"

"I tried to. He was very polite when I introduced myself. Then he threw me down the stairs."

"I heard he's terribly temperamental."

"And he's always chomping on those stinking cheap cigars. And his teeth!" Henkel displayed his own and Werner shuddered. "He has the most awful teeth!"

The soup and the fish elapsed uneventfully. The pheasant under glass caused Haines to comment, "I saw them move." Risa Barron covered her mouth with a hand and excused herself for a few moments. Haines looked across at Garbo and Guiss. He could tell they were holding hands under the table. He wondered why that disturbed him.

He heard Martin Gruber asking, "Do you ever contemplate re-turning to acting, Mr. Haines?"

The question always annoyed him and so he chose a facetious reply. "Why no, I'm thinking of becoming a spy."

His voice carried and he was the cynosure of the table.

Garbo dabbed at her lips with her napkin. "A spy, Billy? You? But that is impossible. You can't keep a secret! Ha ha ha ha ha!"

The only other person who joined her laughter was Billy Haines.

Eight

Within less than a week following the dinner party, Greta and Guiss were the talk of the town. Louella Parsons gushed on her Sunday night NBC radio program at nine-fifteen, following Walter Winchell's breathless and breathtaking fifteen minutes, "Greta Garbo and Albert Guiss seem to have found each other. They met last week at a dinner party to celebrate the start of filming Garbo's comeback film, *Joan the Magnificent*. Since then, my spies tell me they're inseparable. The mysterious financier was seen with Greta at the House of Westmore where she and von Stroheim, who is directing the film, were devising a color makeup for Greta. I've been told some evenings Greta and Guiss take long walks on the beach at Santa Monica where Greta has a pleasant little house. Of course they could only be discussing the film which begins shooting tomorrow, but if they're deeply involved in a romance, well, your Guiss is as good as mine."

Although it was a Sunday night, the Samuel Goldwyn studio was a beehive of activity. Technicians were under pressure to get the lights and the sound equipment installed to von Stroheim's satisfaction. The shooting schedule had to be rearranged to accommodate Peter Lorre's Dauphin, as Jack Warner needed him for a film with Sydney Greenstreet. Because of the use of Technicolor, a heavier-than-usual electrical board had to be installed. The Dauphin's palace had been beautifully designed by Cedric Gibbons, who had been borrowed from MGM with the surprisingly benevolent blessing of Louis B. Mayer. When Garbo heard this, she frowned and said to William Haines, "He's up to something. Why is he being so accommodating? First he lets me have Adrian to design my costume and then he permits Gibbons to design the sets."

"I heard he almost had apoplexy when he heard I was decorating the interiors."

"Which reminds me, Billy. No chintz. They didn't have chintz in those days."

"They didn't have much else either," said Haines glumly, "but they were big on sackcloth and ashes."

Garbo paraded around her dressing room. "I like my costume. Don't you?"

"How'd you get him to get rid of the padded shoulders?"

"My shoulders never need padding. I have a good frame." She studied herself with admiration in the full length mirror she'd demanded be installed and was satisfied.

Haines asked, "What's going on between you and Guiss? Lolly told her millions of listeners tonight that she suspects you're a hot and heavy item."

"We're a little heavy but we have not yet gotten hot." She sat before her dressing table mirror and lit a cigarette. "Don't you think he's very attractive?"

"If you like the type. I think Nils Asther would be better casting."

Garbo exploded. "Oh never never. Nils is too passive. He doesn't have a commanding personality. He does have the softness Albert occasionally displays, especially when we walk on the beach and he talks of the future." She was examining her fingernails. "He plans someday to retire to South America. To Brazil. He has bought a jungle and a river. He is having the jungle cleared and building a little city there."

"You mean a little kingdom, don't you?"

"Sometimes I don't know what I mean and sometimes I don't know what he means. He is such a mass of contradictions."

"Do you think he's in love with you?"

An arch look spread across her face. "But of course he must be. I am so fascinating. I am Garbo, the siren from Sweden. Have you forgotten all the men I've conquered and destroyed in my films? Wasn't I a superb Mata Hari?"

"I couldn't keep a straight face during your love scenes with Ramon Novarro."

"Neither could we. He thought of one of the dress extras he wanted and I thought of a trip to Europe and somehow we got through it. It looked awfully good on film, though, didn't it?"

"Because you made it look good. Christ, when you kiss a man, you devour him."

"But Billy, if you are truly and deeply in love with a man, when you kiss him, it must be to devour him. When I love, I love with an all-consuming passion." She attacked a thumbnail with an emery board. "I've forgotten what it's like, it's been so long. What time is it?"

"It's a little before ten."

"I'm tired. I want to go home."

"What are you hanging around for?"

"Peter Lorre. The first scene tomorrow is the dauphin and Joan. I wish Erich would reschedule it for after lunch. It's such a difficult scene. We need to rehearse it." There was a knock at the door. "Maybe that's Peter now. Come in!"

Lisa Schmidt entered. She said to Haines, "I thought I'd find you here. Himself is on the set and yelling. That miniature statue of the nude gladiator you've placed in the Dauphin's bedroom displeases the master. He wants you on the set."

"That son of a bitch has no eye for beauty!" exploded Haines, "All he digs is distortion and ugliness and physical disabilities. Watch, you just watch. Most of the extras will be blind, missing an arm, missing a leg, dwarfs and midgets and God knows what else. I try to liven things up a bit with a gorgeous, muscular gladiator and he blows a gasket. Which I'm sure is all he blows." As he stormed out to beard the lion on the set, he shouted, "The next scream you hear will be mine!"

They watched his exit, and Lisa asked in a tired voice, "Do you mind if I sit for a minute?"

"Please! Would you like some coffee? It's hot in the thermos there. There's also a thermos of chicken soup and hot chocolate. My housekeeper is a treasure."

"Maybe some hot chocolate."

"Hers is wonderful. She poisoned her husband with hot chocolate."

Lisa said, "I'll have some coffee. Some for you?"

"No, I'll brave the hot chocolate. I think Lottie's poisoning days are long past. Anyway, we are good friends."

"How does it feel to be going back to work?"

Garbo said, "Well, I am no longer a slumbering volcano."

Lisa's face was a study as she poured the hot drinks. "Don't you think this is a strange setup?"

"Strange? Oh, it's a bit exotic. Risa Barron fascinates me. She and Werner Lieb know absolutely nothing about film making and display their ignorance with such authority. And those jewels she wears! My God! They must be worth a king's ransom. But I like her. She amuses me. She doesn't seem to object to the way Albert pays court."

"Between you and me," Lisa said, carrying the cups of hot liquid to the dressing table, "I think she's a taxidermist's masterpiece. Who are these people? Where did they spring from?"

Garbo's eyes were wise and inquisitive as she took the hot chocolate from Lisa. "Are you curious or is von Stroheim curious?"

Lisa laughed and sat. "We're both curious. Guiss is Guiss. I think what little is known about him is all we'll ever know. Or have you managed to penetrate his armor?"

"Oh I don't know. He had to have a mother and father, didn't he?" She contemplated the hot chocolate, which was thick and creamy. No wonder the late Mr. Lynton so greedily went to his death. "Who they were, I haven't the vaguest idea. You know what I think? I think from early in his life he had ambitions to be a very rich and very powerful man. I think he's totally ruthless. . . ."

Lisa feigned shock. "My dear!"

Garbo smiled. "I haven't told you anything I haven't told him. He admits he is self-made, that he always wanted wealth and power, and to attain such vaunted ambitions one has to be at the very least quite ruthless. I'm ruthless. Von Stroheim is ruthless. Every major star and executive in this business, every politician and dictator in the world is ruthless. You have to be to achieve your ambition. But once achieved, you have to be even more ruthless to hold on to it. Take Risa Barron. She told Billy Haines she was once friendly with Hitler and Mussolini. That Hitler wanted her to be his mistress. Do you think this is possible?"

"Why not? With a woman like that, anything could be possible. Jesus, those jewels."

"I'm sure Jesus had nothing to do with it."

"Hitler and Mussolini. That's quite a parlay. And yet she's here on the lam from the fascists."

"I'm sure that was Albert's doing."

"Now that Europe's overrun by the hounds of war, I wonder how badly Guiss has been hit in the pocket. I read somewhere he had vast holdings in Germany, Italy, France and Austria that have been confiscated."

Garbo laughed. "I'm sure he has plenty left."

"I'm told you like Bertolt Brecht's revised script."

"Oh I think it's very good. Now it has wonderful shadings. The lightness doesn't overpower the darkness the way it did in Henkel's. Now it is much more of a parable and therefore it is much more powerful. I'm very excited by it. Oh God, by the sound of that knocking I can tell it's Werner Lieb at the door. I suspect he has trained with the military." Lisa followed Garbo with her eyes as the actress crossed to the door. "He walks, he talks, he bows from the waist and he knocks on doors like a true *Junker.*" She opened the door. There stood Werner Lieb. "I was right. Come in Werner, what's the problem?"

"I came to see your costume." Garbo struck a pose. "Very good, very good indeed." Lisa wondered if he slept with his monocle. She wondered a lot of things about him and his friends and was anxious to share her theories about these people with Arnold Lake and Herbert Villon.

"Dear God, what is all that shrieking?" Garbo went back to the door, opened it and saw von Stroheim brandishing his riding crop in pursuit of Billy Haines. "Oh look at those two fools! And look at Peter!" Peter Lorre, a cigarette dangling out of the side of his mouth, his script under one arm, his jacket hanging somewhat precariously from his shoulders, his hands shoved deep into his pockets, approached Greta's dressing room.

He said wearily, "Von Stroheim will suffer a stroke at the rate he's going." He surveyed her dressing room, which was actually a portable caravan. "I don't suppose I shall be afforded such a luxurious accommodation."

"I didn't ask for it," Garbo said defensively, "Guiss insisted I have it."

"Is he any good in bed?"

"Why don't you ask someone who's been to bed with him? Come in. You're late."

"I was beating up my wife. I do it every Sunday night when she listens to Lolly's program. She loves it. It makes her sleep better. She's an occasional insomniac." He walked past Garbo, who closed the door and returned to the dressing table. "Hello, Werner. Have you done any co-producing yet?"

"I can assure you Risa and I will be quite competent."

Garbo hoped the venom in Lieb's voice wouldn't prove fatal. Lisa Schmidt was trying to make a quiet exit. Garbo asked, "Are you leaving us, Lisa?"

"I thought I might rescue Billy from von Stroheim."

The smoke in his eyes from his cigarette didn't impair Lorre's vision. When Lisa spoke, he turned to look at her, acknowledging her presence for the first time. He liked what he saw. A beautiful figure, gorgeous legs; he couldn't quite see her face as she went to the door. He wondered quickly if she was amenable and available.

"Lisa?" he asked, "Who is Lisa? Why haven't I been introduced to Lisa?"

"I warn you, Lisa. Mr. Lorre is a predatory monster. Possibly because he was brilliant as a child molester in *M*."

Lorre said through a cackle, "But Lisa hardly looks like a child. Turn around, dear, and let's introduce ourselves."

Lisa's fists were clenched. Her mouth was dry. She said a silent prayer, a prayer that begged God to strike Peter Lorre with some form of amnesia, and then she found a lavish smile and turned around and faced him. "Nice to meet you, Mr. Lorre."

"Oh, I am overwhelmed! Such beauty! Such ravishing beauty! Greta, aren't you jealous?"

"No. She makes little of her looks, which makes her a very wise young woman."

Lorre walked to Lisa, slowly, studying her face despite the smoke continuing to cloud his eyes. She folded her arms and waited.

Werner Lieb was intrigued by Lorre's performance. He sensed the actor was up to something, playing a game of cat and mouse with Lisa, who indeed looked as though she was about to be eaten.

"I think we have met before," Lorre finally said. "Haven't we?"

Lisa said firmly, "I have never met you before, Mr. Lorre. I'm quite sure of that."

"I know I'm not crazy. It was about a month ago. Maybe longer."

"I have to go, Mr. Lorre. You'll have to excuse me."

"Now don't be in such a rush. Wait a minute. Let me think." He took the cigarette out of his mouth and held it between two fingers. "Yes, of course. It was *you.*"

Garbo said with impatience, "Oh Peter, stop playing with Lisa. Make friends with her. You'll need her. She handles von Stroheim superbly and is very useful. Lisa, don't look so frightened. Peter is harmless. Peter, behave yourself."

Lorre was annoyed. "I *am* behaving myself. Lisa and I have met before. We have, haven't we, Lisa?" She said nothing. She wished lightning would strike, she wished anything would happen that would rescue her, the way she had prayed to be rescued that night she was pursued on the beach. "We have and we know you know. Remember that night on the beach, Greta?"

"Oh? So now I'm a part of this plot?" She flung the emery board aside. "Peter, will you please sit down and let Lisa get on with her work. Go, Lisa. I'll see you later."

Lorre suddenly raged. "I will not be treated like a fool, Greta! This is the girl on the beach, the one who was running away from something and hid behind your rose bush under your patio. The one your neighbor saw, what's his name . . . ?"

"Saloman." Greta looked perplexed.

"That's right, Saloman. And she sought refuge with me. She asked to use the phone. When Toth . . . you know . . . with the private police guard we pay for . . . when he knocked at my door I hid her in the closet in the living room . . . the one my wife never looks into . . . and when I went to speak to Toth, she fled. Damn it!" He pointed an accusing finger at Lisa Schmidt as Werner Lieb watched the scene with fascination. "You are that woman! You're the one who was being chased and it had something to do with the house in which that strange Wolheim family used to live."

Desperately, Lisa found a laugh. "I'm awfully sorry, Mr. Lorre. You have me confused with someone else. I have to go." She fled.

"But I swear on my wife's head," Lorre insisted to Garbo and Lieb, "she's that woman! Look how frightened she is!"

"I'd be frightened too if you attacked me the way you just attacked Lisa. Oh really Peter, I remember that night now. I'd had drinks with Marion and then went home. I did see someone running from under my patio but only vaguely because of the blackout. And as for you, you were probably in a cocaine haze at the time. There probably wasn't any girl at all."

"Are you trying to convince me I'm insane? I tell you," he said, pointing a finger in the general direction of Lisa Schmidt's departure, "that was the woman who came to my house that night!"

"This is all terribly dramatic," Werner Lieb interrupted, "but I must get back to the office. I promised Albert I would see your costume and report to him. I shall tell him I'm very satisfied with it."

"It doesn't matter. I'm satisfied. That is all that is important where this costume is concerned."

Lieb clicked his heels and gave her the stiff bow from the waist. *"Auf wiedersehn."* To Lorre he said, "Nice to see you again."

A strange look crossed Garbo's face. She saw Lorre react to Lieb's acknowledgment in much the same way Lisa Schmidt had reacted to Lorre when he fingered her. She watched Lieb depart, wondering if he also slept with his body stiffly rigid. Lorre flung his script down on the couch and crushed his cigarette in an ashtray. When they were alone, Garbo asked, "When did you meet Werner Lieb?"

"Lieb? You mean the man who just left? I've never met him before."

"He said, 'Nice to see you again.' "

Lorre shrugged. "Recognizes me from my film. Everybody recognizes me. I never have any privacy anymore."

"Peter," said Garbo gravely, "you've never met him before the way Lisa Schmidt claims she's never met you before." She picked up a hairbrush, faced the mirror and began stroking. "You all intrigue me so. How exciting life is becoming again. I suspect now this film is a hotbed of subterfuge and hidden secrets. Possibly dangerous secrets. Am I right, Peter?"

He was lighting another cigarette. "Let's go over our lines, Greta. I'm a little shaky with them."

"Peter," she spoke his name softly, "I suspect you're a little shaky with things other than your lines." Then in rich tones, she spoke her dialogue, having in just a few days committed Brecht's rewrite to memory, " 'My dauphin, my prince, majesty, I am a simple peasant girl who has come to serve you. My voices . . . my voices have entrusted you in my care . . . oh sire . . . you must believe in me. . . .' "

She didn't hear Lorre speaking his opening lines. She was wondering what she could believe in. She was worried, and she was a little frightened. She needed to talk to Salka Viertel.

Nine

Lisa Schmidt needed to talk to Arnold Lake and Herbert Villon. She found Arnold at his hotel, the Garden of Allah on Sunset Boulevard and Crescent Heights. It had once been the estate of the tempestuous and exotic silent-screen star Alla Nazimova. When she fell on hard times, the estate was sold and remodeled into a series of lovely bungalows and was often home to such literary luminaries as Robert Benchley, Dorothy Parker and Robert Sherwood and a smattering of stars when they were between spouses. It had a popular bar and anyone who didn't drink was looked upon with suspicion or denounced as subversive.

Arnold in turn left messages at various checkpoints for Herb Villon, who was soon located and joined Arnold and Lisa at the Garden of Allah.

In Arnold's bungalow, they listened to Lisa's story of her encounter with Peter Lorre. When she was finished, she said, "I don't think anyone saw me leave the lot. I should go back." Neither of the men said anything. "Werner Lieb is one of Guiss's henchmen. I'm positive he was in that meeting at the beach."

Arnold finally spoke. "Going back could be dangerous."

Villon said, "Not going back could be equally as dangerous."

"That's what I think," said Lisa. "I'm all for going back and brazening it out. What's the worst that could happen to me?"

"You could be killed," said Arnold. Lisa exhaled and reached for the scotch on the rocks he had poured her. "We know for sure there's something subversive and dangerous going on there. The movie's a front for some kind of undercover activity and it smells to high heaven."

Lisa didn't try to disguise her skepticism. "You don't think Garbo would be part of any subversive activity, do you?"

"Who knows? Look at some of the fifth columnists we've been rounding up. Respected politicians, pillars of society, the country's one big nest of underground communist activity."

"I thought the reds were our allies," offered Villon.

"Lately, but with that mother Stalin, who the hell can be sure of what's next? Garbo lived and worked in Germany back in 1925. That picture she made . . ."

"The Joyless Street," said Lisa.

"Didn't she tell you some of those actors she worked with became Nazis?"

"She did," Lisa said, then added hotly, "but there were some of them who didn't. All that happened years after Greta came to the U.S. I tell you she's absolutely apolitical. She's not dumb, but she's not all that smart. What she is is shrewd and very self-protective. The lady isn't quick to give an inch, let alone a yard. I think she's been suckered into this deal and it was easy to land her because she was so confused and upset at parting company with Metro."

Arnold persisted, "What about her romance with Guiss?"

"I don't think she's serious. It amuses her. She finds him and his gang funny. You heard me, to her they're one big collective laugh. She's getting a million bucks, she can afford to laugh." Lisa lit a cigarette. "What I'm wondering is, how does Lorre fit into this scenario? I heard his name mentioned out at the beach. It was he who brought Guiss's offer to Garbo."

"And it was her two girlfriends who steamrollered her into finally giving the deal the nod," added Arnold.

Villon asked Arnold, "Viertel and de Acosta are clear, aren't they?"

"On the surface it would seem so," said Arnold. "They contribute heavily to antifascist causes. They work on a lot of committees. Garbo doesn't."

Lisa said, "Garbo is Garbo. I told you. She's not a political animal. You know she's always shied away from the public eye. She's very choosy about who she associates with. I'm amazed that she seemed to take to me immediately."

"You're a direct line to von Stroheim. She can make use of that."

"She tried to get Lorre off my back. She didn't have to do that."

Villon asked, "This Werner Lieb . . ."

Lisa said, "I'm sure he believes Lorre. That bunch took after me that night, at least some of them. Now they see I've weaseled my way into the production. I'm sure they see me as a threat."

Arnold said gravely. "Look, toots, you're my girl. You're important to me. But we're painted into a corner. If you disappear, they'll be positive we're on to them and we'll never learn another thing."

"Don't you think I know that?" She smiled. "Garbo could be a help."

Villon chuckled. "Are you crazy? Garbo doing cloak and dagger, you've got to be kidding."

"She sure knows how to dig for information, and get it." Lisa sipped her drink. "Keep her in mind. She's going to cross-examine me about Lorre's accusation. What do we do about him?"

Villon said, "I know him slightly. We sweat it out in the same steambath on Thursday night where the celebrities go. You know, Bogart, Eddie Robinson, Vic McLaglen. . . ."

Arnold said sharply, "You be careful of McLaglen."

"That big idiot?" Villon had an incredulous look on his face.

"Don't you know he has his own private army? Cavalry. They meet every week and go through maneuvers and they wear black shirts. McLaglen's Irish. And the Irish are very much on Hitler's side. Hitler's ships and submarines use Irish ports for repairing and refueling."

"I'm flabbergasted," said Villon.

"It's no big secret. Northern Ireland especially. They've no love for Great Britain. They want their independence."

Lisa said, "They're lousy lays."

Arnold smiled. "We can send you to Mexico until this blows over."

"The food doesn't agree with me. No, gentlemen, the lady is frightened shitless but she's going back to the studio. If anything happens to me, at least you know where to investigate, and who to investigate. By the by, this Risa Barron, the one with all the jewelry, she blabs to everyone she's been intimate with Hitler and Mussolini."

"So was Guiss." Arnold had them riveted. "And Hitler offered Garbo his world if she'd return to Germany."

Villon said, "Well it's obvious she turned him down."

Arnold Lake was very tired. "It's way past my bedtime." He asked Lisa, "You sure you want to go back tonight? Why don't you go home and get some sleep. You start shooting tomorrow and it's going to be a rough day."

"You're right. I'm going home. And I'll be in constant touch." Arnold kissed her. "And Arnold, be sure to tell my mom and dad how much I love them."

"When?"

"I don't know. Just in case."

"I got here as fast as I can. Driving in the blackout is hell. Is there any coffee?" Salka Viertel took off her suede jacket and flung it across the back of a chair.

"In one of those thermoses." Garbo watched her friend opening and closing thermos bottles until she found the coffee.

"What's wrong? You're terribly tired. You should go home. What time's your first scene?"

"It will be in the afternoon now. Von is having serious technical problems. Sit down, Salka. I have something very important to discuss with you." She told her of Lorre's confrontation with Lisa Schmidt.

"So? What do you think this means?"

"I think it means something dangerous is going on around here. Maybe Lisa Schmidt is involved in some kind of espionage."

Salka laughed. "You overdramatize everything."

"Oh no. Not this. Not her being pursued on the beach, if it really was her. How we suspected that Wolheim family were a strange bunch because none of them resembled each other. Guiss and his cohorts. And this ugly Gustav Henkel. I don't think he ever wrote the first script of *Joan.*"

"Now really, Greta."

"I mean that, Salka. What writer doesn't fight to do his own rewrite? He calmly sits back and lets them put Brecht on the job? He only wrote one draft. At least demand the right to do the first revision. But no, he sits back without uttering a peep and lets himself be replaced. And Risa Barron with that fantastic jewelry that would make Maria Montez suicidal with envy. She brags about having relations with Hitler and Mussolini. And Guiss. How he woos me. How he promises me the world if I would become his lover."

"Have you?"

"I don't want the world. It's difficult enough to cope with Hollywood." She thought for a moment. "They sent Peter with the offer. They hired von Stroheim when they supposedly couldn't get anyone else, not even von Sternberg. But he's Jewish."

Salka was confused. "What are you getting at?"

"But von Stroheim's also Jewish. He and Joe weren't born to their 'vons.' They added the 'von' to their names when they were getting started, to make themselves sound like aristocracy. Ha ha ha! How does Greta von Garbo sound to you? Ha ha ha!" Garbo settled into a chair and crossed her legs.

"It sounds perfectly awful. Greta, what are you suspicious of?"

"These people. I think they are frauds." She leaned forward and hypnotized Viertel with a steady, piercing look. "Why did you and Mercedes work so hard to convince me to play Joan? Why?"

Salka tasted her coffee, but it was tepid. She put the cup back in the saucer. "We did it for von Stroheim. The three of us—Peter, Mercedes and myself. Without you, there would be no film. Guiss set up this project to get to know you. He is besotted with you. He has been for years."

"Five million dollars for Greta Garbo? Compared to that, what Louis paid me was a pittance and yet I'm a millionaire. Fate is so ridiculous. Really, Salka. Is that all? Is that really all? Has Guiss severed all his ties with the Germans?"

"I don't know anything about that. I don't know what his ties were to the fascists other than he claims they've confiscated billions of dollars worth of his property. You should know more about this then I do! Louella says . . ."

"Oh to hell with Louella." She was on her feet pacing, wringing her hands agitatedly, eyes darting about like a frightened sparrow's. "I have such a presentiment, Salka. Something terrible is going to happen."

"You're being very silly, Greta. What's in those other jugs? They must still be hot. Drink something and then we'll go home."

"Home. Yes, home. Home to my Lottie. She'll protect me."

"This hot chocolate smells wonderful."

"That's how Lottie poisoned her husband. With hot chocolate."

"Forget the hot chocolate. Ah! Chicken soup. It smells scrumptious. What's Lottie's stand on chicken soup?"

"Oh Salka, Salka. I fear for Lisa Schmidt. Oh that fool Peter. Accusing her in front of Werner Lieb."

"Lieb?"

"Another flunky. Supposedly the co-producer. If anything happens to Lisa . . . oh God!" She flung herself onto the couch. "I should go to Switzerland, where they're neutral." She looked up at Salka. "Believe me, Salka, there's something rotten going on in this studio. I'm not sure what it is, but it's going on. I have a lot of thinking to do. Yes, I think I'll go home."

Ten

Lisa Schmidt an American agent?" Albert Guiss swallowed the information Werner Lieb gave him, took time digesting it, and then said, "Are you quite positive?"

"Quite positive, no. We have only Peter Lorre's word for it."

"Lorre's word, as we well know, could be as shaky as his health. Well, if she was the spy at the beach house, she couldn't have heard all that much. We only discussed the film. Risa, what do you think?"

Risa was thinking she'd rather be in her bed getting some much-needed beauty sleep. She was staring at Gustav Henkel, who seemed to be dozing in his easy chair, but with that one you never could tell. Perhaps he was feigning sleep. He did that frequently when conversations were too deep and over his head. "I think Gustav is asleep."

Guiss looked at the writer and smirked. "Perhaps not, perhaps his mind is wandering."

"Not without a road map," offered Risa, who didn't like Henkel. She thought him common and quite ordinary and wished he'd do something to improve his teeth.

"Let's get back to Lisa Schmidt. What's your opinion of her, Risa?"

"Opinion? Opinion? Opinion about what?" When she was tired, she became testy. "Is she a spy? How do I know? I only know her from her work on the film. And she's terribly competent. I know von Stroheim is very pleased with her and when his wife visited the studio last week I don't think she was happy to see that Lisa is so beautiful. Greta seems to like her."

"Very much so," added Lieb as he polished his monocle with a silk handkerchief.

"That's important," said Guiss. "Greta relates to so few people."

Henkel spoke softly. "She asks a lot of questions."

Guiss arched an eyebrow. "Greta?"

"Lisa Schmidt."

"What kind of questions?" pursued Guiss.

"How long have you been here. Where do you come from. Where is your family. How long have you been with Guiss, et cetera, et cetera, et cetera. Sometimes it is dizzying to be evasive. I have made up a whole new biography of myself just to satisfy her inquisitive nature. And the trouble with that is, I can't remember half the lies I fed her."

"If she's really an agent with the FBI, your lies have been recorded and examined. And you're such a brilliant liar I'm sure they find your information most entertaining."

Werner Lieb interrupted. "What's the decision about Lisa Schmidt?"

"To act against her now on such flimsy evidence as Lorre's would in my opinion be very stupid." Guiss had left his position behind his desk and crossed to a map of the world framed and hanging on the opposite wall. The inevitable cigarette in the pearl holder was clenched tightly between his teeth. He studied the map and then, with his hands clasped behind his back, paced the length of the study. "We must do nothing that could jeopardize the progress of the film. We are heavily invested in it and our fate lies in the hands of an egomaniacal director and a manic-depressive actress who, for reasons beyond my capabilities to understand, wants to become a saint."

Risa was studying Guiss. Lover, friend, philanthropist, sadist, bon vivant. Truly a mess of contradictions. She said, "Albert, I agree with you. To move against Lisa would mean doing away with her, and that will mean the police, and if she is really an agent, it will mean the FBI. We don't desire the company of either. We will just have to be very careful. We must somehow convey to Lorre we'd appreciate he keep his mouth shut about her. . . ."

"That's easy," said Werner. "We could threaten him with an inferior brand of narcotics. Like that swamp grass some crooked dealers import from Central America."

"It's after one A.M.," Risa announced impatiently, "let's get some rest. We have to be on the set early tomorrow morning. It's the first day of shooting. How about that? We have at least accomplished that! I feel very satisfied!"

"Feel very satisfied," said Guiss, "but don't feel smug. Good night."

At seven the next morning, Martin Gruber met Lisa Schmidt for breakfast in the coffee shop in Culver City, a safe distance from the Goldwyn Studios, where no one would see them. She told him about the encounter with Lorre, and although Gruber was crumbling his prune Danish instead of eating it, this was the only sign that the incident disturbed him. His mouth wasn't twitching the way it usually did when something disturbed him. She continued with her meeting at the Garden of Allah and, when that dissertation was over, finally took a bite of her buttered bagel.

Gruber motioned to the waitress for coffee refills, asked her to remove the destroyed prune Danish and replace it with a whole-wheat muffin with raisins, cream cheese on the side. They sat in silence for a while, Lisa chewing her bagel, Gruber looking past her outside the window at the Metro studio down the street, which was beginning to hum with activity. Finally he spoke. "Guiss had a meeting late last night. Werner, Risa, Henkel. I was excluded."

"Does that worry you?"

"Not at all. It's a pattern I've grown to recognize. When it's top secret, I'm excluded. But I can guess you were the topic under discussion." He waited until the waitress deposited his muffin and refilled their coffee cups, and then continued. "Guiss is too clever to engage the police or the FBI right now. Sooner or later it will probably have to happen, but not right now. Because if they suspect you're an agent and kill you, then they are the targets of an investigation they positively don't want. After all," he said with a coy smile, "remove the *r* and the *e* from *corpse* and you are left with *cops*."

"Cute. Give me a bite of your muffin, it looks good."

"Help yourself." He sipped his coffee. "Go to the studio. Do your job. From the snatches of conversation I hear, you are liked. Certainly Risa Barron speaks well of you."

"Well that's a comfort."

"You see, it would be easier to ease you out of your job, and avoid the possibility of your continuing to be a threat to them, than kick over a hornet's nest by killing you. To me that would be the sensible move to make."

"If they haven't thought of it themselves, don't you suggest it."

"Don't be ridiculous."

"Supposing Lorre doesn't let up on me?"

"It is my calculated guess, Lisa, he will no longer be a problem. Lorre is himself in a difficult situation. His family and his wife's family are still in Europe. Lorre's a Jew. As long as he plays nice with Guiss, the families are protected."

"He's been trying to get them out, you know. He's petitioned the White House."

Gruber chuckled. "The White House! It's too late for that even with the White House. The war is on and there's no exit for anyone except Axis agents." He looked at the wall clock over the counter. "Isn't it time you got going to the studio? I know Guiss will soon begin to miss me. I'll get the check. We go dutch as usual, yes?"

"Next job you get, ask for an expense account."

*　*　*

At the studio, Goldwyn and Sophie Gang were crossing the lot to the set of *Joan the Magnificent.* He always greeted the start of a new rental production by personally appearing on the set to welcome the newcomers. He liked activity; he thrived on seeing actors and technicians going about their business with alacrity. Making films was his life's blood and he was as enthusiastic about rival producers' projects as he was about his own. "Sophie, take a memo."

"I don't have my book."

"So put it in your head!" he fumed. "Later we'll take it out. I have come to a mountainous decision. I am going to make *The Brothers Karamazov.*"

"But Mr. Goldwyn . . ."

"Don't 'but' me. My decision is final and irreverent!"

"But Mr. Goldwyn," said Sophie in a voice that pleaded with her boss to be reasonable, "the exhibitors are begging for women's pictures. They're up to their projectors in war films. They want romantic films desperately. Pictures the women will go to see!"

Goldwyn thought for a moment and then his face brightened. "All right! So we'll call it *The Sisters Karamozov!* And what's more, I'll offer the part of Grushenka to Greta! How's that?"

"Mr. Goldwyn, how can there be a Grushenka if you change them to sisters? She's the woman they fight over."

He thought for a moment. "Then Greta can be one of the sisters. I'll change Grushenka to Goldfarb and offer it to John Wayne. There's that rotten von Stroheim. A terrible man, a very terrible man. Hello Erich! Why haven't you come to visit me and say 'hello'?"

Von Stroheim had been about to chew out an electrician. "Well, Sam. Nice of you to drop by."

"Tell me Erich, do you know *The Brothers Karamazov?*"

"Not intimately." He collared the electrician, who was trying to sneak away.

"Come by and see me. I may have for you an interesting preposition. Where's Greta? I don't see Greta. Look at all the people, Sophie. This is really going to be a gigantic *eppis.* Look at all the actors and actresses! It looks like a *Who's What* of everybody who isn't working. Look Sophie, there's Eddie Quillan, and Mary Gordon. Over there, look. Cliff Edwards, by golly. What's Ukelele Ike doing in a movie about Joan of Arc?"

"Maybe they found out she liked ukeleles," said Sophie.

"You think so?" He stared about in amazement. "And this set. It must have cost a pretty penis. You know, Sophie, I think I should get to know this Albert Guiss. What do you think?"

"That's him over there with his entourage." Guiss was standing in the middle of the set accompanied by Risa, Werner and Gustav Henkel. Sophie led Goldwyn to the group.

Goldwyn confronted Guiss. "Mr. Guiss, I assume. Let me introduce myself. I am Samuel Goldwyn. I own this studio."

Guiss and Goldwyn shook hands, and then Guiss introduced the others.

Goldwyn continued, "Good luck. A lot of good luck. I smell you're going to have a big hit on your hand."

"Thank you very much, Sam."

"Of course you won't see much until the war is over and you can display it in Europe. In Europe Garbo is a big name, a very big name. But until then, you'll have to march time." Goldwyn was warming up. "I want this to be a big hit for you so it'll be like spitting in the face of that rotten Hitler. Joan will conquer the way the Allies will conquer. They'll push Hitler's nose into horse menus and then I have already suggested they put him in a cage and take him on a world tour for everyone to see. They should charge of course a nominated sum and they'll clean up a fortune. Maybe I can get in on it." He hadn't noticed he had lost his audience.

Sophie remarked as they strayed away, "A very strange bunch."

"Not very polite either," huffed Goldwyn. "Come, let's give a hello to Greta."

Garbo was pleasantly astonished as she entered her caravan dressing room followed by Lottie Lynton and Mercedes de Acosta. "Look at all the flowers! It is like a greenhouse in here! Look Mercedes, there is no room for us! And champagne!" There were at least half a dozen buckets of champagne and bottles of whisky, vodka, and brandy. "And look! Chilled caviar just the way I love it with chopped onions and chopped eggs and sour cream. Lottie, my dear, please fix me one."

Mercedes said, "Look over here, Greta. From Louis B. Mayer, a plate of chopped liver. He probably made it himself."

Garbo struggled out of an oversized sweater. "We must send the flowers to hospitals. But the food we keep for ourselves," she said as she rubbed her hands together and grinned lasciviously. She took the caviar-drenched biscuit from Lottie and bit into it greedily, while Mercedes found her a paper napkin to wipe the dribble from her chin.

"Greta Garbo!" said Goldwyn sternly as he and Sophie entered. "Why aren't you making Joan of Arc for me instead of for these foreigners?"

Garbo liked the man; she had always enjoyed him and his beautiful wife, Frances. She swallowed her mouthful and said, "You didn't ask me. And besides, you already did Joan years ago as a silent. Why would you want to do it again?"

His hands were spread out palms up, "So I can hear her talk! I don't mind chewing my fat twice. Didn't I make *The Dark Angel* and *Stella Dallas* twice? Who sent all these flowers?"

Out of the side of her mouth Sophie warned him, "You sent the white carnations."

Like the crack of a whip, his tongue worked. "Look at my white carnations, aren't they municipal?"

Garbo giggled. "Very municipal, Sam. They're also lovely. But I am so perplexed by all these flowers! Is this for starting a new movie or for a funeral?"

Lisa Schmidt had entered unobtrusively. Mercedes was the first to spot her and admire her beauty. She didn't know her but she assumed she was on the production staff. She very much liked Lisa's beauty. Mercedes wanted to know her better. She heard Garbo babbling about flowers and food and what a trial the first day of shooting can be and would Lottie pour her some hot chocolate and, as she held up the hanger holding her costume, asking Goldwyn and Sophie if they didn't approve, which Sam didn't but held his tongue, and then she commanded Mercedes' attention and Mercedes cooed that it was an absolutely brilliantly designed piece of work and it might just start a new fashion in women's clothes.

That sobered Garbo. "I never thought about that. It's possible, isn't it? Remember how popular I made the pillbox hat and I never saw a nickel of it. Mercedes, remind me to have a talk with Adrian."

Now Goldwyn took the spotlight with his offer for her to do *The Sisters Karamazov* and he would forever puzzle why this brought on a fit of hysterical laughter. Sophie Gang came to his rescue reminding him they were late for a writers' conference with Aldous Huxley and Christopher Isherwood. Goldwyn explained to Garbo, assuming she might never have heard of the two British writers, "They're not only good writers, they're allies. I want them for a picture I'm planning about Bulldog Drummond, you know, the safecracker." (He actually pronounced it "Bullfinch Drumming.") "It's for my new comedy star, Danny Kaye."

"Mr. Goldwyn, we're late," insisted Sophie.

"So what? I'm Sam Goldwyn, aren't I? Did I know one day I'd be Sam Goldwyn? I have a right to be late. Goodbye, Greta. Good luck. I'll bet Mayer sent the chopped liver. And if I'm right, hire a food taster. Stop pulling my sleeve, Sophie!"

When they were out the door, Garbo slumped into a chair. "Yes, the first day is always the hardest. And the last day is always the saddest. But we are a long way from the last day. So Lisa Schmidt, why do you stand there like a lonely mouse?"

Lisa came forward. "I wouldn't dare compete with Sam Goldwyn for your attention."

"Where did you disappear to last night? I tried to find you."

"I was tired and very upset by Lorre. I went home."

"Yes, Peter was very naughty teasing you the way he did. Peter is not celebrated for his handling of women." She crossed to the dressing table and sat there. She saw Mercedes ogling at Lisa. "Oh where are my manners?" She introduced the women to each other while Lottie unpacked several cases of knickknacks which Garbo brought to make the dressing room homier and cozier. There were canned goods and an assortment of cheeses, cold cuts and biscuits to be stored in the kitchenette closets and refrigerator. Garbo was asking Lisa, "Was that you on the beach that night?"

Lisa smiled. "It certainly was not."

Mercedes wondered, "What do you suppose this woman was spying on?"

"Not 'what,' but 'who.'" Garbo thought for a minute. "Whom?" She dismissed it with a wave of her hand that just missed swatting a fly. Mercedes repeated her question.

Garbo said, "That house has been uninhabited for a long time. I wonder who owns it?"

Lisa wanted to blurt out, "Guiss!" but said, "Wouldn't the real-estate people in the neighborhood know?"

"Possibly," said Garbo. She told Lisa, "A very strange family lived in the place for a while—the Wolheims. It's really such an ugly mess, the sort of architecture they favored thirty years ago. Strange house, strange family." She was cleaning her face with cold cream. "Salka and I saw them a few times. A father, a mother, three sons and a daughter. But they bore no resemblance to each other."

"Maybe the children were adopted," suggested Mercedes.

"Salka thought that a possibility too. Funny," she said, wiping the facial cream away with tiny pads of cotton, "they materialized from out of nowhere and then disappeared just as mysteriously. You know, come to think of it, it was early last December when I realized the house was no longer occupied. I remember asking my neighbor, Mr. Saloman, if he knew when the strange family had left and he said they went away December eighth. The day after Pearl Harbor was attacked."

Lisa, who had helped herself to some of Lottie's coffee, said in a strange voice, "Maybe they were German spies." Lottie flashed her a look, startled.

"Do you think it possible?" asked Garbo, eyebrows arched.

"In this town, anything's possible. Do you recall what these people looked like?" Mercedes was applying a match to a cigarette.

"Not really. The youngsters were very ordinary looking. The mother, the mother come to think of it . . . ," she laughed with a faraway look in her eyes, ". . . come to think of it she looked as though she would be perfect as a *bürgermeister's* wife. You know, the wife of a small-town mayor in Germany. I saw lots of them when Mauritz and I used to motor about on weekends when I wasn't needed in front of the camera. And as for the father, I only once got a real look at him." She repositioned herself so she no longer had to address their reflections in the mirror.

Mercedes asked. "Tall, short? Thin, fat? Bald maybe?"

"You know something funny. Now I know who Kriegman reminds me of."

Mercedes asked, "Who's Kriegman?"

"He's Albert's butler. That night at dinner, when I first saw Kriegman, I had a sense of déjà vu. Yes, he reminded me of Wolheim. Isn't that funny?"

Eleven

Kriegman."

Arnold Lake was in Herb Villon's office. "Who's Kriegman?" asked Villon.

"Guiss's butler. That was Lisa I was talking to."

"So I gather. No repercussions from last night?"

"Not from Lorre. He hasn't shown up on the set yet. He doesn't film until the afternoon. Lisa saw Gruber this morning. He felt the same way about Lisa's position as I do. They won't make a move against her until they think it's absolutely necessary. He's sure they don't want the cops or us feds swarming all over the place."

"What about Kriegman?" Villon persisted.

Arnold told him what Lisa had heard from Garbo about the possibly bogus family Wolheim. "I think we ought to have a look at that house."

"Easy enough to get a search warrant."

"Why don't we just go down there and pry open a window?"

"Shame on you, Arnold. That's breaking and entering. That's against the law. It's a felony."

Hands on hips Arnold asked, "You've never done it before?"

"Sure I have. But this house is on Santa Monica Beach. Right there with the big moving-picture stars. Very classy. The Santa Monica boys aren't crazy about us common L.A. cops. We have to move carefully and legitimately. I'll arrange the warrant. There's a pretty good seafood joint out there. We can lunch."

On the Goldwyn lot, in the office prepared for Albert Guiss, Guiss was seated at his desk dictating a memorandum to Martin Gruber. "And in addition," he said very precisely, clipping each word like a stock coupon, "I think it will be detrimental to the film to overpublicize it so early in production. What's the word for that, Martin?"

"Hype."

"Hype." He was amused. "Hype. I like it. Where was I? Oh yes." He leaned back in his chair and contemplated the ceiling. It was a warm day and the windows had been opened wide. He could hear the activity outside and, as someone never before associated with a motion picture, felt that wonderful charge so exclusive to the initial excitement of producing a film. Soon he would be bored to tears with the endless waiting for scenes to be shot, the daily chore of sitting through the rushes, especially von Stroheim's rushes, which would be thousands of feet of film more than other directors would need to shoot. He continued with his dictation. "True, the return of Garbo and von Stroheim is big news, but we can assume in time the excitement will die down and be replaced by other items of fresh interest, so that we can do a concentrated campaign after the picture is completed and edited to everyone's satisfaction and ready to be released, of course, with great hoopla. . . . Hoopla is right?" Martin nodded. "With great hoopla and fanfare and hopefully to huge profits."

"Shall I read this back to you?" asked Gruber.

"Not necessary. You're always very competent."

"Thank you." Guiss wasn't always given to compliments. Praise didn't come easily from his lips.

"Lisa Schmidt."

"Nice girl," said Gruber, without taking his eyes from his notebook.

"I'm not asking for a recommendation, Gruber. I want you to find out who she is."

Gruber was an excellent actor and had once trained with the immortal Max Reinhardt. But Reinhardt found his backside too fat and his voice too thin. "I can get her employment application from personnel."

"I want you to dig deeper then that, Gruber."

"I see. May I ask, is there something suspicious about her?"

"If there weren't, would I be asking you to find out more about her than a ridiculous job application can tell us? Most of those are lies anyway."

And most of what I find out for you, herr Guiss, will be lies anyway, but oh what the hell, they will be delightful lies.

Guiss continued, now at the window and looking out, all the while jamming a cigarette into the favored pearl holder. "Get to know her. Take her to lunch. Perhaps she's uninvolved. Play up to her. That shouldn't be difficult with someone as beautiful as she is. Look. There she is now." Gruber joined him at the window. Lisa was facing Peter Lorre.

Lorre said to her with wide-eyed innocence, the look he employed in films after committing a particularly gruesome murder, "You must forgive me, Miss Schmidt. How could I have embarrassed you the way I did last night? I am so ashamed of myself. I was so upset when I got home I kicked my wife in the shins."

"No matter, Mr. Lorre. It was a bit startling, the idea of me on a beach in a blackout in the dead of night. I'm like the old maid who looks under the bed before she gets into it at night."

"Oh really?"

She was beginning to understand why there were women who found him attractive. He was rumored to be having an affair with a German refugee actress, Kaaren Verne, and she was an exquisite beauty.

"Perhaps one night soon you'll let me come and help you look under the bed?"

She laughed a very husky laugh with difficulty.

"Perhaps one night you'll look under your bed and there I'll be waiting to be trapped. Anyway, Greta was very upset with me and she was right. There was a hunter's moon that night and there was a lot of mist and perhaps I had indulged just a soupçon too much of happy powder. Now we are friends, yes?"

"Of course."

"Good. Why don't we go to the Mocambo tonight? Xavier Cugat's orchestra is playing and I do a dangerous rhumba."

"I'm sorry. But we're working late tonight."

"Oh yes. Of course. I forgot. Oh dear. Greta will be furious. We're supposed to be rehearsing. I'll see you later." He scurried off like Alice's White Rabbit, very late for a very important date.

Something made Lisa look up to the second floor of the executive building. She saw Guiss and Gruber at the window, looking down at her. Guiss didn't notice Gruber's wink. Lisa hurried away.

In Garbo's dressing room, Lottie Lynton asked, "Shall I prepare lunch, Miss Garbo?"

"Let's wait until Mr. Lorre gets here, if he'll ever get here," she added with irritation. "Mercedes, you're so sweet to keep me company but if you have better things to do . . ."

Mercedes was too intrigued with intrigue. "Are you thinking Kriegman was really Wolheim?"

"Oh? Are we back to that again? Good. I like puzzles." She put a finger to her cheek. "Was Wolheim also Kriegman? I don't know. I didn't say he was, did I? I think I said Kriegman reminded me somewhat of Wolheim. Lots of people remind me of lots of people. There were times when I thought Goldwyn and Mayer were interchangeable, but then I'd remind myself how much they despise each other, so they can't be the same person."

"I wonder who rented to the Wolheims? That party ought to know something about them. They had to have references."

"That's an interesting thought." She clapped her hands. "Oh Mercedes? Do you think we should play detective?"

"It's an idea," said the small woman, puffing on a cigarette.

"It could also be dangerous," commented Lottie from the kitchenette.

Garbo reminded Mercedes, "Lottie knows a great deal about detectives. She doesn't like them."

There was a knock at the door and Peter Lorre didn't wait for an invitation to enter. "Something smells good," said Lorre.

"Yes it does," said Garbo with a frown. "Lottie! I thought I said to wait on lunch until Mr. Lorre gets here."

"He's here, isn't he?"

Garbo shrugged. "Never argue with a treasure." To Lorre she said, "Why are you always late?"

He settled into a chair. "This time I ran into Lisa Schmidt. Don't give me such a look! I was very sweet to her and I apologized for last night and I invited her to go dancing tonight but she declined."

"Very wise of her."

"Don't be unkind, Greta. Am I to understand you're inviting me to lunch?"

"It will save time, so let's get to work." She reached for her script on the dressing table.

Lottie passed around a tray of appetizers. "Your favorite," she said, terribly pleased with herself, "skinless and boneless sardines on buttered toasted wheat bread."

Garbo popped one into her mouth and the look of pleasure on her face reminded Mercedes of an advertising logo for a milk company's Elsie the Cow. Garbo asked Lorre, "Do you like the revisions?"

"Very Brechtian."

"What does that mean?"

"What do you mean what does that mean?" retorted Lorre, bristling. "Have you never read Brecht?"

"Salka made me read something he wrote called *Mother Courage*. She wanted me to play it. I'm too young. It bored me."

"Brecht, as a writer, is a law unto himself. He's very sardonic, very bitter and very witty. I have a print of his movie version of *The Threepenny Opera*. He wrote that with Kurt Weill."

"Lotte Lenya's husband?" asked Mercedes.

"Yes," replied Lorre. "I'll run the movie for you if you like, Greta."

"Will it be instructive?" asked Greta.

"It will familiarize you with the man's work. On the other hand, it's very slow and a bit tiresome. It's better on stage. I was at the premiere in Berlin before I fled to England."

"Why haven't we met Brecht?" asked Garbo.

"You wouldn't want to," advised Lorre. "His teeth are worse then Henkel's, his breath is deadly and when he decides to bathe, they raise flags from half mast."

"Charming," said Mercedes. "But he's a damned good writer."

Lottie was whipping up individual omelets. The odor was intoxicating. Lorre sniffed some cocaine and said, "Greta, let's get started. I always have trouble with lines on the first day of shooting."

"There's something else that's bothering you," the astute actress said.

"Oh no. Nothing. I didn't sleep very well last night." He lit a cigarette. There's plenty bothering me, he thought. My family trapped in Europe. Guiss's hold on me. And Lisa Schmidt. Who is she working for? Who?

Marion Davies and William Randolph Hearst were sitting across from each other on the second-floor veranda eating lunch. Her eyes were slightly bloodshot, a souvenir of some lonely, heavy drinking the previous night. She lifted a glass and drank.

"What's in that glass?" Hearst squeaked sternly. His voice was so abnormally high-pitched that whenever he spoke, people looked around in fear that there was a displaced rodent on the loose.

"Same thing that's in yours. Vichyssoise." She always drank vichyssoise from a glass. This one was heavily laced with gin. She held it out to him. "Want a sip?"

"I've got my own. What are you staring at?"

"There's two guys fiddling with the front door of that monstrosity next to us. Why don't you do something about having it torn down?"

"I have to own it before I can tear it down."

"So why don't you buy it?"

"Because I don't want it."

"Okay, then I'll buy it."

"No you won't."

"Yes I will. I've got plenty of cash of my own." She wondered if he'd found out she'd bought into the skyscraper on the southeast corner of Park Avenue and East Fifty-seventh Street in New York. She'd bought it in her sister's name.

"I don't want you wasting your money on unprofitable property."

"I don't want to profit from the damned monstrosity, I want to tear it down. By Christ, they're going into the house. Do you suppose they're planning to move in?" She made a move to shout at them, but they were already in the house, out of sight, out of earshot.

Inside the house, Herbert Villon said to Arnold Lake, "We should have brought swimsuits and taken advantage of the weather."

"We should have brought gas masks." A noxious odor permeated the place. Arnold signaled Villon to open the windows. This Villon did with difficulty. The window seams were warped and misaligned from lack of use. The front door led into a huge living room seemingly furnished and decorated in early Caligula. Arnold pried into sideboards and end tables while Villon nosed into closets and behind pieces of furniture. There was nothing to interest them. Arnold opened a door at the far side of the room. "Hey, the library."

"Oh goody," said Villon, trying desperately to ward off suffocation, "let's hope there's a wall safe. I love cracking wall safes, especially if they're hidden behind a framed print."

There were no books in the library. There was a big desk and an assortment of furniture that defied description. Nothing matched. Villon gurgled happily when he found the wall safe behind a poorly framed print of "Whistler's Mother." While Arnold rummaged about in the desk drawers, Villon worked on cracking the safe. Over his shoulder he asked Arnold, "Find anything?"

"So far a dog-eared paperback of the collected works of Schiller . . ."

". . . Whoever that is . . ."

". . . Some grocery receipts, a rotted half-eaten pear . . ."

". . . Somebody was a slob . . ."

". . . A dead roach . . . rigor mortis must have set in weeks ago . . ." He opened the last drawer, ". . . a jock strap . . ."

". . . In a desk drawer of all places?"

"Somebody was a lousy housekeeper or had a perverted sense of humor. Where the hell is that stench coming from?"

"Maybe from the cellar."

"The house doesn't have a cellar."

"Maybe from the attic."

"No attic either."

"Well somebody was a cheapskate. Voilà!" The safe door swung open. Arnold joined him at the safe. Villon murmured, "Just like Old Mother Hubbard. When she got there, the cupboard was bare." He moved away from the safe with disappointment. He crossed to a door and opened it. "I have found the kitchen."

"Chalk one up for you." They entered the kitchen and attacked the cupboards and the refrigerator. "Cheap dishes, dime store pots and pans, cutlery handed down from some forgotten dynasty . . ." Arnold continued the inventory, to include frayed dishcloths, tasteless tablecloths and napkins, while Villon examined the interior of the refrigerator.

"It's just as discouraging in here," said Villon. "Some old piece of what might have been cheddar, a half-empty jar of peanut butter, likewise apple jelly, some blob on a dish that defies description and I'm not up to the challenge . . ."

Arnold said with disgust, "Whoever these Wolheims were, Mrs. Wolheim was a lousy housekeeper." He opened a door. "This is a pantry. Do you hunger to examine the pantry?"

"Well as long as we're here, it shouldn't be a total loss." They entered the pantry. It did not elevate their spirits. It also revealed nothing of importance or interest other than a shelf that held several brands of laxatives. Villon commented, "Somebody has problems." The door next to the pantry led outside to an enclosed garden. There they saw a marble birdbath, a variety of garden furniture that ranged from wicker to iron grillwork, and what looked like the remains of either a dog or a coyote.

Arnold asked, "Are coyotes known to come down from the hills and invade the beach?"

"Only when they're longing for a dip." Villon led them back into the house. "The animal isn't the reason for the smell. It must be upstairs. I better warn you in case you're unfamiliar with the odor. There's every probability there's a corpse up there."

"Oh please. Not before lunch."

They found her in what they assumed was the master bedroom. She was laid out on the bed, her eyes open with what was either fear, horror or just plain old-fashioned surprise. Villon studied the corpse while a nauseated Arnold forced windows open. Villon said, "She was probably in her fifties. Just about five feet in height, very very plump and she mistreated her hair. It's sort of a dung-brown color. She's wearing a thin, very cheap wedding ring and the wristwatch is a Farber."

"German make," said Arnold, who reluctantly joined Villon at the bed.

"I don't know why I'm thinking this is probably Mrs. Wolheim."

"She looks like a forgotten German potato dumpling. Do you suppose with any luck that phone works?"

The phone was on an end table on the opposite side of the bed. Arnold lifted the receiver, listened and smiled. "Allah is good. The operator to get your team?"

Villon took the phone from him. "That would be very naughty. This is Santa Monica's territory. But I'm feeling very wicked today. This stench is causing my senses to reel." He called his precinct and requested a photographer, a forensic team and the coroner.

"What will you do if the Santa Monica cops turn up before your boys get here?"

"I'll feign amnesia."

"Say Willie." Marion Davies was at the railing of her veranda, now wearing a sailor hat and carrying in her right hand a glass of cold *scharv* laced with a healthy infusion of vodka.

"What, honey?" he tweeted while trying to read Louella Parsons's column.

"There's something going on at that house. For chrissakes will you come over here and look? You're supposed to be a newspaperman, aren't you curious? Those cars are unmarked but if them ain't cops swarming into the place then Greer Garson's my mother."

Hearst stood behind her, saw a number of men get out of a Ford and a Chevrolet and enter the house. "Well," he finally said, "that certainly looks like it might be police activity."

"Well it sure ain't a meeting of the local B'nai B'rith."

Hearst left her and went inside to phone his managing editor. Marion went to her bedroom to use her private phone. She called the Goldwyn Studios and asked to be put through to Greta Garbo's dressing room.

Lottie Lynton took the call. "Oh hello, Miss Davies. Miss Garbo is on the set. I don't know how long she'll be. It's the first day, you know, and everyone's nerves are on edge. Mr. von Stroheim slapped an extra who punched him in the jaw, you know, little incidents like that . . . but wait . . . wait . . . here she is. . . ."

Garbo came storming through the doorway, a dangerous tornado. "That son of a bitch. That hideous Hun. How dare he tell me how to play comedy. His idea of hilarious is dissecting a cat while it's still alive!"

Lottie had her hand discreetly across the mouthpiece of the phone. "I have Miss Davies here."

"I can't talk to anyone now. I'm too upset."

Lottie repeated Garbo's words efficiently. Then she listened and, eyes wide with excitement, reported, "She says . . . er . . . the place is swarming with the fuzz . . ."

"Fuzz? What fuzz?" Garbo was lighting a cigarette and puffing it ferociously.

"The police!"

"What place? What are you talking about?"

"Where the Wolheims lived!"

Intrigue quickly replaced anger. Garbo took the phone and asked, "Marion? What's going on?"

She heard Davies saying, "I saw two guys go in there about an hour ago. Then all of a sudden a couple of cars show up . . ." In the distance she could hear the wail of an ambulance siren. ". . . With what certainly were more cops, plainclothes guys, and one carrying a little black satchel so he had to be the sawbones . . . you know . . . um . . . uh yeah . . . the coroner. So they've probably found a stiff in the joint." Marion was enjoying herself immensely. "How about that! Murder right next door! Oh Christ, Willie's phoning his editor and that means reporters and photographers and they'll be questioning me and I look like shit warmed over! Ethel! Ethel!" she shouted for her maid, "Come in here and make me look young! There's going to be photographers! Greta? I'll keep you posted!"

Marion Davies slammed the phone down and hurried into the room she'd had refitted as a beauty parlor. Ethel had preceded her and was mixing magic potions in pharmacy bowls. "And get the clamps to pull my skin back behind my head. I'll wear a gold brocade turban, that'll hide them." She shouted at another maid who had entered the room. "Get over to the house next door and try and find out who was murdered." The ambulance had arrived and the shrieking siren was abruptly choked off. "The meat wagon's here! I haven't been so excited since I got screwed by Charlie Chaplin!"

The police photographer photographed the corpse from every angle while the forensic team went to work on the room. The coroner, with a practiced eye, took one look at the texture of the dead woman's skin and said she'd probably been dead anywhere from five days to a week.

"Any idea what killed her?" asked Villon while Arnold Lake stood next to him, hands in his pockets, foreseeing that the woman's murder would soon lead to a large-scale explosion of international intrigue. If she was the putative Mrs. Wolheim, and if the Wolheims

were German agents, then her murder could possibly trigger a string of killings confined to the family of agents.

He heard the coroner saying, "If you'll look at her head, you'll notice there are patches on the skull where she's lost clumps of hair." He cleared his throat. "There are certain blood disorders that can cause that. But in this case, I'll put my money on thallium nitrate. That's a highly toxic metal." They stood to one side as the meat wagon orderlies entered with a stretcher and prepared to remove the body. "It's rarely used in one dose. It's usually served a little at a time, like cyanide, so it takes the victim a few weeks to die. The symptoms, in addition to the loss of hair, include a painful burning in the feet. I'll know more when I've cut into her." He watched the corpse being carried out of the room and then said to Villon admonishingly, "Herbie, aren't you being a bad boy? Doesn't she belong to the Santa Monica boys?"

Villon said with an innocent look, "Finders keepers."

At the studio, Martin Gruber made it his business to encounter Lisa Schmidt on the set. "Ah Miss Schmidt. Just the person I've been looking for."

"Mr. Gruber? How can I help you?"

He walked her out of earshot of the personnel setting up for the next scene. "Guiss has ordered me to find out everything I can about you."

"So he's still suspicious?"

"He's tenacious. And very thorough. So I thought we might meet and concoct a biography for you that will satisfy all of us. Nothing too outrageous, mind you. But something that will tell him something but will really tell him nothing. And then he'll be satisfied and compliment me for a job well done. He might even give me a raise."

"Shall we meet and do it together? What do you suggest?"

"Why don't I draw up a rough treatment, and then you can add or subtract or embellish. You're twenty-four, right?"

"Right."

"Orphaned early in life and raised by a cruel spinster aunt?"

"No, it was actually a cruel maternal grandmother who claimed I was illegitimate."

"That bothered you?"

"Oh not at all. I remember mother used to introduce me to a wide variety of uncles at breakfast frequently. They came in all shapes and sizes and a variety of denominations and I adored almost all of them, especially the ones who'd give me some money if I'd let them cop a feel. All kidding aside, I was born in Cleveland, my parents were Bavarian immigrants, and they were killed in a train crash about three years ago."

Gruber thought for a moment. "Nah, too mundane. Let me work on it and I'll soon have a rough draft for you."

In an exaggeratedly loud voice she said, "I'll have those notes typed up for Mr. Guiss, Mr. Gruber. I'll get to it immediately."

Von Stroheim had come upon them unseen by Gruber. "What notes?" he growled.

Gruber took over. "Mr. Guiss wants a daily progress report."

The director's eyes narrowed. "Why?"

"Why, to know how you're progressing. Isn't it usual for the director's assistant to keep a daily report on how many minutes have been filmed each day?"

Von Stroheim's skin turned purple with rage as he exploded, "I will not be persecuted! We have only just begun shooting today and already the vultures are gathering to plague me!"

"Please, Mr. von Stroheim," placated Gruber.

The director shouted, "If you wish to please Mr. von Stroheim you'll keep to hell away from my kingdom! This set is my kingdom! I am the absolute ruler. If Mr. Guiss wants a daily progress report, tell him it cannot be provided with any degree of accuracy because from one day to the next I'm never sure what I have accomplished until I have studied the rushes and decided what is usable and what needs to be reshot and I am a *very slow study!* Now get the hell out of here!"

Gruber fled.

Von Stroheim took Lisa by the arm and hustled her to one side. "What's going on between you and Peter Lorre?"

She felt the blood draining from her face. "Nothing," she managed to say.

"He's very upset. He's giving a very poor performance. I'm told there was a confrontation with you last night that led to circumstances that have left him upset and nervous and unhappy, and I will not tolerate that."

Lisa told him about the previous evening's confrontation and then Lorre's apology earlier that afternoon. "That's all it was," she said in conclusion, "an innocent case of mistaken identity."

Von Stroheim was just about her height, about five feet four or five. They were standing almost nose to nose. "Tell me the truth, young woman. Are you involved in an undercover activity? Are you a spy for Hedda Hopper?"

She collapsed with laughter and von Stroheim smiled. She's a good girl, he thought, a very good girl. I must lure her to a nondescript motel in Laguna Beach and ravage her.

Twelve

When it seemed a small war was about to erupt between Herb Villon and the Santa Monica Police Department, Arnold Lake arranged for his superiors to come to Villon's assistance, which resulted in an uneasy truce. The Santa Monica police smarted from the illegal invasion and threatened revenge.

William Randolph Hearst succeeded in scooping his rival newspapers and bought Marion a diamond tiara that would later be inside the bag of jewelry she gave him to pawn when his newspaper empire was tottering on the brink of bankruptcy.

When Garbo came home from the studio that night with Lottie Lynton, she found Herb Villon and Arnold Lake waiting for her in Villon's parked car. Villon apologized for the invasion of her privacy but since she and Salka Viertel were the only people he knew to have seen the Wolheims, it was possible she could make an identification, if the dead woman was indeed Mrs. Wolheim.

Wearily, Garbo said, "Come inside, gentlemen. Salka Viertel, my good friend, will be here any moment now. Perhaps she can assist in identifying the woman." Lottie took Garbo's coat and bustled out of the room to prepare drinks. Villon and Arnold watched Garbo cross to the couch and slink down onto it. This is the fabulous Garbo, thought Villon, here she is in the flesh, and she's even more beautiful and seductive then she is on the screen.

So this is Garbo, thought Arnold Lake. Big deal. Later, he would dine out on stories about his pal Greta until all of Washington, D.C., stopped inviting him to social events in hopes he would now have the time to find a new routine.

They heard Garbo say, "I'm sure Saloman also saw the Wolheims. He's one of my neighbors. A retired insurance broker. A widower. He lives alone." She indicated with a tired wave of a hand in which direction they might succeed in locating Mr. Saloman. "I'd phone and invite him here but I have never invited him here and I see no reason to upset a precedent. I assume you have a photo of the dead woman, so why not take it to Mr. Saloman, since Salka might be a while yet and I would like some time to pull myself together. The first day of a film is always very trying. You are working with actors mostly you have never worked with before, and you have to learn to accommodate yourself to so many of them. It's like being given a new and unfamiliar family, you understand?"

They understood. Villon volunteered to go see Saloman. Arnold stayed behind and eagerly took the scotch and soda Lottie brought him. Garbo just as eagerly sipped her vodka on the rocks and kicked her shoes off. She studied Arnold for awhile, her inquisitor eyes making him so uncomfortable, he thought she'd put Torquemada to shame. Finally she said, "You are a federal agent, you say?"

"Yes."

"A G-man."

"Yes."

"Like James Cagney?"

"He's not a G-man."

"He was one in a movie I saw years ago. He was a cute G-man. Are there other G-men who are cute?"

"We don't see ourselves as cute."

"I think you're cute." She grinned. "Don't take me seriously. After a day with Erich von Stroheim and Peter Lorre it is understandable that I'm feeling a bit quixotic." She paused and then said, "I should like to play that part."

He could barely keep up with the way her mind jumped about. "What part?"

"The character from which the word 'quixotic' evolved. Cervantes's Don Quixote. But the correct pronunciation is 'Kee-ho-tay.' See, you are surprised. Garbo is educated." She laughed. "Not really very much. I was a poor student. As I grew older, I learned and absorbed from others. That is why I am most frequently quiet. I am quiet because I am listening and learning. Ah! I hear Salka's car! Lottie! Mrs. Viertel is here! Bring her a dry sherry to compliment her dry wit." Garbo crossed to the door and Salka Viertel entered. Garbo introduced her to Arnold just as Herb Villon returned.

Salka liked both men at once. They were handsome and of the no-nonsense type she appreciated.

Villon told them, "Mr. Saloman gave me a positive identification."

"Yes?" Garbo's head was cocked to one side. "Show me the picture." It was in the manila envelope he was holding. She and Salka examined the photograph. Garbo grimaced. Salka said, "Yes that's the poor dumpy thing." Garbo agreed. Salka asked, "How was she killed?"

"The coroner has tentatively suggested the possibility of a toxic metallic poison called thallium nitrate. You'll notice she's missing patches of hair. That's one of the symptoms."

Garbo left them and walked to the window that overlooked the ocean. "Look, Salka, look! The dolphins are out there playing!"

Salka explained to the men, "She dotes on dolphins."

Lottie came from the kitchen with a tray of hors d'ouevres, and offered them to Garbo's guests. She smiled at Villon. Villon thought, I know this woman. I've met her before. But I can't remember. It'll come to me. It usually does.

"You have the weirdest look on your face, Herb."

He told Arnold that he thought he'd known Lottie at another time.

Arnold suggested, "Why don't you ask her. Did she look as though she recognized you?"

Villon couldn't answer because Garbo and Salka returned from their dolphin watching and began bombarding him with questions. Salka took the lead. "Was there any evidence in the house as to her real identity? Obviously Wolheim is a pseudonym."

Villon told them, "There was nothing. No purse, no identification whatsoever. The labels on her clothes were store-bought, cheap store-bought, downtown L.A., not easy to trace. Forensics have dusted the house but found nothing of any importance. A few fingerprints have been sent to D.C. for possible identification. The lab is examining some leftover peanut butter and apple jelly we found in the refrigerator for possible traces of the poison."

Salka asked with interest, "The refrigerator was connected? The electricity hadn't been disconnected?"

"And the phone was working," contributed Villon.

"Then you must investigate the utility companies and find out who pays the bills." Garbo was back in the spotlight again. "Well, shouldn't you?"

Villon was abashed. "Chalk one up for you, Miss Garbo. We should have thought of that ourselves."

"But the people who have paid the bills probably aren't real." She was stroking her chin. "Yes? I'm right? It's logical, yes? If the Wolheims were German agents, whoever paid the bills didn't use a real name. Oh my God!" Her hand flew to her mouth.

Alarmed, Salka cried, "What's wrong? Greta, what is it?"

"Kriegman!"

Arnold asked, "Who's Kriegman?"

"Guiss's butler. Lottie, I need more vodka." Garbo sat. "Earlier today, I was discussing the Wolheims in my dressing room with Peter Lorre and my friend Mercedes de Acosta. There had been some misunderstanding on Peter's side when he thought one of the girls who works with von Stroheim was a mysterious woman in need of rescue on our beach several weeks ago. Nice girl, Lisa Schmidt." Villon and Arnold refrained from exchanging glances. "Anyway, in discussing Mr. Wolheim, I had this feeling I had seen someone who resembled him, and then I remembered who that was. Kriegman!"

Again Arnold asked, "Who's Kriegman?"

"He's the butler who works for Albert Guiss!"

Now Villon and Arnold exchanged glances. Villon said, "We'll have to meet this butler Kriegman."

"I can phone Albert for you if you like," offered Garbo.

"Oh no no. We need the element of surprise here." Villon was adamant. "We'd prefer to drop in on Mr. Guiss by surprise."

Garbo sounded mournful. "Mr. Guiss is not easily dropped in on. He lives in a fortress in Bel Air equipped with very sophisticated electrical equipment to keep intruders out. I have been there several times. I know." Lottie brought her the vodka refill.

Suddenly Villon asked Lottie, "Excuse me. But have we met before?"

Lottie rewarded him with a lavish smile. "But of course we have. Almost ten years ago. You arrested me."

Garbo's mouth hung open. Salka said, "He *what?*"

"He arrested me," insisted Lottie. "And I'll never forget, he was terribly polite and very nice." She reminded Villon, "You had that blonde girlfriend of yours with you."

"Hazel Dickson."

"That's it. Hazel Dickson. She was a gossip writer or something."

"That's right."

"What's become of her? You dump her?"

"No. She joined the army. She's a WAC Captain."

"She ought to do right good at that."

"Right now she's having a bit of trouble keeping a lot of the girls serving under her from getting engaged to each other. Say, what's your name again?"

Her hands were on her hips with annoyance, as though *How dare he not remember her.* "Lottie Lynton, for crying out loud!"

"Lottie. . . ."

". . . *Lynton.*" She underlined her name with impatience. Salka, shaking her head in disbelief, went to the bar to refresh her sherry.

Garbo was delighted at the unexpected confrontation. "Lottie has been with me over two years now. Her parole officer entrusted me to her care. She belongs to me now. She's a treasure."

It was coming back to Villon. "You killed your husband."

"And how, the mean son of a bitch. I kept warning him to stop beating up on me. The damn fool called my bluff so I killed him. I still carry a lot of those scars."

"I remember now," said Villon. "You poisoned him."

"You got it!"

"It was something like cocoa, something like that, right?"

"It was hot chocolate," shrieked Garbo, unable to contain a sudden fit of laughter.

"That's right!" cried Villon. "Hot chocolate!"

Lottie stood tall and proud. Poisoning her husband would be a feat about which she would crow for the rest of her life.

"It was cyanide, right?" said Villon.

"Wrong." She folded her arms. "It was thallium nitrate!" Garbo's laughter died. Lottie couldn't understand the sudden silence. "Well that's what it was. I read up on it in a book of poisons I found in my local library. The poor bastard. It took weeks for him to die. And I had to listen to him yelling in agony, how his feet were on fire and then the clumps of hair began coming out when he combed himself and I tell you, watching him go just about took my appetite away. But he finally went and they caught up with me and I'm out on good behavior and here I am."

"Yes indeed," agreed Villon, "Here you are."

Thirteen

A few hours later over dinner at Musso and Frank's popular restaurant on Hollywood Boulevard, Villon still couldn't get over Lottie Lynton's brazen performance in Garbo's living room. "The way she carried on about poisoning her husband, you'd think she'd invented the safety pin. Have a potato pancake."

Arnold declined the offer. "Do you think she did in Mrs. Wolheim?"

"No motive. Why would she? Just to keep in practice?"

"Well, we have a thallium nitrate killer living in the vicinity of a thallium nitrate victim. How coincidental can a coincidence get?"

"Thallium nitrate's very popular. I had a case a couple of months ago involving some nut case who got rid of his wife, her mother and father, and three teenage children. He claimed God told him to do it."

"Which God?"

"In his case? Probably Buddha. The family was Chinese. They owned a restaurant."

Arnold speared a boiled carrot and was about to consign it to his mouth when he lowered the fork and said, "Martin Gruber."

"What about him?"

"The butler. Kriegman."

"Come on, man, make sense."

"Gruber can take a picture of Kriegman and get it to us. We've got a new camera that works sensationally indoors. They're sure to have one in the local office."

"Arnold, you're a genius."

"I'll get after it first thing in the morning."

"Supposing Gruber balks? He can't go chasing after Kriegman yelling 'Hey Kriegman baby, watch the birdie!' "

"He's clever. He's one of the best informants we've ever had. He comes from a long line of traitors. He didn't need much training when Lisa brought him to us."

"He's that good? You sure he isn't double-headed?"

Arnold gave it some thought. "Work for us and work for them? Anything's possible in this game." He shook his head. "No, not Gruber. He's given us too much stuff over the past year that's been pure gold. He's helped us crack two codes, he got us a great list of fifth columnists working in the country, and the Germans don't pay all that good. We pay *real* good."

"How long has he been in the Guiss camp?"

"Over a year now."

"And he still hasn't been able to nail Guiss and his satellites?"

"Herb, you're such an innocent. When we're out of this place, I'll tell you some bedtime stories."

"What's wrong with here?" asked Villon, while challenging a limp, overcooked asparagus spear.

"You never know who's in the next booth."

"I know who's in the next booth. A couple of French actresses, Fifi D'Orsay and Yola D'Avril. Nice girls."

"Are they Free French?"

"Don't know. I've had no call to make them an offer."

* * *

"I swear, herr Guiss, I swear I didn't kill her! The last I saw of her was over a week ago when she was packing to leave for Canada." Kriegman was dabbing at his damp forehead with a handkerchief. "It was arranged for our people in Toronto to get her back to Germany. Isn't that so, herr Henkel? You passed the message on to them."

In addition to Henkel, Risa Barron and Werner Lieb were in Guiss's office, all of them worried about what consequences might result from Mrs. Wolheim's murder. Henkel stifled a nervous yawn. "Yes, that is so. They didn't particularly want her back."

"Why is that?" asked Guiss.

"They had no further use for her back home. They would have preferred she stay here. They were arranging for her to work with a family in Boston, I believe their name was Kennedy. But Anna wanted to go home. She was frightened."

"Yes," bellowed Kriegman, "she was very frightened. She was gorging herself on peanut butter and apple jelly sandwiches when she wasn't wringing her hands and muttering *'Achtung, achtung'* over and over again. And she was complaining how her feet were burning and she began losing her hair."

"Nerves," said Risa Barron flatly, "nothing but nerves. I had a sister who lost her eyebrows, her eyelashes and her pubic hairs when her husband left her for a houri in Morocco. Of course it all grew back later when she fell in love with a pharmacist. Nothing but nerves."

Kriegman was babbling away again. "You said yourself an agent is hopeless once they begin to lose their nerve. Perhaps if we had stayed on in that house, if you hadn't forced our disappearance after Pearl Harbor was bombed. . . ."

"Your usefulness in the house was finished. I needed you here, just as I needed the boys to join my armed guards." Guiss asked Risa, "The girl? Does she still dissatisfy you?"

Risa was busy fiddling with the clasp of a bracelet. "She tries hard. She's so ordinary. How did she get into undercover work? She's so plain, so ordinary. She should marry a butcher's assistant and have babies."

"She knows Mrs. Wolheim has been killed?"

"Of course she knows. She reads the newspapers."

"Did she say anything to you?"

"She said plenty to me. She's frightened. There were people who saw them on the beach when they took their nightly stroll, that Jew Saloman who lives next door to Greta. And Greta too, and her friend Salka Viertel. And I think Marion Davies when she and Hearst played tag on the beach. *Gott in Himmel!* We should send them all back to Germany and the sooner the better."

Kriegman paled. "Please! Don't send me back! I don't want to go back. There's nothing there for me."

"Oh shut up, you fool!" shouted Guiss. He got up and moved away from his desk, thinking aloud. "She was packed to leave for Germany. Was someone to escort her to the train?"

"I was," said Henkel. Then he smiled, "She was rather fond of me."

"Why didn't you take her to the train?"

"When I went to get her, she was gone. Nobody saw her leave."

"And nobody knows how she got back in the house."

"Her murderer knows." Risa Barron spoke sweetly, mellifluously. "Do you suppose the federals killed her? Do you suppose they murdered her and put her back in the house as a warning that they're on to us?"

Guiss said matter-of-factly, "When they're on to us, they'll come and get us."

Risa's eyes widened. "That prospect doesn't frighten you?"

"I don't frighten easily."

Werner Lieb asked, while polishing his monocle with a tissue paper, "Has it occurred to you that the murderer might be among us?"

"It most certainly has," said Guiss, "but who among us had a reason to kill her?"

"Do all murderers have to have a motive?" asked Lieb. "Aren't there killers who kill just for the thrill of killing? She was of no further use to the cause, right? Therefore, she was expendable."

Risa leaned forward in her seat. "You make it sound so plausible. Maybe you're the one who killed her."

"I'm a pragmatist, Risa. I think the investigation should be left in the hands of the police. The newspapers don't say how she was murdered, just that the body of a woman known as Mrs. Wolheim was found in a bedroom of a Santa Monica beach house in the vicinity of the homes of some very important celebrities. Hearst himself scooped his rivals. I think we should be more concerned with the poor showing on the part of our artists on the first day of shooting. Von Stroheim managed less than two minutes of usable footage. That's very bad."

"From what I saw of the first scene with Garbo and Lorre," contributed Risa, "their performances look very disappointing."

"They will improve," said Guiss with confidence, "and von Stroheim promises to get the lead out. They're all nervous. A first day, they tell me, is never easy."

"That's right," said Risa with a wicked grin, "it's like the first night of a honeymoon. All clumsy fumbling."

Guiss lit a cigarette. "We'll see what we've got when we view the rushes tomorrow. Maybe Greta won't sound good, but she'll certainly look good. Her color tests were remarkable." He smiled at the recollection. "How I would love to make love to her."

For the first time since she'd met Guiss, Risa felt sorry for him. Deep in his thoughts of the elusive Garbo, Guiss looked like a sad and vulnerable schoolboy.

On their way to Arnold's bungalow to continue their discussion of Guiss and company, Arnold and Villon paused in the Garden of Allah's busy bar for a drink. It was crowded with celebrities and Herb Villon was a sucker for important names. Dorothy Parker was sitting at a table with her husband, Alan Campbell, and the comedian Charles Butterworth. They heard Butterworth asking Mrs. Parker, "Have you read Steinbeck's new book?"

"Some of it."

"What's it like?"

She replied, "I've found more substance in tea leaves."

From another table writer-director Preston Sturges was having drinks with actor-humorist Robert Benchley. Benchley was discussing an actor Sturges was considering for his upcoming movie. "I think he's rather mediocre," Benchley said.

Sturges replied with a thick tongue, "He's not talented enough to be mediocre."

At the bar, actress Miriam Hopkins was trying not to look bored with her companion, actor Vince Barnett, who said to her from out of the blue, "Y'know Miriam, I think I lived in another life."

She said brightly, "Where you swung by your tail?"

Arnold nudged Villon. "Let's go to my bungalow. I've had it in here."

In his bungalow, Arnold removed his jacket and poured drinks for them. Villon settled into an easy chair and lit a cigarette. Arnold said, "You know what I think, Herb? I think the lady was done in by one of her own bunch."

"I think you may be right."

"I have to be right. As far as we know, she was just part of her phony family. She probably didn't know anybody else in L.A."

"What bugs me," said Villon, "is where was she holed up from the time she left the beach house December eighth until her murder? That's two months at least."

"They probably had her stashed in one of their safe houses. They've got at least three that we know of in the area." Arnold thought for a moment. "Somebody must have thought she was a threat or else she was of no further use to them and it was simpler to kill her than send her back to Germany. They have a route back through Canada, you know."

"So I've heard. Our friendly neighbors to the north realize how hospitable they're being to the Nazis?"

"They know, trust me, they know."

"Okay, now what about Guiss and his playmates?"

"We know," said Arnold, "that Guiss is Viennese and that he served as a lancer in the Viennese army. In that period he showed an amazing talent for diplomacy and won the friendship and admiration of some very powerful people. Now that's about twenty years ago. It's reasonable to suppose he was a war hero but I doubt we'll ever get the opportunity to see and admire his decorations. Then there's a five-year lapse and when he re-emerges, he is a very very wealthy man enveloped in a cloak of mystery."

"No wife? No children?"

"No nothing. Lots of rumors of mistresses. Risa Barron has been filling that bill for the last couple of years. He's showered her with a fortune in jewelry."

"What about Barron? Have you ever met her?"

"I've only seen photographs, newsreels: She's an ugly broad who's learned how to look good. Her features are all wrong but put them all together the way she does and you have what the pulp writers call a fascinating adventuress. She's played footsie with a lot of bad boys. Hitler and his gang, Mussolini and his pasta patrol. It's rumored she served time in a harem and came away with the title to an oil well. She was really nuts about Guiss but I hear there's the suspicion that it might be cooling. He's after Garbo."

"I'll bet he doesn't get her," said Villon.

"Then there's Werner Lieb. Everything about him is phony. His name, his monocle, his position as co-producer of the movie. What he is is Guiss's aide-de-camp. Guiss picked him up in South America about ten years ago where he was on the lam from Germany on a swindling deal. He took money from old ladies."

"So do department stores."

"There was also a charge of pederasty. Guiss cleaned his slate for him. He recognized in Lieb the kind of toady who wouldn't go bad on him. Guiss is very fond of him and Lieb is smart enough to know he'll never do better then he's doing now."

"And Henkel? What's his story?"

"He used to be an accountant. He tried writing short stories but never sold any, at least not to our knowledge. We don't think he's German. How's your drink?"

"It's fine. Tell me more. I'm fascinated."

"We doubt Henkel's his real name. The boys have studied his photographs and suspect he's a Slav, or a Pole, or even a Latvian. There's a candid shot of him grinning at some bathing beauty pageant and God Almighty those teeth of his look like they've been bombarded with buckshot."

"And then there's our boy Gruber. Mustn't forget to get that camera to him."

"There's also our girl Greta."

Villon sat up. "You're certainly not suspecting her of killing Mrs. Wolheim."

"Oh no way. But she spent time in Germany. She knew a lot of people there who today are active Nazis."

"So what? Pola Negri's back in town trying to make a comeback, remember her?"

"Silent pictures?"

"Right," said Villon. "But do you know where she was before the war broke out in Europe? She was in Germany starring in pictures for our boy Goebbels. Does anybody put her in a hot seat and grill her?"

"We've got a complete dossier on her. She's harmless. She worked in Germany because it was the only offer she had on the burner and she was running out of jewels to hock."

"You can't tell me Garbo might be a sympathizer. She was pretty damned smart tonight. 'Check out who's paying for the utilities!' Why didn't *we* think of that?"

Arnold shrugged. He was tired. He wished Lisa Schmidt would check in. He would need her to get the camera to Gruber. He wished he didn't feel so uneasy about her safety. There wasn't a fascist fanatic he knew about who didn't operate with a short fuse. Today it's "Don't kill her" and tomorrow it could be "What, she's still alive?" These people frightened him. They weren't human the way he'd been taught about humanity in Sunday school. They weren't real. He said it aloud and startled Villon. "Guiss isn't real!"

"What the hell is that supposed to mean?"

"I just had a hunch. There's something about Guiss that makes me suspect he's a fake."

"You mean he isn't really rich?"

"I mean, maybe it's not his money."

Villon was helping himself to another drink. "I know what you're getting at and it's an interesting premise. He was planned and created a billionaire, a mystery man. To act as a go-between. The mobs used to do that back in the twenties. Did you know they created George Raft and paid to make him a star just to get a foot inside Hollywood? Did you know that?"

"He's still a star, isn't he?"

"Go figure that one out. No talent and his name is still above the title."

"Figuratively, so's Guiss's. But what's his talent? Why has he been told to pour five million dollars into a turkey about Joan of Arc? Why is it costing five million? Lisa Schmidt says the sets aren't inexpensive, but they're not lavish. Outside of Garbo's million, the other members of the cast are working for their usual fees, nothing out of the ordinary there. She thinks maybe two or two and a half million would more than cover the cost of the production. So who's pocketing the difference?"

The phone rang. It was Lisa Schmidt. Arnold told her about the camera ploy and she assured him it would be no problem getting it to Gruber. She told him about Guiss ordering a thorough investigation into her background. Then they moved on to discuss the murder.

"Have you figured out how the body got into the house?" Lisa asked. "Was she still alive when she was in the house? Did she inconveniently die there and the killer decided he might just as well leave her there?"

"Good thought."

They discussed the utilities. Lisa said, "It's Guiss's property. Gruber told me that a long time ago. That's why the utilities are still connected. Why else did they have the meeting there? Why else were the Wolheims in residence for so long? I'll bet you a week's salary they had a shortwave sending and receiving set and were a relay station. Damn it, Arnold, it's in one of my reports that Guiss owns the house."

"I can't remember everything I read," Arnold snapped. "I get so many damned reports from J. Edgar I sometimes wonder when he finds time to hate so many people."

"I think it's a good chance one of her own people killed her. Maybe Guiss ordered it. If Kriegman really is Wolheim, maybe for one reason or another the lady was threatening to blow the whistle on the boys. Oh Christ I'm tired. I can't think. Let me know when you have the camera, we'll make arrangements to meet."

"What kind of a biography have you and Gruber cooked up for yourself?" asked Arnold.

"It's a beaut. Maybe we can sell the movie rights."

"Maybe. Get some sleep. Sorry I snapped at you. I'm a little punchy."

"We're all a little punchy. See you tomorrow."

"And Lisa, bolt your door and windows."

"I'm way ahead of you. I already have. It's very stuffy in here. Good night."

Villon poured another drink for himself and Arnold said, "You better go easy on that stuff. You'll have a bitch of a hangover in the morning."

"I never have hangovers. And I don't have an easy time falling asleep. The booze helps. I've got to work on this Guiss theory of yours. What did Lisa have to say?"

Arnold told him about Lisa's questioning if the woman was dead on arrival or conveniently expired there.

Villon said, "You're forgetting something. The poison was administered over a period of time. Somebody knew her favorite foods and laced them with the poison. I'll give you odds on that."

"Maybe peanut butter and apple jelly?"

Villon looked at his wristwatch. He knew the men in forensics would probably still be at it. It was only a little past ten. There were times when they conducted their experiments throughout the night, especially when they were facing an overload. He phoned his precinct and got through to one of the men in forensics. He advised him to test for thallium nitrate in the peanut butter and the apple jelly.

Jack Kelly of forensics told Villon, "That's just what we found. She must have eaten the stuff over a period of weeks, two, maybe less if she gorged on the stuff."

"Thanks, Jack." After he hung up, Villon said, "If she left the stuff behind in the refrigerator and doted on it that much, she had to get herself a fresh supply when she moved to the safe house."

"It was probably bought for her," said Arnold, "as a farewell gift."

Villon sighed. "Arnold, it's getting too late for irony. I'm going home. Could you point me to the door?"

Garbo sat in the darkness of her living room, puffing a cigarette, staring out at the ocean, watching the waves rise and crest against the shore, while harboring thoughts that until now had been strangers to her. Poison and murder and corpses in a neighboring house. Lottie Lynton and the joy she took in being a husband killer. Villon had identified himself as a detective, but what about the other man? His name, his name . . . she prodded her memory. Oh yes. Arnold Lake. Did he say he was a detective? No, he didn't. Then who is he? Still, he didn't have to say he was a detective, he was with the other one. They were quite chummy. They enjoyed each other. They worked well together.

Peter Lorre flashed into her mind. They hadn't worked well together today. Yes it was the first day and that old chestnut about the first day of a film being the most difficult always holds true and her nerves were genuine, but Peter's nervousness, she was convinced, was due to something else.

Fear.

Fear? But of what is he afraid? Could it be Lisa Schmidt? Could it be possible he really saw her on the beach that night? Right in his own home asking for help? Perhaps she never thought that someday she would confront him again. Peter was so positive at the studio that she was the woman in question, he was almost frantic about it. And then today, the very next day, he says he was mistaken. Yesterday's angry puppy is today's darling pussycat. And it's wrong.

She stubbed the cigarette out and went to the bar for a vodka on the rocks. With the glass in her hand, she opened the back door and went out to the patio. From where she stood, she could see the house of mystery. Bathed in the eerie glow cast by the full moon, it looked sinister and threatening. Mrs. Wolheim.

Mr. Wolheim. Kriegman. Now in the new guise of Guiss's butler. Does Guiss suspect that Kriegman is an enemy agent?

"Oh my God," she whispered, "I am so dense. I am so stupid. Of course he knows!"

She hurried back into the house, shut the door, drew the curtains to protect the blackout, and phoned Salka Viertel. Salka listened closely and absorbed the information and suspicions her friend was pouring out. Finally she said, "Listen to me, Greta. Whatever you suspect, you keep to yourself. It could be dangerous."

"When have I ever been afraid of danger? Didn't I co-star with John Barrymore?"

"Please Greta. If these people are what you think they are, and they suspect you know, your life could be in danger. God in heaven, it's already been in the papers we identified Mrs. Wolheim. So it stands to reason we'd also be able to identify *Mr.* Wolheim. And if it really is Kriegman, and he is now working for Guiss . . . oh my God Greta. We might at this very moment be marked women!"

"Stop being so melodramatic, Salka. You've written too many scripts. Who would dare kill Garbo?"

"Albert Guiss."

"You really think so? But how enchanting. This makes him a bit more interesting."

Salka said with irritation, "Stop talking like a fool. Maybe we should phone those detectives who came to the house. Maybe you should tell *them* what you suspect."

"Don't you think they are smart enough to have figured that out by themselves? They seemed quite intelligent. Oh Salka. How wonderful!"

"What's wonderful?"

"To be in danger! I don't think I have ever been in danger before. Oh Salka, it's a whole new emotion for me and I have been so desperately looking for something fresh in my barren life! I'm in danger! How marvelous! I'm tempted to phone Louella and Hedda but no, I will not. This emotion is mine, all mine, and I shall keep it to myself like the greedy, selfish little brat I am. I shall have another vodka and think about this. Go to sleep my darling. Go to sleep. We'll talk tomorrow." Gently, she replaced the phone on the receiver.

* * *

Go to sleep? Is she mad? Salka threw a pillow across the room and knew she was in for a restless night.

Garbo poured the vodka she had promised herself and then went back out on the patio. Did she think she had fooled Salka? Had she overplayed? Did Salka truly believe that Greta was not afraid of danger? The night air caused her to tremble. The night air? Or was it fear? God, you fool. Go back inside. Get off the patio. You're an easy target out here in the moonlight. She hurried back into the house. She latched the door securely. She hurried to her bedroom and came to a decision to share her suspicions with Villon and Arnold.

Fourteen

They were delighted she had phoned early that morning and asked them to come to the studio. Villon and Arnold sat with Garbo in her dressing room drinking hot chocolate catered by Lottie Lynton. Garbo wondered if they'd forgotten it was hot chocolate that had brought the curtain down on Mr. Lynton's life. Lottie also served a plate of Toll-House cookies she had baked early that morning. The men had nothing but admiration for the actress. Her deductions were intelligent and carefully thought out. Hers was a shrewd brain camouflaged by immortal beauty. They admired her and told her so.

Garbo clapped her hands with joy, a little girl winning the approval of her teachers. "And what is that interesting-looking camera you have there Mr. Lake?"

"Um, it's something I picked up in South America when I was down there a couple of months ago."

"It looks terribly sophisticated. I only have a little Brownie. Still, it takes very nice pictures. May I examine the camera?" Arnold handed it to her and she looked through the viewfinder and laughed. "You both look so serious. Is there film in it? I'd like to take your picture." Lake asked her not to and she pouted. "I take a very good picture, you can trust me. I have been taught by masters. Cecil Beaton, Louise Dahl Wolfe, Robert Capa who has gone off to photograph the war in Europe. But still, if you don't want your picture taken . . ." Her voice trailed off in childish disappointment as William Haines joined them. She introduced him to her visitors and then said to Haines, "You are out of sorts. What is wrong?"

"As Dr. Jekyll once said, I'm not myself today. Von Stroheim is in a bitch of a mood. He watched the rushes this morning with the wiener schnitzel gang and they were in an uproar." Haines grinned. "I knew he'd eff this movie up the way he effs up everything else. He shot thousands of feet yesterday and there's maybe a minute or so that's usable. You should have heard Guiss chewing him out. I almost felt sorry for Von but by God he gave as good as he got. He told Guiss where to put the rushes if he was that dissatisfied."

He treated them to a wicked impersonation of the director, strutting back and forth while slicing the air with an imaginary riding crop. "Who are you amateurs to tell me what looks good and what looks bad? You know nothing about judging rushes. Only the experienced eyes of the director and his editors know what can be used and what should be discarded. And sometimes even *we* miss a good shot and have to go back and run the rushes again and again until we have enough snippets that will piece together superbly. You have hired von Stroheim?" Haines puffed out his chest and stuck out his chin. "Then you must totally trust von Stroheim! I am not a hack like von Sternberg, who is finished in this business!" Garbo winced. She and Haines knew if it wasn't for this lucky throw of the dice, von Stroheim would be probably sitting in his agent's office listening to reason about returning to the front of the camera to portray any number of villainous Nazi roles now being offered him. Surely the man must recognize the industry was astonished that anyone would ever trust him with directing a movie again.

Haines continued his impersonation. "So if you want me out, I am out. Otherwise, go away and leave me to conduct the progress of the film. Greta is gorgeous and Lorre will improve . . ."

Greta squealed with delight. "Did he really say I was gorgeous? Oh Billy, how that pleases me. Then Lorre and I will be wonderful today. I'll grab Peter by the throat and make him give a performance. He broods too much about the mysterious woman on the beach."

Weirdly on cue, Lisa tapped at the door, which was wide open as Haines had left it, and joined them. "Good morning all." She said to Greta, "You'll be pleased to learn the monster thinks you look great in the rushes. I agree."

"You saw them?"

"Of course. I'm the director's assistant. I have to sit next to him with my notebook and translate his growls."

This amused Garbo. "Erich growls?"

"He provides a large variety of sound effects, few of them pleasant."

"You don't like him?"

"Oh I'm growing very fond of him." She was helping herself to coffee and accepted a cookie from Lottie Lynton. "He's growing on me. His insults are becoming melodious, and his complaints deserve a harp accompaniment." She took a bite of cookie and a sip of coffee. "All that bluster is a cover for his fear."

"But what is he afraid of?"

"Failure!" snapped Haines. He explained to Villon and Arnold, "Failure is the bubonic plague of Hollywood. Fail and you're out and the job offers decine and disappear and you're no longer needed as the extra man to complete somebody's dinner table arrangements, so you either take to drink or dope or both if you're not already hooked or else you go to Europe to look for a job, except these days there's a paucity of European want ads."

"Or you're very wise to turn to interior decorating and make a whole new career for yourself," Garbo said while smiling at Haines with admiration.

But Haines was now off on a tack of his own. "Or you're crazy enough to go into set decorating and spend the day dodging the slings and arrows of a demented martinet." He suddenly shrieked, *"Fuschia!"* Arnold's eyes widened at the outburst while Villon, with his eyes, caught Lisa's attention and subtly indicated the camera Arnold was holding. "The sunnuvabitch doesn't like fuschia! It reminds him of his mother's bedroom. How could a mother allow a son like that in her bedroom!"

Garbo reminded him mournfully, "But he was once an innocent little boy like you were."

Haines said haughtily. "I was never innocent. I was the smartest kid in the neighborhood. I slept with all the right people and got free ice cream and candy and didn't have to pay for my movie tickets. Oh the hell with it. I survived Louis B. Mayer, I'll survive Erich von Stroheim." He turned on Lisa. "I suppose he sent you here to find me?"

"No, he's busy excoriating Mr. Lorre. He's threatening to replace him with Donald O'Connor."

Garbo was horrified. "A teenage tap dancer as the Dauphin of France?"

"Why not?" asked Lisa, amused that Garbo would take von Stroheim's threat seriously. "Remember he tried to make a dramatic actress out of Fay Wray, but she ended up frustrating a big ape."

Haines asked from out of left field, "What's with that murder on the beach? Did you know the woman, Greta?"

"Only by sight. I assume you've read the papers. They say Salka and I recognized her. How tragic to die alone like that. But then, I shall also die alone, I think. Let us not dwell on death. We are surrounded by too much of it and it is inevitable and I am happy to be working again and I want to stay in a happy mood at least until I finish my scenes with Peter. They are supposed to be funny and I can't be funny if I'm not happy. And here's Alysia. Come in, Alysia. Am I needed on the set?"

Alysia Hoffman came in and Garbo realized there had been a dramatic change in the woman since the day Mercedes had introduced them to each other. She wore new clothes, simple but becoming. Where once her movements had been timid and tentative, she was now assured and straightforward. Garbo wondered if she had ever been a gym teacher before turning to acting. Alysia told her von Stroheim was still fussing with the camera setups.

Hearing the word "camera" reminded Arnold of their real mission to the studio. He heard Garbo introducing him and Villon to Alysia

Hoffman and wondered why her expression seemed to change when Garbo identified them as detectives. He wondered how Hoffman would react if he corrected Garbo and unmasked himself, albeit foolishly, as a government agent. Garbo further explained they were investigating the murder on the beach. Arnold asked matter-of-factly, "I don't suppose by some long arm of coincidence you might have known Mrs. Wolheim?"

"Me? How would I know her? You mean because I am also German?" She laughed and it was a very small laugh that could have used some energy. "We refugees don't all know each other. There are so many of us." Villon refrained from commenting "too many." "Anyway, since coming here, I have lived in a sort of self-enforced isolation caused by an economical situation. Now that has improved and I shall attempt to get out in the world a bit more, no?"

Lisa complimented her on the smart suit she was wearing. Alysia thanked her. Haines in his smart-aleck way asked the lawmen, "You guys got any hot leads?"

Villon folded his arms and said, "We're rounding up the usual suspects."

"Which is by way of telling me to mind my own damn business." Haines sighed and said to Greta with a finger to his cheek and with a little boy's voice, "Why is it the big boys don't want to play with me?"

Garbo ignored the question and told Villon and Arnold, "Alysia has been very kind in consenting to be my stand-in." Lisa admired Garbo for the generosity of the statement. Garbo continued, "In Europe she was a much bigger star then me."

"Oh no no," Alysia remonstrated, but not too strongly, thought Lisa.

"Oh yes yes. Alysia made pictures in all the major studios in Europe." Garbo ticked off the list and Villon and Arnold looked interested, though they were anxious to be alone with Lisa and get the camera to her without arousing suspicion. "It was being brought to Mexico for a film that sadly did not materialize that brought her to this end of the world. She had a hard time getting into America. Oh my heavens!" Her hands flew to her temples in a familiar Garbo gesture. "If I ever left the country now, they might not permit me to return!"

"Why not?" asked Villon.

"I'm not a citizen! I too am an alien!"

Villon asked, "Don't you want to become a citizen?"

"Oh yes. I should, shouldn't I? I've been here seventeen years, it's time I did something positive. I shall write to Eleanor Roosevelt and ask her to tell her husband to make me a citizen. You know," she began giggling, "she has sent me several fan letters. After seeing me as Camille, she asked for a lock of my hair." The giggle matured into a roar of laughter.

Arnold said through the din, "Mrs. Roosevelt asks for lots of locks of women's hair."

Garbo stopped laughing and raised an eyebrow. "Oh really? Well, now that you tell me this, I am no longer unique. Oh dear, how disappointing." Then she giggled again, "It wasn't my hair I sent her anyhow. I snipped off one of Freddie Bartholomew's curls and sent her that instead. Ha ha ha ha ha!"

Lisa Schmidt said, "I'd better get back to the set. If von Stroheim's missing me, he might blow a fuse."

Arnold interjected swiftly, "I don't suppose we could get a look at the set? I've never been in a movie studio before."

Lisa said, "But of course. Come with me."

Greta walked the three to the door. She said to Villon and Arnold, "You will keep me apprised of your progress?" Villon reveled in her conspiratorial tone of voice. "I feel so much a part of your case, now that I helped identify that poor woman."

"You'll certainly be hearing from us," Arnold assured her.

Alysia Hoffman mumbled something about probably being needed on the set too and followed the three out of the dressing room. Garbo said sadly, "They wouldn't let me take their picture."

Haines said, "Maybe they're on the lam?"

Garbo said indignantly, "Oh don't be so childish. What are you going to do about the fuschia?"

With hands on hips and a pout on his lips, he said, "I shall scrub the fuschia and shower the fucker with electric pink and with any luck it'll give him a deadly case of diarrhea." With a chuckle, he left.

Garbo was preoccupied with her own disturbing thoughts. Looking back on the previous half hour, she had the uneasy feeling the atmosphere had been charged with strange undercurrents. What was there about Arnold's camera that disturbed her? He said he had bought it in South America, but there was no manufacturer's identification to be seen anywhere. She had examined the camera carefully because cameras fascinated her, she had faced so many of them in the lifetime of her career. She demanded of her photographers complete and thorough details about how they were focusing on her and what were they trying to achieve. She had wanted to ask Arnold if it was possible to secure such a camera for herself, but she had a suspicion it was a make only an officer of the law could obtain. She knew cameras and that was a very special camera.

She accepted another cup of coffee from Lottie Lynton, who recognized the expression on Garbo's face and returned to the kitchenette, leaving Garbo to her thoughts. Garbo was now dwelling on Alysia Hoffman. Was Garbo crazy or had the woman seemed annoyed when Garbo was telling Villon and Arnold how famous Alysia had been and how she came into this country through Mexico?

Garbo was sitting at her dressing table and caught a glimpse of her dark expression. "Oh my, Greta! You must look happy. You must think happy. You have to play a happy scene! Did you hear what Lisa said, Lottie? I look wonderful in the rushes. I must phone Salka and Mercedes and tell them. Mercedes is a little cross with us today. She's jealous that we identified Mrs. Wolheim. Poor Mercedes. Perhaps she'll be lucky and find a murder victim of her own to identify."

Samuel Goldwyn said to Sophie Gang, "I'm grudging him but you have to hand it to von Stroheim. He's still an original." He had seen the morning's rushes from a clandestine position in the projection booth, his cigar smoke polluting it and nauseating the projectionist. "He's a master of composition. And that Greta, she's all by herself. There's nobody like her."

"I hear Peter Lorre's disappointing."

"He'll get better. Von Stroheim will show him the rushes and Lorre will be ashamed of himself and do better today. He's a wonderful actor. Here in Hollywood he's wasted. He should play Hamlet . . . ," he said, pronouncing it "omelet", "and maybe that king . . ."

"Lear?" asked Sophie.

"That's it, Lear. And also in that play about the *schwartzer* . . ."

"*Othello?*"

"Yeah, what I saw Paul Robeson play on Broadway. He should play the troublemaker . . ."

"Iago."

"Say listen, smarting pants, how do you know so much about Shakingspeares?"

"I majored in English literature in college."

"You went to college? I didn't know you're a college graduate. Well well well. So I really got a bargain when I hired you." He sounded as though he had just pulled off a big deal on Wall Street. "Anyway, Peter will improve. You should face it, for him, acting is like water off a dike's back."

It was all done so swiftly, no one noticed the progression of the camera from Arnold to Lisa and from Lisa to Martin Gruber. Gruber hurried away quickly, passing Alysia Hoffman as she returned to the set, ignoring her "Hello, Martin" in his anxiety to get to his office and secrete his contraband in the tote bag he'd brought with him to the studio. Strange, thought Alysia, he's never rude.

Fifteen minutes later, Gruber was in Guiss's office where the financier and his three associates were holding a council of war. Lieb was saying, "Perhaps we should admit von Stroheim is a mistake."

Guiss replied, "Don't be so quick to think of replacing him. We've only seen one day's work. Perhaps the man's right. We have to wait until he has more footage to work with, until he has what he calls the beginning of an assemblage. Then we'll be in a better position to judge what he's accomplishing."

Lieb insisted, "But look at all the waste! If that continues every day then the film will be vastly over budget and that must not happen."

Guiss exploded. Martin Gruber just jotted down notes, amused by the way these amateurs were at each other's throats already, and only a miniscule amount of footage in the can. Guiss shouted, "Since when have you become an authority on budgets? On a film you don't calculate money spent on a day-to-day basis, you have to wait a few weeks and *then* see where you are. Right, Henkel?"

"How should I know? This is my first movie."

Risa looked at him with undisguised revulsion. Guiss sometimes had incredibly strange tastes in associates. Where had her lover found this creature, she wondered. He was in residence long before her arrival and it was not easy to weasel information about himself out of him. He was as agile at evading answers as a farmer was crossing a field and avoiding piles of cow dung.

Guiss slammed a fist down on the desk. "I'm right and I will not be disagreed with!"

Ah, thought Gruber, he's already gone Hollywood.

Risa lit a cigarette, blew a smoke ring in Guiss's direction, and then said in a firm, strong voice, "Gentleman, we are avoiding a more pressing problem."

"And what is that?" asked Guiss, trying to control the trace of anger still left in his voice.

"Kriegman. What do we do about Kriegman? If Greta and Salka Viertel recognized Hannah Baum . . ." which was the name of the woman who had posed as Mrs. Wolheim ". . . surely Greta will have recognized Kriegman as having impersonated Mr. Wolheim."

Guiss was uneasy in his chair and finally crossed his legs. "She's seen him several times. She has said nothing."

"Perhaps she's playing a game," said Henkel. "She likes games, doesn't she?"

"She's a whiz at Chinese checkers," conceded Guiss.

"It's unfortunate it was she who had to be one of the group who recognized Hannah. That could pose a serious problem," said Risa.

"Meaning?" Guiss was obviously not happy with this conversation.

"Meaning sooner or later, if it already hasn't dawned on her, she will recall that Kriegman was indeed Wolheim. Those three oafs who posed as the sons are barely recognizable in those operetta costumes you have them wearing when they carry the spears, but again, there might come a time when she'll recognize *them*. And as for that tower of quivering jelly who is now my maid, Greta might realize at some point soon that *she* posed as the Wolheim daughter."

Guiss said, "Greta will not be coming to the house for a long long time. She had made it quite clear she doesn't accept social engagements when she is engaged in filming."

Risa commented sarcastically, "Such dedication to one's craft is only to be admired."

Werner Lieb said, "Miss Garbo has become dangerous. She is a threat to us and our assignment."

Guiss was lacing and unlacing his fingers. Martin Gruber cursed himself for perspiring. Guiss said, "Are you suggesting we consider eliminating her?"

Lieb said nothing. He watched Henkel stifling his perpetual nervous yawn.

"And what becomes of this project? What becomes of *Joan the Magnificent?*" asked Henkel.

Lieb said matter-of-factly, "If we play with fire, we'll get burned."

Guiss exploded again. "You damn fool! Murder Greta? Would you dare dynamite the Lincoln Memorial?"

"It's under consideration."

"Dummkopf! If Kriegman and the others are unmasked, it is simple to deny any knowledge of their background. Our story is that they were recently hired to augment my staff. How should I have suspected they are subversives? They came with excellent references and it is very difficult in these trying times to get competent household help, and so I was grateful to find them and hire them! Is that understood? And not another word about eliminating Greta, do you hear? Not another word!"

Henkel stifled another yawn.

Fifteen

It had taken courage and patience and cunning, but Martin Gruber got his picture of Kriegman. He happened upon him walking in the garden and in an agitated state, talking to himself. Gruber, unseen by Kriegman, positioned himself behind a privet hedge and got a succession of candid shots that, had Kriegman seen them, might have fired him with the ambition to become a professional model.

Gruber arranged to meet Lisa Schmidt to give her the roll of film. It had been agreed he was never to contact Arnold at the Garden of Allah or Villon at his precinct, for fear of being seen in either place and recognized by a German agent. As Arnold impressed on Gruber, they were all over the place. One of them was making a small fortune as a masseur to the stars and had developed a profitable sideline feeding items to the town's hungry gossip columnists.

Lisa dropped into the Garden of Allah for a drink the next evening, after leaving the studio, and found a seat at the bar next to Arnold Lake. As they chitchatted amiably, Lisa slipped the roll of film into Arnold's jacket pocket. After her third sidecar, Lisa was amenable to seeing the interior of Arnold's bungalow and so the evening was not a total loss for either one of them.

After the first day, the rushes improved considerably, and Peter Lorre was giving the kind of performance that made his fellow actors feel he was definitely a contender for an Academy Award nomination. They spoke of Garbo's work with awe, albeit reminding themselves that the Academy had never honored the actress and probably never would. Hollywood disapproved of mavericks. Mavericks made the Academy voter uneasy and uncomfortable.

Mercedes de Acosta was succeeding in making Greta Garbo uneasy and uncomfortable. Garbo managed successfully to camouflage her true feelings, asking her friend "So you think . . . how did you put it . . . I might be on the spot?"

"Now look Greta, it's quite obvious these Wolheims, or whatever the hell their names were, were answerable to higher authorities. And these authorities are undoubtedly fearsome and ruthless and dangerous. They'll stop at nothing to save themselves and they don't give a damn who they kill to protect themselves. Greta," she pronounced the name like a rumble of thunder, "I'm a Cuban and I have survived the overthrowing of power. My family fled Cuba because my father's life was in danger." Greta was thinking, Mercedes should have pursued an acting career. A little on the hammy side but she sure knows how to sell a point to the audience. "Greta," said Mercedes, with more thunder, even more fearsome, "we are none of us invincible. If you identified one member of that bogus family then they fear you can identify the rest of them."

"But I only know where Kriegman is. I don't know where the sons and the daughter are."

"Would you recognize them if you saw them?"

"I think so. Yes."

"Then you are *positively* dangerous to them. If Kriegman is working at Guiss's castle, how do you know the others aren't there too? You said yourself that the first time you went there for dinner there was a horde of extras and walk-ons working as guards, spear holders, maids, a large kitchen staff. Those four could have melted quite easily into that crowd."

"Yes," Garbo agreed, "anything is possible in Hollywood."

Lottie came out on the patio and announced Villon and Arnold. The sun was taking its own sweet time setting on the horizon and the moon was already struggling for position. Mercedes politely declined Lottie's offer of hot chocolate, although there was a chill in the air, and instead asked for a bourbon neat. Greta greeted her visitors and introduced them to Mercedes. As Lottie prepared and served drinks to the four of them, Garbo repeated Mercedes's apprehensions and suspicions.

Arnold said, "I can assure you they won't make an attempt on Miss Garbo's life. And as for the whereabouts of the so-called sons and daughter, we already suspect they're doing service in Guiss's place, but their only importance would be if one of them were a witness to the murder and that's highly improbable. Herb and I think Mrs. Wolheim was brought back to the house because the killer was getting impatient. She was taking too long to die. He felt the poison should have taken effect by then because she had gobbled such huge quantities of it. We think he took her to the house to finish her off."

Garbo suppressed a shudder. He was so cold and matter-of-fact in detailing this theory of the snuffing out of another human being's life. Whatever this Mrs. Wolheim had been, she had been a person and a person who died a horrible death and so, in Garbo's estimation, was worthy of some pity.

"So some days some guys get lucky," said Villon, taking over the narration from Arnold. "Once he got her in the house, probably complaining about her burning feet and her bouts of nausea, she suddenly collapsed, her eyeballs rolled up into her head, her skin turned grey and clammy . . ."

"Mr. Villon, please," pleaded Garbo.

"Sorry. I didn't mean to get so graphic." How he ached to hear her call him Herb. How he pined to call her Greta. How he wondered it would be like to caress and kiss her toe. He didn't care how big her feet were, these were the feet of Greta Garbo and if it was up to Herb Villon, they'd be declared a national treasure.

He heard Arnold say, "So he carried her to the master bedroom, laid her out and left her there."

"Where is her luggage?" Garbo had their attention. She smiled. "If she was supposed to be leaving the country, she would have to have luggage. Certainly a handbag. A passport?"

Arnold said, "You don't need a passport to board a submarine." To Garbo's inquisitive look he explained, "It's the usual transportation for getting their people in and out of North America. So Herb, where's the lady's luggage?"

"Either checked at Union Station or at a bus terminal. My guess is Union Station. Anyway, I'm ahead of you. I've got a couple of boys working on it."

Arnold fished an envelope from his inside jacket pocket. "And now Miss Garbo, would you please examine these?"

She took the envelope and found the pictures of Kriegman. "He's very photogenic, isn't he? In person he seemed so nondescript, but here he is, very imposing and very impressive. Obviously when these photos were taken he was in a state of agitation. But yes, this is Kriegman alias Mr. Wolheim. I'm sure even Kriegman is a false name." She stared at Mercedes. "Why are you so upset, Mercedes?"

"You're getting yourself in deeper and deeper! Is there no stopping you?"

"But Mercedes, I am not just Greta Garbo the actress. I am also Greta Garbo the soldier. I am serving my country. If Louella and Hedda knew, they'd stop writing those terrible lies about my lack of patriotism, but we don't dare tell them, do we gentlemen?"

"Certainly not those two," said Villon, and he thought of his Hazel Dickson soldiering for her country and wondering what she would have made of all this: him, Herb, sitting on a patio with Greta Garbo. It was as momentous to him as taking aim at Lincoln must have been to John Wilkes Booth.

"You're a damned fool," said Mercedes. "I need another bourbon." Lottie was called for and pressed into service. She had drawn the blackout curtains and they now sat in darkness, none of them inclined to move indoors.

Garbo told them the filming was finally accelerating, with von Stroheim giving it the pacing Guiss so desperately desired. Lorre's performance was now a vast improvement and she was feeling very good about her own. Then she asked the inevitable. "When do you plan to arrest Kriegman?"

"Why?" asked Villon.

"Because he's a spy!"

"We've got no proof."

"But I have identified him as Wolheim. And I'm sure so will Salka and Mr. Saloman."

"That's just identifying him as the man who passed himself off as a mysterious man named Wolheim. We don't know positively they were spies. We're very suspicious . . ."

"To say the least," interjected Arnold.

"But we haven't a shred of proof. Anyway, Miss Garbo . . ."

"Oh please, I'm Greta. We are working together. And you are Herb. And you are Arnold. After all, aren't we comrades in arms on the battlefield?"

Villon was aglow. Herb. Greta Garbo had pronounced his name aloud. Herb. It had a different sound, a different meaning. If his mother knew that her beloved Herbert had heard his name spoken by the glorious Greta Garbo, she would rise from her grave and materialize above them miming benedictions.

Arnold wondered why that stupid look on Herb Villon's face. He looked like Stan Laurel silently crowing about a major victory against Oliver Hardy.

Mercedes was speaking. "I don't see how you can minimize the threat of these people. They love to kill. I know, I was in Hamburg when that maniac was on the loose murdering at random, and he's still on the loose. Didn't any of you read about him? He was a poisoner. Oh my God, he wiped out a dinner party in a restaurant by tampering with their *spetzel.*" Herb thought, I wouldn't want my *spetzel* tampered with.

"Mercedes, are you suggesting this Hamburg poisoner has come all the way from Germany to poison sad Mrs. Wolheim?"

"Don't scoff, Greta. In this day and age anything is possible! Look at the success of Abbott and Costello!"

Garbo smiled. "They amuse me. 'Who's on first?' Ha ha ha ha ha."

"There's a fresh outbreak of killings in Dusseldorf," Arnold told them.

"How do you know this?" asked Garbo. How would he know what's going on inside Nazi Germany?

Arnold cleared his throat. "I happen to have access to certain information."

"Because you are a G-man?"

"You got it."

"Can I be a G-woman?"

"You have to be a graduate lawyer to join us."

Mercedes was doubly unhappy. A G-man, for crying out loud.

Herb was thinking Arnold should bite his tongue. Was it his fascination with the star that made him make the slip in front of the de Acosta woman, probably overheard by Lottie Lynton, or was it deliberate?

Garbo was asking Mercedes, "Where can I study law, Mercedes?"

Mercedes could no longer contain herself. She exploded. "You're talking like a god damned fool! You don't need to study law, you need a psychiatrist!"

Garbo said calmly, and with a trace of a smile, "I would only drive a psychiatrist insane. I visited one once a long time ago. He asked for my autograph." She explained to the others, "I never give autographs." She said to Arnold, "Wasn't the fact that you're a government agent supposed to be privileged information?"

Arnold said. "My superiors decided it was time to let the word out and make some people doubly uncomfortable."

"I wish you had let me in on that," said Villon.

"I was going to, but it was Greta who beat me to it by giving the game away."

"Oh my God," she gasped, "so I did! Forgive me, please forgive me."

Is this genuine or is this an act? Villon wondered. He heard Arnold assuaging Garbo and caught the look of confusion on de Acosta's face.

Garbo slapped her knee. "Aha!" She was pointing a finger at Arnold. "You want your true identity to become known to Guiss and his people. You led me into the slip of my tongue! By saying you have ways of knowing what's going on inside Germany. You knew my curiosity would get you to . . . ," she screwed up her face searching for the correct expression, ". . . to . . . to . . . I have it . . . blow your cover." She looked at them triumphantly. "So this is what it is to have your cover blown! It must be an exciting experience. But wait!" She was on her feet and pacing, circling them like a lioness about to pounce on her prey. "This is why the Wolheims were removed from the house, for fear that they might blow their cover. Then they actually were considered dangerous! They were afraid for their safety, my God, for their lives." She spun on Arnold. "Don't they execute spies in wartime? Oh poor Mrs. Wolheim. She didn't want to die. She wanted to go home and be a *hausfrau* again. She didn't want to be caught and executed. And I'm sure she didn't want to be poisoned. Arnold? Do you think she knew she was being slowly murdered? The burning feet, the nausea. Do you think she recognized she was being cruelly put to death? Oh the poor woman. I wonder if she is survived by children."

"Consider this, Greta," said Arnold. "Consider that in the course of her assignments, Mrs. Wolheim might have caused a number of deaths herself. She might have passed on information that sank ships and caused the destruction of ammunition factories or landing fields, she might have caused the deaths of thousands of soldiers and sailors."

"Oh what a terrible woman! Let's go inside. It's so dark out here I can't tell who is who. Lottie! Turn off the lights in the living room. We're coming in!"

"Are you going out?" Lieb asked Martin Gruber, who was carrying the tote bag that contained Arnold's camera.

"Yes, I have a dinner date. Mr. Guiss doesn't need me tonight."

"What a good-looking carryall. Did you buy it here in L.A.?"

"Yes. I found it in a shop on Beverly Boulevard."

Lieb reached for the bag. "It has an interesting pattern. May I take a closer look?" Gruber relinquished the bag. Lieb held it up, making a meal of presumably admiring the pattern. "Oh how clumsy I am." He had dropped the tote. The camera spilled out. "Oh my, I hope I haven't damaged the camera." He made a swipe at it and grabbed it before Gruber could retrieve it. Lieb examined the camera closely. "Very interesting. What make is this?"

"I think it's South American," said Gruber. "It's not mine. It belongs to a friend. I borrowed it to shoot some photos on the set."

Lieb screwed his monocle into his eye. "It takes pictures indoors?"

"Only when there is sufficient light, and the sets are brilliantly lit."

"How interesting. I should like to see some of these photos."

"They're being developed now. When they're ready, I'll show them to you." Damn, thought Gruber, damn this man. Now I have to hold on to the camera and do some shooting on the set. "I must go now, herr Lieb. . . ."

"*Mr.* Lieb. Don't make that slip again. Why are you so nervous? Why are you perspiring?"

"I'm going to be late. I don't like being late."

"I'm sorry if I detained you. Don't keep your lady waiting."

Gruber found a slight laugh. "Did I say I was meeting a lady?"

"Oh, I assumed you were meeting Lisa Schmidt. You seem so chummy at the studio."

"That's because we're working together. We have no other interest in each other, I can assure you."

"Why do you have to assure me?" asked Lieb coldly. "Your private life is your own business. I just happened to make a comment, that's all." He smiled, a thin, icy smile. "She's very beautiful. I wouldn't blame you if you were trying to make out with her. I wouldn't mind a taste of honey myself. Goodnight, Gruber." He dismissed Gruber abruptly and left the downstairs hall where they had run into each other.

Gruber hurried out of the house and found his car. Once behind the wheel, the tote bag placed at his side, he gripped the wheel tightly and waited for the panic to subside. Then he had the feeling he was being watched. He relaxed his grip on the wheel and turned on the ignition. From the corner of an eye he could have sworn someone at a window had pulled back a curtain slightly and was watching him. He pulled out into the road that led to the iron gates, perspiration dripping down his face. Perhaps it was nothing, he hoped, perhaps I'm getting paranoid. Perhaps Werner Lieb is smarter than we think he is. Perhaps he guessed the camera was a very special camera. I must go to the studio tonight with Lisa and photograph the set. God damn the man! *Mr.* Lieb. Not *herr* Lieb. He suddenly felt giddy. Oh well, what the hell. Herr today, gone tomorrow.

Lisa Schmidt wasn't happy about Gruber's encounter with Lieb and she knew Arnold and Villon wouldn't be either. She was even less happy about returning to the studio with Gruber and having to sign in with the guard on duty at the gate. Oh well, she'd concoct some excuse for their having to return after the others had gone. Fortunately, night shooting wasn't scheduled until the following week. It was now seven o'clock. Von Stroheim had called it a day shortly before six. He wanted to spend a few hours with his editors. He was probably closeted in an editing room with them now, preparing the next morning's rushes. After the first unpleasantness with Guiss, he now made a point of editing the rushes down to a reasonable length and carefully excising his excesses. He didn't want to lose this movie. He needed the quarter of a million he'd been guaranteed. He was heavily in debt. He needed to make money and start saving. The war wouldn't last forever. If this was his ultimate directing job, then he'd have to go back to playing Nazi villains. And when the war was over, such parts would be redundant.

This was the first time von Stroheim had taken her into his confidence. She sympathized with him. She wanted him to come up with a winner. But there was something she knew that von Stroheim didn't know and she was not about to share this ugly confidence with him. Arnold Lake's superiors suspected the film would never be completed.

Sixteen

Promptly at eight P.M., Guiss entered the dining room. There was no one seated at the table. The majordomo who oversaw the dining room greeted him with a warm smile and pulled back his chair at the head of the table, expecting Guiss to sit and be served.

But Guiss was perplexed and annoyed. "Where are the others?"

"I don't know, sir. I'm sure they're on their way."

"Where is Kriegman?"

"I don't know, sir. I have been in the kitchen the past three hours. I've seen no one but the staff there."

Abruptly, Guiss turned and left the dining room. The majordomo said something nasty and pushed the chair back into place. He looked at the serving table groaning under the weight of trivets and chafing dishes and serving plates covered to keep the heat in, an overabundance of food that could feed the starving people of Europe and leave some over for a nosh tomorrow. He had a feeling no one would arrive to eat this sumptuous dinner.

Guiss had buttonholed Risa Barron's maid, Agathe, who had impersonated the Wolheim daughter. Her hands fluttered like the wings of a frightened butterfly expecting to be pinned and exhibited under glass. "She didn't tell me where she was going. She put on her diamond and ruby bracelets and her amethyst necklace and, dragging her sable on the floor behind her, she left her suite saying she needed to be by herself tonight."

"And Henkel? And Lieb? Do you know where they are?"

"If they're not here, sir, then they're gone, sir."

"And Kriegman? What has become of Kriegman?"

Fear had dampened the palms of her hands and she was trying to dry them by rubbing them on her apron. "I haven't seen him in several hours, sir. He . . . he's been acting and talking very strangely, sir. He . . . he's frightened. Ever since Hannah was found murdered, he's been frightened. Oh sir," she blurted out as tears sprang to her eyes, "I'm frightened too. If Hannah was killed then they want to kill all of us."

"Stop blubbering like an idiot, you idiot. Who is this 'they' who you think wants to kill all of you?"

"The people up there. The people who give orders." She was pointing at the ceiling.

"You're a fool, Agathe. *I* am the people up there, the people who give orders. Do you think I want to kill you?"

Now she cowered. "I hope not. Oh please, can't I go home?"

"Shame on you, Agathe, shame on you. When you were being trained, they told me you had a great potential. Now look at you. Weeping, wringing your hands, afraid of your own shadow. You disgust me." He left her cowering in the hallway, and wondering where indeed Kriegman had disappeared to.

As Agathe hurried to her room, she thought back to her conversation with Kriegman in the library, which was always a safe haven for them to meet in when the others were at the studio.

Kriegman had said, "One of them murdered Hannah. It had to

be. I'm positive. And if they considered her a threat to them, then all of us who posed as Wolheims are in danger."

"But I think she was murdered because she wanted to go home, and they didn't want her back there."

"Don't you want to go home? *I* want to go home. I hate this rotten place with its palm trees and tennis courts. And look at me. He makes me play the butler. 'Kriegman do this, Kriegman do that, Kriegman kiss my backside.' Me! A graduate of Hamburg University with a degree in philosophy. And I let them draft me into espionage. What a fool I am, what a fool. Well let me tell you this, Agathe, I'm not going to wait around waiting for the axe to fall. One of *them* killed Hannah. Maybe Guiss himself."

Her eyes widened. "You think?"

"It's possible," he insisted. "The man is a cold-hearted brute. He has no ethics, he has no morals, he's a party machine. Who is he anyway? Where does he come from? I think he was invented."

"What?" She was incredulous.

"He's not real. The man is not real. There is something about him that does not ring true. I always feel he is acting a role. And some day he'll be unmasked. If I could only find out who it is that *he* answers to."

"You mean he's not the big cheese?"

"He's a big cheese, all right, but of a very inferior brand. Be cautious, Agathe. Be careful. We are in danger. You, me, the boys. We are in terrible danger."

Now she was in her room, but she couldn't lock the door. She jammed a chair under the doorknob and sat on the bed, palms wet again, hands in her lap and trembling, and wondering what to do. Try and run away, but where would she go? Turn herself in to the authorities and plead for mercy? They would put her in jail, but so what? Jail is preferable to death. She had seen those American pictures about women's jails. It wouldn't be so bad, not if kindly Jane Darwell was the warden.

"What are you doing here so late?"

Von Stroheim startled Lisa and Gruber. He had entered the set quietly and Lisa was surprised to see Alysia Hoffman was with him. They found Gruber in the act of photographing the Dauphin's throne. Lisa was a good actress. "You're still here?"

"Obviously. I was just taking Alysia to dinner. What are you doing, Gruber?"

"I'm taking snapshots of the set for Miss Garbo." Quick thinking, thought Lisa.

"And what does she want with snapshots of the set?"

Lisa answered for Gruber. "For her scrapbooks. She keeps insisting this film is her swan song and she wants snapshots for the future to jog her memory of the good time she's having now."

"She's enjoying doing this film?"

"Hell yes," said Lisa, "it's got her in a marvelous frame of mind. Can't you see it in the rushes?"

Alysia finally spoke. "Yes, it's very evident. She even looks younger. Come on, Von, you see it, admit it."

Von, thought Lisa. The lady moves fast. She wants to be a star again. Good luck to you, dearie.

Von Stroheim laughed. "Yes, she's magical. All right, take your pictures and I'll see you in the morning. Wait a minute. I'd like to have a look at that camera." Gruber handed it to him. Von Stroheim held it up so that Alysia Hoffman could have a closer look at it. "I've never seen anything like it before. It's certainly not an American make, is it?"

Lisa said, "I think Greta said it came from South America. Some friend or some fan sent it to her."

"It has to be foreign," agreed Von Stroheim, "it's much too sophisticated to be one of our brands." He handed the camera back to Gruber. "Lisa, remind me to ask Greta where she got it. I'd like to get one for my son. Come Alysia. How's about Romanoff's? I feel in a festive mood tonight. Maybe Bogie will be there. I enjoy trading insults with him."

Lisa watched them leave as Gruber stood, seemingly immobilized. Lisa said, "Our Alysia is a smooth worker."

Gruber answered, "Very smooth. We have enough pictures. Let's get out of here."

"Greta has to be primed about the camera and the snapshots.

Let's go to the office and phone her, then we can drop the film off at Schwab's drugstore. Maybe some movie producer is there waiting to discover me like Lana Turner."

Guiss sat in his study, staring into the fireplace at the pyre of crackling wood which reminded him of Jeanne d'Arc's fate. Between the palms of his hands he warmed a brandy snifter. He was preoccupied with the sudden defection of his comrades and annoyed at having been abandoned without warning. True, they frequently went about their private business without advising him of their plans, but the past month they had been almost inseparable and now he was feeling a mortal emotion, loneliness, and he didn't like being alone. How does Garbo manage it? She relishes it, she treasures it, she husbands her loneliness like a miser, like the miser ZaSu Pitts so brilliantly limned in von Stroheim's *Greed.* He sipped the brandy and was so preoccupied with his thoughts that he did not hear Henkel enter.

"Drinking alone?" Guiss was startled and made a noise that sounded like a puppy's yelp. "That's very bad."

"You startled me." Then sternly, "Where did you disappear to?"

"I felt like some gefilte fish, so I drove to Cantor's on Fairfax Avenue."

"I won't put that in my daily report."

Henkel was lighting a cigar. "Who cares. You admit, there are a few things the Jews have given the world that are a worthwhile legacy. Gefilte fish, knishes, stuffed derma, bagels and lox. I think I'll join you in a brandy."

"Kriegman has defected," said Guiss.

"Oh? Are you sure?"

"I missed him at dinner, which I ate alone." Henkel didn't look guilty. "I went to his room. It was in complete disarray as though he had packed hastily. I looked for his passport but it was also gone. He has fled, the fool. And Agathe is frightened too. I had a talk with her. I hope she isn't thinking of doing anything foolish."

"Why don't we make sure she doesn't?"

"Gustav, would you want it to appear that the Hamburg monster has relocated to Hollywood?"

Henkel shrugged as he crossed to a seat near Guiss while taking a sip of his brandy. "There's only been one murder, Hannah's. That hardly constitutes an epidemic. Did her murder cause you to take any flak?"

"Strangely enough, no."

"Well then. . . ."

"I wonder where Werner has gone. He rarely goes off by himself," said Guiss.

"Perhaps he felt an urge to patronize Madam Frances tonight." Madam Frances ran movieland's favorite house of prostitution.

"I wouldn't mind a visit myself. Risa has been rather cold to me lately." Guiss sounded petulant.

"Well, you're so obvious about Greta, can you blame her?"

"Nothing will come of a relationship with Greta. I think the woman's asexual."

"That's not what I've heard. I hear she possesses quite a scrap-book of sexual memories." He contemplated his cigar and then said. "We have never discussed the detectives, Albert."

"Villon and Lake? They're a music hall act."

"I have taken the liberty to investigate Villon and Lake."

Guiss was surprised and pleased. "So? What have you found? Anything incriminating?"

Henkel spoke slowly and deliberately. "Villon is a highly respected police officer. On some cases I find he was as ruthless in tracking down a killer as Javert was in his pursuit of Valjean." He took a puff of cigar.

"And Mr. Lake?"

"He is not a member of the Los Angeles Police Department."

"Perhaps he's a reporter."

"Reporters can't afford to live in the Garden of Allah. I think he's a federal agent."

Guiss's face hardened. "If he is, he's no match for me."

"Still, if he is, then it means we are in danger."

"Why so? We're producing a film. Lots of aliens have set up

independent production here. So it stands to reason we have too."

"But if they investigate where our funds are coming from?"

"Yes, there's a danger there. But still, that's part of our job, no? Danger is always with professionals like us. Come Gustav, I'm still hungry. Let's go raid the refrigerator."

"You think?"

"I positively think," said Arnold.

They were in Villon's office. After leaving Garbo, they'd decided to do some work and picked up sandwiches and coffee for their dinner. Now it was three hours later and they had put on paper everything they knew about the *Joan the Magnificent* production. They listed the cast of characters involved: not just the actors, but also those who were participating behind the scenes. Arnold was waiting to hear from Washington as to the true identities of the Wolheim family. Surely one of their operatives in Europe, and there were a brilliant assortment risking their lives in Germany, would soon provide them with that information.

Now Arnold had posited the theory that Guiss wasn't the head of this operation. He had a hunch Guiss was taking his orders from someone superior. "And that someone had Mrs. Wolheim murdered. And murder can be infectious. It can spread. I think we're in for a few more killings."

"How tiresome, dahling," said Villon archly and then stretched his arms. "What about von Stroheim and Alysia Hoffman?" Lisa Schmidt had phoned them and told them of hers and Gruber's encounter with the director and the actress, after which she phoned Garbo and advised her to back up the lie that she had requested photos of the set and that the camera was her property.

"Von Stroheim, who knows? Alysia, an unknown quantity. Obviously she's on the make with von Stroheim. She was once a big star, she wants to be a big star again. She ain't the kid she was twenty years ago, but then, in the movie business, who can make a safe guess?"

"I must admit," began Villon, "I was quite impressed by her having worked all over Europe. I suppose in the silent days it didn't matter. She must have piled up a big list of contacts."

"Indeed. It got her to Mexico and then into the States."

"Do you suppose she might have known Guiss or any of his bunch back there in Germany?"

Lake rubbed his nose. "We could ask her. But I'm sure she'll say she didn't. Lisa says she's not at all chummy with them at the studio. In fact, the only one she relates to is Greta."

(My Greta, thought Villon, with a silly grin.)

"There's that dumb look on your face again."

"Hmmm? What? Oh, sorry. You were saying?"

"I said the only one she relates to is Greta, who got her the job." He wondered if Herb was suffering a touch of indigestion. "Now she's working on relating to von Stroheim. Well, he spent a lot of time abroad before the war began."

"He made some good pictures in France," said Villon. *"Grand Illusion* is a knockout. And very anti-war. The Nazis didn't make anti-war propaganda films."

"They only made a lot of anti-semitic crap and infantile operettas with Zarah Leander. She's a Swede but she works exclusively for the Nazis. Real weird, them Europeans." Arnold scratched the back of his hand. "Could von Stroheim be a part of this gang? Nobody would touch him for years. Not since 1933 when he was kicked off *Walking Down Broadway* by Fox. After that it was hard times for him. Quickies on Poverty Row. Then all of a sudden he turns up in France and he's a star above the title again."

Villon nodded. "They're much more faithful to the old timers over there. Here we throw them on the ash heap and make believe they never existed. Why is it in this country that aging is an embarrassment?" He picked a crumb from his desk and licked it off his finger. "I don't think von Stroheim's tainted. He just got lucky all of a sudden, and I hope he's prepared to see this whole damn thing blow up in his face. Arnold?"

"What?"

"Couldn't you get Greta a special G-man's badge?"

"Come on, Herb. Grow up!"

"Okay, now as to Alysia Hoffman. . . ."

The lady in question was reading her director's palm. The lighting at Mike Romanoff's restaurant in Beverly Hills was subdued and flattering and there was no Humphrey Bogart for von Stroheim to trade barbs with. In fact the restaurant was suffering a paucity of celebrities, which it usually did on a midweek night. Working actors were at home learning their lines or grabbing some much needed sleep; non-working actors couldn't afford to eat out, let alone at Mike Romanoff's, Mike being a fraud from Brooklyn who claimed to be a scion of Russian royalty. Hollywood was amused by him and the restaurant's food was good.

"What else do you see?" asked von Stroheim, as he signaled the waiter for more champagne. He did not believe in palmistry or astrology or black magic or in an afterlife, but he decided it was politic to humor the woman, who was obviously eager to resume her former station in films as a star.

"I see a very confusing future."

"With a war on, that's inevitable." He moved his hand from hers to his champagne glass. "Tell me, Alysia, when it ends, will you stay here or go back to Germany?"

"Will the war ever end? And Germany. Germany will be in ruins. It will take the film industry a long time to renew itself. By then I'll be forgotten."

"Here they hardly got to know you, your films were rarely exported. But there, you're still a big star."

"You think so? You remember Lil Dagover and Dorothea Wieck?" He did. "Well, they were brought here in the thirties with big hoopla and big fanfare. They were brought as threats to Greta and Marlene. A big laugh. They failed miserably, so back they went to Germany. And back to what? Character roles, small supporting parts, and early retirement."

"Your face changes when you're bitter."

She smiled lavishly. "Is this an improvement?"

"A vast one. Alysia, did you know Guiss or any of the others back in the homeland?"

"Not at all, why do you ask? You sound like the detectives."

"Guiss disturbs me. There's something not right with him."

"How so?"

"I find him terribly unreal. I feel he's an actor who reads his lines well but with no emotion. It's as though someone out of sight is directing his every move, his every intonation."

"You make him sound like he's a robot."

"That's what I think he is. A robot. Now then, my dear, this has been terribly charming, but it's getting late and we have to be on the set bright and early. So, your place or mine?"

"But Miss Garbo, you mustn't go out walking by yourself. It's not safe."

Garbo waved away Lottie's apprehension. "I can look after myself. I have to think. I can't think in the house. The walls are closing in on me. The private guards are all over the beach since the murder. I'll be all right."

"At least carry a blunt instrument! Take this butcher knife."

Garbo laughed. "I wouldn't know how to use it. I'd cut myself and wouldn't that be foolish?"

A few minutes later she was trudging along the beach. She heard an argument between Hearst and Marion Davies as she passed their house, Hearst tweeting away like a cornered canary, Marion shouting epithets that made Garbo cringe. Then a man emerged from out of nowhere, out of the night's blackness and she stood still waiting for him to identify himself. He said nothing, so she spoke. "Who are you? What do you want?"

"Oh it's you, Miss Garbo." Tom Toth recognized that familiar husky voice. "It's me. Tom Toth."

"Oh good, Thomas. You're on the job. You're protecting us."

"I wouldn't wander too far, Miss Garbo. It's a very cloudy night."

"I see that. I just need a little walk. I'll be all right." She continued on her way. He decided to follow her at a safe distance. Soon he was wondering, What's so fascinating to her about the murder house?

What fascinated Garbo was that the front door was slightly ajar. And she could see the faint reflection of dim light, not enough to spill out into the blackout and cause an alarm. It wasn't a matter of overcoming fear or a display of false bravery, it was just her incurable curiosity. She widened the door enough for her slender body to enter the room.

Now why the hell is she going in there, wondered Toth. The murderer returning to the scene of the crime? Murderer? Garbo? Crazy.

Garbo was appalled by the ugliness of the furnishings. There was just enough light for her to regard the room with a look of distaste. The light was coming from the room beyond. She heard no movement there. She was unaware that Toth was at the front door watching her. He saw her push open the door to the next room. It was the kitchen.

Garbo sniffed. Someone had cooked something here. She saw an opened can on the kitchen sink. She crossed the room to investigate. It was a popular brand of corned beef hash, cheap but tasty. She had Lottie prepare it for her every so often. The light came from a small lamp above the stove. It was shaded. Terrible room. Who had come here to eat corned beef hash? she wondered.

And then she knew.

He was seated in the breakfast nook, a terrible look of agony on his face. On the table in front of him were the remnants of what she suspected had been corned beef hash. He still clutched a fork in his right hand. His left was clasped in a fist. He looked like a judge presiding over a courtroom, but the condemned was himself.

Behind her, Tom Toth said, "Jesus Christ."

"No," Garbo corrected him calmly, "this is Kriegman, who has also been Mr. Wolheim. I hope the phone is still working. We have to phone for help."

Seventeen

"**B**y God they found another stiff in that joint!" Marion Davies shouted from her balcony. "Greta found it, for crying out loud. Greta of all people! Silent Sam who wants to be alone. Don't that take the cake!" She took a swig from her glass of borscht, which held a healthy jigger of tequila. Hearst came charging onto the balcony.

Hearst tweeted, "She's not talking to any reporters. She's barricaded in her house with those two harpies of hers, Viertel and de Acosta. Go over there, Marion. See if she'll talk to you. She trusts you."

"Oh God. That means I have to get dressed. I can't tramp over there in these pajamas." She shouted for her maid. "Get me that blue pailleted special out of the closet, my pink picture hat with the yellow ribbons and my pink slippers with the sapphire buckles. No you can't have this glass, I'm not finished with it!"

Hearst now sounded like a piccolo. He asked sternly, "What's in that glass?"

"Borscht!" she yelled. "The Reds are our allies now, right? They drink Borscht. Now I drink borscht. It's all for the Allied cause." She took a healthy swig, smacked her lips, and blessed Hearst for buying all her lies. Now that's true love.

Kriegman's murder cornered the airwaves. It was broadcast across the country and around the world by short wave. The Santa Monica Poison Case had taken on significant importance now that there was a second victim. There were those who considered that, wherever Kriegman's soul had landed, he should be flattered his body was discovered by the great Garbo. Kriegman caused no tug of war between Villon and the Santa Monica police force. It was tacitly agreed to leave the case in the very capable hands of Villon and Arnold Lake. Actually, Santa Monica's force was a small one, and they couldn't successfully tackle a murder case.

The scene of the crime was of necessity, because of the late hour, basking in the glow of an arc light, breaching the blackout policy. The authorities doubted there would be any Japanese planes in the area. They were capable of making it to Hawaii, but getting to the California coast was considered an impossibility. Villon's team were all over the place. The coroner was grumbling something about why can't bodies be discovered at a reasonable hour. He also told Villon and Arnold he wouldn't be a bit surprised if this was another case of thallium nitrate poisoning.

This murder gave Villon and Arnold a fix on the killer's modus operandi. Villon said, "It has to have worked this way. Mr. X, that's our killer . . ."

"Why not Madam X too as a possibility?"

Villon agreed, "Definitely a possibility. But for clarity's sake, since clarity begins at home," Arnold grimaced, "let's stay with Mr. X. So he is known and trusted by both victims. He offers them safety until they can disappear out of L.A. and into the hinterlands, the boondocks, South America, wherever they think they'll be safe. Safe not from us, but from their own people. Mr. X, of course, is a fake. His assurances are lies. He has orders to murder the defectors. He knows poisons. He sends Mrs. Wolheim . . . what did you say they told you her real name was?"

"Hannah Baum."

"Let's stick with Wolheim. It simplifies matters. Where was I?"

"He sends Mrs. Wolheim . . ."

"Yes. Right. He sends her to that big undercover operation in the sky gradually; there's no rush at first. But when she begins to become a big pain and an even more dangerous threat, he gets her packing, deposits her luggage at Union Station where we found it and brings her here, presumably to hide until it's time to catch the train. Probably frightens her into thinking the town is crawling with Nazi operatives on the hunt for her. She dies. He leaves her here. Why not? It's as good a place as any and there are no traces left behind that might incriminate him."

"He was obviously in a big rush with Kriegman." Arnold watched the coroner's assistants trying to pry the fork out of Kriegman's hand.

"Obviously. The spokesman at the castle . . . which one was it?"

"Gustav Henkel, the scriptwriter."

"Sure he is. Anyway, he says Kriegman was last seen by one of the maids around three in the afternoon. There's clothes and a suitcase missing from his room, so he must have decided to take it on the lam on the spur of the moment."

Arnold screws up his face, heavy in thought. "How about this? Try this scenario. When Martin Gruber took those candids of him in the garden, he was in a state of agitation, Kriegman. Worried. Frightened. Mrs. Wolheim's death triggered the fear he might be the next target."

Villon spread his hands and said, "And he was right, right?"

"The killer recognized the danger signal. He worked on Kriegman and won his trust. The same routine as with the lady victim. But he had to work fast. He convinced Kriegman he could provide him with a safe exit, but he had to hide out here until it was time to go. Then when they're here, he's conveniently brought along the corned beef hash, offers to fix some for Kriegman, who undoubtedly hasn't had his dinner, and the killer puts enough poison in the food to kill a football team."

"You know that for sure?"

"It has to be. It had to work fast."

The coroner was telling his men as he stood with one hand on Kriegman's shoulder, "Okay, boys. Wrap him and file him."

Villon asked the coroner what he thought killed Kriegman. Could it be thallium nitrate again?

"Absolutely," said the coroner. "A poisoner always stays with the same brand. I assume they feel comfortable with it, it's like the company of an old friend. Oh yes, it was a very heavy dose. Look at his face, if you can stand it. I assume he was wolfing the food down, so before it took effect, he'd finished most of it. Then whammo, it got him and you can see the pain must have been ferocious. Look at the way his legs are splayed under the table. Boy what he must have suffered in his feet." His men were having difficulty removing Kriegman from the breakfast nook. Rigor had set in remarkably fast. "Gently boys, let's try not to bust any bones."

Villon led Arnold out of the kitchen. "What do you think, Arnold? Who's next?"

"Logically, the boys who impersonated the sons and the girl who impersonated the daughter."

"I'm going to assign Greta some protection. Now that she discovered the body, somebody may think she knows more than she really does know, and set her up for a farewell tour. Anyway, there's nothing else we can do around here. I'm sure the killer left no trace. The boys are taking the hash can back to the lab to test for prints, but I doubt they'll find any. Let's drive over to Greta's. I'd walk, but I can't stand sand in my shoes."

Arriving at Garbo's house, they faced a barrage of questions from a small army of reporters and photographers encamped outside. They gave them very little satisfaction, Villon promising them a big break later in the day. Inside the house they found Garbo with Salka and Mercedes. To their pleasant surprise, Marion Davies was there looking like a Christmas tree ablaze out of season. She was drinking from a glass of hot chocolate laced with slivovitz from a flask in her handbag. Greta introduced her to the men and then Greta suggested that Tom Toth, who was guarding the rear of her house with several of his men, escort Davies back to her house. What Garbo had to say to her friends was for their ears only. If Davies heard there was the danger she'd pass it on to Hearst.

"The bum's rush, eh?" said Davies, as Toth offered her his arm. She wasn't too steady on her feet. "It's okay, Greta. I understand. Thanks for the interview. I did interview you, didn't I? That's what Willie sent me to do. Did I get any information? What year is this? Where am I?" She admonished Toth. "Not so fast, Buster, I'm not wasting any of this. Slivovitz is hard to come by these days. Them Poles ain't exporting it anymore, under the circumstances." She downed the remnants of her drink in one gulp and handed the empty glass to Lottie. Then she took Toth's arm and with her free hand waved at the others and said, "See you in church." Toth managed to guide her out to the patio. Lottie shut the door behind them and wondered when Miss Garbo would get any sleep.

"Lottie, you'd better go to bed. I won't be needing you anymore tonight."

"What about yourself? You've got an early call."

"I'll be fine. Please go. There is much for us to discuss here."

"Yes ma'am." This was said peevishly. Lottie was very annoyed at being excluded. She wanted to offer to brew fresh hot chocolate, but since poison was the killer's method, she decided it was wiser not to remind them she too had had a go at it once upon a time.

After Lottie left, Arnold told the ladies Kriegman had been killed in a similar manner as Mrs. Wolheim. Arnold told them Mrs. Wolheim's real name was Hannah Baum. Villon retrieved the narrative and explained how he and Arnold thought the murders had been committed. They were convinced the murderer was in residence at the castle.

Greta accepted a light from Villon and paced about the room, puffing on her cigarette. She was troubled and she saw no reason to disguise her feelings. She recognized there was a possibility that she herself was in danger but sloughed the danger off with a shrug of her shoulders.

Garbo the fearless, thought Villon, wishing desperately to overpower her with passionate kisses. Then he thought of his beloved Hazel Dickson, somewhere in the war zone with her unit, and him left behind because of a punctured eardrum.

Arnold was wishing Villon would wipe that idiotic look off his face.

"I have spent a lot of time with Guiss," said Garbo, now positioned in the center of the room under a grey cloud of cigarette smoke. "I have studied him very carefully and I positively feel there is something wrong with the picture he presents of himself."

"The man is dangerous, Greta," said Mercedes. "Stop playing detective. These men are perfectly capable of solving the murders, I'm sure." Villon refrained from blowing her a kiss.

Garbo said, "My dear, there is more to this situation than the murder of two enemy agents. We must also consider, and most importantly, what further damage the survivors can do to our country. Isn't it possible there are others who pose a threat and must be eliminated? Isn't it possible their subversive activities will continue to spread unchecked like a frightening epidemic? And most importantly of all, certainly very important to me," she said, now directly addressing Villon and Arnold, "What is the truth behind this production? Why are they doing it and for such an absurd sum of money? What's really going on behind the scenes?"

Arnold spoke up. "Greta, as of a couple of hours ago, my office knows a great deal more. We know the real identities of the Wolheims." He told them. "We know the purpose of the production. Certainly the entire five million isn't being spent on the film."

Salka laughed. "Oh no? Wait till von Stroheim gets through with it." Mercedes nodded agreement knowingly.

Said Arnold, "He's begun to economize. My informants tell me he's tightening his belt."

"Yes," agreed Garbo, "he's shooting less unnecessary footage. I think he's averaging three to four minutes of film a day. That's very good for a production like this where there are battle scenes and panoramic episodes that require scores of extras. So Arnold, where is most of the money supposed to go?"

"To continue financing their various organizations in this country. It's as simple and as obvious as that. They have to channel funds here to feed their espionage ring."

"But how did they get these millions into the country this time?" It wasn't a question from Garbo, it was a demand.

"The Germans get the money to Northern Ireland. The Irish have set up dummy corporations in America who receive the money and disburse it."

"But that's terrible!" said Salka.

"Look, Salka," said Arnold. "Northern Ireland has been fighting in vain for their independence for almost three decades. They hate the British. They'll go to any lengths to see them defeated. With Britain overthrown, independence is theirs."

"What are these dummy corporations?" asked Mercedes.

"Sorry," said Arnold, "that's positively privileged information. But just wait until the war is over. The world, and especially Wall Street, will be in for a big shock when we start unmasking the villains."

"So Arnold, here we sit in the eye of a hurricane." Garbo was nibbling absentmindedly at a Hydrox cookie. She looked at her girlfriends and giggled.

"What's so funny?" asked Mercedes.

"Here we are, the three witches of Shakespeare." She intoned spookily, " 'Double double toil and trouble, Cauldron boil, cauldron bubble.' I wanted to play the wicked witch in *The Wizard of Oz* but poor Louis B. had a fit when I asked him. I would have done it for nothing." She sighed a very heavy sigh. "How often am I plagued by minor defeats." Then she tossed the cookie aside onto a table and said to Villon and Arnold, "Boys, let's get back to Albert Guiss. Something about him preys on my mind. He's larger than life. Much much much larger than life. The way he lives, his exaggerated eccentricities. The castle. The dozens in service there, most of them unnecessary. Like who nowadays hires a majordomo to oversee the

·kitchen? Utterly ridiculous. And those spear holders in their silly uniforms." She laughed. "It's all so dumb. But when the magazines ask to photograph the interiors, they are met with an iron curtain of silence. No publicity, thank you very much. This pompous and ridiculous display is for our own pleasure. Tell me if I'm wrong, chaps, but don't you get the suspicion that Guiss is not his own master?"

"Smart lady," said Arnold, expecting Garbo to preen with pride, but she was too anxious to get on with other matters bothering her.

"Don't misread me, I'm sure that in many ways Albert Guiss is a very powerful man, but tell me, Arnold. Your people were so magnificent in uncovering the identities of the Wolheims and so many other facts of importance, why don't they know the source of Guiss's wealth? Or do they?"

"We don't know for sure. We strongly suspect he's a front for a powerful group of financiers."

"Well then, who are these financiers?" Garbo looked at the women, anxious for them to share her curiosity.

"We don't know," Arnold replied truthfully. "We can take pot-shots and guess, but we don't know for sure."

Garbo asked provocatively, almost flirting, "So what do you guess?"

Arnold played the game. "You're a smart lady. What do you think we guess?"

"Ha ha ha. All right, I'll tell you. I think Albert Guiss was created to be an investor in the overthrow of the free world. I think over the past decade or whatever it took, the members of the Axis made Albert Guiss into this overblown financial creature who could travel the world freely and without suspicion, making the necessary investments they needed to build the powerful war machine intended to destroy the Allies. Do I make sense?"

"Greta, have you had access to our files?" Arnold was impressed.

"You know I haven't. I'm just having a wonderful time discovering sections of my brain I've never had any reason to use before. Salka, Mercedes, let me be an example to both of you. Worry less about scripts and refugees and concentrate more on activating your minds into fresh areas of discovery."

"Smugness doesn't become you," said Salka. "It's late, I think it's time we all went home and let Greta get some sleep. Gentlemen, I'm sure you realize Greta herself might be in danger. Since she's so quick to share her delightful deductions with everyone, it's bound to occur to Guiss and his odious satellites that she might just deduce herself into a proper solution. Oh God, Greta, must you be so suicidal?"

"How can I help myself? I'm a Swede. We have the highest percentage of suicide in the whole world. Can you imagine that? It must be all those months of winter darkness. Goodnight, my darlings. Get home safely. No Arnold, you and Herbert wait a few moments. I'm not finished with you."

Villon thought of offering to spend the night, but what would happen if he ever was invited to share her bed, he wondered, and immediately supplied the answer. He'd be a nervous, fumbling wreck and she and her friends would have a big laugh over it.

Now the three were alone. "I had to get rid of them," said Greta, "they fuss and fret over me as though I was something fragile. I'm not. I'm a pretty strong fellow. Feel my muscle, go ahead, feel it." It was a very strong muscle. Villon wondered if she'd be interested in some Indian hand wrestling.

Feeling re-energized now that they had humored her, Garbo resumed a serious demeanor. "Now then, men, there is a murderer out there who is a threat to our friends. Lisa and Gruber are certainly in danger, aren't they?" Arnold nodded. "Do you know something, I have this intuitive feeling Guiss is very angry about these murders. I am sure to him they were unnecessary."

"What makes you think that?" asked Villon.

"Murder attracts the wrong kind of attention, doesn't it? Like here Kriegman is murdered and Kriegman was Albert's butler and I'm sure this brings the police and the press to his doorstep and it is certainly attention he does not want. Right, men?"

"Absolutely right," said Arnold.

"So Guiss is not the murderer. It could be Werner Lieb, or Gustav Henkel, possibly Risa Barron. . . ." She thought for a moment. "What do they say about poison? Poison is a woman's weapon, yes?"

"Yes," said Villon, "poison can be catnip to a woman. There's been a lot of them dosing their victims."

"And Risa Barron is so charming, I truly find her charming. I envy her that ability. I have to work so hard at it."

Faker, thought Villon.

"Risa is the kind that could lull a person into a false sense of security. She could convince a frightened person that she will help them to safety, she has that way with her. Sad, under other circumstances, she and I might have become friends. I am always attracted to strong women, strong people. Salka and Mercedes are very strong. Take Salka, as an example. Her house is where all the brilliant minds in exile converge. Some day I will take you to one of her salons. There you'll see Einstein and other great scientists. The world's greatest authors. Thomas Mann, Lion Feuchtwanger, Ferenc Molnár. The conversation is dazzling, overwhelming, and I, I the supposed great Garbo, I shrink into a corner and pray they will not notice me."

"After your display of knowledge tonight," said Arnold, "I think if you want to, you could hold your own with them."

"Don't let me kid you, I do hold my own. After all, I'm Garbo. They aren't. But Garbo is a façade created by Hollywood. Behind that façade, as I'm sure you have guessed, hides a very frightened little girl. But enough of this." She paused to light a new cigarette. "Arnold, Herbert, I'm going to say something that you're going to think, quite possibly, is very silly. It's very melodramatic, something that belongs in a film starring Basil Rathbone."

"Let's hear it," said Arnold.

"I think the person who gives Albert Guiss his instructions is here, here in Los Angeles. I really believe such a person exists, and we probably have met this person. This person is much more powerful than Guiss, and therefore much more dangerous. What do you think? Is it logical or is it foolish melodrama?"

Arnold Lake said, "I think you're right on the nose again, Greta."

She clapped her hands. "Well then, I think it's up to me to find and unmask this mysterious creature." Her eyes narrowed. "And I'm pretty sure I can do it. Don't try to discourage me. It's an incentive to do something for my country. Oh yes, it's my country. I shall become a citizen." She smiled sweetly, "And when I do, I hope you'll be there as my witnesses." She clapped her hands again. "And then we'll go to some quiet saloon near the courthouse and get pleasantly drunk and maybe reveal secrets about ourselves to each other that are better left . . . ah well. What are secrets really? They are so unimportant. Do I sound foolish?"

Villon spoke from his heart. "You sound wonderful. And I love you."

"Of course," said Garbo, "of course."

Eighteen

In less than a week, the unsolved murders were consigned to near limbo by the press. The war reclaimed the headlines. The *Joan the Magnificent* company was working at full speed. Von Stroheim astonished everyone, especially Guiss, with his accelerated energies. It was almost at a point where the set builders couldn't keep up with him. He shouted less and was politer when he demanded something. He wasn't subtle about his feelings for Alysia Hoffman, and no one was too surprised when he elevated her to the featured role of one of the Dauphin's courtesans. No longer was she in danger of being beheaded as one of Joan's fellow prisoners. There was doubt, anyway, in the research department, that any form of guillotine existed as yet; otherwise, why not lop Joan's head off instead of burning her at the stake?

Garbo was pleased for Alysia and told her so. "Are you in love with Von?"

Alysia didn't commit herself. "He's been nice to me. He's separated from his wife. He adores his son. He doesn't seem to have many friends and I have a very good time with him. Is this wrong?"

"Of course not," Garbo reassured her, "as long as you recognize that Von is not a man given to permanent commitments. He had a number of mistresses when he worked in France and believe me, I'm not being catty if I warn you there might be some competition of yours in the vicinity."

Alysia laughed. "That doesn't bother me. I live only for the day."

"How wise. Just as I do."

Martin Gruber materialized. He was carrying a large florist's box. Lottie Lynton sniffed and said, "More flowers."

"From Mr. Guiss of course," said Gruber with a small smile.

Garbo said to Alysia, "He inundates me with flowers. I send them to local hospitals. What has come over him?"

"Oh you're very funny, Greta. This past week you've gone off with him after the day's shooting at least three times that I know of."

Garbo assumed a haughty air. "You mustn't count, Alysia. It's bad luck." She said to Gruber, "The snapshots were excellent, Martin. You're a very good photographer."

Alysia said, "Didn't Von want to know where he could buy one of those cameras?"

"That's right, Martin asked me. But I'm totally in the dark. I haven't the vaguest idea if they're available in this country."

Gruber said, "I've made some inquiries. I canvassed some camera shops. They offer no hope. It seems to be of a kind not available here."

Alysia said, "Maybe it's one of a kind."

Garbo was at the dressing table, lightening her eye shadow. "Wouldn't that be unusual? Surely it is unprofitable just to manufacture one camera, one teeny teeny camera. Imagine if General Electric manufactured only one refrigerator, or one toaster. Ha! There would be economic chaos. You know, I was thinking of offering the camera to Erich as a gift when the picture finishes, but now I can't find it. Lottie and I hunted high and low for it, but we can't find it."

Lottie said from the kitchenette, "Well I don't recall ever seeing the damn thing in the house. Are you sure Mr. Gruber gave it back to you?"

"I'm very sure," said Garbo.

"I remember returning it," said Gruber. "Lisa was there when I gave it to you."

"Don't worry about it, Martin. It doesn't matter. I have plenty of other cameras and this one will turn up again. I'm always misplacing things and then find them days later. Martin, tell Mr. Guiss I will thank him in person for the flowers. Later."

Martin left and Alysia watched Lottie arranging the long-stemmed roses in a vase. The others didn't notice her arcane expression.

Sam Goldwyn was listening to Sophie Gang's litany of memos.

"Mrs. Goldwyn called and said she's received a cash donation for her children's relief society. It's a large sum but there was no card or anything and she doesn't know who to thank."

"So why should she bother? It's a synonymous donation."

"I gave Mr. Guiss your budget for *Up in Arms,* and he said he'll let you know in a few days if he's interested in investing."

"The hell with him. Who needs his money? You know I always do my own financing. Go get the budget back."

Sophie was aghast. "I can't do that. That would be impolite."

"I don't like that man anyway. There's something wrong with him. He never eats in the dining room with the rest of us pheasants. Who does he think he is? Hitler? The bum."

Sophie cast a "Heaven help us" glance at the ceiling and returned to her notes. "New York called. They're sending us a very interesting set of galleys. A book Random House is publishing next fall. They're very high on it."

"So what's it about?" He bit off the end of a cigar.

"It's about euthanasia."

"Oh for heaven's seven, Sophie. Why would I want to do a picture about Chinese teenagers?"

Werner Lieb was in Guiss's office in the studio with Henkel and Risa Barron. Guiss was exuberant about the picture's progress and said, "Von Stroheim is really doing an extraordinary job. It's a vast improvement on those first awful days."

Risa said, as she fingered her necklace of lapus lazuli, "Alysia Hoffman has had a tonic effect on him. Now she has a bigger role. Greta better look out. Soon Hoffman might be playing Joan. Don't make such a face, Henkel."

"She doesn't have it in her to be Joan. What are those pictures you're looking at, Werner?"

Lieb removed the monocle from his eye, blew breath on it, and then polished it with a handkerchief. "These are pictures of the set taken by Martin with a very strange, very unique camera." He told them about his incident with Martin and the camera earlier that week, in fact the day Kriegman was murdered.

"So these are the photographs he took?" said Guiss. "He gave you this set?"

"Yes he did. He promised I'd have a look, I found the camera so unique. He said he took them at Greta's request."

"That's right," said Guiss. "She showed them to me. They're quite good."

Werner Lieb agreed. "They're excellent." He handed the set to Risa, who wasn't very interested in the pictures and passed them on to Henkel. Lieb continued, "Kriegman was murdered on the fourteenth. The developers always date the film on the back. Turn one over, Henkel. What's the date?"

"The sixteenth."

"Yes. So these are not the snapshots from the film in the camera when I spoke to Martin in the hallway. These films were shot at a later date. So what he had on the film in the camera was obviously something entirely different."

Henkel asked, "You think he used the camera to photograph something else?"

Lieb said, "Am I the only one among us who has noticed that Martin and Lisa appear to be very very friendly?"

"Well, what's wrong with that?" asked Risa. "She's young and pretty and he's young and handsome. How did they used to say in silent pictures, 'Youth calls to youth?' "

Lieb continued. "Peter Lorre thought she was the woman on the beach the night we were spied on."

"So?" questioned Guiss. "He just as quickly said he was mistaken."

"Much too quickly," said Lieb. "Supposing she really was that woman. And they got to Lorre in order to protect her. His eyesight is damned good."

"He's on dope, Werner," said Risa wearily. She was bored with actors. She was bored with film making. She wanted to be in Brazil, in Rio, where most of her friends had decamped to. Where they were living high on the hog. She was bored with international intrigue. She was tired of looking over her shoulder to see if she was being followed. And she was bored with the men in this room and their constant presence.

Lieb spoke calmly, coolly and with authority. "I think Lisa Schmidt was that woman on the beach. I think Martin Gruber was given that sophisticated camera to photograph Kriegman because Greta suspected he was Wolheim. Gruber got his photograph and Garbo made a positive identification and so Kriegman was eliminated."

Guiss leaned on the desk with his elbows and made a pyramid of his fingers. "Why would they eliminate him? Why not arrest him? The sensible thing would be for the federals to take him into custody and interrogate him mercilessly. You know, the way we've seen Edward G. Robinson do it. It makes no sense that they killed Kriegman and Hannah Baum. It makes no sense at all. It's totally illogical."

Risa Barron had a new cigarette holder. It was decorated with tiny chips of valuable gems. She took a puff, a long and languorous one, exhaled, and then said matter-of-factly, "Now Greta is a threat to the others." She was enjoying the look of annoyance on Guiss's face. "She can identify Agathe and the three boys. If Agathe is arrested, I think she'll go over to the other side to save her neck. Kriegman's murder didn't do much to improve her shaky morale." She chuckled. "The smallest sounds make her jump with fear. Do you know, just this morning she likened the clatter of the lawn mower to a machine-gun attack. Can you imagine that? And Albert, why do we need so many gardeners? They're all over the place. It's impossible to stroll the grounds without one of them popping out from behind a tree or a bush to scare the hell out of me. But I must say the pool crew are so young and attractive. Don't you agree, Albert? Greta is a threat to our security?"

"If she ever was, she no longer is."

"You sound so positive," said Risa.

"I have reason to believe Greta regrets having cooperated with the authorities. You know how she treasures her privacy. Since finding Kriegman's body, her life has been hell. She is besieged by reporters and cameramen at her beach house. You've seen them yourselves at the entrance to the studio, lying in ambush for her. Now she's impatient to complete the film and leave Hollywood."

"To go where?"

They had been strolling the castle grounds a few nights earlier, Garbo with her arms folded, a sweater around her shoulders to fend off the night chill, Guiss with his arm around her shoulder. Of late when he made that move she didn't shrug it away. It was obvious to her he was in love with her. She recognized the signs. She was still a master at the art of creating lovers. She said huskily, "There is an unhealthy atmosphere here in Hollywood. It's not just the war, it's the industry itself. The Jews have a stranglehold on the industry. Mayer, the Warner brothers, Sam Goldwyn. Now there's this influx of Jews from Europe and they too have become infected with this need, this sick desire for power. I don't like it. I have to get away."

"Where will you go?"

"I'm giving that some thought. For a while I'm thinking of relocating to New York City. There I'll wait for the war to end. Then I will go to Switzerland. Salka has a house there in Gstaad."

"And Salka is one Jew who does not seek power?" He had removed his hand from her shoulder and was lighting a cigarette.

"Have you never known a Jew you liked?"

"I've never had much traffic with them."

"You're pulling my leg!"

"I wish I was."

"Be serious. You haven't dealt with Jewish financiers? How could you avoid that, you silly man."

Guiss's face froze. "I am not a silly man. Those who I deal with in finances mean nothing to me. I don't care what their origins are, only the financial condition of their empires. I learned long ago to be emotional about nothing. I'm a tough trader, Greta, and that's because socially I keep those in power at arm's length. Yes, I have a drink with them, of necessity I dine with them, there have been occasions when I took trips with them, but I have a strict rule: never become intimate with them."

She laughed. "You're so contradictory. Here I am, alone with you under the stars, in a garden that is heavenly scented, gloriously scented, you have had your arm around me, this is not intimate?"

"This is not a business transaction. This is a man and a woman," he took her hand and kissed it, and then he whispered, "I want to give you the world, Greta."

"I don't want the world," she said impatiently. "It is much too much to manage. And besides, to offer me the world now is to offer me damaged goods. If the world was mine I'd be responsible for repairing and reconstructing all the ruined cities, the ruined nations. What an appalling thought."

"I will make you the queen of the European film industry."

"Ah, now you are diminishing your offer. First you offer me the world, and now you narrow your offer down to Europe." She decided the time was right to take the plunge. "Tell me the truth, Albert. You're a friend of Hitler's, aren't you?" They were standing in the shadow of a gazebo. There was little light from the stars and the crescent moon. She couldn't see his face clearly, but from his intake of breath, she knew she had struck a nerve. "I need to know, Albert. It's important to my future."

"Why?" The manner in which he spoke the word gave her no clue as to his feelings.

"I'll tell you why and you will respect this confidence, as I certainly will respect yours. Before the war, Hitler made me an offer through his embassy here to return to Germany and make films there. He promised me the run of the UFA studios. Magnificent real estate. I hope the Allies don't bomb it into oblivion. I think of some day owning it. I turned the offer down because not only did I then think it was presumptuous, but because my career was on an upturn thanks to the success of *Ninotchka*."

"You were surrounded by Jews on that one."

"Very gifted ones—Lubitsch, Billy Wilder, Melvyn Douglas."

"Ina Claire?"

"Good God no, she's a *shicksa*. A very wicked woman. Did you know she married my John Gilbert after I stood him up at the altar? Never mind, it's not important. It's ancient history and I am not a historian. What I have been doing of late, Albert, is a lot of thinking about myself and my future as an actress. If there is a future for me, it's no longer in this country. It will have to be in Europe. I speak many languages. My native Swedish, French, my Spanish is not bad, and I'm very fluent in German. If you have a direct line to Hitler, and his offer is still open, then I am interested."

"Bravo! Bravo Greta!" He took her in his arms and kissed her with a fervent passion that took her by surprise. She struggled for air.

"Why Albert, your ardor is such a revelation!"

"I'm insane about you!"

"Oh don't be insane, insanity is so difficult for me to cope with. I always thought my father was insane and he was such a brute."

He continued holding her in his arms, strafing her ears with words she was anxious to repeat to Villon and Arnold. "Bravo, not becuase you are ready to return to the Fatherland, but Bravo because your words fill me with confidence, that you feel sure we will win the war . . ."

Fatherland. We will win the war. And yet why do I not struggle out of his arms? Why? Because I'm a good soldier. I am also a spy, and if I must say so myself, a damned good one.

". . . that we will prevail," continued Guiss without pausing to take a breath, "Greta, Greta, my enchanting Greta, my exquisite jewel, when all this is finished, marry me, oh my darling, marry me."

"When all what is finished? You mean the picture? Surely there will be retakes."

He released her. She patted some stray hairs back into place. "You're jesting," he said. "You're making fun of me."

"The thought of marriage usually disturbs me. I am not a person to be bound by a ring and a piece of paper. If we must, we will talk about it some other time. I'm sorry, Albert. Marriage has never been for me and I don't think it ever will be. So if our relationship is predicated on that, then perhaps we should both forget this conversation, try to make believe it never took place."

He watched her as she strolled away from him. His words brought her to a halt. "I will not forget this conversation. I love you too much. I will contact Goebbels and he will tell Adolf. I'm sure despite severe losses on the battlefields, they will be very pleased. Eva Braun is a great fan of yours." Garbo shuddered. "I'm sure you girls will have a great deal to talk about when you meet."

"If we find something in common," said Garbo. She led him back to the castle.

She was frightened. She had learned too much. Guiss will tell his unholy threesome what they discussed and someone in that group won't buy her desire to return to Germany. But still, she reminded herself, I'm a soldier on a mission and I knew when I accepted it that it would be terribly dangerous. I am no longer frightened. I am proud of myself. Very proud of myself. And Villon and Arnold Lake will be proud of me too. And perhaps if Arnold can't make me a G-woman, he'll make me a Junior G-man. I eat the breakfast cereal that sponsors them and I listen to that radio show religiously, along with "Portia Faces Life" and "Just Plain Bill."

Risa Barron couldn't stop laughing. She had this hilarious vision of Garbo and Eva Braun exchanging dress patterns.

"Control yourself, Risa," said Guiss sternly.

"I can't help it. Eva Braun is such an idiot!" The laughter continued.

Werner Lieb said, "Well, now Miss Greta Garbo might know just a bit too much about us."

Guiss slammed his fist down on the desk. "She's completely trustworthy! I'm sure of that! Last night we became lovers."

Risa paled and jammed a cigarette into the holder. She said coldly, "Congratulations." She wasn't provoked by jealousy. She wasn't given to the common, ordinary emotions of her sisters. To women like Risa Barron, men were a commodity, especially very rich men. There had been others before Guiss and there would be others succeeding him. She'd done very well by him, her treasury of jewels, the investments he made for her. She was extremely well off, and was determined to survive the war and whatever consequences of Germany's defeat. She had arranged a safe exit to South America months before the conflict became a reality. She had something else on her mind and she voiced it. "So now there are three to occupy our attention. Lisa Schmidt, Martin Gruber and Miss Greta Garbo."

"Risa, I'm warning you." The threat in Guiss's voice was unmistakable.

There was a trace of a smile on the woman's face. "Love can be so destructive." Then she raised her voice, "It has paralyzed your brain! You, the great genius created by even greater geniuses, you've become a lovesick schoolboy. It's a cliché but it's true."

"There must be no more murders." Guiss had their undivided attention. "It was foolish to murder Hannah and Kriegman. Absolutely foolish. The police and the federals wouldn't be on our trail now if they had continued to live." No one refuted his statement. "Did you hear me, Werner?"

"I've heard an awful lot," said Lieb, while Gustav Henkel stifled one of his nervous yawns.

"And I will hear nothing further about Greta Garbo. We've seen von Stroheim's assemblage. This film is their masterpiece, and in a way," he added with pride, "it is *my* masterpiece too!" He stood up and proclaimed proudly, "Around the world, millions will read," he said, waving his arm like an orchestra conductor, "Albert Guiss presents Greta Garbo in Erich von Stroheim's *Joan the Magnificent*. If I must say so myself, it sounds most impressive." He sat down, a faraway look in his eyes. It did not bother him that his associates were displeased and angry. He was not aware he was seated on a powder keg. He was wrapped in his selfish thoughts of future glory, of a future to be shared with Greta Garbo, and it did not occur to him that these dreams were the components of his Achilles' heel.

Garbo had a rendezvous with Villon and Arnold at Salka Viertel's house. It was agreed that they would not meet at the studio ever again, unless there was an official reason for a police visit. The beach house would remain out of bounds until the press would abandon their pursuit of the star.

"So now Salka, you are part of the war. Your home is our safe house! Don't you feel proud that you are contributing something?"

Salka sniffed and went to the study and her enemy, the typewriter. She hated working but she needed money to survive. She had to support a variety of friends who were down on their luck. She worked hard so they would never be down on *her* luck. She sat at the typewriter, let herself dwell on Garbo for just a few more seconds, and then erased the word "danger" from her mind and tried to compose some dialogue for Joan Crawford.

Garbo told Villon and Arnold everything. She had a powerful memory and she acted out brilliantly the scene in the garden with Albert Guiss. She heavily underlined "Fatherland" and "We will win the war" and insisted it was now quite evident to her that he was a creation of the Axis allies. She didn't tell them she had slept with Guiss. Something like that called for discretion and she was the master of discreet.

Arnold said, "It's not as though we weren't pretty positive they were German operatives, but at least now we've got it from the horse's mouth."

"What? Garbo? A horse's mouth?" she said with mock indignity. "Salka thinks I'm the other end of the horse! Ha ha ha! So I have done well, yes?"

"Absolutely brilliant," said Arnold.

"So now I can become a Junior G-man?" She had come to the rendezvous with Lottie, directly from the studio, and Lottie had immediately commandeered the kitchen to prepare snacks and her inevitable hot chocolate. While she laid these out on the coffee table in the living room where they were conferring, Arnold marveled at Garbo's contradictions.

She was a great star, a strong woman seemingly in command of herself and her destiny, whatever that might be, and yet there was this charming and amusing childish side of her. Calling them "chaps" and "men" and wanting to be a "G-woman" or even a "Junior G-man". Or was she kidding the pants off them? She wasn't a particularly witty woman, but she had a marvelous sense of humor. Her friends adored her and she seemed to adore them in return. Still, there was something about her he found sad and touching. Her desire to be alone. Her fierce determination to remain her own person. Did she have relatives? he wondered. And if so, would they be there for her should she ever need them?

Villon was saying, "Interesting they selected Goldwyn's studio to do the production. I mean Sam Goldwyn, how Jewish can you get? I don't suppose you've heard Guiss refer to him as 'that yid' or something equally unpleasant?"

"No, not Guiss, he's quite gentlemanly about his dislikes and distastes. But you remind me. It was someone else who referred to Jews as 'yids.' I ignored it then, but now . . . it makes me wonder. Hot chocolate, anyone?"

Nineteen

The bottle of milk was on the floor in the hallway next to the door to Lisa Schmidt's apartment. The milk was delivered early and Lisa enjoyed her varieties of dry cereal and milk for breakfast. Occasionally there wasn't enough time and she'd wait until she got to the studio to eat. This morning there was plenty of time. She brought the bottle of milk to her small dining table and poured it over the krispies. She noticed the bottle cap was slightly awry; it had been like that several other times. She must leave the milkman a note and tell him to stop being so careless. He was a replacement, she learned from a neighbor. The war had claimed his predecessor.

As she ate slowly, she dwelled on many things. The Guiss gang, as she privately referred to them, the picture, and von Stroheim's interest in Alysia Hoffman. Then there was Hoffman herself, a dethroned movie queen desperately in search of a new kingdom. Martin Gruber and the chances he took with the camera, hell, the chances they were all taking, and there was that burning sensation in her feet again. It came and it went, all week long, always in the morning when she ate breakfast at home. Burning sensation in the feet . . . *oh my God.*

She phoned Villon. She was positive she was being poisoned, she told him. Her breakfast milk. No, she wasn't panicking, but she was frightened. She didn't know how much poison was in her system. She wasn't sure how much milk she had drunk, but she got a quart a day. She had a sweet tooth so she made custards and chocolate puddings and she ate much too much of them. "Hurry, Herb, hurry. I feel faint. I'm nauseous. My feet are on fire. Herb . . ."

Villon recognized the sounds. The phone dropping, Lisa slumping to the floor. There was no time to call Arnold. He summoned one of his detectives and drove like a demon to what he prayed would be Lisa's rescue. They used a skeleton key to enter her apartment and found her prone on the floor. Villon picked her up in his arms and directed his detective to bring the milk bottle with them. They rushed Lisa to a hospital emergency room, where Villon identified himself and told the examining doctor he suspected Lisa had been poisoned with thallium nitrate. The doctor whistled, slightly off key, and had Lisa prepared for a stomach pumping. Her breathing had become unnatural and he feared for her life.

Villon sent the detective back to the precinct with the milk bottle, cursing the fool for not having held it with a handkerchief. He phoned the Garden of Allah but Arnold had left. Villon left messages for Arnold at his precinct and with Garbo in case Arnold phoned her.

Garbo paled when she heard of Lisa's condition.

"There's Gruber to worry about," said Villon. "You must get to him and caution him. And Greta, there's yourself."

"Well yes, but I only eat and drink what Lottie prepares for me. And I don't believe she is considering poisoning me. Are you, Lottie?"

Lottie smiled and continued with the tunafish salad she was preparing.

"I will alert Gruber," said Greta, and hung up. On the studio phone, she asked the operator to page Gruber, and then rescinded the request immediately. If they hear I am paging Gruber, they will suspect I'm up to something. The killer will guess that the poison has taken its effect on Lisa Schmidt. The killer. The poisoner. This madman, or is it a madwoman? There was a knock at the door and Lottie opened it. There stood Martin Gruber carrying a florist's box. Garbo didn't thank God, she thanked Guiss. "Come in, Martin. Lottie, shut the door. Put those foolish flowers aside." She told him about the attempt on Lisa's life. The bottles of milk.

"What are Lisa's chances?" Martin asked. He had fallen in love with her and only now that her life hung by a thread would he admit it to himself.

Garbo said, "Who would know where she lived?"

"Just about everyone connected with the production. There's always a list of personnel issued to everyone with addresses and phone numbers."

"And of course they would have access to it. Those monsters who are Guiss's associates. Martin, we are in terrible danger. You must be very careful."

"Don't worry about me. I will look after myself. I don't think they're on to me."

"Don't be so sure. They made much of a drama about the camera. Don't underestimate them. I have gotten to know them very well this past week. There isn't one of them who isn't capable of murder."

"I don't think it's Guiss. I have memorandums he has dictated about his displeasure at Hannah Baum and Kriegman's murders."

"I wonder if it's been noticed Lisa hasn't shown up for work. I have it! I will phone the lot and disguise my voice and say I am Lisa's girlfriend and she's been rushed to the hospital. A good idea, yes?" She was smart enough not to use the studio phone. She was connected to the set and gave an assistant the news. After which her face glowed and she said, "I'm a very good operative, aren't I? After all, I was an espionage agent in *Mysterious Lady,* and I was a pretty good Mata Hari, even if they had to hire June Knight to dance for me. Ha ha, how Marlene will be jealous when she hears about this!"

* * *

From FBI headquarters in downtown Los Angeles where he had been summoned for what proved to be a momentous meeting, Arnold Lake searched for Herb Villon by phone. He was directed to the hospital, where Herb told him Lisa Schmidt was putting up a tough struggle for survival. Villon had ordered additional protection for Garbo and assigned two detectives to go to the studio and bring in Martin Gruber for his own safety.

"I hope she pulls through, I'm crazy about her," Arnold said. Lisa might have been heartened by her burgeoning list of admirers. "Herb, I'm at headquarters. I've been there since early this morning. We got word the Germans are planning to call home a number of their agents, so we've got to move in on them and fast. We're closing the books today on Guiss and his bunch."

"This means shutting down the movie! What a blow that'll be to Greta and von Stroheim."

"Sorry, buddy. That's the toss of the dice."

"When does the operation begin?"

"It's underway at the castle right now."

Several weeks earlier, Agathe, who had posed as the Wolheim daughter and was now one of Risa Barron's maids, had found the courage to sneak out of the castle and turn herself in to Herb Villon. Herb and Arnold in turn convinced her she was more important to them at large in the castle than in custody.

"But I will be poisoned!" Agathe had protested tearfully.

Herb lied, "You could be executed as an enemy agent."

"Oh my God, wherever I turn lies death."

"You have nothing to fear in the castle. They won't kill anyone there. They don't want to give us an excuse to enter it. Be smart, Agathe, be as smart as they, say you've been in the dossier we have on you. . . ."

"Dossier." She repeated the word in a ghostly tone.

Arnold said smartly, "We're very big with dossiers. Go back to the castle. Watch what goes on carefully. Report to our boys who are inside."

"Boys? Inside?"

"Do you agree to go back?" persisted Villon.

Agathe said gravely, "How do they say it in England, 'In for a penny, in for a pound.' Okay. In espionage school they said I was the girl with the greatest potential. Well, I wasn't. I was no good as Fraulein Wolheim. Now I have an opportunity to redeem myself. You shall benefit from my training, ha. Ironic, isn't that so? Now, who are these boys inside?"

She was surprised and then delighted to be told that various gardeners, kitchen help, members of the swimming pool crew and the gardener who operated the lawn mower were all federal operatives who had carefully infiltrated Guiss's employ to prepare for his downfall.

"The man who runs the lawn mower? That's funny."

"What's so funny?" asked Herb.

"I have slept with him." She shrugged. "He's better with the lawn mower."

Villon phoned Garbo and told her Arnold's news. She exhaled, as though she'd been struck a blow in the stomach. Then just as quickly she said, "It's better this way. But Herbert, how will you know who is the poisoner? Will you ever find out who is Guiss's superior here in Los Angeles?" She thought for a moment and then said, "You know, I think I know who that might be. I shall confront this person."

That alarmed Villon. "Greta! Don't do anything foolish! You're no match for these people!"

"No match indeed! Haven't I outsmarted them! Haven't I outwitted them! I most certainly am their match!"

She didn't hear the door open. Lottie was clattering pots and pans in the kitchenette. He came in carrying an opened bottle of champagne. Then Greta saw his reflection in the dressing-room mirror, the bottle of champagne, and thought quickly and wisely. "Why how nice of you, Mr. Henkel. Champagne! And my favorite brand!"

"Don't drink it!" shouted Villon.

"Goodbye, Herb," she said sweetly. "Lottie, Gustav Henkel

brings me champagne. Gustav, it's so early in the morning for champagne. Wouldn't you prefer some of Lottie's exquisite hot chocolate?"

Henkel had been in his office when he heard Villon's two detectives arrive to take Martin Gruber into "custody." He knew then that time was running out and swiftly. He'd taken care of Lisa Schmidt, Martin Gruber would elude him, but there was Garbo, and she belonged to him. Her murder would give him immortality. He had a bottle of champagne laced with poison prepared for himself and the others. The authorities would never take him alive, he'd promised himself that a long time ago. He would be the savior of the others too. Lieb was a megalomaniac, and desperately in need of Henkel's help.

Guiss has been good to him. He'd spirited him out of Hamburg when the police were beginning to close in on him. Oh how he enjoyed killing people! It was wonderful to know they were dying in awful agony, with feet on fire and innards bursting with nausea and he was the master of their fates. Now it would soon be finished, but there was still much to accomplish. He went to Guiss's office with the bottle of champagne which contained more than enough thallium nitrate. He was killing Lisa Schmidt with small doses to prolong her agony; he had never liked her after she had unsubtly given him the name of a good local dentist.

Only Guiss was in the office. He was in a terrible state over Gruber's "arrest." Henkel sympathized. Guiss was busy emptying the files and desk drawers of what might be incriminating evidence. "Champagne? You choose now to drink champagne?"

"Why not?" said Henkel airily. "I've been saving this bottle for just such an occasion!" He brought two glasses from the bar, took them to the desk and filled them. "Come, Albert, this may be our last chance to drink together."

"I shouldn't drink with you at all. You murder Hannah Baum and Kriegman, and before Gruber was taken into custody, he told me Lisa Schmidt is in serious condition in the hospital. Oh Gustav, you have so much to account for. Where the hell is Werner? Where the hell is Risa? The fools."

"Come Albert, drink up." Henkel lifted his glass in a toast. "To absent friends!"

Guiss downed his in one gulp. Henkel refilled it. "It's very good stuff, Gustav. Did you bring it all the way from Hamburg?"

"No, it's from our cellar in the castle. Drink up."

Guiss said as he prepared to down the second glass with its lethal contents, "You know, I should have told you this a long time ago. But really, Gustav, you've got to do something about your teeth." He downed the glass and felt dizzy. He sank into his chair. "Gustav. Something's wrong with me. Do something. Call someone. I feel terrible. My feet are burning. This awful nausea . . . Oh Gustav! You rotten son of a bitch!"

The castle was taken over in an orderly fashion. The federal agents posing as employees knew who were German staff and who were innocents supplied by employment agencies. Werner Lieb had barricaded himself in his bedroom, where he disappointed Risa Barron by committing suicide with a bullet to his right temple. Risa Barron heard the shot, shook her head sadly, and wondered why Agathe, who was usually in a nervous and agitated state, stood so calmly at the window watching the federal agents leading their captives out of the castle into police wagons. Risa had her box of jewelry and a small suitcase. She planned on replenishing her lavish wardrobe at her next port of call. In a rare moment of kindness, she asked Agathe, "Look, do you want to come with me? To South America, to Rio? You can have a whole new life there."

"No," said Agathe. "But *bitte*. Thank you. I want to stay here in America. I think I will like it here."

Risa smiled. "You cooperated with them, didn't you?"

"To save my life, yes. I neutralized the electronic machinery. I had to sleep with the engineer to find out how, but he was pleasant. Are you sure you will escape them?"

Risa pressed a panel in a wall that revealed a hidden passage.

"Dear girl, I rented this place. And I chose this bedroom because of this hidden panel. The castle was built by a celebrated and delightfully perverted silent screen director. This is how he sneaked his girlfriends in from the outside under his wife's unsuspecting nose. Good luck to you, Agathe. Perhaps we will meet again." She hurried into the hidden passage and into the arms of a federal agent who had discovered the entrance to the passage in the gazebo in the garden.

"You do not drink the champagne, Greta?"

"It's too early for me. I told you that." She was sure Villon was on his way. Lottie came out of the kitchenette with two steaming cups of hot chocolate.

Lottie said to Greta, "Don't you dare drink that champagne. This morning they burn you at the stake. You must have a clear head. You must remember your cues for the fire. It can be very dangerous. I don't care how much precautions they said they've taken. Accidents can happen. Here Mr. Henkel, forget the champagne. I'll see to it that she drinks it after the scene is shot. Here," she said jovially, "join Miss Garbo in my special hot chocolate." She waved a cup under his nose. "Isn't that tempting?"

"Oh yes. Very tempting." He took the cup from her. Lottie took the bottle of champagne to the kitchenette. Henkel watched Garbo sip her hot chocolate and close her eyes in ecstacy. He drank some of his. It was truly delicious. He said to Garbo, "The police have arrested Martin Gruber." She said nothing. He drank more hot chocolate. "You're not surprised. You knew all about us. You led Albert on. You made him believe you loved him, that you wanted to come to Germany after the war." He drank again. "You were very clever, Greta. Did you guess I was the Hamburg poisoner?"

"Actually, I suspected Werner Lieb. He went to school in Hamburg. Guiss knew you murdered the Wolheims?"

"Yes."

"He protected you. Why? He was against the murders."

He chuckled and he drank more hot chocolate. Lottie was returning from the kitchen with a jug in her hand. "We are brothers. We loved each other." He grinned and the teeth looked more repulsive than ever. He held his cup out to Lottie. "You're anxious for me to enjoy more hot chocolate. It's so hot, like my feet. I know what you're doing to me." He winked at Lottie. "I know about your past, Lottie Lynton. We did a complete check on you. Isn't thallium nitrate wonderful?"

Lottie said matter-of-factly as she refilled his cup, "Sometimes it is and sometimes it ain't. When I tried it out on a horse, it worked real fast. She was an old nag and we had her in the barn behind the house. She pulled my husband's wagon. He was a junk dealer. He was planning to get rid of the animal anyway, she was old and near blind."

Garbo covered her mouth with a hand. Henkel was in the throes of agony, but she admired the way he never spilled a drop of the liquid, never took his eyes from Lottie's face.

"But Henry took forever," Lottie said, admiring her fingernails. "He had the constitution of an ox. He was over two hundred and fifty pounds and it was solid muscle. It seemed to take forever for him to die. Let me have the cup. It's beginning to spill." She saw the look of horror on Garbo's face. She was paralyzed by the sight of the dying man.

Henkel clutched his stomach. His eyes were on Garbo. Poor bitch. She has no stomach for this. She should have seen what Hannah Baum and Kriegman went through before they gave up the ghost. My feet, my feet, oh dear God in heaven, my feet. So this is what it's like? How could I. What a beast I am. He blurted, "Albert is dead. He drank the champagne. She would have had him killed anyway. He would not have survived. She ordered me to kill Hannah and Kriegman. She had a list and she was determined to wipe them all out. The Schmidt woman, Gruber and you, Greta Garbo, she despised you . . . oh my God . . . oh my God . . . despite her power in the Nazi party . . . she wanted to be *you*. . . ." He looked into Lottie's eyes. *"Danke."*

"Bitte," rejoindered Lottie as she watched him sink onto the floor.

Villon came rushing into the dressing room followed by Arnold, Villon shouting Greta's name.

Garbo was on her feet. "I'm all right. I'm fine. Lottie has the bottle of champagne." She pointed to Henkel's body. "He told me everything. There he is, chaps, the stiff. Do you know, he was Albert's brother? And there is a person who was more powerful than Albert."

"We know," said Arnold. "His wife. His widow."

The pyre was piled in the center of the sound stage. The outdoor set reminded Peter Lorre of the early impressionistic silent German films. It had the feel of *Caligari* and *Warning Shadows* and, for a while, Lorre was struck with a nostalgia for his homeland. Perhaps after the war. . . . His thoughts were interrupted by the entrance of Garbo with Villon and Arnold. There were over two hundred extras present. The actors impersonating the inquisitors were mostly impatient. Boris Karloff chafed at the heat of the lights needed for Technicolor shooting. Bela Lugosi, not needed in this sequence, came to see how von Stroheim would handle the burning. Von Stroheim was fussing with Alysia Hoffman, who looked stunning as the haughty noblewoman he had her portraying. She watched Garbo arriving. She saw Villon and Arnold. She grabbed one of von Stroheim's wrists and held it tightly.

"What's the matter with you, Alysia?"

"It's warm. Is my makeup running?"

"You look terrific. I'm going to shoot your big close-up before I set fire to Joan. Then I'll repeat it with the flames flickering on your face. The critics will praise that, take it from me. What's the matter with you? Why are you trembling? Oh it's you, Greta. I didn't send for you. I won't need you for at least another hour."

"You are wrong, Erich, I am needed now. You know Mr. Villon and Mr. Lake. They have come with very sad news. Erich, I'm sorry to have to tell you this, but there will be no *Joan the Magnificent.*"

Von Stroheim saw Sam Goldwyn and Sophie Gang materializing. Goldwyn had just learned that his studio had been overrun by an enemy spy ring, and almost suffered a stroke. Sophie Gang had calmed him with a stiff hooker of brandy after he demanded the spies be "determinated."

"Exterminated," Sophie corrected him.

Greta wanted to throw her arms around von Stroheim and comfort him. He was in a state of shock; his private world had collapsed. Goldwyn astonished her when he came forward and said, "I'm going to take over. I've been watching the rushes. I think they're mostly magnificent. Here and there a little too fussy, a little too fancy shmancy," he said, putting his arm around von Stroheim, "and we'll have a lot of disagreements, just like in the old days, okay Erich?"

Von Stroheim was so overcome with emotion, he struggled for words. "Sam, Sam, I . . . I love you Sam . . ."

"Careful!" cautioned Goldwyn, "there will be gossip. Better Greta should love me. At last we're working together. Where is she? Where did she go?"

Garbo was talking to Alysia Hoffman, who was surrounded on each side by Villon and Arnold. Alysia stood regally, hands at her sides, fists clenched, a look of pure arrogance and defiance on her face. "And I'm sorry to be the one to tell you, Albert is dead. His brother poisoned him."

Alysia's voice was shrill. "So? So? So now you know everything, *hein?* I suppose now I am to be taken into custody, ha! What a laugh." She said with a sneer, "For years I traveled Europe's capitols setting up the powerful structure of Albert Guiss. Guiss! Ha! He was Reinhold Henkel when I chose him to become the richest man in the world. Goering didn't like that but I have more power than that obese pig, more power than that odious cripple Goebbels; there are times when even Hitler fears me. And you, Greta Garbo, I molded you and your friend Mercedes like putty. You played into my hands so easily!"

Von Stroheim said to Goldwyn, "We may have to reshoot all of her scenes. How can we release a movie starring a master spy?"

Goldwyn was elated. "Are you mad? The publicity will be sensational. *Life* and *Look* and all the other magazines will fight for an exclusive. And I'll give it to all of them."

"But I need the close-ups I was going to do today! Now I won't be able to get them."

Goldwyn patted von Stroheim's shoulder. "Oh no? Just leave it to Irving."

"Your name is Sam, Mr. Goldwyn," Sophie Gang reminded him, eternal suffering etched in her face.

"I know my name, you silly woman."

Garbo studied Alysia's face as Goldwyn approached Arnold Lake. The woman's lips were working, but no sounds emerged. Her eyes were blinking wildly and for no reason whatsoever, she was fussing with her elaborate coiffure. Garbo moved back and took Villon's hand. It sent a tingle throughout his body. "Herb, Herb, look at her. Look at Alysia Hoffman. I think she's breaking down. She's going mad."

Alysia Hoffman began walking slowly toward von Stroheim. She looked around at her audience. The set had gone quite still. Someone was laughing maniacally. She didn't realize it was herself. And then she spoke in a voice underlined by hysteria. "I'm ready for my close-up, Mr. von Stroheim!"

Epilogue

The media went wild with the story of the cracking of Alysia Hoffman's spy ring. There was heavy speculation as to who else in the country might be working for the enemy. Risa Barron, in return for a promise of sympathetic treatment, gave the FBI an extensive list of traitors in their midst. There was quite a fuss over the confiscation of her fabulous jewel collection, Risa storming, "Damn you! I worked like hell for them." She wasn't doubted, but they were held in custody until after the war, when a shrewd Jewish lawyer won her her freedom and the return of her property, and she fled to Brazil, where she opened a chain of jewelry stores.

After *Joan the Magnificent* was completed, Greta Garbo left Hollywood, little realizing she would never make another film. She did do a test for a projected Walter Wanger production years later and there was talk she would accept a cameo role in a possible filming of Proust's *Remembrance of Things Past,* but instead she traveled the world like the Flying Dutchman, doomed to keep on the go, until finally she settled into an apartment in New York City.

While *Joan* was still shooting, Garbo stayed in touch with Villon and Arnold. They were good friends now, and although she had every reason to believe Herb Villon was hopelessly in love with her, she did nothing to encourage him. Strangely enough, while work continued on *Joan,* there was no longer a fire or a passion in either Garbo's work or von Stroheim's direction. He would admit to no one how deeply he had become committed to Alysia Hoffman, and he seemed listless and unhappy.

Mercedes de Acosta wrote a sizzling autobiography, *Here Lies the Heart,* published in 1960 by Reynal, in which she shamelessly and sizzlingly claimed or implied lesbian relationships with not only Garbo, but also Dietrich, Claudette Colbert and Eva Le Gallienne, to name just a chosen few. There were some eye-popping photos to illustrate her allegations, including several of Garbo nude on an isolated island.

Salka Viertel retired to Switzerland. Her son Peter, who had worked on the screenplay of *The African Queen,* wrote a book about John Huston and the filming, *White Hunter, Black Heart,* which in turn was eventually filmed by Clint Eastwood, who directed and impersonated Huston. Peter had the good taste to marry Deborah Kerr.

Peter Lorre and Bela Lugosi died of their drug addictions, in the later stages of their lives reduced to appearing in cheap quickies. They were almost unrecognizable.

Von Stroheim returned to acting, featured mostly as nasty Germans until the war ended. He returned to Europe, where he continued acting, mostly in France, and then in 1950 Billy Wilder brought him back to Hollywood to co-star in Gloria Swanson's brilliant comeback film, *Sunset Boulevard.* The film did little to revive their careers.

William Haines was arrested after the war on charges of impairing the morals of a minor. He escaped a jail sentence but his life was ruined. Six months after his death, his grief-stricken lover committed suicide.

Agathe, whose last name was Schulman, sold her memoirs of her life as a spy to an eager publisher in New York. It sold well and was the basis of a successful television series. The book was pure fabrication, but it made Agathe wealthy and she married a Mexican playboy who beat her regularly and succeeded in divesting her of most of her savings.

Marion Davies never succeeded in buying the house which was the scene of two murders. Shortly after the war, Hearst was on the verge of bankruptcy and in danger of losing his vast newspaper empire. Marion, gallant and loyal to the very end, handed him a paper bag filled with her jewel collection, the sight of which would have caused Risa Barron to hemorrhage, and Hearst was rescued.

Arnold Lake returned to Washington, D.C., married a dried-out debutante, and tried to run for office as president of the United States. He did not succeed and returned to his law practice and sired three sons, all redneck anti-Semites. He continued to send Christmas cards to Herb Villon.

Hazel Dickson returned from the war a changed woman. Herb Villon expected to marry her, but she was having none of it. A former gossip columnist for a newspaper syndicate, she moved from gossip writing to political analyzing and became a terror in print. Herb never married. He retired to Las Vegas and, until her death, kept in touch with Garbo.

Before Billy Haines's death and her permanent move to New York, Garbo invited him to the Beverly Hills hotel where she was temporarily in residence, to have lunch with her. When he arrived, she realized he wasn't the same Billy Haines she used to know.

"You are so sad, Billy. Why don't you come to New York with me? There is no Hollywood any more. Here, you are a dinosaur."

"Worse. I'm a leper. I can't even cry on Crawford's shoulder. She's moved to New York. Oh what the hell. I've got a house, I've got money, I'll just be that perverted old man on the hill. By the way, whatever became of *Joan the Magnificent?*"

Garbo stroked her chin. "I'm not quite sure. Goldwyn said it was too terrible to release, so now it sits somewhere in storage, unwanted, unloved, like me."

"Albert Guiss loved you."

"Yes, he really did. Very tragic. He could have been a great man, but he ran with the wrong crowd." She laughed. "You know, I've never told this to anyone before. Billy," she leaned forward with a sly look, "I went to bed with him. Ha ha ha."

Haines raised an eyebrow. "So did I dearie, so did I!"

They enjoyed sharing a laugh after so much gloom. "You should have heard the comments of my beloved Lottie Lynton when she suspected I'd caved in to Albert's advances. Poor, dear Lottie."

"Say, whatever became of her?"

"Oh don't you know? She fell in love with a man who owned a service station in Pasadena. But very soon the marriage went sour and so you know what?"

"No. What?"

"He poisoned her! Ha Ha Ha Ha Ha!"